TOM CLANCY
ZERO HOUR

TOM CLANCY

ZERO HOUR

DON BENTLEY

RANDOM HOUSE
LARGE PRINT

Cover art and design by Eric Fuentecilla

The Library of Congress has established a Cataloging-in-Publication record for this title.

ISBN: 978-0-593-60774-9

www.penguinrandomhouse.com/large-print-format-books

FIRST LARGE PRINT EDITION

Printed in the United States of America

1st Printing

This Large Print edition published in accord with the standards of the N.A.V.H.

PRINCIPAL CHARACTERS

UNITED STATES GOVERNMENT

JACK RYAN: President of the United States

MARY PAT FOLEY: Director of national intelligence

THE CAMPUS

JOHN CLARK: Director of operations

DOMINGO "DING" CHAVEZ: Assistant director of operations

GAVIN BIERY: Director of information technology

JACK RYAN, JR.: Operations officer / senior analyst

LISANNE ROBERTSON: Former director of transportation

OPERATIONAL DETACHMENT ALPHA 555

CAPTAIN ALEX BROWN
MASTER SERGEANT CARY MARKS
SERGEANT FIRST CLASS JAD MUSTAFA

1-6TH CAVALRY SQUADRON

LIEUTENANT MIKE REESE
**CHIEF WARRANT OFFICER THREE
    KASSI SHAW**
**CHIEF WARRANT OFFICER THREE
    JAY HOGG**
CHIEF WARRANT OFFICER TODD ASKINS
**CHIEF WARRANT OFFICER
    MATT ISAACSON**
**CHIEF WARRANT OFFICER
    BUDDY AUTEN**
**CHIEF WARRANT OFFICER
    RON THOMPSON**
**CHIEF WARRANT OFFICER
    DAMON NICOLAS**
LIEUTENANT COLONEL J. D. JACK

DEMOCRATIC PEOPLE'S REPUBLIC OF KOREA LEADERSHIP

CHOI HA-GUK: Chairman, Democratic People's Republic of Korea, Supreme Leader
CHOI MESUN: Sister of the Supreme Leader
EUN PAK: Member of the Politburo

GENERAL IL-SEONG PHYO: Chief of the general staff of the Korean People's Army

OTHER CHARACTERS

DR. CATHY RYAN: First Lady of the United States

ISABEL YANG: Potential Campus helper

KIRA SIDOROVA: Russian scientist

LIEUTENANT BRANDON CATES: United States Navy SEAL

TOM CLANCY
ZERO HOUR

PROLOGUE

MUSUDAN-RI MISSILE TEST FACILITY, NORTH KOREA

"HOW IS HE?"

The innocuous-sounding question was anything but. In fact, to refer to the man in question simply as **he** without the accompaniment of one of his many honorifics was grounds for execution. But for Eun Pak, that ship had long since sailed. He remembered what was at stake with every breath, and Pak intended to ensure that his coconspirators did as well.

"The same."

Pak examined the man standing before him, considering.

Choi Ha-guk, chairman of the Democratic People's Republic of Korea and its Supreme Leader, had been incapacitated for the last week. One week since the Russians had unexpectedly handed Pak the opportunity of a lifetime. In most other places on earth, one week was not a significant amount of time.

Seven days.

The length of a typical American vacation.

But in the Democratic People's Republic of Korea, or DPRK, one week was time enough for an empire to fall.

Or rise.

But only if the weak-kneed man standing before him was telling the truth.

"And how is your baby daughter?" Pak said, coloring the question with a smile. "Her name is Seo-jun, correct?"

Of course it was correct.

Though Pak was an unremarkable middle-aged man with a slight build, hairless scalp, and thick glasses that magnified his watery eyes, he was also a member of the Korean Workers' Party. More important, Pak was a ranking member of the Politburo. A role with no parallel outside of the hermit kingdom. But here, in the land that time forgot, Pak was a minor deity. Certainly not on the same scale as the Supreme Leader, but powerful in his own right. Even a minor god such as Pak could erase an entire bloodline with a single telephone call.

Judging by the pasty look on the man's face, this knowledge wasn't lost on him. The man was a party member also and a doctor to boot, but in the DPRK, science was no match for deity. Either way, the doctor's time on earth was finite. If Pak was successful in his endeavor, there would be no witnesses. If he wasn't, well, Pak didn't intend to die alone. But just because the doctor had to be silenced didn't mean his infant daughter had to share the man's fate. Pak might be thorough, but he wasn't a monster.

Not without reason, anyway.

"She is fine, comrade," the doctor whispered. "Just fine."

"Good," Pak said with a nod. "Then let's ensure she stays that way. Tell me again his status."

Even here, in the sanctity of his temporary office located at the Musudan-ri Missile Test Facility, over six hundred kilometers from the seat of government in Pyongyang, Pak refused to speak the Supreme Leader's name. Past generations had attributed mythical qualities to the nation's ruling dynasty, and while Pak didn't subscribe to such superstitious nonsense, he was cautious for a different reason.

Unlike many of his fellow ruling elite, Pak made it a point to keep track of the advancements taking place beyond the DPRK's borders. He'd heard of listening devices that activated based on the utterance of a specific word. While Pak had his office swept for bugs regularly, one of the Supreme Leader's sycophants in the Ministry of State Security might have hidden some technological marvel that activated only when the Korean dictator's name was spoken. Pak hadn't risen to his current station through cowardice, but neither did he spit in the face of fate.

The man huffed out a breath, his lips smacking together like a horse's.

Pak thought the gesture something that a peasant might do. A mannerism unworthy of a doctor who attended to the Supreme Leader, but Pak let it pass without comment. Pak had ascended to his current station through meritocracy, but not the kind that resulted in promotions for bureaucrats in other corners of the world. No, Pak's skill was in a discipline much more basic.

Survival.

As a sitting member of the Politburo, Pak worked in the DPRK's decision-making apparatus. The Politburo's members were second only to the Supreme Leader and his family when it came to governance authority. Contrary to his predecessor cousin who'd championed the concept of **Songun,** or military-first as it pertained to DPRK politics, the Supreme Leader had vested more authority in the Politburo. The Supreme Leader had assumed power in a military-backed coup. He evidently didn't want to lose his position and life in a similar manner. This restructuring of the government had muted the all-consuming influence of the Korean People's Army and increased the influence of Pak and his fellow cabinet members.

But Pak's high-profile position wasn't without risk. Members of the Politburo who fell out of favor with the Supreme Leader often just disappeared. A single misplaced word or misunderstood facial expression could mean death. And when it came to the deaths of those who disappointed them, the leaders of the DPRK both past and present were anything but boring. In his three decades of service to the Korean Workers' Party, Pak had seen men stabbed to death by bayonet-wielding soldiers, burned alive by flamethrowers, mauled by attack dogs, and torn limb from limb by antiaircraft guns.

The Supreme Leader's lust for capital punishment wasn't limited to hapless paper pushers or military officers. Several branches of the dictator's family tree had been pruned in a manner only slightly less morbid. In addition to the cousin who predated him, the Supreme Leader had consolidated his power by dispatching a team of killers equipped with an experimental nerve agent to Malaysia to deal with a wayward half-brother. Pak had survived the lethal palace intrigue this long because he'd learned how to read people, how to recognize their tells. For instance, the doctor standing before him was as prone to hedge against relaying bad news as anyone, but when the man mimicked a horse, his words were true.

"Outwardly, his condition hasn't changed. But I think he's getting better."

"Why?" Pak said.

Pak was careful with the amount of influence he placed on the question, maintaining a stoic face while his heart raced. Much hung on the doctor's answer.

The doctor ran a hand through his sparse hair as he hunched forward, his thin frame sagging under the question's weight.

As a medical attendant charged with the Supreme Leader's health, the man ranked much higher in North Korea's unofficial caste system than the average citizen. In practical terms, this meant that the man and his family rated rations in great enough quantity that they wouldn't starve and living quarters with both power and running water.

But the effects of malnutrition were evident all the same.

Though only in his mid-thirties, the man looked two decades older. The wispy patches of hair sprouting from his scalp were prematurely gray, his shoulders stooped, and his skin sallow. While the median height and weight of their cousins to the south had steadily increased since the Fatherland Liberation War ended seventy years earlier, North Korea's population had withered both figuratively and literally. Life expectancy, weight, height, and overall health had all been in a steady decline for years.

The frail men and women surrounding him were constant reminders to Pak that an existence separate from the murderous undertones surrounding the politically elite was no guarantee of a longer life. In fact, the opposite was quite often true. Pak might live with one eye always open, waiting for a dagger thrust at his back, but he wouldn't starve to death.

That was something.

"His respiration and heart rate have begun to spike at increasing intervals during the day. This indicates that the patient is healing. His mind is slowly walking the path toward consciousness."

"How long until he wakes?" Pak said.

The doctor shrugged, his bony shoulders barely lifting his shirt. "There's no way to be sure. The periods between the increased heart rate and respiration are growing shorter and the manifestations longer. If the patient continues on this trajectory, I expect him to regain some semblance of lucidity in as soon as forty-eight hours."

"Two days?" Pak said.

Another huff.

"It could take longer. Conservatively I'd estimate a week, but I think he will be conscious much sooner."

Two days.

The words crashed against Pak's carefully constructed façade like a howling typhoon. Up until this point, everything he'd done was explainable or deniable. There would still be loose ends to clean up, like the good doctor, but on the whole Pak's exposure was minimal. Or as minimal as could be expected in the hermit kingdom, a place in which entire families ceased to exist at the whims of a boy-king.

Over the last several days, Pak had edged around the opportunity the ancestors had provided him. It was not unreasonable to think that the Supreme Leader's incapacitation might even have been staged. An elaborate stunt to test his inner circle's loyalty in preparation for yet another purge. Now that he was convinced that Choi really was incapacitated, Pak faced an ultimatum—act or watch the opportunity of a lifetime disappear.

Pak's gaze settled on the polished brass shell casing situated at the corner of his desk. Unlike his spacious office in Pyongyang, Pak's current quarters were decidedly more Spartan. If the scientist Pak had displaced to claim the space had a personal life, it was not evident. No family pictures or knickknacks graced the walls or shelves. Instead, every spare meter was devoted to academic books, charts and graphs covered with indecipherable equations, or reports detailing the successes and failures of previous missile tests.

Pak's brass shell casing was the one exception.

The cartridge was from a 7.62-millimeter round commonly fired by the AK-47. Though Pak had long ago learned the value of keeping his public workspace sterile as to not provide potential enemies with anything that could give them a deeper insight into his motivation, such decorations were not uncommon. The shell casings were supposed to serve as a remembrance of the regime's martial history, but to Pak, the length of brass signified something more.

The cartridge had been passed down to him by his father, who in turn had received it from his father. A man who'd been slated for execution in one of the many mass killings orchestrated by the boy-king's grandfather. Learning of his fate from a trusted friend, Pak's grandfather had arranged for his own death. A farm accident that was plausible and therefore not considered suicide. With this gift, Pak's grandfather had maintained his family's status in the Party and shielded his lineage from further harm. This selfless act defined Pak's life in two ways. On one hand, Pak wanted to honor his grandfather's sacrifice. On the other, Pak had vowed to make himself and his descendants immune to a single man's homicidal urges. This was quite simply the opportunity of a lifetime.

Two days wasn't much time, but it would have to be enough.

"Excellent," Pak said, sweetening the word with a rare smile. "You've brought honor to yourself and your family."

"Thank you, comrade," the doctor said, bowing at the compliment. "I am honored to serve."

"Yes, you are," Pak said. "And this is how you will ensure that honor passes from you to your daughter."

The doctor's hopeful expression faded more with each word Pak spoke. By the time Pak finished, the doctor's face was again the color of ash. This was to be expected. Pak was a man of his word. The doctor's daughter would reap the benefits of her father's sacrifice, just as Pak had with his grandfather.

Unfortunately for the doctor, the similarities wouldn't end there.

1

JACK RYAN, JR., CONSIDERED HIMSELF A MAN OF culture. Even so, he'd never before experienced a flash mob. At least he thought it was a flash mob. This was South Korea. If there was anything Jack had learned in the handful of hours he'd been on Korean soil, it was that things here were a bit . . . **different.**

And that included flash mobs.

One moment Jack had been contemplating the towering stone statue of Admiral Yi Sun-sin, the next he was body-to-body with a plaza full of chanting Koreans. Though the early-afternoon sun had yet to burn through a gray overcast sky, and scattered puddles of oily water from the morning's rain still coated the pedestrian area's stone walkways, the iffy weather did little to deter the growing crowd. People poured into Gwanghwamun

Plaza from adjacent streets, spilling past the office buildings lining the west and east sides of the plaza and threading around the concrete barriers and stone planters designed to keep frisky Korean drivers at bay.

Jack had taken Domingo "Ding" Chavez's advice. Rather than renting a car, Jack had grabbed a cab at the airport. Once again his mentor and co-worker had provided Jack with safe counsel. While he wasn't exactly a stranger to driving overseas, as near as Jack could tell, Korean traffic signs were merely suggestions. In fact, none of the Western driving norms Jack was accustomed to seemed to apply. After he and the cabbie experienced two near misses before even leaving the airport proper, Jack had decided that feigning sleep and reciting the Rosary was the best way to allow his jet-lagged mind to cope with the sudden onslaught of stimuli. Lisanne Robertson had followed suit, cradling her head against Jack's shoulder and closing her eyes. With the feel of her thick, dark hair against his cheek and the smell of her olive-toned skin just inches away, the traffic hadn't seemed quite so horrible.

Or maybe Jack had just come to the realization that dying with a beautiful woman's head on his shoulder wasn't such a bad way to go. In any case, the avalanche of bodies now pouring into the plaza made the taxi ride's madness seem like a Sunday drive.

At six-foot-two, Jack had no problem seeing over the crowd, but he was less successful in locating an avenue of escape. The people really were coming from everywhere, and the first human wave had washed up against the statue and was now pooling in swirling eddies. Jack was a big man even by American standards. His two-hundred-twenty-pound athletic frame usually ensured that bystanders kept their distance.

Not in South Korea.

Like in many Asian countries, Koreans didn't subscribe to the Western idea of personal space. Though to be fair, flash mobs by nature were all about crowding as many people into a confined space as possible. Assuming of course that this gathering actually was a flash mob. Jack was not the hippest guy when it came to social media, but the videos he'd seen tended to feature impromptu concerts or dancing, not chanting people holding signs. Which meant this probably wasn't a flash mob at all. Koreans had a long history of protesting government abuses, both real and perceived, and this tradition far predated Instagram or TikTok.

Using the lifelike rendering of Admiral Yi Sun-sin as a reference point, Jack pressed through the crowd until he arrived at the statue's elliptical-shaped base. Mounting the two steps leading up to a viewing platform of sorts, Jack assessed the situation from his newly found observation post.

The plaza was oriented north-to-south, with the

statue of Admiral Yi Sun-sin on the very southern tip, surrounded by an array of decorative fountains and specially designed stones commemorating the admiral's victory over a Japanese fleet back in the 1500s. A second statue sat to the north of the admiral, this one a golden rendering of King Sejong the Great seated on his throne. Beyond the throne, a long stretch of closely cropped grass pointed to a traditional temple-style building framed by a pastoral set of mountainous foothills, an unexpected sight in the center of a city of more than nine million people.

But there was nothing pastoral about the press of bodies surging into the plaza or the ranks of riot police taking up station between the demonstrators and the office buildings. For the first time since he'd set off on his solo sightseeing trip, Jack was glad that Lisanne was back at the hotel. She'd elected to crash in her room for a short nap before dinner.

Her room.

Those two words carried with them a world of significance.

Pushing away his romantic quandary for the moment, Jack focused his sluggish brain on the task at hand. While he was all for experiencing as much of South Korea as possible during his short trip, participating in a riot wasn't on his list. He was wearing a hat to hide his dark hair and sunglasses to conceal his blue eyes, but Jack was under no illusions that he somehow blended into the crowd. Between his height and girth, he stuck out like a sore thumb, and if there was one place where blending in mattered, it was in a rambunctious crowd, especially one overseen by riot policemen looking for an excuse to make an example out of someone.

While his potential escape route to the south was clearly untenable, the north looked more promising. Much like the National Mall in Washington, D.C., this area of Seoul was packed full of cultural icons, museums, and the like. In fact, the Blue House, the Korean version of the White House, was only a couple kilometers to the north. It stood to reason that security measures would become progressively more restrictive in that direction of travel.

Jack figured this meant that if the crowd became unruly, the demonstrators would confine their activities to this section of the plaza rather than risk the wrath of the Presidential Security Service, whose security cordon would tighten the closer one came to the president's residence. Besides, if things truly got out of hand, Jack could always seek refuge at the U.S. embassy conveniently located on the eastern side of the plaza. Though they might tolerate a bit of social disobedience directed at their own government, the South Korean National Police Agency would take a dim view toward anyone targeting a foreign embassy.

His decision made, Jack moved north using the giant golden statue as his guide. As he pushed through the crowd, he was careful not to let the riptide of bodies drag him down the steps to his right. The stairs led to a lower tier and the recessed entrance of a museum dedicated to Admiral Yi Sun-sin. The lower landing's high walls to the east and steps to the west were channelizing terrain, and Jack instinctively knew to avoid it.

These were not the thoughts of an average tourist.

Very little about Jack was average.

2

AS JACK EDGED THROUGH THE BYSTANDERS, HE SENSED the crowd's energy changing. The gathering had begun with an orderly vibe. Though the plaza's pedestrian space was limited, the press of bodies had felt benign, more like the spectators lining the corner of Broadway and 34th Street for the Macy's Thanksgiving Day Parade than the chaos of a riot. In a way he couldn't really explain, Jack would have almost termed the mass of people polite.

But not anymore.

Now a sense of menace permeated the air like the smell of ozone after a lightning strike. Jack would be hard-pressed to articulate what exactly had changed, but he believed what his sixth sense was communicating all the same. The chants sounded angrier, people's expressions looked harsher, and the shoving and pushing were more pronounced.

Something was about to happen.

Something malignant.

Jack had no intentions of being close by when it did.

A scream echoed to his right.

Jack looked toward the sound, watching as several bodies tumbled down the recessed steps, like boulders eroded by a flash flood. Two of the bodies, a portly middle-aged man and a twenty-something hipster, both pushed themselves to their feet. The third, a teenage girl, lay where she'd sprawled, clutching her ankle. For a moment, the mass of humanity parted, and the girl's fearful eyes found Jack's. Then a cloud of tear gas drifted skyward from the row of riot police lining the street to the west.

The crowd convulsed as protesters swarmed.

The stricken teenager vanished.

Cursing, Jack grabbed the metal railing and vaulted into the makeshift mosh pit. Like a stone splashing into a pond, Jack's bulk sent ripples through the crowd. He capitalized on the disruption, charting a path through the humanity with the subtlety of an icebreaker's bow. In four quick strides, Jack smashed his way to the still-screaming girl, scooping her up with powerful arms and dislodging two of the people trampling her in the process. With a drowning swimmer's desperation, the girl wrapped her arms around Jack's thick neck, babbling in Korean between tear-filled hiccups.

"It's okay," Jack said, cradling the teenager to his chest. "I've got you."

While Jack did in fact have the girl, the situation was a long way from okay.

As Jack had feared, the recessed area leading to the museum had become a choke point. People were fleeing the lurking tear-gas clouds spiraling in from the west with none of the discipline and consideration for others the demonstrators had initially displayed. As Jack watched, a man was crushed against the railing above him, crying out in pain. The demonstrator shoved back against the encroaching bodies, freeing himself, but Jack knew that the next person wouldn't be so lucky.

Though humans liked to think of themselves as enlightened beings, the primal animal lurking beneath the veneer of civilization was closer to the surface than most people realized. When a fight-or-flight situation arose, the average **Homo sapiens** didn't react all that much differently than a stampeding bovine. To make matters worse, the ramp sloping from the upper plaza to the museum's entrance was acting like a funnel, channeling the surging crowd into a whirlpool of swirling bodies. Turning behind him, Jack looked toward the museum's entrance just in time to see a protective metal accordion drop over the glass doors, sealing the antiquities in and the crowd out.

No help that way.

The girl murmured something Jack could neither hear nor comprehend. When he didn't respond, she said it again, this time pointing. Following her outstretched index finger, Jack understood.

Up.

The panicking crowd made escape up the stairs to the west or the sloping ramp to the north impossible. Likewise, with the entrance to the museum barricaded, evading to the south was out. But perhaps Jack needed to think three-dimensionally. The eastern wall was made of smooth cinder block, unclimbable to anyone not part spider. But the top of the barrier was lined with metal railings, presumably to keep street-level pedestrians from accidentally falling into the recessed area.

That was a possibility.

Grunting, Jack push-pressed the girl over his head toward the tubular railings, shoulders quivering with the effort. The teenager stretched for the barricade, her fingertips just brushing the cylindrical railing.

Too far.

A series of distant screams brought another avalanche of bodies tumbling into the already confined space. Jack cradled the girl against his chest an instant before the surge smashed him against the cinder-block wall. He took most of the impact across his back and shoulders, but the collision whiplashed his head into the masonry, causing him to briefly see stars. Somehow Jack kept his footing, but the bodies compressed him against the wall, making it difficult to breathe. The girl squirmed in his arms, shrieking as an overweight Korean man used her damaged ankle as leverage to pull himself upright.

This had to end.

Now.

Turning so that he faced south, Jack backpedaled, forcing his way up the ramp. People groaned and cried out to either side, but Jack no longer had the luxury of caring. The compounded force of thousands of bodies was just too strong. Sooner or later, the girl would be ripped from his arms and trampled to death.

Jack wasn't going to let that happen.

The first several yards were relatively easy going, but Jack's good fortune quickly ended. Like a spring compressed to its limits, Jack's progress was abruptly halted by a wall of unyielding human flesh.

He wasn't going any farther.

Looking up, Jack eyed the railing, judging distances. By shouldering his way up the ramp, he'd lessened the height to the metal barrier. Not as much as he'd have liked, but maybe enough. Transferring his grip, Jack shoulder-pressed the girl upward. This time she got her fingers around the bar, but the smooth metal slid from her grasp.

His shoulders and arms quaking, Jack lowered the teenager back to his chest.

He had to lift her higher.

Another round of screams echoed from the west, but Jack didn't bother to look. He already knew there wasn't enough room for the coming wave of people. Either he was lifting the girl free or they'd both die in this hellhole. Jack crouched and then exploded upward, driving from his heels. Rather than trying to just lift the girl, this time Jack hurled her into the air like he was squat-thrusting an Olympic bar piled with weights.

The teenager rocketed upward with a shriek.

The apogee of the girl's flight brought her even with the top railing, but her flailing arms missed the silvery metal completely. Jack cursed even as he prepared to catch her deadweight, but the girl surprised him. With a move that might have been equal parts skill or desperation, she snagged the bottom section of the rail, wrapping both of her thin arms around it. The teenager didn't look like she had the strength to haul herself the rest of the way over the railing and onto the street, but she was safe.

For now.

Seeing the girl's leg dangling invitingly down the cinder-block wall, a man several people down from Jack grabbed hold as if to pull himself out of the churning pit. Or at least Jack assumed that's what the Korean was trying to do. Jack's Korean was extremely limited, so he persuaded the man of the inadequacies of this plan using a more universal language.

Violence.

Leaning over the swirling mass, Jack struck the man once at the base of the neck with his closed fist.

Once was enough.

The man crumpled soundlessly, but the damage to the teenager was already done. The Korean's weight had yanked the girl off her somewhat secure perch. Now she was hanging the length of the wall, her grip on the railing slipping.

Figuring that turnabout was fair play, Jack planted a boot on the fallen man's back and vaulted upward. He too snagged the lowest section of railing, but unlike the girl, Jack had the use of both legs. Grunting, he turned perpendicular to the wall, placing his feet flat against the cinder block. Then he pushed off the rough surface, trading grips for a crossbeam slightly higher than the one he'd previously held. This gave him enough room to loop his leg over the lower railing, winching himself up and over the concrete lip.

The little maneuver had taken more out of Jack than he cared to admit, but he hadn't earned a rest just yet. Crouching on the street level, he threaded his arms between the railing and snared the girl's wrist just as her grip faltered. She screamed as she hung by one arm, but this time Jack was ready for the weight. Clamping both of his massive hands on her slender forearm, Jack stood, taking her mass with his legs.

Once again, the teenager surprised him. The girl grabbed Jack's wrist with her free hand, solidifying their link. Then, as she drew even with the top railing, she looped her uninjured leg over the metal, easing some of the load on Jack's traps and hamstrings. The maneuver caused her broken ankle to bang against the cinder-block wall, and while the girl cried out, she didn't loosen her hold on Jack or on the railing.

Tough cookie.

Jack wrenched the girl's wrist skyward as he pushed with his legs, executing a hang-clean lift that would have done his strength coach proud. The girl rocketed over the railing and into his arms. Now they were on the street above the roiling crowd. Jack took a shuddering breath and started to lower the girl to the ground until he caught sight of her ankle for the first time.

The flesh was swollen and deformed—broken for sure.

He needed to get her to help.

Turning, Jack saw a scattering of police officers forming up on the eastern five-lane road separating the plaza from the north/south running line of office buildings and hotels. As Jack watched, a white van with a green light bar, green stripes, and a prominent green cross nosed up to the sidewalk.

Taking the ambulance's arrival as a sign, Jack started across the street, the girl once again cradled against his chest.

Several of the police eyed Jack, but no one attempted to interdict him. While Jack knew firsthand that riots could be nasty business, the South Korean National Police had a reputation for professionalism. They were here to do a job, and that job was to prevent looting or damage to the businesses and cultural icons lining the plaza, not rough up a man carrying an obviously injured girl. But while they weren't actively preventing Jack from leaving the site of the riot, neither were they rushing to help.

Fair enough.

Jack could certainly understand the sentiment behind their actions. As Ding was fond of saying, if you're gonna be stupid, you'd better be tough. Ding was one of the original members of the storied Rainbow counterterrorism team.

When he spoke, Jack listened.

Adjusting his course, Jack tracked toward the green-and-white ambulance. The vehicle had parked about seventy-five meters south of the nearest police picket line, perhaps so that the medics wouldn't be caught up in a potential melee between police and protesters. This meant Jack had significantly farther to carry the teenage girl, a situation emphasized when his foot caught an unseen pothole and he stumbled, jarring the girl's leg.

"I'm sorry," Jack said as the girl whimpered. **"Joesong haeyo."**

This along with **please, thank you,** and **excuse me** formed the bulk of Jack's Korean vocabulary.

In this case, it was enough.

"Thank you," the teenager replied hesitantly.

"No worries," Jack said, hoping a reassuring tone would comfort the girl even if his words didn't. "These medics will fix you up. Once they get a splint on your ankle, you'll feel right as rain."

Right as rain.

Who talked like that?

The answer came a millisecond later—his mom, the indomitable Cathy Ryan. Apparently, holding a child transformed Jack into his mother.

Fantastic.

"Oh-kay," the girl said, spacing out the word's two syllables. She tightened her arms around Jack's neck even as she gritted her teeth.

If her ankle truly was broken, by now the initial shot of adrenaline had to be wearing off. The poor kid must be in agony. Across the way, two medics hopped out of the ambulance. Jack assumed that the pair would be moving to help, but neither man so much as glanced his way. Instead, the driver rounded the front of the vehicle and headed east, disappearing from view. The second medic yanked open the ambulance's side door before sticking his head inside.

"Hey," Jack said, bellowing to ensure that his voice was heard. "A little help here. **Dowa juseyo.**"

Who would have thought that he'd exhaust all his Korean phrases in his first five minutes of conversation? That said, either the language app he'd selected was defective or Jack was dealing with the most disinterested paramedic ever to take the Hippocratic oath.

"Over here," Jack yelled. "This girl needs help."

This time he put enough umph in his voice to attract the attention of the nearest policeman. The man turned to his partner and exchanged words. The partner shrugged. Setting his riot shield and baton on the ground, the policeman trotted toward Jack.

Which was more than could be said of the paramedic. The man's head popped out of the ambulance's cabin as Jack's second bellow echoed across the street, but what the paramedic did next was puzzling. Rather than follow the policeman's lead, he locked gazes with Jack as he stood in front of the ambulance, unmoving.

Then he smiled.

Though it was a heartless gesture, Jack could understand why the medic might react that way to rioters who'd injured themselves while breaking the law. But Jack would have thought that even the most hardened first responder would feel compassion for a suffering teenage girl. After all, the riot policeman had to be every bit as jaded, and he was still coming to help.

Or maybe the ambulance was meant to serve as a casualty collection point. In this case, perhaps the medic had been instructed not to leave the vehicle for fear that he would become lost in the crowd and unreachable when those with truly life-threatening injuries were discovered. While Jack didn't agree with this logic, he at least understood it. But here again, the medic's actions were indecipherable. After holding Jack's gaze for a beat, the man walked around the vehicle and disappeared to the east, retracing his partner's footsteps.

Jack stopped mid-stride, finally understanding.

To his left, the policeman was halfway across the street.

To his right, the ambulance's passenger door was still swinging open.

No help there.

Spinning in a complete circle, Jack saw them.

A series of concrete planters lining the metal railing behind him.

With a grunt, Jack sprinted for the planters even as the teenager pounded her fists against his chest. The policeman called out, but the totality of Jack's being was focused on the rectangular concrete structure steps away. He could see every indentation in the chipped surface, count every blade of grass in the green foliage sprouting from the dark soil.

Just three more steps.

Then two.

Jack dove across the planter, banging his knee on the jagged edge as he sailed over in a headfirst, Pete Rose slide. He careened into the metal grating on the other side of the structure like a pinball bouncing off a bumper. Then he was on the ground, the girl squirming beneath him. Shrieking, she clawed at his face and neck, no doubt convinced that her American savior had lost his mind.

For a long moment, Jack found himself agreeing.

Then the world exploded.

3

THE BLAST FOUND JACK IN PIECES.

First, an eye-scorching flash of light. Then invisible fists of heat that pummeled him with searing haymakers. Finally, an all-consuming roar. Jack curled around the girl in the fetal position as debris fell from the sky, waiting for the ground to cease trembling. After a moment he realized that it was his equilibrium, not the earth, that was still trembling.

With a groan, Jack pushed himself to his knees, using the planter for support.

Or what was left of it, anyway.

A piece of metal had shattered the thick concrete like a children's sandcastle, embedding itself in the potting soil that had formerly held foliage of some kind.

Now only charred stalks remained.

Another couple inches and the shrapnel would have scythed into Jack's head.

This sobering thought did much to propel Jack the rest of the way to his feet. Though the world was still tilted slightly off axis, he could stand. This meant he could walk.

At least in theory.

Reaching down, Jack gathered the teenager in his arms.

"You okay?" Jack said. "Okay?"

Tears streamed down her face, but she nodded.

Tough cookie didn't even begin to describe the teen's grit. When this was over, he might just have to introduce her to Ding. Cradling the girl, Jack turned to where the ambulance had once stood. This was not a natural disaster or some kind of horrific accident.

It had been a bombing.

An attack.

Which meant that there were no assurances that the ambush was actually over. In Jack's experience, a bomb was more often than not the precursor to the main event. A way to soften and disorient the target before the real killing began. He needed to get off the X and vacate the kill zone.

The devastation on the opposite side of the street was reassuring in an odd way. Though bodies were strewn around the ambulance's wreckage, and several of the neighboring buildings showed damage from flying debris, the structures were still standing. Likewise, the vehicle itself, while engulfed in flames, was recognizable and not at the bottom of a crater. Either the explosives hadn't detonated properly or the bomb was smaller than Jack had originally thought.

In some ways, it was the difference between a tragic event and a catastrophic one. If the entire ambulance had been loaded with ammonium nitrate and fuel oil like the rental truck used in the Oklahoma City bombing, nearly everyone in the plaza would have been injured while those in the outermost ring would have been killed by flying debris, the bomb's shock wave, or both.

Including Jack.

While he didn't know why the bomb's explosive yield had been abnormally low, Jack wasn't going to look a gift horse in the mouth. Putting one foot in front of the other, he stumbled toward the line of policemen. This time, he didn't have to bother asking for help. Like the best of law enforcement officers the world over, the Korean police were running toward the death and destruction wrought by the car bomb with little regard for their own safety or injuries. A female officer sprinted up to Jack, her cap missing and her short black hair disheveled. As she drew closer, Jack saw a wicked gash across her forehead that was still leaking blood. Nevertheless, she pointed at the girl while jabbering in Korean.

"It's broken," Jack said, loudly and slowly. "Her ankle."

He realized the idiotic statement for what it was when the teenager responded to the police officer with a rush of Korean.

Way to live up to the American stereotype.

"Take her over there," the policewoman said, her English accented but easily understandable. "We have to help the most injured first."

The officer pointed toward a street corner that was fast becoming a casualty collection point. Jack nodded. While the bomb's blast had been far less damaging than it could have been, the ensuing destruction was still significant. Not to mention the injuries, which must have resulted from the tear gas–induced stampede Jack had barely escaped. The girl's broken ankle was no doubt painful, but it wasn't life-threatening.

For that, Jack was grateful.

Walking across the street, Jack tried to keep his stride even and measured, as much to keep from falling as to avoid jarring the teenager. The poor girl had been through a lot already today. Jack didn't want to add getting smothered by an American to the list.

In a first, he made it to the casualty collection point without incident and placed the teenager gently on the ground. A frazzled-looking man rushed over wearing a paramedic's uniform and blood-soaked gloves. The medic barked a question, and Jack responded by making the break sign with his hands and then pointing at the girl's ankle.

The man knelt, triaging the leg with quick, efficient motions even as he conversed with the girl in Korean. After finishing his examination, the man looked at Jack and asked a question in halting English.

"You friend?"

Jack shook his head. "**Aniyo.** Just helping."

The medic nodded. "She stay here. Then go hospital."

"Sounds good," Jack said.

The medic was on the verge of leaving when the girl accosted him with a deluge of Korean. The man nodded twice and then turned back to Jack.

"She say you saved her. She say thank you."

The girl grabbed Jack's hand with both of hers as the medic spoke.

"Thank you," she said, again pausing between the words.

"You're very welcome," Jack said with a smile.

After giving the girl a final wave, Jack turned and headed east, away from the destruction and chaos engulfing the plaza.

Though his first inclination was to stick around to tell the South Korean authorities what he'd seen, Jack decided against that course of action. The bombers had been dressed as paramedics, and the crowd had been herded into the kill zone, presumably by additional coconspirators who looked like police. Until he could better tell friend from foe, Jack intended to get as far away from the site of the bombing as possible. If anything, he and Lisanne would probably be on a plane headed back home by this time tomorrow.

Then his phone rang.

4

"HELLO," JACK SAID, ANGLING HIS FACE TOWARD THE ground as he walked.

Though he was wearing bulky clothing and a hat to conceal his hair, there was nothing Jack could do about his fair Irish skin or light-colored eyes. In a city as homogenous as Seoul, different stood out. This was not the time to draw the attention of law enforcement.

"Jack? It's Lisanne."

The husky voice brought the beginnings of a smile to Jack's face, despite the craziness surrounding him. He and the half-Lebanese, half-American woman were currently in the relationship equivalent of no-man's-land. They were something more than friends, but not yet lovers. Jack had brought her home to Mom and Dad twice now, and that was significant. First, because Jack could count the number of romantic interests he'd seen fit to introduce to his parents on one hand.

But that wasn't all.

Jack's parents had the honor of being the First Lady and the President of the United States. With this in mind, bringing a date home for Sunday dinner took a bit more coordination than it had before Jack Ryan, Sr., had been elected to the nation's highest office.

And then there was the fact that he and Lisanne were coworkers.

Or at least had been coworkers.

Jack and Lisanne were both clandestine employees of The Campus—a private organization technically outside the umbrella of the American intelligence community. Though Lisanne's director of transportation title sounded ordinary enough, like most things Campus-related, there was more to Lisanne's role than what met the eye. As a former Marine whose Lebanese mother had ensured she was fluent in Arabic, Lisanne had quickly proven herself operative material. In fact, the legendary John T. Clark, director of operations for The Campus and plank owner in the storied Rainbow organization, had been supervising her field training when an operation in China had tragically gone wrong. Lisanne had sustained a grievous gunshot wound that had required the amputation of her arm and almost cost her her life.

Now Clark and his second-in-command, Ding, were trying to decide what to do with Lisanne.

Or perhaps it was more accurate to say that Lisanne was trying to figure out what to do with herself.

With just one arm, her career as a gunfighter was over before it had really begun.

But that didn't mean her utility to The Campus had ended.

"Hey, Lisanne," Jack said, his smile widening. "I thought you were taking a nap."

"I am. Or at least I was. Every emergency siren in Seoul seems to be blaring. Know anything about it?"

"Well . . ."

"Holy crap, Jack," Lisanne said. "You serious?"

"Afraid so," Jack said.

"You need to come in?" Lisanne said.

Once again Jack found himself appreciating the way Lisanne thought. Rather than asking for a play-by-play of what had happened, she went straight to the most pertinent question—was Jack operationally compromised. Jack thought that it was this, more than her martial prowess or linguistic proficiency, that had impressed Clark. Lots of people knew how to shoot and fight. Someone who could think while enduring the crushing pressure that went hand in hand with clandestine operations really was a diamond in the rough.

"I don't think so," Jack said, angling down yet

another side street. "But we should move up our schedule if possible. I didn't cause this nonsense, but I had a front-row seat."

Jack had briefly entertained the idea of heading to the U.S. embassy. The mission was only a block or two from the riot and subsequent car bombing and would offer refuge if things really went sideways. But that safety was a double-edged sword. Foreign intelligence services routinely tasked watchers to log the comings and goings of embassy visitors. Jack and Lisanne were in South Korea for operational purposes. He wanted to stay under the radar, and that meant avoiding the embassy.

"Agreed," Lisanne said. "That's why I'm calling. Well, and because I half expected you to have something to do with the sirens."

"Seriously?" Jack said, a smile in his voice.

"Let's face it, friend. Subtlety isn't your thing. Anyway, Isabel texted. She wants to meet today instead of tomorrow."

"She say why?" Jack said.

"No. And since we're still in the dating phase, I didn't push. You know how people can be about commitment."

The double entendre, intentional or not, gave Jack pause.

He and Lisanne were also standing at the commitment precipice. For the first time in his life, Jack found himself intentionally going slower. This was partly because Lisanne was a Campus colleague and Jack knew that the nature of their work relationship would permanently change if they became intimate. But his hesitation ran deeper. Jack's history with women wasn't stellar. For far too long he'd lived the playboy life, never thinking past the moment.

This attitude had gotten him nowhere.

During his last assignment to Israel, Jack had done some soul-searching. He was no longer the junior Campus guy who needed hand-holding from Clark or Ding. He'd finally achieved what he'd spent the last decade chasing in one form or fashion only to find it . . . wanting.

By this point in his life, Jack's dad had already met and married his true love and had fathered two children. Jack always assumed he'd follow in Senior's footsteps. He'd meet the right girl and start a family. Now that he was in his thirties, Jack had finally realized that he wasn't going to just bump into the future Mrs. Ryan while running clandestine operations for The Campus. To quote his surgeon mother, a change in results necessitated a change in behavior. Jack hadn't yet worked out exactly how to make that change, but he knew the series of flings and casual relationships he'd pursued in his twenties had not led to happiness.

With Lisanne, he had the chance to start over. To court a woman who could very well be the future Mrs. Ryan. Though their relationship was still in its infancy, Jack knew that Lisanne was something special. He wasn't going to mess this one up by repeating past mistakes, even if that meant sailing into uncharted territory.

"Sorry," Lisanne said, breaking the silence, "I didn't mean—"

"Lisanne Robertson, you're the only girl I've brought home to Mom and Dad," Jack said, smiling into the phone. "Ever. I'm not afraid of commitment, but I want to do this right. You deserve it."

For a long moment, Lisanne didn't reply. Jack forced himself to remain quiet, even though he desperately wanted to speak. Patience wasn't something that came easy to Jack Ryan, Jr., but maybe even old dogs really could learn new tricks.

"Jack Ryan," Lisanne said with a chuckle, "you are something else. We spend the better part of a fifteen-hour plane ride trading magazines and talking about nothing. But now that you're on a cell phone and dodging the police, you want to have the relationship discussion. You sure know how to make a girl feel special."

"Wait a minute," Jack said, coming to a stop on the sidewalk. "I—"

"Joking, Jack," Lisanne said with another soft laugh. "I'm joking. And also a little flattered. I can't say I've ever had this talk with emergency sirens for mood music. Tell you what, I'll give you credit for starting the conversation, but let's pick this up later. We need to focus on the girl we're jointly dating instead."

In the lexicon of espionage, The Campus was very much still **dating** Isabel Yang. The twenty-six-year-old Ph.D. student had come to The Campus's attention via a handoff from Adam Yao, a CIA case officer and sometime Campus collaborator. Adam had originally considered making the approach himself, but hadn't. Isabel had already turned down a recruitment offer from the buttoned-down agency once. Perhaps she would respond more favorably to a different organization.

An organization like The Campus.

As an off-the-books, quasi-government entity, The Campus did not have access to the formidable recruiting tools available to the acknowledged members of the intelligence community, even though its operational tempo was greater than that of many of its sister entities. The recruitment and training of new Campus personnel was a monumental task the organization struggled to handle. After experiencing the rigors of onboarding new operatives firsthand, Ding Chavez had come up with a novel idea—utilize the Israeli Mossad's model of "helpers" to augment The Campus's operational staff.

With this in mind, Jack and Lisanne were given the task to follow up on Adam Yao's lead by flying to South Korea and conducting an assessment of Isabel's current and future utility to The Campus. While nothing in her already extensive file suggested that the scientist was asset material, Isabel was deemed worth the trip. An American female academic who spoke three languages, lived in South Korea, and could pass for half a dozen nationalities wasn't exactly a four-leaf clover, but she was pretty darn close.

"Deal," Jack said, "but this conversation isn't over."

"It took fifteen hours to get here," Lisanne said. "I'm pretty sure it'll take at least that long to fly back. We'll keep until then. Isabel, on the other hand, wants to meet in less than an hour."

"Where?" Jack said.

"Itaewon," Lisanne said. "She sent an address to a coffee shop off Hoenamu-ro Street."

Jack pulled up Google Maps and entered the address. The establishment was a fifteen-minute walk from his current location, just southeast of the sprawling Namsan Park, famous as the home of the iconic Seoul Tower. The mountainous terrain would act as a natural buffer to the chaos enveloping the Gwanghwamun Plaza Jack had just left and the shopping and dining mecca that was Itaewon.

Better still, the U.S. Army garrison of Yongsan was just to the southwest of the café. At this point, Jack wasn't expecting trouble, but he hadn't been during his earlier sightseeing excursion, either. The longer he spent in this business, the more Jack subscribed to the operational belief attributed to legendary Marine General James N. Mattis—be polite, be professional, but have a plan to kill everyone you meet.

In this case, Jack wasn't on a mission to kill anyone, but that didn't negate the need for contingency planning. Though much of the U.S. footprint originally stationed at Yongsan had been relocated to Camp Humphreys, the installation still housed armed American soldiers.

Good enough for Jack.

"I can make that work," Jack said. "What about you?"

"Shouldn't be a problem. I'll take a cab and text you when I'm on the way."

"It's a date," Jack said.

Another soft chuckle.

"This is work, Jack. Not a date. Someday I hope you learn the difference."

Jack scrambled for a witty reply, but he was too late.

Lisanne had already hung up.

5

SEOUL, SOUTH KOREA

"I HAVE A QUESTION," SERGEANT FIRST CLASS JAD Mustafa said, placing his Sac Sac can on the faux-wood table.

"For the last time, I don't know how they squeeze the grape past the little hole in the soda can," Master Sergeant Cary Marks said, flipping over the strips of meat sizzling on the boxy grill separating the two men. "Maybe the same way they get those little sailboats into bottles."

"Nah," Jad said, adding bits of garlic to the smoking meat, "the little ships are collapsible. Everybody knows that. Besides, that wasn't my question, though I think I just swallowed an entirely intact grape. I have a much more pressing inquiry—why are we here again?"

Cary sighed as he rescued a slice of **bulgogi** from the hungry flames, slapping the spitting beef on the lettuce he'd appropriated for this purpose. Or at least he hoped it was lettuce. In Cary's opinion, the greens the waitress had deposited on the men's table bore a striking resemblance to the trimmings left on the sidewalk last time he'd weed-whacked his front yard.

To be fair, this was a long way away from Cary's front yard, which was located just minutes from the 5th Special Forces Group's home of Fort Campbell, Kentucky. Cary and his best friend and fellow sniper were in a barbecue restaurant in Seoul, South Korea. And while the two Green Berets were accustomed to spending time in far-flung places around the globe in the company of their fellow Operational Detachment Alpha, or ODA, teammates, this was something new.

The two men, along with the ten other members of ODA 555, or Triple Nickel, had traded their MultiCams for civvies and left their field gear and weapons in the team room. From Cary's perspective, their current digs were a good deal better than baking in the Syrian heat while lying shoulder-to-shoulder under a smelly sniper hide site. But Jad had a point, and Cary owed him the courtesy of an honest reply.

"Do I look like an officer?" Cary said, adding some mostly cooked garlic strips to the meat. "We're here because we were told to be here. Now eat."

Jad swiped a piece of charred meat from the grill

with his chopsticks, showing a surprising amount of dexterity. He studied the dangling strip for a second before adding the beef to his own stack of lettuce.

"Do you think it's—"

"No," Cary said, "I don't."

"How do you know—"

"Because I do," Cary said. "That's a delicacy here. They wouldn't just serve it to us out of the blue."

"Okay, but—"

"Are you a Green Beret or not?" Cary said, sandwiching the lettuce around his meat. "'Cause if this is too much culture, you can always eat at McDonald's with the SEALs."

Physically, the two Green Berets couldn't have been more different. Cary Marks was a blue-eyed, blond-haired farm boy from New England whose vowels gave away his Yankee roots under moments of duress. Jad Mustafa's dark complexion and SoCal surfer accent lent itself to kidding from his teammates, who often accused him of being a SEAL in disguise, a sentiment Jad's affinity for hair gel and fashionable clothes didn't help. Even so, the men's differences in skin color or nationality had ceased to matter long ago. After more than a half a dozen shared combat deployments, Cary and Jad were brothers in a way that transcended birth parents or family lineage.

And like brothers, they enjoyed picking at each other.

"That was uncalled for," Jad said, his brown eyes twinkling. "As a proud Libyan, I have more culture in my little finger than you do in your farm-boy—whoa, now. Boss, I think our dinner plans just got interesting."

Cary had shared more meals with Jad than he could count. Some of these had been of the beers-and-burgers variety typical of American friendships, but most had not. Far more often Cary and his spotter had spent mealtime huddled over the remains of a meal, ready-to-eat, or MRE, passing the tiny allotment of Tabasco sauce between them as they alternated duties behind an M151 spotting scope or the SIG Sauer Tango6T optic mounted to Barrett Advanced Sniper Rifles.

Sitting on the back deck with a cold one while jawing about the Titans' chances at a Super Bowl ring was one way to gain the measure of a man. Trying to ignore sand fleas munching their way up your inner thigh while maintaining surveillance on a target compound in one-hundred-degree heat was another. Cary had been the team sergeant for Triple Nickel long enough to do both with Jad, and with that familiarity came knowledge. In this case, the knowledge that when Jad used the word **boss,** the time for bullshitting and ass grabbing was over.

"Whaddaya got?" Cary said, resisting the urge to look over his shoulder.

As was the case with most folks who lived at the pointy end of the spear, Cary hated sitting in a room with his back to the door. Unfortunately, his spotter was of the same philosophy, and had been a little fleeter of foot when the two men had entered the restaurant. This meant that Jad was now positioned with his back against the wall, leaving Cary dependent on his spotter.

Which, now that Cary thought about it, wasn't all that different from the situations in which the two men usually found themselves.

"Important dude just arrived," Jad said, pitching his voice low enough not to carry. "Dark suit, blue tie, glasses. Three protective agents with him— two men and a woman. All three are giving yours truly the hairy eyeball."

"Let's face it," Cary said, folding the lettuce around the meat strips and roasted garlic slivers, "you are a shady-looking dude."

"I don't know, white boy," Jad said, his voice barely a whisper. "Neither of us really blends in here."

The pair were in a nondescript Korean barbecue restaurant off an unnamed side street in the Itaewon section of Seoul, within walking distance of the U.S. Army garrison at Yongsan. The establishment was no-frills, but clean. The tables were made of fake laminated wood and the plastic chairs were clearly not meant for lingering. Patrons cooked their meal on the boxy grills that formed the centerpiece of each table, ate, and then made room for the next customer.

Judging by the lack of English signs, the restaurant's off-the-beaten-path location, and the waitstaff's general indifference, this was not one of the places that catered to American soldiers and their ready supply of dollars. This was a refuge for Koreans looking for good food without the exuberance that often accompanied large groups of U.S. servicemen.

In other words, a perfect place for Cary and Jad to set up a command post for the exercise the rest of the team was currently conducting on Seoul's crowded streets. But when it came to escaping the notice of perpetually suspicious bodyguards, the BBQ joint wasn't quite as perfect. Though the two Green Berets had the wide shoulders and broad backs typical of those who called the Special Operations community home, there wasn't anything particularly noteworthy about their appearance.

At least back in America.

In Korea, Cary's blue eyes and blond hair were as atypical as Jad's Arab complexion. Which was exactly the point of the exercise. Like it or not, the Chinese Dragon's ever-expanding sphere of influence was on a collision course with America's interests. Sooner or later, the two biggest kids on the block were going to slug it out. When that happened, people like Cary and Jad needed to know how to operate in an environment in which they stuck out like sore thumbs.

Environments like the dimly lit BBQ joint, for instance.

"Smile," Jad said. "We got company."

6

ONCE AGAIN CARY RESISTED THE URGE TO TURN, EVEN as his shoulders and back tensed. This was the last time he would let his spotter beat him to the seat facing the door, even if he had to resort to drastic measures like kicking a fellow Long Tabber in the shin. Whoever had coined the phrase **ignorance is bliss** had obviously never sat unarmed in a Korean restaurant with trouble at his back.

"Good afternoon."

The greeting was spoken in accented but understandable English by a woman standing just behind Cary's right shoulder. He turned, acting surprised even as he pondered his response. On one hand, he could go with the tried-and-true Loud American stereotype and reply in a manner the Korean would dismiss as rude but ultimately harmless. Or he could embrace his Special Forces heritage and attempt to start winning hearts and minds.

Cary chose the latter.

"An-nyeong-ha-se-yo," Cary said, giving the woman his best New England farm boy smile.

She didn't seem impressed. Though to be fair, she didn't look like a woman who was easily impressed. She stood a little over five feet tall and probably weighed about a hundred pounds soaking wet. Like her principal, she was dressed formally, but her dark suit was considerably less flashy—white blouse, dark slacks, and a jacket. A wardrobe meant to deflect rather than demand attention.

The apparel of protective details the world over.

"Are you enjoying your meal?" the woman said.

Cary turned all the way in his seat before answering, providing him with an excuse to survey the rest of the room. The Important Dude, as Jad had so aptly termed him, was clearly the center of attention. The shop's proprietors, who hadn't so much as looked up when Cary and Jad had taken their seats, both came out from behind the counter that ran the length of the far wall, chattering in Korean.

The restaurant's other occupants, a gray-haired man and woman at the opposite end of the room, were similarly engaged. Though the older couple hadn't risen from their seats, their collective attention was focused on the middle-aged Korean man with an expensive suit, perfectly coiffed hair, and a camera-ready smile.

But Cary gave the man no more than a passing

glance. The Green Beret's interest was professional in nature, so it was the woman and her two
muscle-bound companions who garnered his attention. The trio had divided forces. The woman
and the shorter of the two men had actioned on
the room's only possible threat—Cary and Jad—
while the third bodyguard stood facing the door.

He was the first to die.

One moment the man had been peering out the
front entrance, the next his head exploded in a
splatter of brain matter, skull fragments, and gore.
The accompanying pistol reports were soft, more
coughs than the thundering barks Cary expected.

Which meant that the firearm was suppressed.

Which told Cary quite a bit about the shooter
or shooters.

But he stored this information away for a more
in-depth examination later. Right now, Cary had
a more pressing concern.

Survival.

Cary was out of his chair before the bodyguard's
corpse hit the floor. Since he was already turned to
the right, that was the direction he moved, desperate to vacate the fatal funnel formed by the restaurant's door. Jad had the same idea, though he
moved in the opposite direction, instinctively putting distance between the two targets the shooter
would have to neutralize.

Or at least the two secondary targets.

The remaining bodyguards would be the shooter's first priority.

With two bodyguards and a single entrance, that would normally be easier said than done. The door served as a natural choke point that would force attackers to enter one at a time, exposing themselves to the deadly crossfire two trained defenders would produce.

Assuming, of course, the bodyguards were actually facing the threat.

They were not.

Instead, the woman and man were both oriented on the Green Berets.

Jad and Cary's movement further contributed to the fog of war, causing the bodyguards to spend precious milliseconds determining whether or not the two men represented a threat. Milliseconds that put them even further behind the attackers' actions. After realizing the true threat was behind them, the pair turned and drew their pistols with admirable speed.

But not quickly enough.

Action beats reaction every time.

A man shouldered his way through the swinging glass door, submachine gun firing as he moved.

The two protective agents had converged on Cary. This made sense when the encounter was likely to be physical. But now the equation had changed, and their proximity worked against them.

While space bought time, the converse was also true. The lack of physical separation between the bodyguards meant the shooter was able to easily shift aimpoints between them.

The man went down first, with the woman following him to the scuffed floor a split second later. The pair fell lifelessly in a tangle of limbs like marionettes whose strings had just been cut. In the space of five violence-filled seconds, the shooter had eliminated the room's threats.

Or so he thought.

Unfortunately for him, the shooter's body hadn't been the only one in motion.

As he swung the K7 submachine gun tucked against his shoulder toward the Important Dude still standing frozen at the front of the restaurant, two things hit him in quick succession. The first was the still-flaming grill Jad had hurled with the accuracy only a former high school discus thrower could manage.

The second was Cary.

As any proficient shooter knows, panning a firearm left or right is infinitely easier than adjusting an aimpoint up or down. Left and right allows the shooter to keep a stable firing platform. Up and down requires the realignment of several major muscle groups. This was why the attacker made such quick work of the two bodyguards. It was also why Cary tackled the man at the knees.

Well, that and the fact that the grill had caught

the shooter dead center in the chest. While it was too much to hope that the gas-powered flame was somehow still intact, judging by the shooter's scream, the metal grating was plenty hot.

Cary wanted no part of that.

Rather than the full-on at-the-knee block he'd perfected in high school football, Cary slanted his attack so that his shoulder hit the shooter at an oblique angle. This was done both to better collapse the knee joint and to make it harder for Cary to end up on the business end of the submachine gun. To bring his weapon to bear, the shooter now had to track the muzzle over his own body.

Cary wasn't about to let that happen.

The Green Beret exploded upward as he connected with the shooter's knee, driving toward the ceiling and lifting the gunman. Then, with an agility that reflected long hours in the combatives gym, Cary pivoted, pile-driving the man into the floor face-first. The shooter's nose or neck or maybe both broke with an audible pop, but Cary was leaving nothing to chance. Threading his fingers through the man's hair, Cary smashed the gunman's face against the floor three times. Probably overkill, but in Cary's world, safe was better than sorry.

A point driven home milliseconds later by a pistol firing repeatedly inches from his head. Cary instinctively jerked up, but a hand pressed on the center of his back, preventing him from moving.

Jad's hand.

The pistol fired twice more.

Then the pressure eased.

"Okay, boss," Jad said. "Second shooter's down."

Only then did Cary see the form slumped in the restaurant's doorway.

Scooping up his dead shooter's K7 submachine gun, Cary moved to the right in a tactical crouch even as he knew Jad was doing the same in the opposite direction.

Contrary to popular belief, surviving a gunfight wasn't only about speed and violence of action. Though those two precepts had their place, Cary had learned firsthand the value of tactical patience, especially after the element of surprise was forfeit. Rather than charge through the door like he was breaching a target, Cary inched to his right in controlled increments, peering over the submachine gun's sights in a maneuver known as **slicing the pie.** This controlled way of clearing the area beyond a door was much more time-consuming than a standard entry, but as a defender, Cary had all the time in the world. Every second brought the authorities closer in a realignment of forces that would stack the odds in Cary's favor.

Or so he hoped.

"Contact rear," Jad shouted, as the sound of muffled gunfire echoed through the room.

Cary crouched, instinctively presenting a smaller target while leaning against the wall, his muzzle still oriented on the danger represented by the front door. Trusting your partner was one of the hallmarks of effective close-quarters battle, or CQB. As much as Cary wanted to turn toward the perceived threat behind him, his job was to trust Jad and pull security on the other likely avenue of approach.

But knowing what to do didn't make doing it any easier.

Then a man barreled through the front door, and Cary had something else to think about.

The shooter turned to his left as he entered, his stubby submachine gun already spitting flame. Ignoring the stream of bullets snapping past his head and the accompanying concussive muzzle blast, Cary angled his submachine gun upward while firing. He put one burst into the man's torso and a second into his neck and head.

This was not the time to assume the attacker wasn't wearing body armor.

The shooter crumpled in the doorway, sprawled half in and half out of the restaurant. Trading one CQB technique for another, Cary moved his head around the doorframe for an instant, executing a quick peek.

Nothing but empty sidewalk.

"Clear, front," Cary said.

"Clear, rear," Jad said. "Room clear. Boss, we've got trouble."

"I'm really starting to hate it when you say that," Cary said, dragging the dead shooter inside before closing the front door and throwing the bolt. Just because the front was now clear of shooters didn't mean it would stay that way.

Turning, Cary surveyed the room.

What he saw wasn't good.

Besides the three shooters and the two bodyguards, the shop's husband and wife proprietors and the elderly couple were lying on the floor in rapidly expanding pools of crimson. Jad was crouched over the Important Dude's prone form, but even from across the room, Cary could see that his teammate's efforts were in vain. In addition to his blood-soaked shirt, the Korean man had a grievous head wound that was clearly not survivable. Blood stained Jad's hands to the wrists as the Green Beret frantically applied pressure to the man's multiple wounds, but it was a losing battle.

The man shuddered once, and then lay unmoving.

"This is trouble, all right," Cary said, still coming to terms with the room's carnage.

"I'm not even talking about the KIA," Jad said, standing. "Did ya see what the shooters are wearing?"

Cary looked from the victims to the perpetrators and began to swear. The dead men were dressed in the blue-on-blue uniforms of the Korean National Police.

"What's the play, boss?" Jad said.

That was a very good question. Technically, U.S. forces in South Korea were protected by the Status of Forces Agreement, or SOFA, a set of rules governing how the Korean justice system could interact with servicemembers.

Technically.

That said, Cary was not an idiot.

In a room in which multiple people were dead, he and Jad were the lone survivors, and the only ones holding weapons. Not to mention that if the Important Dude merited three armed bodyguards, it was probably safe to assume that some very influential people in the South Korean government were going to be unhappy about his untimely passing.

Perhaps unhappy enough to delay implementation of the SOFA rules long enough for the Korean police to take a crack at Jad and Cary.

Ally or not, Cary knew from experience that angry interrogators tended to see what they wanted to see. There was no way he was placing his and Jad's well-being into Korean hands. If there was ever a time for asking for forgiveness rather than permission, this was it.

The scream of approaching sirens only served to underscore Cary's decision.

"Snap pictures of the shooters with your phone," Cary said, even as he did the same for the protective detail and the Important Dude, "then we're out of here. We'll sort out what's what from the American side of Yongsan's gates."

"Tracking," Jad said. "What about the weapons?"

This did give Cary pause.

South Korea had extremely restrictive laws governing the possession of guns. Then again, the nation presumably also had a law or two against murdering people in a BBQ shop. The Yongsan garrison wasn't that far away, and Cary would be more than willing to surrender his illegal firearms to the military police manning its gates.

Until then, forewarned was forearmed.

"Take 'em," Cary said. "If shit goes sideways again, I don't want to rely on your grill-tossing skills."

"That was a great throw, though, right?" Jad said, heading for the restaurant's back door.

"A little higher would have been good," Cary said, following his spotter through the kitchen. "You almost caught my hair on fire."

"Please," Jad said, "scorching the mop sprouting from your skull would have done the world a favor."

"You should talk. Captain Brown has been on your ass to get your mane trimmed for weeks."

"First of all, as a proud Libyan American, my relaxed grooming standards differ significantly from your unsophisticated farm-boy bowl cut. Second, my hairdo will be the least of his worries once Reaper 6 hears about this cluster."

As the two men spilled into the alley behind the restaurant, Cary had a feeling his spotter was right.

7

THE COFFEE SHOP WAS ON THE STREET LEVEL OF A multistory building. An outdoor seating area/deck behind the shop offered an amazing view of the needlelike Seoul Tower perched atop the rolling hills that formed the backbone of Namsan Park. As Jack had hoped, the chaos engulfing the plaza hadn't made the transition southeast.

But that didn't mean it had gone away.

Jack had stretched the quarter-of-an-hour walk to the coffee shop to forty-five minutes so that he could conduct a surveillance-detection route, or SDR, to check for watchers. Jack could think of no reason why he would be under surveillance, but tradecraft was tradecraft. Besides, like it or not, he and Lisanne's relationship had already begun to change. Exhibit one was the giddiness he'd felt after talking with her. A giddiness that made him completely overlook a very pertinent point about the car bombing—the perpetrators had been Asian and dressed as first responders.

This wasn't an attack by Islamic fundamentalists or disaffected citizens.

In fact, the more Jack thought about what he'd witnessed, the more the incident changed from a one-off scene of violence to a meticulously planned and orchestrated event. The crowd had been herded into the car bomb's kill zone by riot police employing tear gas. But as he reviewed mental footage of the event, Jack couldn't recall hearing the dull **thump** a riot gun made as it launched tear-gas canisters skyward. Jack remembered the screams and the distinctive odor of CS agent, but he couldn't recall warnings by loudspeaker or the other escalation techniques that typically precipitated unleashing tear gas.

After all, the plaza was already near the bursting point and the riot police would have known about the death trap posed by the recessed museum entrance to the east. Why not drive the crowd west instead? Or better yet, push into the crowd and use tear gas to divide the protesters, sending them fleeing to the north and south. And that was assuming that the dispersing agent had been warranted at all. From Jack's perspective, the protest had been peaceful up until someone had employed CS gas.

Jack was thinking through the implications of this new development when his phone vibrated with a text from Lisanne. But instead of a message confirming she'd secured a cab, Jack read something else.

Hotel locked down. No one allowed in or out. Lost Wi-Fi. Recommend Zulu protocol.

Jack's thumbs hovered over his phone's virtual keyboard as he thought.

Zulu protocol referred to a Campus standard procedure employed when operating in environments in which normal communications were monitored and/or compromised. Typically, the protocol was instituted when Campus members were operating in near-peer threat environments such as China, Russia, and the like. While South Korea certainly had many of the technological capabilities of a near-peer threat, they were an allied nation, which meant that Campus operatives had little to fear.

Normally.

But there was nothing normal about the chaos enveloping Seoul. Jack thought of two explanations for what was occurring. Each was equally stark. Either a series of operatives with the skill and precision to pull off a complex ambush beneath the nose of the Korean National Police were running around the city, or the Korean government had just taken a very authoritarian turn.

Or both.

In any case, like Jack's use of an SDR, Lisanne's suggestion to implement Zulu protocol was right on the money. Until the emergency communications SOP was lifted, there would be no voice calls or e-mails. All comms would be text-based and utilize an app specially designed by The Campus's IT guru, Gavin Biery. Though truly unmonitorable communication was all but impossible on a commercial phone, the app provided the next best thing. Messages traveled through encrypted servers, and the communication threads were deleted immediately after transmission and masked. If a truly near-peer foreign intelligence service got ahold of the phone and knew where to look, they'd eventually find and decipher the text messages. But in the absence of NSA Suite B encryption and mil spec radios, Gavin's app was the next best thing.

Agreed, Jack typed. **Zulu protocol until further notice.**

Roger that, Lisanne responded. **You keeping your date?**

Another excellent question.

Isabel was a high-enough-priority prospect to merit two Campus operatives traveling thousands of miles for what could just be a fifteen-minute conversation. Though he couldn't put his finger on exactly why, Jack couldn't shake the feeling that his meeting with Isabel was important. Maybe even critical. That she'd asked to bump up the timeline just provided more fuel to the fire. In the running risk/reward calculus that was a constant part of every espionage professional's life, Jack felt that he had more to gain by keeping his meeting with Isabel.

Yes, Jack typed. **I think it's the right play.**

Me too, Lisanne responded. **Text me when you're done.**

You're going to wait up for me?

Will it be worth my while?

Jack felt another smile tug at his lips. This was insane. He was about to perform an operational assessment on a potential asset after narrowly surviving a combination riot and car bombing. And what was he focused on?

Flirting with Lisanne.

He needed to get a grip.

Especially since Isabel had just walked through the door.

8

ADAM YAO HAD INCLUDED ISABEL'S PICTURE AS PART
of the target package, but Jack didn't need to consult his phone to recognize her. As per standard procedures, Jack had arranged the coffee date under false pretenses. This was done for two purposes—one, in the event that another foreign intelligence service had already compromised Isabel's phone, Jack wasn't going to advertise the true nature of his interest in the young scientist.

But that was only one part of the reason.

Equally important was Isabel herself.

The Central Intelligence Agency was one of the most well-known, albeit least well understood, entities in the world. Each year, the Agency's website had more applicants than any government organization, and more than many of them combined. Even if the potential recruit didn't fancy a career in espionage, they normally felt proud that they'd been asked to join such a prestigious entity. Almost everyone took the time to at least consider the offer before responding.

Not Isabel.

As a woman of mixed Korean and Chinese descent who spoke both Korean and Cantonese fluently, Isabel popped up on the CIA's radar early on in her collegiate career. An Agency talent spotter at Texas A&M University engineered a chance meeting with Isabel at the university's Memorial Student Center. The recruiter's goal had been to persuade the college coed that her linguistic skills and considerable intelligence would be best put to use at the Central Intelligence Agency.

Isabel had turned the recruiter down flat.

The rejection wasn't due to Isabel's lack of patriotism. Her Chinese American father had met her Korean mother during a tour of duty in South Korea. Shortly after Isabel had been born, he'd attended the Army's grueling selection course and become a Green Beret assigned to the 10th Special Forces Group. Twelve years later, he'd been killed in Afghanistan. Accordingly, Isabel was attending college via a scholarship from the Special Operations Warrior Foundation.

Isabel's love for her country wasn't in question.

But her heritage was steering her choices in other ways. As a young girl, she'd promised her father that one day she would obtain her Ph.D. It was a child's promise, and if her beloved dad had lived, it probably would have remained as such.

He hadn't.

So rather than accepting the CIA's offer of employment, she'd attended graduate school to obtain her master's and Ph.D. Now she was spending a year overseas doing postdoctorate work for Seoul National University. Russian intelligence officers liked to joke that there was no such thing as former KGB, and while the CIA wasn't quite as draconian, it did have a long memory. This memory extended to promising young candidates. As such, Isabel's application for a South Korean visa had once again garnered the Agency's attention.

But this time it was Jack's turn to take a shot.

Isabel's reason for declining the CIA's initial offer was feasible but also troubling. As any case officer worth their salt knew, assets who worked for ideological reasons were always the riskiest. People who spied for money, or grievances, or sex were lower on the scale of humanity, but much preferable to those motivated by love of country or fervent beliefs. In order for the handler/asset relationship to be successful, the case officer needed to **own** his or her agent. They had to be able to reach into their target's soul.

Someone who betrayed their country for money or sex could usually be persuaded with access to more of the thing they craved. Like a drug dealer servicing a heroin user, a case officer's job was to manage their asset's addictions, providing a fix only when the asset produced. But a spy motivated by ideology was much more difficult to run. This person's seemingly pure motivation made them harder to corrupt.

If the asset really was a true believer, the case officer's job was easier, since motivation was never a problem. But as with love, the ardor of ideology sometimes cooled once the asset confronted the cold, hard reality that was the profession of espionage. In this manner, a true believer added a level of uncertainty to the relationship that an agent runner would avoid at all costs if given the choice.

This is where Jack stood with Isabel. Though she'd turned down the recruiter's initial pitch, she wasn't out of the game completely. Isabel was the daughter of a fallen Special Operations soldier, and Jack was willing to bet that there was a streak of patriotism in the girl. A streak he could use. But on the off chance that he was wrong, Jack needed to be able to exit the conversation without the scientist being any the wiser. Pitches from the CIA recruiter were to be expected, but an offer to work for a semilegal clandestine organization was in a category all its own.

Jack needed to tread carefully.

Fortunately, in the forthcoming dance between asset and handler, Jack held a slight advantage. While he had requested the original meeting,

Isabel had asked to change the date and time, moving the appointment forward rather than attempting to push it off. This meant that she wanted something. Now it was Jack's job to find out what.

And then exploit it.

As Mary Pat Foley, master spy, family friend, mentor, and current director of national intelligence, had reminded Jack on numerous occasions, in the profession of espionage, nice guys finished last.

Or dead.

"Are you Jack?" Isabel said.

Though she'd entered the coffee shop several minutes ago, Jack hadn't beckoned her over or even acknowledged her presence. Their first interaction would set the tone of the relationship, and Jack wanted to stoke the subconscious idea that this meeting was Isabel's idea. She needed to approach him rather than the other way around.

"Yep," Jack said with a smile. "Please, join me."

Isabel slid into the seat across from him, and Jack was struck by how correct Adam's appraisal of the girl had been. She was dressed Western style in a bulky maroon Texas A&M sweatshirt, form-fitting jeans, and sandals. Her black hair was in a high ponytail, framing a pretty face and dark, luminous eyes. The slender woman's features were decidedly Asian, but she could have passed for several different nationalities.

Isabel was a case officer's dream.

"Would you like a coffee or something?" Jack said, gesturing toward his cup. "I honestly don't know what this is, but it tastes incredible."

Jack was determined not to let the craziness of the last several hours dictate the pace or tone of their conversation. Isabel was a completely separate topic from car bombings, riots, or a potential foreign adversary operating on the streets of Seoul. The meeting needed to be calm and thorough, and Jack intended to conduct it as such. He'd learn what he needed to know, but he'd ease into the relationship with a deftness that would do Mr. C. proud.

"No coffee," Isabel said, her diction rapid and clipped. "Are you with the CIA?"

Or maybe not.

"That's a strange question," Jack said.

"I'd say it's pretty binary," Isabel said. "A simple yes or no will do."

Jack thought about his response.

One of the first things he'd learned about running assets was the concept of rapport. Mary Pat said that a handler's job was to build rapport with his asset for the same reason that a car salesman asked about your dog while extolling a vehicle's award-winning gas mileage. People were relational beings. Relationships influenced transactional behavior far more than the average person realized. Building rapport wasn't difficult, but maintaining it was another matter.

Case in point, lying to an asset was one of the easiest ways to burn a bridge you'd spent countless hours building. Isabel wasn't an asset or agent in the truest sense of the word, but she was being groomed as a Campus helper, which was pretty close to the same thing.

As such, Jack needed to be delicate with his answer.

"No, I'm not with the CIA," Jack said, "but my work does have national security implications. Why do you ask?"

"I might be naïve to the cloak-and-dagger life, but I'm not an idiot. My background and expertise were attractive enough to warrant a visit from the CIA once already. I'm guessing my worth has only increased since I moved abroad."

"If I thought you were an idiot, I wouldn't be here," Jack said.

"Why are you here?" Isabel said.

"Not to check in with you on behalf of the State Department, as I'm sure you've already guessed," Jack said. "The organization I work for is much smaller and more agile than the CIA. We don't have the personnel or financial resources that they do, but we still do some pretty interesting work. We're always on the lookout for folks who could help with that work."

"So this is a job interview?"

"Nope," Jack said, shaking his head. "This is a get-to-know-you session, nothing more."

Jack had intended his response to be reassuring, but judging by Isabel's frown, it was the opposite.

"You seem disappointed," Jack said. "You told the Agency recruiter you had no intention of leaving your academic studies. Did you have a change of heart?"

"More like a change of circumstances," Isabel said. "I received a text this morning. A concerning one."

Jack kept an interested expression in place even as he fought against a wave of frustration.

Of course.

The CIA was infinitely more famous for what it didn't do than what the organization actually accomplished. This was mostly by design. Clandestine operations were kept secret for a reason. But just like nature abhors a vacuum, the American populace wasn't so great with agencies that undertook secret missions. If the CIA wouldn't tell people what it actually did, then Hollywood would do the job for them. Like many case officers, Mary Pat Foley had worked in the Agency's recruitment department, and the questions from potential applicants were legendary. Everything from aliens to JFK assassination theories.

Jack could only imagine where this conversation was heading next.

"From who?" Jack said.

"A friend of mine. We were roommates my last year at A&M. She was an exchange student. A Russian exchange student."

Okay, so Jack hadn't seen that one coming.

"What's her name?" Jack said.

"Kira. Kira Sidorova."

"You guys stayed in contact?" Jack said.

Isabel nodded. "She was really nice and a bit older. Kind of like a worldly big sister. She'd already finished her undergraduate and master's and was doing a study-abroad semester as part of her Ph.D. program."

The hair on the back of Jack's neck began to stand up. Now he was worried about where the conversation was heading for an entirely different reason.

"Has she asked you for anything specific in your correspondence?" Jack said. "Information about your work, research, even stuff that's publicly available?"

"No," Isabel said, her frown returning. "Like I said, I'm not an idiot. My dad was a Green Beret. I know that Russians are the bad guys. But if Kira's a spy, she's a terrible one. She's been providing me with information."

"What kind?" Jack said.

Isabel shrugged. "Like all scientists, Kira has to publish or perish. Most of the leading academic journals still reside in English-speaking countries. She asked me to review papers she was planning to submit for publication on several occasions. It's a pretty standard practice among scientists, but to be on the safe side, I still had the university security folks look over my comments before I sent them. Anyway, a month or so ago I let her know I was coming to Seoul. She travels quite a bit internationally, and I was hoping we could meet up. This morning I got a text from her out of the blue. It has me worried."

"What did it say?" Jack said.

"Run."

9

IN A CONVERSATION FULL OF TWISTS AND TURNS, KIRA'S instruction to **run** should have commanded Jack's full and undivided attention.

It didn't.

This wasn't because Jack doubted Isabel or had any misgivings about her account. If anything, the woman had become more compelling the longer she'd talked. No, Jack was no longer focused on the potential Campus helper for an altogether different reason—the three Korean men who'd just come into the coffee shop.

At first glance there wasn't anything terribly riveting about their appearance other than the fact that they were wearing the light blue top and dark blue bottom uniform of the Korean National Police. On the heels of the riot and car bombing, the streets had been positively crawling with police. A coffee shop was as good a place for a couple of Seoul's finest as anywhere else. After all, the counter display held an assortment of pastries, and the stereotype about cops and donuts wasn't all wrong.

But the three uniform-wearing men didn't seem interested in sugar or caffeine. Rather than making their way to the register and the glass case full of goodies, they flowed across the shop's open space. The first two men cleared the shop's corners while the third man dominated the center of the room. They ignored the proprietor's string of Korean as they searched the café, looking for something.

Or someone.

The number-two man locked onto Isabel's ponytail.

Then he glanced up, noticing Jack.

His eyes narrowed.

In an instant, Jack remembered where he'd last seen the flattened nose and cauliflower-deformed ears.

The car bombing.

"Time to go," Jack said, reaching across the table to grab Isabel's hand.

"What—"

Jack didn't give the scientist time to finish. Instead, he yanked her around the sticky table.

"Go," Jack said. "Now."

Jack pushed Isabel toward the wooden railing separating the deck from the drop-off below. The scientist had an athletic build and an agile mind.

Hopefully that would be enough to get her onto one of the neighboring roofs and down to safety. Either way, Jack couldn't help her any longer.

He was otherwise occupied.

The Korean with the cauliflower ears charged toward the doorway separating the café from the outdoor seating area, reaching for the pistol holstered at his waist.

In a strange way, Jack found this comforting.

South Korean police were notoriously reluctant to use their firearms because they could be held legally liable for excessive force. If the man was already drawing his weapon, he wasn't a policeman.

This meant that Jack was under no obligation to play nice.

Jack froze for a second, ensuring that the bomber's wide shoulders were squarely in the choke point formed by the doorway.

Then he acted.

Jack grabbed the table and tossed it, sending the cheap furniture tumbling end over end toward the bomber. For the first couple rotations, the projectile was on a perfect trajectory to smash into the bomber's chest. Then one of its spindly metal legs found traction on a crack in the floor. The table still collided with the bomber, but at a significantly slower velocity. The plastic surface clipped Cauliflower Ear's knees, causing more annoyance than injury. Fortunately, Jack's two hundred and twenty pounds of righteous rage was close behind.

Conscious of both the gun clearing the man's holster and the shooter's two companions stacked behind him, Jack turned at the last second, aiming for the Korean's side.

Had Jack still been a college football hopeful, the ensuing hit would have made his highlight reel. He exploded upward, lifting the shorter man from his feet while driving the bomber's neck and shoulders into the metal doorjamb. The man grunted as his head ricocheted off the door with a satisfying **thud.**

For one glorious moment, all felt right in the world.

Then Jack remembered the other two gunmen.

Jack headbutted the Korean in the mouth and twisted to the right, using the bomber's body as a shield.

The gunman had other ideas.

The bomber fired a jab at Jack's throat with his left hand while rotating the pistol in his right toward Jack's midsection. Jack saw the strike coming and tucked his head, taking the blow on his chin rather than on his vulnerable Adam's apple.

The Korean had cinder blocks for fists. Even with his bell rung and nose streaming blood, the bomber still punched like Mayweather. Jack felt the jarring impact pop through his vertebrae, but it was the bomber's other hand that worried him.

The one with the gun.

Gripping the man's shirtsleeve, Jack buried his

front two knuckles in the tender part of the bomber's wrist even as he bludgeoned the Korean's forearm against the doorjamb. The bomber was tough, but steel was tougher.

The man's fingers opened.

A pistol clattered to the floor.

Progress.

At least that's what Jack thought, until the stubby form of a second pistol poked over the gunman's shoulder.

Not good.

Jack shoved the bomber toward his partner, creating space for a front kick. He leaned into the blow, stomping his size-thirteen boot into the man's chest, and then thrusting with the ball of his foot. Jack's toes, knee, and hip snapped into linear alignment like a cracking whip, delivering the strike's tremendous force directly to the bomber's vulnerable solar plexus. He'd never have Bruce Lee's finesse, but mass and acceleration were two things Jack possessed in spades.

The bomber spun through the air, arms and legs windmilling.

Grabbing the metal door, Jack wrenched the edge free and shouldered it closed. The improvised barrier bought him time, but not much. The locking mechanism was on the café side, and there was no way Jack could hold the improvised barricade closed against the three angry Koreans. As if hearing his thoughts, the door shuddered as someone hurled themselves against it.

Jack lowered his shoulder and set his legs, straining against the men as he looked for options.

In his head, Jack kept a running tally of items he wanted to add to his operator low-profile kit. A doorstop just went to the very top. His eyes settled on the table he'd kicked at the bomber. The laminate surface was now cracked from the furniture's rough treatment and peeling away in large strips. Hooking a foot around the table, Jack dragged it within arm's reach even as the pounding against the door grew more pronounced.

More bodies were being added to the equation.

Flipping the table over, Jack wedged one end beneath the doorknob and the other against the wooden deck. It held for a second, but then began sliding across the deck's smooth surface.

No help there.

The door jumped beneath Jack, partially opening before he slammed it back shut.

The Koreans were locking in their timing.

Jack had just moments.

Grabbing the table, Jack banged it against the deck one-handed, breaking several of the laminate pieces free. He crouched, keeping his shoulder locked against the door even as he grabbed the shards and wedged them beneath the doorjamb. Once the scraps found purchase between the metal and decking, Jack seated it with several well-placed kicks.

The door shuddered again, the metal seeming to bow outward, but the makeshift doorstop held.

For now.

Sprinting to the back of the deck, Jack vaulted over the railing and hurtled into space.

10

SOUTH KOREA HAD ONE OF THE GREATEST POPULATION densities in the world, and Seoul led the nation, with more than forty thousand people per square mile. Faced with increasing growth rates coupled with decreasing space, builders and architects expanded in the only direction available to them.

Up.

This meant that while the café's deck was a good two stories above the ground, Jack didn't have near that far to fall.

At least not all at once.

Leaping from the wooden railing, Jack cleared the narrow crevasse of open space separating his building from the one immediately behind it.

Mostly.

A single Korean pine reached its twisting limbs skyward from a planter behind the building, and Jack encountered the green foliage face-first. He grabbed for a limb, snared a fistful of branches, and heard them snap as he fell. Fortunately, while the fickle tree did not arrest Jack's descent, it did change his trajectory. Rather than slamming into the pavement, Jack bounced off the flat roof of an older nearby building before rolling to the edge.

While this structure was only a single story high, the decrease in height didn't come with a corresponding increase to the softness of the lurking asphalt. As he tumbled toward the roof's lip, Jack saw a gutter leading to a downspout. He wrapped both hands around the metal's slick surface and then added his legs for good measure. The pipe groaned under his weight, but held long enough for him to shimmy to the ground.

Where he found Isabel standing at the building's corner, watching his performance.

"I thought I told you to run?" Jack said, again grabbing the woman by the arm.

"I'm not much on running."

Isabel shook her arm loose as she spoke, breaking Jack's grip with a simple wrist-lock escape.

The message was subtle but clear.

Isabel wasn't helpless.

Fair enough.

But that didn't make the three men in the café any less deadly.

"Look," Jack said, changing tack, "you don't know me, but from one child of a veteran to another, you might want to hear me out. The guys upstairs are killers, and my trick with the door isn't going to hold them. I'd like to learn more about your Russian friend, but if you want to go your own way, feel free. I'll do my best to draw off the shooters to give you a head start, but I can't promise anything. What's it gonna be?"

Isabel stared at Jack in silence, her dark eyes searching his.

Then the café door slammed open.

"Okay," Isabel said, "we'll give your way a try. What next?"

"Put distance between us and them," Jack said, gesturing upstairs.

"Follow me," Isabel said, grabbing Jack's hand.

"Thought you'd never ask," Jack muttered as they sprinted down an alley.

11

"REAPER 6, THIS IS REAPER 7," CARY SAID, FOLLOWING Jad through the press of bodies clogging the alley.

The crowd had steadily thickened as the two men made their way toward the Yongsan garrison. While no sidewalk in Seoul was ever empty, the number of people out and about was clearly unusual. Cary had hoped to find somewhere quiet to call in a sitrep to his team in the clear. This wasn't going to happen.

Triple Nickel was currently scattered across Seoul in teams of two, taking part in an exercise meant to mimic the conditions that came with operating clandestinely in a densely populated Asian country. As the team sergeant, Cary would traditionally be co-located with the team leader, Captain Alex Brown, call sign Reaper 6, managing the action from a tactical operations center, or TOC.

But Alex was about as far from a traditional team

leader as Cary had ever served with. In the Special Operations community, that was saying something. Army Special Forces had a unique mission set. A role that differed from any of the other members of the greater Special Operations community. Unlike, say, the Ranger Regiment that specialized in direct action missions, Green Berets were masters of unconventional warfare. Their charter was to train and lead indigenous forces, winning wars by, with, and through their students.

This was why every Special Forces soldier learned a language as part of their qualification course in addition to the more typical tactically based skills. As such, the Green Berets tended to collect people who differed from the kick-in-the-door-and-shoot-bad-guys-in-the-face mold found in the Navy SEALs or Marine Raiders. People like Jad Mustafa, a Libyan American surfer from Southern California, and Cary Marks, a blue-eyed, blond-haired farm boy from New England.

And then there was Captain Alex Brown, a former Army Apache helicopter pilot and college lacrosse player. Since this was an exercise, Alex had opted to fall in with one of the operational teams and stick Cary and Jad with the command-and-control role. Alex really did put the **special** in Special Forces, but like all officers, the young captain was coming to the end of his time as a team leader. In another couple months, he'd have to rotate off the ODA to a staff job, and he undoubtedly wanted to get in a couple last hurrahs before be-coming a PowerPoint ninja like his peers.

Besides, the aviator turned Green Beret had proven his mettle under fire in Syria, saving Cary's and Jad's lives during an engagement with a com-pound full of Shia cult members dead set on bring-ing about the apocalypse with a little help from Iran. To Cary's way of thinking, this more than earned Alex the right to have some fun in what would probably be his last tactical assignment with Triple Nickel.

Now that the exercise had morphed into some-thing more resembling the dumpster fire that had been Syria, Cary could think of no one else he'd rather have answering the call sign of Reaper 6.

"Go for Reaper 6," Alex said.

The transmission came via the wireless speak-ers all members of Triple Nickel had been issued for the exercise. The devices were akin to earbuds, but sat deeper in the wearer's ear canal so as to re-main out of sight. The speakers were connected via Bluetooth to what looked like a standard iPhone, but in reality featured much heavier encryption and some interesting hardware and software add-ons. The communications setup was designed to make the Green Berets look like innocuous and, perhaps more important, harmless civilians rather than battle-tested warriors.

Camouflaging the men's physical appearance took a bit more doing.

Thanks to the glut of post-9/11 movies and TV shows, by now everyone knew that operators wore long hair and bushy beards. As such, Cary's teammates took care to groom themselves in ways that didn't scream "military." Their physiques were a bit more challenging in that operators tended to have broad backs, wide chests, and heavy shoulders. Fortunately, the men were able to garb out in baggier shirts and looser-fitting pants. Their wardrobe wasn't going to get the Green Berets second glances at a South Korean nightclub, but the bulky garments were ideal for hiding Daewoo K7 submachine guns, which, coincidentally, was exactly what Cary had stuffed beneath his shirt.

"Six, this is 7," Cary said. "I'm calling an emergency ENDEX, over."

ENDEX stood for end of exercise, an event that normally occurred once the training iteration had run its course. But every exercise had a contingency plan for ending early due to injuries or potential real-world mission constraints.

Like gunmen shooting up a restaurant.

"Copy ENDEX," Alex said. "Can you clarify the reason, over?"

"Roger that," Cary said, choosing his words carefully. "Real-world scenario. Will explain in person. Reaper 7 and Reaper 23 were in contact. Eleven KIA. Heading for Rally Point Shiner. I say again, Rally Point Shiner, over."

If Alex resembled any semblance of a normal

team leader, this was when the proverbial shit would hit the fan. Cary had just told his commander that two of Alex's Green Berets had been in an incident ending with eleven people dead. To make matters worse, the incident had occurred during a training event that was being conducted in a foreign country.

But Captain Brown wasn't normal in any sense of the word.

"Roger that, 7," Alex said, "copy all. Be advised that Rally Point Shiner is unusable. Agitators are gathering outside the gates and have been harassing cars and pedestrians attempting to enter. Anticipate an imminent lockdown. Suggest you try for alternate Rally Point Yuengling, over."

As with every operation, the names assigned to graphics and waypoints followed a particular theme. This one was beers. Cary was certainly a fan of America's oldest brewery, but he couldn't for the life of him remember what the brevity code signified.

"What's Yuengling?" Cary asked as he drew even with Jad.

The two men had been moving south toward the Yongsan garrison and had now put several blocks between them and the proverbial crime scene.

"It's an outdoor market," Jad said, bringing up the operational graphics on his cell phone. "About three klicks to the northeast."

Cary eyed his spotter's phone and shook his head.

"Don't like it," Cary said. "The location is great, but we'd have to backtrack north, and I don't want to chance running into any police, real or otherwise."

"How about this one," Jad said, stabbing an icon due west of their current location.

Cary eyed the choice and slowly nodded. The distance was farther away—about five kilometers from their current location—but the rally point was a luxury hotel that catered to Americans. The establishment boasted two bars and a restaurant, any of which would be perfect for lying low until the situation at Yongsan quieted.

"Six, this is 7," Cary said. "Recommend Rally Point Sam Adams instead. It's a good distance from our compromised site, and it specializes in Western clientele. We'll be able to blend in, over."

"Speak for yourself, white boy," Jad said. "I don't think we'll see too many of my people."

Cary replied with the one-fingered salute.

Though he'd spent his early years in Libya, Jad was as American as apple pie and baseball. When people asked his country of origin, the easygoing Green Beret usually responded with one word— SoCal. Over the course of the numerous years they'd served together, Cary had heard his spotter bring up his heritage for only two reasons— operational utility or the opportunity to tweak his team sergeant.

The latter was much more common.

"Copy Sam Adams," Alex said. "Head that way, but take your time. I'll collapse the rest of the team. We'll get stage ahead of you and set up a couple observation posts. Once we're in place, I'll text you a surveillance-detection route that runs by us. If you've got watchers, we'll pick them up."

"Sounds good, 6." Cary released the transmit button, thinking for a second.

While he still believed his decision to hold on to the K7s was correct, the submachine guns added a level of complexity to the recovery operation. A level of complexity his team leader should know about.

"Six, this is 7," Cary said. "One more thing— Reaper 23 and I are armed with the assailants' weapons. Taking them seemed a good idea at the time, but this has gotten bigger fast. If you want us to ditch them, we will, over."

"Seven, this is 6. If you think you need the guns, keep them. If you want to ditch them, do it. I'll back you either way. I'll see if I can rent us a couple adjoining rooms at Sam Adams. We can sort this out properly once all our boys are together safe and sound, over."

Once again, Cary paused before transmitting his response. This time the delay wasn't because he was considering what to tell his team leader. It was because Cary was mentally cursing whatever Army genius decided that team leaders should stay with their teams for only two years. In that moment

Cary was convinced that if he could just hold on to Captain Alex Brown for another twenty-four months, Triple Nickel would be able to conquer the world.

"Roger that, 6," Cary said. "We're proceeding to Sam Adams."

"Reaper 6 copies all. Stay safe, 7. Six out."

Cary intended to do just that.

But the officers manning the checkpoint at the end of the block had other ideas.

12

"WHAT'S THE PLAY, BOSS?" JAD SAID, COMING TO A stop at the alley's mouth.

Cary moved up behind his spotter, wondering the same thing.

Itaewon was more a warren of interconnecting alleys and side streets than a city proper. With a reputation for food, shopping, and debauchery all within an easy stroll of Yongsan, the little collective saw no shortage of American faces. Though prostitution was officially illegal in South Korea, enforcement was often lax, especially in so-called red-light districts. In Itaewon, this took the form of a sloping stretch of road populated on both sides by brothels and bars featuring juicy girls—young women in revealing clothes who worked as prostitutes or cocktail waitresses.

Appropriately named Hooker Hill, the infamous section of road had been deemed off-limits by countless American commanders, but regulations did little to stem the flow of human traffic up the decrepit pavement. As long as the establishments were permitted to exist, American servicemembers would brave military punishment to darken their doorsteps.

Occasionally, Korean police and their U.S. military counterparts ran joint operations in an attempt to discourage patrons. These took the form of sting operations inside the brothels as well as checkpoints located at the mouth of the avenue and at random locations throughout the walkways stretching between the more popular bars and eateries. At these checkpoints sobriety was assessed and warnings given reiterating the off-limits status of the establishments of ill repute.

At first, this is what Cary thought he and Jad were seeing—another not-so-subtle reminder of exactly what liberties were permitted during a servicemember's time off. But though the pedestrians queuing in front of the checkpoint were primarily Caucasian, the men and women manning the blockade were Korean National Police, absent their American counterparts.

The Green Beret's suspicions deepened as Cary watched a skinny American soldier of no more than nineteen approach the barricade. Rather than performing a sobriety check or warning him away from Hooker Hill, the police officer asked for his military ID, which the kid readily supplied. The officer checked it against a handheld device while his partner frisked the soldier.

"They're looking for someone," Cary said, thinking out loud. "An American soldier."

"Or two," Jad said. "Something tells me that we don't want to make their acquaintance. Any ideas?"

Cary looked from the checkpoint to the ever-growing line of servicemembers. As he watched, several Koreans approached the barricade and were waved through without a second glance. The police were definitely after Americans, which meant there was no way he and Jad were going anywhere near that checkpoint. Jad might be able to pass through unmolested, but without knowing what images the police had on their handheld devices, Cary wasn't willing to run that risk.

"We could try and find a way around the checkpoints," Cary said, turning his back to the trio of police officers, "but I don't think that's a winning proposition."

"Agreed," Jad said. "What's Plan B?"

"Plan B requires a little help from the locals."

"Unconventional warfare," Jad said. "I like it."

"You might want to reserve judgment until you see where we're going," Cary said. "Also, I hope you're not too attached to those shoes."

"These shoes would follow you anywhere, boss."

"We'll see."

13

MUSUDAN-RI MISSILE TEST FACILITY, NORTH KOREA

PAK ALWAYS THOUGHT THAT THE LOCATION OF THE Musudan-ri test facility was a bit of a paradox. On one hand, the unobstructed view of the surf crashing against the rocky shore and the sight of seagulls circling the tide pools was good for the soul. On the other, the rickety-looking gantry of crossed steel that sat upon a soot-blackened concrete pad seemed out of place. A man-made stain on what would otherwise be a pristine beachfront view. But there was a reason the test site was located in such a remote location.

As the army of white industrial trucks and hazmat-clad workers could attest.

"How are we progressing?" Pak said.

"Precisely on schedule," said General Il-Seong Phyo, chief of the military's general staff.

"I'm afraid the schedule must be expedited," Pak said.

"What do you mean?" General Phyo said.

Pak and Phyo represented the pillars of North Korean society—Party, State, and Army. Not coincidentally, the two men would also be first on the chopping block should the boy-king decide to institute another one of his infamous purges.

"Exactly what I said," Pak replied, his calm voice contrasting with the general's anxious one. "We knew that our time to act was coming. It has now arrived."

"Be more specific," General Phyo said.

The general's response had the tone of a demand. Understandable, given that the general commanded the 1.2 million–strong Korean People's Army, or KPA. In his world, he was accustomed to obedience.

But this was no longer his world.

It was Pak's.

"The boy-king will soon regain consciousness," Pak said. "Full awareness could come in as soon as forty-eight hours. He is currently under guard and lightly sedated, but the Russian specialists intend to conduct a full evaluation of his health in two days' time. We must move before then."

Unlike the North Korea physician in charge of the Supreme Leader's care, Pak had no leverage over the foreign doctors. In this, the Russian visitors to the missile testing facility were both a blessing and a curse. A blessing in that the catastrophic failure of their prototype weapon had presented Pak and his conspirators with a window of opportunity. A curse in that, in their shame, the Russians had dispatched a full medical team to care for those injured in the explosion—most notably the Supreme Leader.

"Impossible," General Phyo said, his corpulent cheeks reddening with bluster. "I told you that we needed—"

"Three days' notice," Pak said. "I know. You have fifteen hours. It must happen tonight. Military men do what they're told. Give the order."

"We can't just—"

Turning from the ocean view for the first time, Pak fixed the entirety of his attention on the worm in a warrior's garb. As was the case for all of the top-tier military leaders, General Phyo was almost never without his dress uniform. Today was no exception. An assortment of badges and ribbons covered both sides of his olive-green suit jacket. The man had never seen combat, but he could have been mistaken for a war hero.

Like Pak, he was nothing of the sort.

"Listen to me carefully," Pak said. "Do your part and share in the reward, or die where you stand. It makes no difference to me. Don't for a moment make the mistake of assuming you're invaluable.

You're not. Your vice chief of staff, General Go, already expressed his willingness to do whatever is asked of him. Choose your course."

He didn't put much emphasis on the command, but his voice cut through the general's response just the same. Pak was someone to be feared. Unlike the general, whose influence began and ended within the ranks of the KPA, there were no limits to the scope of Pak's authority. The Politburo managed absolutely every aspect of society. Next to the boy-king and his family, Pak was one of the most powerful people in the DPRK.

A very dangerous position to occupy.

General Phyo slowly shut his mouth even as his eyes slid from Pak to the cadre of plain-clothed bodyguards standing behind him. Rough, scarred men who held their weapons like they knew how to use them. Unlike the peacock of a general, Pak's men were intimately acquainted with combat.

"I will give the order," Phyo said, "but I command the conventional forces. The Korean People's Army Special Operations Force is outside my purview."

"But not mine," Pak said.

A convoy came into view, snaking along the gravel road that led to the test stand complex. Though the vehicles were about two kilometers to the south, Pak could make out the boxy form of cargo trucks. They would be joining the decontamination teams laboring on the remains of the launchpad as well as the efforts going on behind the closed doors of an innocuous-looking building situated near the wood line. A building with a deceptively high ceiling and massive steel blast doors that guarded the entrance to its cavernous interior.

Blast doors that had protected the building's contents from damage.

"You are going to secure the old war dog's co-operation?" Phyo said, not bothering to hide his disbelief. "How? He has no aspirations beyond his current post and no family. He lives like a pauper. What could you possibly use to persuade him?"

Something you would never understand is what Pak wanted to say. He didn't. Though the sentiment rang true, Pak saw no reason to further rile the pompous man. Instead, Pak provided the reassurance the coward-in-a-hero's-uniform needed.

"Nothing breeds success like success. Do not trouble yourself with this matter. It's under control."

Which was not precisely true.

But General Phyo didn't need to know this pesky detail.

"All right, then," General Phyo said, turning with a huff. "I'll be getting back to Pyongyang. Conventional forces will be issued marching orders within the hour."

"Excellent," Pak said. "Two of my bodyguards will accompany you."

"What?" the pudgy man said, stopping in his tracks.

"You said it yourself, General," Pak said with a

smile. "We are at a critical juncture. A misfortune suffered by either of us could damn us both. You're too valuable to go unprotected."

The general stared at Pak, his Adam's apple bobbing up and down on his fleshy throat.

"Of course," Phyo said, recovering his voice. "I'm grateful for your concern."

"Just for the next fifteen hours," Pak said with a smile. "After that, we will never know fear again."

The general nodded a second time and then turned to where his aides were huddled on the far side of the hill, out of hearing range. He bellowed instructions to the men as he strode toward his waiting helicopter. Without being told, two of the men in Pak's protective detail peeled off, following the general.

Pak looked again at the soot-blackened concrete pad.

He no longer saw a stain.

He saw opportunity.

14

SEOUL, SOUTH KOREA

"DO I NEED TO TAKE OUT THE SIM CARD, TOO?"
Isabel said.

Jack shook his head. "Removing the battery should be good enough. If that doesn't do the trick, they've got a beacon in your phone. Ditching the SIM card won't help."

"Who's 'they'?" Isabel said.

"That's the million-dollar question," Jack said, removing the battery from his own phone as he spoke.

The device hadn't been out of his possession since he'd arrived in South Korea, so he couldn't imagine it had been compromised. Even so, the killers had found him and Isabel somehow. In situations like these, Jack agreed with the old Sherlock Holmes adage—after eliminating the impossible, whatever remains, however improbable, must be the truth. As an espionage practitioner, Jack wasn't a big believer in coincidences, but only a fool would consider running into the same man twice in a city of nine million a coincidence.

Jack, or Isabel, or both were being hunted.

The questions were why and by whom.

Jack intended to get answers.

"You think my Russian friend Kira has something to do with it?"

Isabel lowered her voice as she spoke, and while Jack appreciated her focus on operational security, he didn't know that it was wholly necessary.

AFTER RACING THROUGH A SERIES OF ALLEYS, JACK HAD again found himself heading toward the southern base of Namsan Park. But the hilly green space with its wide-open expanses and broad pedestrian walkways was the last place Jack wanted to go. Until he had a chance to put together some of the day's missing pieces, he didn't want to be somewhere that might make the killers' jobs easier.

Normally, this would be cause to head for the operation's safe house, but no one, Jack included, had seen the need to lay on such a property for what should have been a simple interview. This was why he and Lisanne were staying at a hotel. But even if the facility was no longer locked down, Jack had no intention of inadvertently compromising his operational partner by dragging a surveillance team, or the killers themselves, to Lisanne. Until he had a better handle on who the men were and how they'd found him, Jack needed to hole up somewhere secure and think.

Somewhere like the Seoul Metro.

After Jack voiced his thought to Isabel, she'd led them east along the southern edge of Namsan Park. Though she'd lived in the city for only a handful of months, Isabel moved like a native, swimming through the crowds and navigating the confusing network of streets without so much as a glance at her phone.

Jack was impressed.

Present craziness aside, Jack had no doubt that Adam was onto something.

Isabel would be a fantastic Campus asset.

After buying tickets for them both, Isabel had handed Jack his and then showed him the way to the multistory escalator that moved people from street level to the underground station. From there, it had been quite easy to disappear into the bowels of Seoul's almost six hundred miles of mass transit. Only after changing subway lines twice, each time picking stops and directions at random, did Jack feel comfortable enough to shift his focus from staying alive to determining why they were in this predicament in the first place.

"Has your Russian roommate ever sent you a text like this before?" Jack said.

Isabel shook her head.

"Then I'd say it's safe to assume she's a piece of the puzzle."

"Do you think she was talking about the men in the café?" Isabel said.

Jack shrugged.

"I'm not sure," Jack said. "I guess that depends on whether they were tracking you or me."

"You've seen them before?"

Jack nodded. "Yes, briefly. You following the news about the bombing?"

"In downtown Seoul?" Isabel said. "Of course."

"The men who just attacked were responsible."

"Why?"

"No idea," Jack said. "I saw them just as they pulled up in the VBIED."

"VBIED?"

"Sorry—Vehicle-Borne Improvised Explosive Device. They were driving an ambulance and wearing paramedic uniforms."

"Sure it was the same guys?"

"Yeah," Jack said. "Their leader has a wrestler's cauliflower ears. It was him. I'm positive."

"What do we do next?" Isabel said.

That was a very good question.

Jack eyed the subway map mounted to the wall above Isabel's head as he thought.

The safest course of action would be to head for the U.S. embassy. If the demonstration and subsequent bombings were one-off events, Jack could hand Isabel over to a CIA case officer, round up

Lisanne, and jump on a plane heading home. If they weren't, and a greater sense of unrest was enveloping South Korea, the embassy would be an excellent place to shelter. In fact, if things were bad enough, Jack was sure he could persuade the U.S. ambassador to cut loose a detachment of Marines in order to escort Lisanne from the hotel. The embassy was a hardened structure and considered American soil. If there truly was a storm coming, Jack should take refuge at the embassy.

Except that Jack wasn't much of a take-refuge kind of guy.

The train slid to a stop, and the glass doors opened. Half of the passengers disembarked, making way for the crowd of incoming riders. Though "making way" was perhaps too charitable a description. Straphangers the world over weren't known for social niceties, but in the Western world, there was at least an unspoken order of how the process should work.

Not in South Korea.

Rather than an orderly exit of outgoing passengers followed by an influx of new ones, the doors opened and a melee ensued. The crowd didn't so much surge as explode. To Jack's American eye, the maelstrom of bodies didn't look much different from the earlier riot, but none of his fellow commuters acted like anything was wrong. Men, women, and children forced their way in and out of spaces that shouldn't have been able to accommodate them, the doors whisked closed, and the train continued its journey.

Two more stops until the U.S. embassy.

"Here's what I think we need to do," Jack said, a plan coming together as he spoke. "The safest place for you right now is the U.S. embassy. But if I drop you off there, you're not getting out until this craziness subsides. The good news is that you'll be safe."

"And the not-so-good news?" Isabel said.

Jack frowned.

"The not-so-good news is that I have a feeling folks inside that building are a bit busy right now. My worry is that you're going to be put on the back burner. But if I'm right, your Russian friend might have an important piece to this puzzle. A piece that will be overlooked in the current hustle and bustle unless we can add more context to it."

"How?" Isabel said.

"Your friend knew you were in South Korea, right?"

Isabel nodded.

"In Seoul?"

Another nod.

"Okay," Jack said, "then it serves to reason she knew something about the riots or the bombing."

"Or something else that's already happening," Isabel said. "Something that we don't know about yet."

Jack stared at Isabel, considering her words.

He hadn't even thought of that possibility. His eyes drifted to the television hanging from the subway car's ceiling. It was tuned to a Korean news station. The volume was turned off, but as expected, the subtitles were all in Korean. Other things could be happening across the city or country, and he wouldn't even know about them.

"That's a great point," Jack said. "Either way, we need to find out more about your Russian friend. What does she know and how does she know it?"

"Want me to ask her?" Isabel said.

Jack shook his head.

"That isn't a question you should ask in a text. Text messages leave trails, no matter how secure the software. If somebody with enough resources and determination gets her phone, they'll be able to piece together even encrypted and supposedly deleted conversation threads. If she truly knows something, then it's safe to assume she put herself at risk by warning you. But maybe there's a way we can ask her questions without endangering her. Can I use your phone?"

"Sure," Isabel said, "but I thought we were trying to keep off the bad-guy tech ninjas' radar."

"We are. But I have my own tech ninja. His kung fu is strong."

Isabel rolled her eyes.

"You know that analogy doesn't work, right?"

"I'm jet-lagged, cut me some slack," Jack said. "Okay, I'm going to give my guy a call. When I tell you to, power up your phone."

"Yes, sir," Isabel said, giving Jack a mock salute.

Jack smiled, as much in response to Isabel's gesture as to hide the knot forming in his stomach. The more he thought about it, the more convinced he was that the trio of killers had been tracking him, not Isabel. Though he didn't know how, his phone was the most obvious mechanism for doing so. He had to assume that the moment he brought the device online, he'd be beaconing his position. Then again, Jack's other option was to scurry into a deep hole and hide.

That wasn't going to happen.

Snapping the battery back into place, Jack waited for the phone to connect to the subway's Wi-Fi system.

Then he made a call.

15

"JACK! HOW YOU DOING, BUDDY?"

As always when he phoned Gavin Biery, Jack did the time-conversion math in his head. Seoul was thirteen hours ahead of Alexandria, Virginia. Which meant it was way too early for The Campus's IT director to be this chipper. Either Gavin had doubled his daily intake of energy drinks or he'd pulled another all-nighter.

Or maybe both.

"I'm in trouble, Gavin," Jack said. "You got a minute?"

"Sure, Jack, just a second. Hey—that last one did not count. My phone vibrated, and it jolted my hand."

A cacophony of angry, mostly male voices answered Gavin's pronouncement.

Jack had long since given up trying to determine what the plump, perpetually single keyboard warrior did in his spare time, but this was a new one even for Gavin.

"Sorry, Jack," Gavin said, his voice muffled. "I was in the middle of a saving throw when you called. Between you and me, there's no way my barbarian could have stood up to that fireball spell anyway, but if you're not cheating, you're not trying, right?"

"If you say so, buddy," Jack said. "Where are you?"

"Game night's at my place this week," Gavin said, "so I'm home. Tell me what you need. If I can't do it with the gear in my office, I can remote into the Campus servers and work it that way."

"Awesome," Jack said. "I've got a phone with a chat thread between two people. Any way you can give me the location of the other person?"

"What app are they using?" Gavin said.

"Signal."

"That's a tricky one."

"Tricky like you won't be able to do it?" Jack said.

"Come on, Jack. Have a little faith. No, tricky like the schmucks in my kitchen might roll without me if I don't get this done fast. The barbarian isn't my best character, Jack. But I've spent six months upping his experience points. I don't want to lose him to some half-elf mage with an attitude."

Again Jack was at a loss of exactly how to respond. Acknowledge his ignorance and face another round of disappointing noises from Gavin? Play along and risk getting dragged further down the rabbit hole?

There was no right answer.

Fortunately, Gavin had already moved on.

"Do you have the phone ready?" Gavin said.

"In a minute," Jack said. "I've been dodging a team of bad guys. I think they might have been using her phone to track us, so I had her remove the battery."

"That's very cute, Jack, but if you're working against a near peer, removing the battery probably won't help. Rumor has it that the Russians have been working on a hack that allows them to store power in the—"

"Gavin. Do you want me to power up her phone or not?"

"Sorry. That elf mage really has me pissed. Yeah, power it up and then send a chat invite to this number once you're connected."

Gavin rattled off a string of numbers.

Jack memorized them and had Isabel punch the digits into the app.

"Okay," Jack said as Isabel hit send. "Text is coming your way."

"Got it," Gavin said. "Man, she's got a lot going on in this phone."

"You see evidence of foreign intrusion?" Jack said.

"What? Oh, no. Nothing like that. But her battery

is only at fifty percent efficiency, and her storage is almost nil. I bet I could triple her processor's speed if I—"

"Gavin—focus."

"Sorry, Jack. Old habits. Okay, ask her the chat name."

Jack did and relayed the information to Gavin.

"Got it. Whoa—this girl she's chatting with's a looker. I know you and Lisanne are about to get married, but if that doesn't work out—"

"Gavin, Lisanne and I haven't even been on a real date. We're not anywhere close to getting married."

"Whatever. I'm just saying you should keep your options open. Don't get me wrong, Lisanne's a hottie, but—"

"The location," Jack said.

"I was coming to that if you'd just let me finish. As I was saying, you should keep your options open because your new friend's chat partner has exotic taste when it comes to foreign locales."

"How exotic?"

"North Korea."

Jack leaned back in his seat, turning Gavin's words over in his mind. While he'd learned long ago that absolutely anything could happen on a Campus operation, even he hadn't seen this one coming.

"You're sure?" Jack said. "Her IP thingy isn't getting routed through cloakers or whatever?"

"Jack, seriously. Please don't string those words

together again. Ever. Usually, you trying to get technical is funny. But that was downright revolting. Yes, I'm positive the IP thingy isn't being routed through cloakers. Your friend's chat partner is in North Hamgyong, North Korea. Ring any bells?"

"Not off the top of my head," Jack said.

"Mine either. But that's why we have our friend Google. I did a quick search while we were talking and it seems like North Hamgyong is the location of the Musudan-ri Missile Test Facility and—holy moly, Jack."

"What?" Jack said.

"You and I both need to brush up on our current events. There's a reason why Musudan-ri is trending to the top of the search results. A little over a week ago, there was a pretty big accident. I'm sure there's Campus high-side reporting I can cross-reference for more detail, but open-source analysis suggests it might have been some sort of nuclear test gone bad."

Jack looked at Isabel, seeing the researcher in a new light.

"What kind of scientist is your friend again?"

Isabel shrugged. "She's a medical doctor, but she's gravitated more toward research. She specializes in treating radiation sickness."

"What's her name?" Gavin said.

"Kira," Jack said. "Kira Sidorova."

"I just queried her in JSTOR. It's a repository

for academic publications. Kira isn't just a scientist. She's one of the world's premier experts in radiation sickness."

"Which makes her presence at a potential nuclear disaster purely coincidental, I'm sure," Jack said.

"Good Lord, Jack," Gavin said. "What have you gotten yourself into this time?"

If history was any indicator, nothing good.

16

"HELLO?"

"Hey Mr. C., it's Jack."

"Your ears must be burning, Junior. We were just talking about you."

"Really," Jack said, scratching his day-old stubble. "Why?"

This question carried more weight than the casual manner in which Jack had asked it implied. While the term **legend** was now thrown around as casually as its linguistic predecessor **hero,** both words applied to John T. Clark. Besides serving as Rainbow's first commander, Clark had been a CIA paramilitary officer, Vietnam-era Navy SEAL, and SOG veteran. He and Jack's father had literally met in the jungles of Colombia during a paramilitary counter-drug operation gone wrong. Now Clark was one of his father's best friends as well as Jack's boss.

When John Clark talked to you, you listened.

When John Clark talked **about** you, a smart person inquired as to the reason.

Doing otherwise was the equivalent of taking your life in your hands.

"I'm sure this isn't news," Clark said, "but South Korea's a mess. A demonstration in downtown Seoul got out of control. Seems like there was also a car bombing."

"I heard about that," Jack said.

Even at night the Itaewon Market was a bustling flood of humanity. Vendors selling "meat on a stick" from mobile stands were interspersed with shops featuring everything from fake mink blankets to knockoff designer luggage and ballroom dresses. A series of winding pedestrian walkways stretched throughout the marketplace, connecting the stalls in a manner more resembling a Vegas casino than a main thoroughfare. Or at least the walkways were pedestrian in theory. Like much of South Korea, the rules of the market were open to interpretation and favored the bold, or reckless, depending on your point of view. Top-heavy motor scooters piled with everything from sacks of rice to towering stacks of produce gently competed for space with the shoppers.

Or maybe not so gently, depending on the driver's urgency. More than once, Jack thought he was about to be run down when he didn't maneuver out of the way fast enough. Much to his chagrin, Jack soon learned the folly of yielding. Like schoolyard bullies, a motor scooter rider who detected weakness seemed to telepathically communicate the news to the rest of his two-wheeled brethren. Soon a convoy of motor scooters was trying to edge past Jack on their way to destinations more pressing. He was forced to adopt the coping strategy practiced by the majority of his fellow shoppers—walk down the center of the road and pretend that the motorbikes and their sputtering engines didn't exist.

The tactic worked.

After a fashion.

A particularly daring scooter edged past Jack without even inches to spare, splashing a foul-smelling puddle across Jack's shoes and staining them a rather unpleasant color. But that was okay. After learning that Kira was texting Isabel from the site of a weapons test gone bad in North Korea, Jack had decided that a complete operational scrub was in order. After sanitizing the two phones, Jack had left his and Isabel's cells on two different subway cars while he and the researcher went in search of a new wardrobe, new phones, and food.

Fortunately, Itaewon Market offered all three.

Now, with a wardrobe that included a different hat and glasses to hide his American complexion, Jack had sufficiently prepared himself for the next, more daunting operational step—coming clean with John T. Clark. Though **prepared** might be a bit too optimistic. Perhaps a more truthful explanation was that Jack had finally run out of excuses to delay the conversation.

It was time to face the music and let the cards fall where they may.

Or something like that.

In any case, while Jack was an absolute believer in telling his boss the truth, he didn't need to tell his boss **all** of the truth **all** at once. If there was one thing he'd learned from working with intelligence operatives, it was the critical nature of controlling the flow of information. This was definitely a case of easy does it.

"You know something about that bombing, Junior?" Clark said.

Or maybe not.

Working with a legend could be downright annoying. Clark had enough raw talent for any two operators. It didn't seem fair to add clairvoyance to his list of skills. Then again, John T. Clark had never been a big believer in playing fair.

"I don't really know anything, sir," Jack said, "but I did experience it. Firsthand."

"Somehow I'm not surprised. Care to elaborate?"

"Not much to tell, Mr. C. I was sightseeing, got caught up in a riot, saved a girl from getting trampled, and then had a front-row seat to the car bombing."

"Good night—why didn't you check in with the local authorities or the embassy?"

"I thought about that, sir, but I got a look at the car bombers before they initiated. The men were dressed as paramedics and pulled the VBIED right up next to the police line. Just before the bombing, police on the west side of the square used tear gas to move the crowd east, into the kill zone. Made me think there was more to this than met the eye. My plan was to try and lay low until I could sort things out."

"Try?" Clark said.

"That's the operative word," Jack said. "The potential helper we're here to evaluate asked for a crash meeting. Today instead of tomorrow. I agreed, but the meet was interrupted by the two men I saw emplacing the VBIED. Except that this time they were dressed as Korean National Police. I escaped with the helper, but running into the same men twice isn't a coincidence. The bombers are either tracking me or the helper."

"Any idea which?"

Jack sighed before answering.

"I've been giving that a lot of thought, and I'm still not any closer to knowing. As crazy as it sounds, I think it really could be either of us. Turns out Adam Yao has a good eye for talent. A number of years ago, Isabel roomed with a Russian scientist named Kira Sidorova. Just before the car bombing Kira texted Isabel and told her to run."

"Did the Russian know Isabel was in Seoul?"

"Yep. And it gets even more interesting. I had

Gavin lock down the scientist's phone. She's currently in North Korea. At the Musudan-ri Missile Test Facility."

Clark let out a low whistle.

"I've got to hand it to you, son," Clark said, "you have an uncanny nose for trouble. Too bad you couldn't turn that talent into something more lucrative—like picking lottery tickets."

"Come on, Mr. C.," Jack said. "It really wasn't my fault."

"Like father like son," Clark said. "Okay. I'm assuming you've already gone through sanitation protocols?"

"Yes, sir."

"Good. Do you think Lisanne's compromised as well?"

Jack thought for a moment before replying.

"Unknown. She hasn't left the hotel, so I wouldn't think so. But until we know who the bombers are and how they tracked us, the most conservative course of action is to assume she's burned as well."

"Agreed," Clark said. "Here's what we'll do— take the helper to the U.S. embassy. I'll get in touch with Lisanne and have her do the same thing. We can regroup once the three of you are safe behind the embassy's walls. I'll get our analysts on the Russian scientist and see what Gavin can pull from security cameras at the scene of the bombing so that you can take a look. If we're lucky, maybe we get an image or two to feed to the facial-recognition software. Clear?"

It was clear.

Exceedingly so.

But in Jack's opinion, it was also the exact wrong thing to do. Jack's history with Clark was both long and complex. On one hand, Jack had Clark to thank for his status as a Campus operative. The former Rainbow CO swung a big stick, and when he decided that his best friend's son had the stuff to be a covert operative, the rest of the Campus staff fell in line.

On the other hand, Jack knew that it was impossible for Clark to separate him from his father, and his father was the President of the United States. As such, Clark often treated Jack with kid gloves. Sure, Jack had been in plenty of scrapes and had more than his share of operational scars, but those tended to come from situations he stumbled into on his own apart from, or sometimes contrary to, Clark's guidance.

This had come to a head recently during an unplanned and certainly unsanctioned operation in Syria. Specifically, Jack had challenged Clark's guidance, and while the older man had relented, it had still shifted the relationship between the two operators onto uncertain ground. From Jack's perspective, his real or imagined probationary period as a Campus operative should have ended long ago. He'd demonstrated the ability to function as a fully capable member of the team. Jack's performance was on par with that of Ding or Dominic, or perhaps even Clark himself. Clark claimed he saw Jack in the same light.

Maybe it was time to put that claim to the test.

"With all due respect, Mr. C., I think that's a bad idea," Jack said. "If we go to ground at the embassy, we lose the ability to stay mobile. To continue to develop the situation. The initial riots were only a stone's throw from the embassy. What if they return or grow in intensity? In my opinion, the last thing we should be doing is huddling behind Marine guards, sir."

The ensuing silence was brief but profound. When Clark spoke again, his voice had lost the fatherly concern Jack had heard earlier. In its place was something different.

Steel.

"What do you suggest?" Clark said.

Jack took a deep breath before replying, even though he'd thought through this exact question in detail before even placing the call. In that moment, he wasn't John Patrick Ryan, Jr. Eldest son to the President of the United States and de facto godchild of the man on the phone. Instead, he was the lead Campus operator in the field, about to make a tactical recommendation to his boss.

Just like his mentor, Ding Chavez, would do.

But Jack wasn't Ding.

"I think we're uniquely postured to take advantage of a fluid situation," Jack said. "Instead of standing down, let's escalate this into a full-on Campus operation. Give me authority to get a command post up and running in the form of a safe house here in Seoul. Task Gavin and his supporting team to me and get the Campus analysts running down everything we know about the Russian scientist, the North Korean weapons site, and possible intersections between the two. If we can get support from acknowledged in-country CIA case officers, have them lean on their Korean counterparts. Understanding the possible threat vectors posed by the bombers is key. My gut says this whole thing is connected somehow. If the FBI legates stationed here liaison with their Korean counterparts to get copies of bombing footage, I can identify the bombers. The Campus has an agility that conventional government entities don't. Let's use it."

Another long pause. Then—"Anything else?"

"Yes, sir," Jack said, "there is. Start moving Campus assets this way. Shooters. I have no indication that this thing's going kinetic, but I'd rather be safe than sorry. Lisanne is great, but she's not a gunfighter. Not anymore. Speaking of which, I could use a weapons cache, too. I've already been caught unarmed twice. I'd rather not go three for three."

"Let me get this straight," Clark said. "You think what you've found merits a sanctioned Campus operation. An operation run out of South Korea and helmed by you?"

"Yes, sir," Jack said, surprising himself with how steady his voice sounded, "that's exactly what I think."

"That's interesting," Clark said, "because I think the same thing. All right, son. This one's yours. I'll energize our logistics cell and find you a safe house. Come up on the net once you're set up and ready. Good hunting, Jack."

Clark ended the call as Isabel returned from her final foray into the market, shopping bags in tow.

"How'd your call go?" Isabel said.

"Well," Jack said, still trying to wrap his head around what had just happened. "Really well."

"What do we do next?"

"Put the band back together."

17

"COMRADE, THERE IS A . . . PROBLEM."

Ju Min-jun looked at the man standing in front of him and suppressed a sigh. Though the atmospheric filtration system inside the Sang-O class submarine had been verified by two separate inspection teams prior to launch, the air had grown steadily staler over the three-day mission. The DPRK submarine was vastly improved over its World War II predecessors, but the thirty-four-meter vessel still ran on electric batteries while submerged. This meant that the boat had to snorkel each night to vent the rank exhaust generated by its diesel-electric engines while they labored to recharge the sub's batteries. The submersible was at its most vulnerable during this maneuver, making the time it spent hovering just below the breaking waves nerve-racking, to say the least.

But that wasn't the worst of it.

South Korean patrols had been especially prominent over the last twelve hours. At one point, the submarine's snorkel had been just seconds from breaking the water's frothing surface when the electronic technician had warned of a P-3 Orion sub hunter orbiting just fifty miles to the east. With this in mind, the Sang-O's captain had made the decision to forgo recharging the engines in favor of creeping south along the coastline at a paltry two knots. The speed provided just enough thrust to maintain steerage while minimizing the drain on the batteries. Unfortunately, this also necessitated diverting power away from atmospheric controls in favor of powering the nearly silent electric motors. The fans charged with circulating breathable air through the three-hundred-and-seventy-ton tin can hadn't blown in the better part of four hours, and the sub's human cargo was now paying the price.

Min-jun and his team of three commandos were in peak physical condition. The four men hailed from the KPASOF, or Korean People's Army Special Operations Force, an almost two-hundred-thousand-strong contingent of elite soldiers trained to infiltrate South Korea and eliminate high-value targets. Even judged by this company, Min-jun and his comrades were a breed apart. Unlike his contemporaries who had wartime missions that ran the gamut from sabotage to assassination of high-ranking South Korean officials, Min-jun and the three men in his charge were part of a national strategy. So sensitive was their mission that Min-jun's reporting structure went through Politburo rather than military channels.

It was not an exaggeration to say that the fate of his nation rested on Min-jun's narrow shoulders, and he'd chosen his men accordingly. Out of an eligible pool of more than one hundred operatives in his command, Min-jun had selected his fellow operatives based on their physical and mental toughness. As such, the men had weathered the sub's deteriorating conditions like warriors.

The vessel's crew was a different matter.

A sheen of sweat covered the sailor's face, and his cheeks puffed and contracted with each breath. He looked like a man who was a heartbeat away from death—an assessment that might be true for a number of different reasons.

"What exactly is the nature of the problem?" Min-jun said.

Though he wanted to vent his growing frustration at the slick-skinned submariner, Min-jun knew it wasn't worth the effort. For one, the crew was already justifiably terrified of the commandos. More important, frightened men made mistakes, and while Min-jun wasn't a sailor, he knew that this mission had no margin for error.

None.

"The boat is . . . stuck."

"Stuck," Min-jun said, his anger coloring his voice despite his best intentions. "On what?"

"Perhaps it would be best if you talked with the captain, sir," the sailor said, stammering. "If you would like to follow me to the bridge?"

Though not quite an order, Min-jun recognized a command when he heard one.

Son Chi-won, Min-jun's team sergeant, had silently observed the exchange from his narrow bunk at the opposite end of the cramped berth the commandos called home. At a decade older than Min-jun, Chi-won was getting close to mandatory retirement age, but Min-jun wouldn't have dreamed of leaving the stocky commando behind. Unlike the other members of the team, Chi-won had infiltrated South Korea a total of three times. In each instance, he'd accomplished his intelligence-gathering mission and successfully exfiltrated north undetected. Chi-won brought a sense of maturity to the team and Min-jun relied on the older man's judgment and martial skills.

As Min-jun got to his feet, Chi-won shot him a questioning glance. Min-jun gave his subordinate a quick nod before following the sailor out of the compartment. Min-jun thought that poor air wasn't the only thing to blame for the sailor's agitation. If Min-jun's suspicions were correct, the commandos needed to be ready.

It gave him comfort knowing that, as usual, Chi-won was one step ahead.

The dank, oxygen-deprived atmosphere hit Min-jun full in the face as he transitioned from the cramped compartment to the even more claustrophobic passageway leading forward toward the bridge. Like most KPASOF officers, Min-jun had made a similar journey in a midget sub earlier in his career before he was granted operational control of a team. But he had nowhere near Chi-won's operational experience. As such, the burly team sergeant had known exactly what to do when the air in the commandos' berth had begun to sour.

Reaching into his ever-present rucksack, Chi-won had withdrawn a small tank of spare air. The device was carried by some of the veterans to supplement their rebreathers in case of an underwater emergency. As the air had become ever more decrepit, Chi-won had eased open the tank's valve, releasing fresh oxygen into the cramped quarters. It wasn't the same as breathing in an ocean breeze, but the supplemental oxygen allowed the men to sleep while the rest of the crew suffered.

Now Min-jun found himself struggling to draw oxygen from the carbon dioxide–saturated air. The ensuing headache did nothing to improve his disposition toward the submarine's captain. If foul air was the only thing wrong with this damnable tin can, Min-jun would still be lying in his bunk. No, a summons to the bridge was indicative of a much more urgent problem.

Min-jun resisted the urge to run his fingers

along the blade secreted at his hip as he walked. He could feel the leather sheath nestled against his skin, but the supple hide, while pleasing, was no match for holding the blade's checkered grip. Like all Navy crewmen, the submarine's captain had insisted that Min-jun and his men surrender their firearms for the duration of the journey. Min-jun knew better than to resist, but that didn't mean he'd relinquished **every** weapon. The twenty-nine-centimeter blade was both simple and elegant— a copy of the Fairbairn-Sykes fighting knife allied commandos had carried in World War II. Not exactly a common Asian weapon, but it was effective, and in Min-jun's line of work, functionality trumped beauty.

By the look in Chi-won's eyes, Min-jun was willing to bet that his team sergeant had concealed more than just a knife. KPASOF operatives were trained to live by their wits in South Korea, a country populated by people who would gladly kill them if given the chance. The first rule Min-jun had learned during the brutal SOF selection process was that not all his enemies were South Korean.

Chi-won lived by the same adage.

Min-jun passed by half a dozen of the sub's fifteen crew members in the short walk from his quarters to the bridge. Though the sailors were all perspiring heavily and struggling just to breathe the thick air, they snapped to attention as the commando moved past. Min-jun had a feeling this had less to do with a sudden adherence to military customs and courtesies and more of a foreshadowing of what awaited him. Naval vessels were infamous for the unofficial communications system that existed among sailors. Bad news always traveled quicker than good.

After stepping through a final waterproof hatch, Min-jun entered the sub's nerve center. He was thoroughly unimpressed by his surroundings. While the Politburo member who'd tasked him with this mission had taken great pains to emphasize that the commando would be traveling aboard the most advanced vessel in the North Korean fleet, Min-jun had his doubts. The Sang-O had been configured for reconnaissance/infiltration rather than attack, but the vessel had been retrofitted at the turn of the century. It looked its age. The bridge consisted of a meager four workstations covered by levers and knobs that would have seemed more at home on a vessel sailing during the Fatherland Liberation War seventy years ago.

The captain's station did have a computer monitor, but Min-jun had stolen a glance at it when he'd first come aboard and had been underwhelmed. During his time in the South, Min-jun had wandered through one of Seoul's many electronic markets. The technology on display bordered on magical. The sub's guidance system was archaic in comparison. The green monochromatic screen flickered incessantly, and the displayed data was largely unreadable to Min-jun's eyes. He wasn't a submariner, but he was willing to bet that the knockoff Samsung in his pocket contained more computing power than the entirety of the vessel.

"You asked to see me, Captain?" Min-jun said.

He'd phrased the question respectfully, but the sub's captain still seemed put off by Min-jun's presence. With a huff, the captain stood from where he'd been squatting behind a series of gauges of indeterminable purpose, eyeing Min-jun like the commando was yet another problem to be solved.

Which was probably true.

Sang-O-class boats were small for a reason. They went where larger submarines wouldn't and did what they couldn't. The vessels and their crews committed acts of espionage and sabotage on the Supreme Leader's behalf. The sailors who manned the subs were good at their jobs, but Min-jun and his team of three represented the most challenging facet of their operational portfolio. A mission that entailed substantially more risk. Even worse, during the infiltration phase, the captain effectively had to cede operational control of his boat to the commandos.

"There has been a . . . **development** in our mission profile," the captain said, glaring at Min-jun.

Though barely one and a half meters tall, the boat's commanding officer, Shin Si-woo, had the self-assured presence one would expect in someone who was the master of his domain. Years of plying his trade in a vessel with a living area little larger than a passenger bus had added a softness to Captain Shin's jowls and a potbelly that slipped over his belted trousers. Even so, the submariner exhibited a certain hardness. Submarine captains operated without supervision thousands of kilometers from safe waters. They were bred to be independent, and Captain Shin was no exception.

But while Min-jun might respect the submariner, he did not fear him. Operating in an enemy's harbor where discovery meant possible death required a rare form of courage. But Min-jun's mission took him behind enemy lines, where every passerby represented a potential death sentence. Captain Shin might be intimidating for a submariner, but he was still just a sailor.

Min-jun was a killer.

"What is the **development**?" Min-jun said.

Min-jun made his question as innocuous-sounding as possible, but he maintained the emphasis Captain Shin had placed on the operative word. The commando wasn't an idiot. He already had a fairly good idea what the captain was going to tell him. The low-frequency vibration that permeated the boat when the sub's driveshaft was turning had been absent for the better part of ten minutes. It didn't take a nautical genius to guess why.

"The puppets have been busy," the captain said,

gesturing toward the map table. "They have created a new obstacle. We have temporarily run aground."

Min-jun suppressed a sigh. The South Koreans had not taken the threat represented by stealthy DPRK minisubs idly. While Min-jun's country-men were incorporating the best technology pur-chased or stolen from Russia and China into their electric boats, the South Korean Navy had made their ports and coastlines more difficult to exploit.

In addition to increasing the number of aircraft and surface vessels outfitted with next-generation acoustic sensor suites, the puppets had borrowed a page from China's efforts in the South China Sea. But instead of creating ad hoc islands out of ex-cavated sand, the South Koreans had done some-thing more ingenious. Like combat engineers creating obstacles ahead of the forward line of their own troops, South Korean naval construction ex-perts had erected a maze of submerged sandbars designed to beach midget subs as they stalked the coastline. The DPRK's intelligence agency, the Reconnaissance General Bureau, or RGB, had been warning of undersea obstacles for the last several months, but the Korean People's Navy, or KPN, had assessed the likelihood of the barriers ensnaring a minisub to be low.

So much for naval intelligence.

"What do you mean temporarily?" Min-jun said, eyeing the navigational chart.

"We're at a depth of thirty fathoms," Shin replied,

tracing the chart's depth contours with a pudgy finger. "In a situation like this, I'd normally empty our ballast tanks to help dislodge our hull from the sand, but we're currently at low tide. If I attempt that maneuver now, we run the risk of inadvertently surfacing. In four hours, this inlet will flood as the tide comes in. At that point it will be safe to blow the ballast. Between the additional thrust provided by our diesels and our positive buoyancy, we will pop off this sandbar like a cork from a champagne bottle."

Min-jun felt the conviction powering the captain's assessment, but he didn't share it. This wasn't because Min-jun was a master sailor—far from it. But the one thing he'd learned in his not-so-insignificant career was that no-fail missions weren't afforded the luxury of waiting for circumstances to improve. Min-jun operated on the assumption that the puppets to the south were already looking for him and his team. Their search could take the form of a P-3 Orion antisubmarine airplane or a frigate making a routine sweep of the harbor. Even worse, at this depth the sub could become entangled in a fishing boat's nets. Previous teams had been compromised in such ways, and Min-jun knew what would happen if he and his men were discovered prior to accomplishing their mission. That the commandos would die was a given, but Min-jun's commander had taken things a step further. To drive home the critical nature of Min-jun's mission, the Politburo member had detailed exactly what would befall Min-jun's pregnant wife and unborn child were he to fail. Min-jun had no intention of failing. So while the stout, sweat-drenched man standing in front of him might be the South Sea god Yongsin reincarnated, Min-jun wasn't betting his family on rising tides and fickle ballast tanks.

"How far are we from shore?" Min-jun said, transferring his gaze from the navigational chart to the captain.

"The currents are notoriously treacherous here," Shin sputtered. "If you'll just wait a couple more hours—"

"How far?"

Min-jun didn't shout the question or shake his fist, but his words knifed through the soggy air all the same. The relationship between submariners and the commandos they carried was complicated to say the least. Unlike Min-jun and his men, the sailors ferrying him into battle weren't trained to operate in South Korea. If the midget sub was permanently stuck or discovered, the crew became a liability. An impediment to the commandos' ability to accomplish their mission.

In this profession, liabilities were dealt with in just one way.

The submariner opened his mouth, shut it, then opened it again. When he answered, his words carried the sound of defeat.

"Three kilometers," Shin whispered.

Min-jun nodded without speaking, even as he raced through the calculations. Three kilometers was not an insurmountable swim, but neither would it be easy. The currents in this part of the peninsula were notorious for their unpredictability. The obstacles the puppets had dug in the sea floor would only amplify this effect. In his mind's eye, Min-jun saw torrents of water careening down narrow channels like invisible avalanches, crushing the breath from unwary swimmers and carrying their lifeless bodies out to sea like flotsam.

The puppets were nothing if not thorough. Undoubtedly these new sandbars held acoustic sensors sensitive enough to detect divers in the water. Next to drowning, Min-jun most feared a beachside welcoming party of Korean National Police or Marines as his men staggered from the surf. And then there was the time of day. Waterborne infiltrations were done under cover of darkness. Sunset came early this time of year, but if Min-jun left now, at least part of the swim would have to be done in daylight. If the sun was still up, Min-jun's chances of detection increased exponentially. But he and his team were going into the water all the same. His subordinates had families, too. Love of the Supreme Leader was all fine and good, but nothing motivated a man like the thought of seeing his pretty wife doused with gasoline and set aflame.

Failure was not an option.

"Three kilometers will suffice," Min-jun said, his voice conveying a confidence at odds with his turbulent stomach. "Prepare the chamber. Your boat will be four crew members shorter within the hour."

Captain Shin mouthed a reply, but Min-jun was no longer listening.

Instead, his thoughts turned to his wife's porcelain skin and the raging sea.

18

THE TASTE OF RUBBER FILLED HIS MOUTH AS MIN-JUN bit down on the regulator's mouthpiece and took his first, cautious breath of air. While the gases that could kill a man were often odorless and therefore undetectable, every diver secretly believed that he would be able to tell if his air source was contaminated. Therefore the first inhalation was always done with caution and always before the diver was committed to the water's unforgiving embrace.

The air flowed into Min-jun's mouth like a cold, clean mountain breeze. He inhaled deeply, filling his lungs before exhaling in one continuous breath. Forming his index and thumb into a circle, Min-jun gave the "okay" signal, which was quickly mirrored by the other three members of his team. With a silent prayer to the Supreme Leader for favor, Min-jun grabbed the handholds mounted to either side of the submarine's dive chamber and pulled himself through the open hatch and into oblivion.

The first few moments were chaos as unseen fingers tried to rip his regulator from his mouth. As he'd been trained, Min-jun made a fortress of his forearms, shielding his vulnerable mask and oxygen source from the violent currents. After several disorienting seconds that felt like being caught in a washing machine's spin cycle, Min-jun found himself in a bubble of relative calm about a meter above the ocean floor.

Free from the current's power, Min-jun began to drift upward, and he quickly adjusted his buoyancy, venting air from his vest until his knees came to rest in the sand. Safe for the moment in the eye of the watery hurricane, Min-jun scanned the abyss for his fellow divers. As his eyes probed the dimness, he finally understood the true nature of their problem.

The minisub hadn't merely grazed the top of a submerged sandbar as the captain had supposed. Instead, the black nose was nearly embedded in a mountain of silt. The collision between machine and earth had caused sand to avalanche down the ridgeline, burying the front third of the sub in sticky mud. In order to break free, the submersible would need to rock back and forth while redlining its engines, a maneuver noisy enough for the puppets to detect.

But that wasn't the worst of the news.

With the ferocity of an alpine wind, the current

coursed over the sandbar as the tide came in, tumbling into countless invisible vortices and miniature whirlpools. In the same manner in which a dust devil revealed the wind's presence, the tumbling patterns of sand and debris kicked up by Min-jun's exit showcased the danger facing his team. As he watched, another form emerged from the dive chamber only to be dashed against the side of the sub before tumbling into the abyss.

Min-jun pushed off from the ocean floor, ready to fin to the swimmer's rescue, when a pull on his harness brought him up short. Turning, he found himself face-to-face with Chi-won's unmistakable visage. Even through the dive mask, Min-jun could see the scar bisecting his second-in-command's furry eyebrows. Locking eyes with his commander, Chi-won gave a single shake of his head.

No.

The simple gesture conveyed a magnitude of truth. A truth that Min-jun knew but didn't want to acknowledge. The other diver was gone. Beyond Min-jun's reach. The collision with the sub had probably knocked the man unconscious. At the very least, the water's fury had torn the regulator from his mouth. Chasing the stricken man felt like the right thing to do, but it was an exercise in futility. Even if Min-jun found the missing swimmer and got him back to the sub, the commando would likely be brain dead from a lack of oxygen.

More important, the mission would fail.

That was unacceptable.

Looking over Chi-won's shoulder, Min-jun saw the shadowy form of a third diver.

His team now numbered three.

He had to accept the inevitable.

With a quick nod, Min-jun tightened the straps on his gear bag and checked the fasteners on his rig. Just because the trio had made it through the invisible hydro-slipstream tumbling over the submarine didn't mean they were home free.

Far from it.

The commandos still had to fin to the beach undetected. The simplest course of action would be to just follow his compass due west, but as was often the case with Special Operations missions, the simplest solution was also the deadliest. Min-jun expected several more sandbar obstacles. Trying to swim over them would mean subjecting himself and his teammates to the punishing surf that had already killed one member of his team. Instead, Min-jun intended to pick his way between sandbars, remaining clear of the current's clutches. With a quick series of hand motions, Min-jun conveyed his thoughts to his men.

Then he set out for what he hoped would be a fairly uneventful swim.

IT WASN'T.

Four hours later, Min-jun dragged himself from

the frothing surf. He'd exhausted his main air supply fifteen minutes prior and been forced to transition to his emergency. The small cylinder of "spare air" got him through the surf break submerged, but Min-jun had still surfaced earlier than planned. Fortunately, in a first for the mission thus far, the beach had been abandoned as planned, but Min-jun still felt the presence of an imaginary rifle's crosshairs with every kick.

Or perhaps not so imaginary.

This stretch of beach belonged to a resort hotel. The semidarkness and time of year meant that the beach should be empty of vacationers. Unfortunately, the potential isolation also meant that there was a chance the rolling dunes would be guarded by South Korean National Police.

In the seventy years since the Eternal Leader agreed to the armistice, the DPRK had perfected the art of submarine infiltrations. Not to mention the occasional abduction of South Korean or Japanese civilians. To compensate, South Korea now employed layered coastal defenses. Air assets like the venerable four-engine P-3 Orion plane or Seahawk helicopter provided the outermost cordon, while coastal patrols and acoustic sensors formed concentric rings of security closer to shore. Roving land-based patrols formed the final defensive line, and the randomness and unpredictability of these sentries were Min-jun's greatest concern.

Fortunately, he had a plan.

Min-jun remained submerged up to his neck to minimize his visual and thermal signatures even as Chi-won and Kwang-ho, the remaining commando, materialized next to him. For the first time, Min-jun noted who had perished while egressing the submarine.

Ahn Gi-ung.

The deceased commando had been selected as much for his martial prowess as a sunny disposition that neither fierce cold nor baking heat could diminish. Now Gi-ung was gone. The first casualty in what was arguably the most important undertaking ever entrusted to a KPASOF team since the unit's inception.

"Is he here?" Chi-won said, spitting out the phrase in between breaks in the surf.

"We'll see," Min-jun answered.

Pulling a small, waterproof box from his harness, Min-jun mashed down on the large button. Though not full dark, the ambient light had decreased enough to allow Min-jun to make use of his night-vision device. Trading the waterproof box for a small monocle, Min-jun held the device to his eye as he scanned a stretch of beach now rendered in shades of green. For several long seconds, he saw only crashing surf and silent buildings. Then, just as his hope began to wane, a single flash of white flared against the sage void like an ember glowing to life. The infrared beacon strobed a sequence of two long pulses followed by a pair of short ones.

The recognition signal was correct.

Now Min-jun had to leave the safety of the ocean and cross one hundred meters of deserted beach, while trusting his life and those of his team to an agent he'd never met.

Simple.

Except for all the ways in which it was not.

"Outcropping to the right," Min-jun whispered after the strobe had gone dark.

"I saw it," Chi-won replied in a gravelly smoker's rasp. "What about our Navy friends?"

Min-jun paused, considering.

The stranded minisub represented a safety net of sorts. While there was no way Min-jun could rendezvous with the vessel in its current location, for the next forty-eight hours the sub would remain in South Korean waters. In a normal infiltration, the submarine would creep to several preplanned egress points just off the coast in case the commandos needed to make an emergency exfiltration.

But as Min-jun's commander had made abundantly clear, this was not a normal mission. The target was real, and the waterproof dive bags Kwang-ho and Chi-won carried weren't filled with ballast. Once the commandos left the safety offered by the rolling surf, there was no turning back.

This meant the beached submarine wasn't a safety net.

It was a liability.

And there was only one way to deal with liabilities.

"Do it," Min-jun said.

Chi-won gave a sharp nod even as he reached for a pocket on his own vest. A moment later, a waterproof box was in his hands. But unlike the device Min-jun had employed, this one had a protective barrier over the transmit button. Snapping the seal, Chi-won broke the plastic away, revealing a large red button. Positioning his gloved thumb above it, the team sergeant looked at his commander a final time.

For the briefest of moments Min-jun hesitated. Then he nodded, the blurry image of Gi-ung's limp body tumbling to a watery grave foremost in his mind. The sacrifices required for this operation would not be borne solely by Min-jun's team. Chiwon depressed the button.

A green light glowed briefly in response.

Then it was done.

Captain Shin might have been able to free the submarine from the sandbar's grasp without detection, but Min-jun couldn't take that chance. It was time to leave the sea and its ghosts behind. The commandos now had just one way home, and that journey began with the agent holding the infrared strobe. Min-jun doffed his fins and strode from the surf.

The fight to liberate the south had begun.

19

SEOUL, SOUTH KOREA

"ABOUT WHAT I SAID EARLIER," JAD SAID, GINGERLY edging around a tacky patch of floor. "I'm going to need another pair of shoes."

"I know you're a sneaker aficionado," Cary said, "but surely you've stepped in beer before."

"First off, these are not sneakers. They're Nike Dunks. Second, if you think that sticky stuff is beer, I've got a bridge to sell you."

Cary smiled even as he tried to mitigate the unpleasant combination of smells by breathing through his mouth. As much as he wanted to pretend otherwise, he was afraid Jad was right. The familiar odors of stale beer, cheap cologne, and cigarette smoke he could tolerate. It was the sour undertones that had him worried. Based on the room's décor, he was betting on vomit, body odor, urine, or something even less pleasant. Then again, one did not come to an establishment like this for the ambience. He and Jad needed help slipping past the series of roadblocks ringing Itaewon.

Help from the kind of people who did this for a living.

Criminals.

But not the sort that robbed banks or sold drugs. No, Cary was picturing a unique type of lawbreaker. One that the police tolerated.

Like the establishments on Hooker Hill, for instance.

In the long and sordid history of the military's association with Itaewon's notorious red-light district, there were many tales of woe. The careers that had been ended behind the crumbling façades lining the filthy stretch of road were both numerous and distinguished. One of the most infamous cases involved a general officer who'd paid his tab with a government credit card. By their very nature, these institutions stayed in business by avoiding the law's attention. With this in mind, Cary thought that Hooker Hill might just provide the avenue for escape he and Jad were seeking.

But that was before he'd seen the red-light district up close.

Now Cary was wondering if he'd been a little too clever for his own good.

"This way. This way."

The instructions came from a tiny Korean woman urging them deeper into the establishment's bowels. Even in the club's purposely dim lighting, Cary could most charitably characterize the woman's appearance as **weathered.** Though she still had the figure for the leather pants and skintight blouse she was wearing, Cary had no doubt that the face beneath the Korean's caked-on makeup bore a great deal of mileage.

Though it was probably a difference without a distinction, Cary had chosen a club that Google labeled a bar rather than a brothel. This wasn't to say that it was an establishment Cary would have frequented, but neither did it offer the peepshow windows or raised dancing platforms common to houses of flesh.

As a Green Beret, Cary had often found himself working within culture norms with which he disagreed. But that didn't mean he shelved his morals. Too often the women employed by Asian strip clubs or brothels had been sex-trafficked or otherwise coerced into this lifestyle. Cary had no intention of providing material support to those who profited from others' misery. The bar was seedy, but it wasn't a whorehouse.

That would have to be good enough.

"Coming, **Ajumma**," Cary said. "Coming."

AFTER IDENTIFYING THE BAR HE INTENDED TO TARGET, Cary had pooled his money with Jad's. Between the two of them, the Green Berets had just over a thousand bucks in a combination of Korean won, dollars, and euros. Not exactly a fortune, but at a place that undoubtedly operated on the very edge of solvency, the cash should be more than enough for the job at hand.

Or so Cary hoped.

After trooping inside and asking to see the manager, Cary had started negotiations. The woman had begun the interaction by professing not to speak English, an affliction she'd rapidly overcome once Cary had flashed his wad of cash. Jad then took the lead, and the bartering began in earnest. As a good New England boy, Cary absolutely hated the back-and-forth that went with trying to get the best price for a service.

Jad, on the other hand, had been right at home.

Harkening back to his childhood frequenting the souks of Tripoli, Jad went after the proprietor with unabashed glee. After a particularly brutal exchange that had strayed across at least three different languages, the Korean had nodded and bowed, cementing the agreement.

Jad was smiling, while Cary was covered in a cold sweat. He'd led jirgas between warring Afghan warlords that had been less stressful.

"Van outside," the Korean woman said. "You go."

She shouldered open a door at the rear of the bar, revealing an alley and an idling panel van. Cary was still a bit unclear as to the purpose of the van. From what he could gather, the woman's establishment rated a place on Hooker Hill because it provided a commodity that was also both greatly in demand and mostly illegal.

High-end American liquor.

The contraband was smuggled into the bar via the panel van, and as such, the owner had developed a **relationship** with local law enforcement. She gave the police a cut of the proceeds and they ignored the comings and goings of a certain battered vehicle.

At least that was the story she was spinning.

There were holes in her explanation large enough to accommodate a bus, but beggars couldn't be choosers. Even so, Cary felt a sense of foreboding as he traded the establishment's relatively safe confines for the unknown represented by the idling vehicle.

Jad seemed to agree.

"Good doing business with you, **Ajumma,**" Jad said, offering his hand and a smile.

"**Ne,**" the woman said, accepting Jad's handshake. "Good business. You go. Now."

In an instant, Jad's expression changed to something ominous as he pulled the woman toward him for a more intimate chat.

"Look at my face, **Ajumma,**" Jad said, the smile long gone. "You don't want to make people who look like me angry. If the police stop our van, the men who sent us will be angry. Very angry. Understand?"

"Understand, understand," the woman said, trying to wrench her hand free.

"Good," Jad said, releasing the woman. "Here's a little extra something to take care of any trouble we've caused you."

The Green Beret pulled the much diminished wad of cash from his pocket, peeled off another hundred, and held it out. The woman hesitated for a second and then snatched the bills.

"Annyeonghi gyeseyo, Ajumma," Jad said with a final smile.

The Korean woman didn't offer a good-bye of her own, but she didn't slam the door and lock it, either. Cary chose to take this as a good sign. The van's driver was separated from the cargo area by the kind of metal webbing often found in work trucks. He acknowledged the two Green Berets with a nod and then accelerated out of the alley as soon as Cary pulled the door closed.

20

"DID YOU TELL THAT WOMAN YOU WERE A TERRORIST?" Cary whispered as he made room for himself on the van's cluttered floor.

"I'm not responsible for what she assumes," Jad said.

"You really are—" Cary said.

"**Amazing** is the word you're looking for," Jad said.

"I'm thinking it's not," Cary said.

The van slowed to a stop, and the driver rolled down his window. Cary could hear the Korean exchange, but with no way to see the driver's face and no understanding of the language, he had little idea what was said.

"What's the play if things go sideways?" Jad said, his earlier levity gone.

Cary hesitated.

Despite the comforting weight of the concealed K7 submachine gun, Cary wasn't prepared to shoot his way to freedom if the police yanked open the van's door. His earlier application of deadly force against gunmen wearing police uniforms had been predicated by their execution of unarmed civilians. But for all Cary knew, the police manning the roadblock were legitimate.

He wasn't a murderer.

"I'll make a duress call to Reaper 6, but we'll comply peacefully," Cary said.

"After all the work I went to convincing the bar owner I was a terrorist?" Jad said.

The words aside, Cary recognized the strain beneath his friend's forced levity.

Reaching over, Cary squeezed the big man's leg.

"Hang tough, brother," Cary said. "We've been in tighter jams than this."

Which was true.

What was also true was that tight jams felt a whole lot less constricting with a SCAR heavy in your hands and a band of rough men at your back. This sitting-in-the-dark-and-hoping-for-the-best shit was for the birds.

The conversation's volume increased as words flew between the driver and the policemen. Not good. Cary reached into his pocket, preparing to key the transmit button. He could feel the nervous energy radiating from Jad even as he began to reconsider his plan.

Maybe they should stash the weapons in the van's clutter.

Or maybe they should just wrench open the door and run for it.

Cary turned to Jad, intending to solicit his spotter's thoughts, when the yelling up front ceased. A moment later the van began to move as the driver pulled smoothly away from the roadblock.

"What'd I tell you?" Jad said, elbowing Cary in the side. "Piece of cake."

Cary smiled, but didn't offer a comeback. It had just occurred to him that while they'd made it through the first checkpoint, there would likely be concentric rings of roadblocks. And the more distance they put between themselves and Hooker Hill, the greater the likelihood of encountering police who didn't know about the **Ajumma**'s special relationship with her local officers.

Honest cops really could be problematic.

THANKFULLY FOR THE TWO GREEN BERETS, THE remainder of the trip was uneventful. Or as uneventful as driving in downtown Seoul could be. Cary was convinced that on more than one occasion the van's tires had crested the curb for the sidewalk. He couldn't see outside from his position on the floor, but neither did he want to stand up to look through the dirty window. While he'd love to get a glimpse of the world beyond the vehicle's thin metal frame, the risk wasn't worth it. Seoul might be a city of unusual sights, but a Caucasian face peering from inside a delivery truck would surely be remembered.

Instead, Cary contented himself with tracking their progress on his phone.

As per their negotiations with the **Ajumma,** the driver was supposed to proceed generally southeast until he crossed the Han River. Then he would stop and drop off his cargo of Americans. Though hardly an expert on Seoul, Cary knew a thing or two about setting up man traps. The snaking river that formed the southern boundary of Seoul proper provided a first-class natural barrier to those looking to escape the city on foot.

If it were Cary in the Korean National Police's place, he would concentrate his resources on the river's northern banks, paying special attention to the many bridges spanning the body of water. With this in mind, Cary intended to part ways with their smuggler as soon as the van was feet dry on the river's southern side.

With no way to keep track of what was happening outside and no desire to engage the driver in conversation and thereby give him more information to provide to the police if he was questioned later, Cary contented himself with watching the blue blip signifying their position on Google Maps progress steadily southward.

Until the blip stopped moving.

Cary refreshed the screen and then swore as the

two most dreaded words in the English language appeared at the top of the display.

No service.

"Hey," Cary said, elbowing his spotter, "you still have service?"

Like all good commandos, Jad had passed the downtime in the van by engaging in every soldier's favorite pastime—sleep. But in tribute to his training, the Green Beret awoke instantly alert.

"What?"

Or at least mostly alert.

"I lost service," Cary whispered. "See if you've still got it."

As he waited for Jad to check, Cary keyed the transmit button.

"Reaper 6, this is Reaper 7, commo check, over."

Cary had decided not to establish communications with the rest of Triple Nickel until he and Jad were out of the van and on their own. If the van was stopped and they were compromised, or if the van driver was the talkative sort, Cary wanted the man to have as little information as possible. Many Koreans spoke decent English, and Cary didn't want to chance the man overhearing bits of his conversation or learning that the two crazy Americans he'd ferried past the roadblock had been in contact with others.

At the time, the decision had seemed sound. Now Cary wasn't so sure.

"Reaper 6, this is 7, commo check, over."

Silence.

"No cell service," Jad said, frowning as he studied his phone. "But I'm more worried about the lack of Wi-Fi."

"Why's that?" Cary said, mentally preparing himself.

In the lexicon of Green Berets, Jad was an Eighteen Echo, meaning that he was a communications sergeant. In addition to the requirement for languages, Army Special Forces members each received a designator denoting their area of specialization. Cary was an Eighteen Charlie, meaning his specialization was in all things explosives. Jad on the other hand was a communicator and his training gave him the equivalent of a degree in RF engineering. Discussions on topics such as wave propagation theory, signal amplifiers, and atmospheric distortion delighted Jad and made Cary want to claw his eyes out. Jad was his brother-in-arms and the best spotter he'd ever worked with, but Cary knew that when the Echo started geeking out on electrons, pain was imminent.

"Seoul went to a citywide Wi-Fi a couple years ago," Jad said, still fiddling with his phone. "But even if that system was down, we should be seeing something. It's like the entire spectrum is gone."

"Jamming?" Cary said.

"Maybe. I'd need a spectrum analyzer to know

for sure. Bottom line is that it would take something state-sponsored to throw out enough juice to black out an entire city. I'd say we're looking at some kind of government-sponsored communications lockdown. Hang on a sec—a Wi-Fi signal just popped up."

Cary looked at his phone and saw what Jad was referencing. A single entry showed on his normally busy networks page. Actually, two entries. One had Hangul characters. The second read SEOUL EMERGENCY in English.

"Do we join?" Cary said.

Jad scratched the stubble on his chin as he thought.

"Keep off and let me join," Jad said. "That way one of us stays clean. Besides, I've got a couple extra firewalls on my phone."

"You're the proton herder," Cary said.

"I think you mean electron, boss," Jad said. "Here goes nothing."

Jad touched his phone with his index finger. His shoulders tensed, as if he were bracing for an explosion.

"Okay," Jad said, "we're connected. Now—"

A long, single note emitted from the phone, sounding a bit like the emergency broadcasting system back home. A moment later, a voice speaking in English emanated from the handset.

"A state of emergency has been declared for the

Seoul Capital Area. You are directed to shelter in place until this emergency is lifted. Further updates will be provided as they are available. Thank you."

"That was interesting," Jad said, as the message cycled through a second time. "I tried texting, calling, and jumping on the Internet, but this network permits one-way traffic only. I'm disconnecting. What next?"

"Reaper 6 said he was going to meet us at the hotel," Cary said. "Let's keep riding this horse as long as we can."

"I know you're a **Yellowstone** fanboy, but you've got to stop with cowboy quotes," Jad said.

"Is it America you hate?" Cary said. "Or just Kevin Costner?"

"I happen to like both. But a sap collector from New Hampshire pretending to be a cowboy is just plain stupid."

"I'll have you know that Granite Staters are the cowboys of New England."

"Just like Libyans are the surfers of Africa," Jad said.

"If the flip-flop fits," Cary said.

"That's just hurtful."

"Cowboy up, amigo."

The change in the van's engine noise kept Jad from replying, which was probably just as well. Cary had learned long ago that he stood no chance against his spotter's verbal ripostes once Jad got warmed up. Judging by the look on his friend's face, the Libyan had been about to unleash a zinger.

"Ahjussi," Cary said, catching the driver's eye in the rearview mirror. "What are we doing?"

"Out," the driver said, as the van slowed to a stop. "Go, go."

Cary peered through the window and sighed.

The good news was that the driver had brought the Green Berets across the Han River as per their agreement with the Hooker Hill bar owner. The not-so-good news was that the two commandos weren't anywhere near the prominent intersection of Hakdong-ro and Yeongdong-daero Roads. Ordinarily this wouldn't be a problem, as the Green Berets had certainly hiked to their destinations more than once, but it wasn't the idea of hoofing it to the hotel that had Cary concerned. Without Wi-Fi or cell connectivity, Cary had no way to update his Google map. Cary was pretty good at terrain association and could navigate overland without the use of a compass if he had a good map.

That became quite a bit more difficult in an urban jungle.

"Where are we, **Ahjussi**?" Cary said, trying again.

"Out. Out!"

The driver was growing animated, and Cary thought he understood why. The English version of the emergency message broadcast over the city-wide Wi-Fi had been pretty unambiguous—shelter in place. The police were probably beginning to enforce this edict on vehicular traffic as well. The driver didn't want to get arrested for bucking the order.

"Okay, okay," Cary said to the driver, "keep your pants on. We're going."

"Ready, boss," Jad said, getting to his feet.

"Giddyup," Cary said, wrenching open the sliding cargo door.

He hopped down to the street, and Jad joined him half a second later. Turning, Cary went to shut the door, but the van accelerated away from the curb before he could reach the handle.

"I don't think he likes us," Jad said.

"Speak for yourself," Cary said. "Mama said I was a very nice boy."

Jad snorted but for once kept his opinion to himself, which disappointed Cary. Though he usually came out on the losing end, Cary would have welcomed another round of sparring. Anything would have been better than focusing on the intimidating and totally unfamiliar buildings surrounding them.

"Recognize that street?" Cary said, gesturing at the Hangul characters.

"Nope," Jad said, "but unless I miss my guess, the structure down thataways is a baseball stadium. Actually, two stadiums grouped together. Ring a bell?"

Cary turned, eyed where his spotter pointed, and

swore. It did ring a bell, after a fashion. Though Seoul had a number of arenas and stadiums, Cary knew of only two clustered together as part of a sports complex.

"I think that's the Olympic Stadium," Cary said. "We have successfully crossed the Han River."

"Fantastic," Jad said.

"Sort of. It also means that the Hyatt is due west."

"How far west?"

"A couple kilometers. After we swim across the canal."

"Swim?"

"'Fraid so."

"The Koreans don't have bridges?" Jad said.

"They do," Cary said, "and there'll be police checkpoints on all of them."

"Boss, if I wanted to splash barefoot in the water, I'd have been a SEAL."

"You can't swim?" Cary said.

"Of course I can. I'm a freaking surfer."

"What's the problem?"

"The problem is I'm having a fantastic hair day."

"You really are a SEAL."

"Hurtful. Just hurtful."

21

UNDISCLOSED LOCATION, SOUTH KOREA

"I CAN'T BELIEVE YOU'RE FINALLY HERE."

The man behind the wheel of the late-model Hyundai said the words with a reverence that bordered on comical, and Min-jun might have found the entire exchange humorous if this hadn't been the third time the phrase had been uttered word for word. In a covert operation, many things could spell doom for the operatives, but nothing was as dangerous as an overly eager asset.

"I've been waiting for this," the driver said again, apparently mistaking Min-jun's silence for encouragement.

"The Supreme Leader thanks you for your service," Min-jun said.

In North Korea, this statement would have concluded any discussion, regardless of the topic. Though Min-jun had his doubts as to whether the leader of the DPRK really was God incarnate, there was no question that the man-child had powers that bordered on the mystical. With a single word, he could end a life or elevate it. His name, when spoken at all, produced an awe that was more fear than respect.

But not today.

"Yes, yes," the driver said, waving away Min-jun's words with one hand as he steered with the other. "And I am happy to serve in this godless land on his behalf. What I meant is that I've been waiting for your team for more than two hours. It's cold and rainy. I'd thought you'd be on time. Also, I was expecting four of you, not three."

"There were four," Min-jun said.

The commando's comment brought the driver up short. The man glanced from the road to Min-jun, seemingly waiting for the commando to elaborate. Min-jun let the uncomfortable silence build for several long moments before speaking.

"Your name is Sung-ho, correct?" Min-jun said.

"Yes," the driver said, frowning.

"How long have you lived in the land of the puppets, Sung-ho?" Min-jun said.

"Ten years," Sung-ho said, changing lanes to pass a scooter packed with boxes that towered over the driver's head. "I've maintained my cover as instructed while staying active in the North Korea Freedom Coalition."

Ten years. For a third of Min-jun's life, his driver

had been going to bed with a full stomach in a warm bed while pretending to be a defector disaffected with the DPRK. A bit more than just a full stomach, judging by the potbelly spilling over the driver's slacks. For Min-jun, the last decade hadn't been quite so prosperous. His father and mother had both starved to death during the latest famine, pooling their allotment of rice together so that his youngest sister could survive.

These tragedies had both strengthened Min-jun's resolve and solidified his hatred for the people who lived in plenty while starving their brothers and sisters to the north with crippling sanctions. Min-jun had volunteered for the KPASOF so that mothers and fathers would never again have to choose between their lives and those of their children. His reasons for embarking on this particular mission were no less compelling. And here this overfed imbecile sat, complaining about the cold. Min-jun wanted to kill the man here and now and toss his lifeless body into a ditch.

But he didn't.

Instead, he asked another question.

"What were your instructions?" Min-jun said.

Sung-ho frowned. "To take you to the safe house."

"Were you told to ask questions?"

"No."

"Then don't."

"Look, all I'm saying is that—"

Min-jun tuned the man out.

Though Min-jun thought about disposing of Sung-ho for much longer than he admittedly should have, in the end he settled back into his seat and vowed to ignore the idiot's prattle. He was warm and dry, and his two remaining teammates and their kit were safely in the car. The loss of Gi-ung was tragic, but not as debilitating to the mission as if the commandos' gear bags packed with weapons and specially designed tools had been washed out to sea.

All things considered, Min-jun and his men were in a good spot. He needed to do everything in his power to keep this place of harmony from being disrupted. As much as it would be good for Min-jun's soul to punch his stiletto blade through the driver's windpipe, for the next twelve hours Min-jun's job was to be invisible. Anything that could potentially interfere with that objective needed to be ignored.

For now, anyway.

But thoughts of invisibility vanished as strobe lights played across the Hyundai's narrow interior.

Strobe lights coming from the police car behind them.

22

"RELAX," SUNG-HO SAID. "JUST RELAX. EVERYTHING'S going to be fine."

In contrast to his soothing words, the driver's fingers drummed a nervous tempo on the steering wheel as his eyes darted to the rearview and sideview mirrors.

Like all North Korean commandos, Min-jun had been briefed extensively on the disposition and conduct of the South Korean National Police. South Korean law enforcement officers were, in a word, tentative. Prior to his last infiltration exercise, a DPRK intelligence analyst had showed Min-jun and his team a series of embarrassing video clips showcasing Korean National Police standing idly by during mass brawls. During the operation, Min-jun had made it a point to observe law enforcement officers as they performed their duties. To a person they'd been polite, professional, and nonconfrontational. In fact, there was just one infraction that he'd seen the police ruthlessly enforce—drunk driving.

"Have you been drinking?" Min-jun said, eyeing the driver.

"What?" the man said, glancing at his passenger. "No, of course not."

"Then relax," Min-jun said. "Everything will be fine."

But it was becoming more apparent by the second that everything was **not** going to be fine. The driver didn't smell of alcohol, nor was he acting intoxicated, but he was certainly more nervous than he should have been for a random traffic stop. Something else was going on. Unfortunately, Min-jun didn't have the time to determine what.

A brilliant shaft of white light pierced the dim cabin. The retina-burning brilliance gave Min-jun an excuse to turn toward the light's source, even as he shaded his eyes from its effect. But the commando didn't direct his attention toward the police car. Instead, Min-jun made eye contact with Chi-won and Kwang-ho seated behind him.

No words were exchanged, but both commandos nodded.

"Okay, here we go," the driver said, speaking rapidly. "Just keep quiet—I'll handle everything."

Min-jun grunted his assent, but he was focused on the two figures exiting the Hyundai patrol car. As per standard procedure, the officers separated, with one covering the left side of Min-jun's vehicle while the other took the right. But in a break with protocol, both officers already had their sidearms drawn.

So much for everything being fine.

"Get out of the vehicle," the closest officer said. "Now."

Min-jun complied, taking an extra-large step as he exited even as Chi-won, who was seated directly behind him, stayed closer to the vehicle's frame.

"What is this about?" Sung-ho said, his voice nearing hysteria.

Kwang-ho, who had been seated behind the driver, responded to Sung-ho's outburst by slapping him across the face. Hard. The **crack** of flesh hitting flesh cut through the night as the driver collapsed against the vehicle's frame, hands flailing against the unexpected violence.

It was perfectly executed.

For an instant, both Korean police officers shifted their attention to the quarreling men.

A fatal mistake.

Just as they'd practiced countless times, Chi-won and Min-jun drew the Baek-Du-San pistols secreted at their waists with smooth, fluid motions. Min-jun engaged the target on his side of the car while Chi-won took care of the officer on the far side. The 9-millimeter rounds were subsonic, but absent a suppressor, the pistol's report was still quite loud. That was okay. There was a time and a place for silent killing.

This wasn't it.

Min-jun fired into his target's center mass as he stalked forward in a shooter's rolling walk. The South Korean tumbled to the ground. Min-jun smoothly followed the man down, continuing to shoot until he was certain the threat had been neutralized.

Beside him, Chi-won ceased fire once his target fell, the vehicle's frame preventing him from administering the coup de grâce. Kwang-ho had no such problem. The third commando drew his own pistol and supplied the necessary head shot. In the space of a single drawn breath, the threats had been eliminated.

Most of them, anyway.

Effortlessly transitioning from one target to the next, Chi-won grabbed the sputtering driver by the throat and rammed his pistol beneath Sung-ho's jaw.

"You have one chance to live," Min-jun hissed as he joined his team sergeant. Behind him, Kwang-ho was already dragging the body of the nearest policeman back toward the cruiser. "Why did the police pull us over?"

"I don't know," the driver said, his wild-eyed gaze bouncing between the two commandos.

"Kill him," Min-jun said.

"Wait," the driver screamed. "Wait. This doesn't have anything to do with you. I make a little money on the side selling meth. I pay the police to look the other way. I was late with this month's payment."

"You were bribing the police?" Min-jun said.

"Yes," the driver said, babbling. "I mean no. I wasn't paying off everyone. Just those two officers. They have the beat where I sell my pills."

"What are their names?" Min-jun said.

"Hyun-ki and Kang-dae."

"Is he telling the truth?" Min-jun said, looking past the driver to Kwang-ho.

The commando looked at the two officers' name plates and gave Min-jun a quick nod.

"You weren't paying off anyone else?" Min-jun said.

"No," the driver said. "No one. I swear."

"Let him go," Min-jun said to Chi-won.

The team sergeant gave Min-jun a quizzical look, but complied.

"Thank you for believing me," the driver said, tears streaming down his face.

"I don't," Min-jun said. "Kwang-ho."

The lean commando extended his arm, the policeman's sidearm in his hand. Faster than the blubbering traitor could speak, Kwang-ho fired the pistol. The driver gasped, then gurgled as he slid to the dirty concrete.

"Good shooting, comrade," Min-jun said, ignoring the dying man's moans. "Put the pistol in his hand once he dies. It's far from the perfect crime scene, but we don't need perfect. We just need to keep the puppets busy until we get to the alternate safe house."

"There's an alternate?" Kwang-ho said.

"This may be your first operation," Chi-won said. "But it isn't ours. Always have a secondary safe house, even if you have to pay for it yourself."

"What about transportation?"

"Here it comes now."

Headlights played across the scene as a single car crested the hill. Stepping into the middle of the road, Chi-won waved his hands. Like a good South Korean, the motorist slowed to a stop and rolled down the passenger window. Chi-won jogged over to the car, forced the man out at gunpoint, and shot him in the head. Five minutes later, the body was in the car's trunk and Min-jun was behind the wheel.

Certainly not the best start to an operation.

Neither was it the worst.

23

SEOUL, SOUTH KOREA

THE GLASS DOORS OF THE PARK HYATT SEOUL BECKONED.
Cary was not a connoisseur of fine hotels, but even he could see that this was a nice establishment. A bright, inviting foyer framed by gargantuan stone slabs formed the entranceway, while a row of floor-to-ceiling windows provided a vantage point for the bar or restaurant located on the second floor. This was the kind of place frequented by movers and shakers—businessmen celebrating after closing a big deal or wealthy travelers accustomed to a bit of pampering. The clientele was smartly dressed, and the cars dropping off the patrons ranged from flashy sports cars to luxurious SUVs. This was not the place for two Green Berets covered in grime.

"We're a bit underdressed, boss," Jad said.

"Nah," Cary said. "Fitting in is all about attitude."

"That's funny," Jad said, "'cause the only attitude I'm sensing is the one coming from the doorman."

As usual, Cary's spotter had the right of things. A dapper man wearing a starched black uniform was eyeing them from the other side of the spotless glass doors. He seemed to be willing the Green Berets not to enter. Cary felt his pain.

Though the canal the two commandos had forded had been a relatively easy swim, the water hadn't been the cleanest. Like Jad, Cary had been able to keep his head above the muck the entire time, but he intended to burn his clothes at the first opportunity. That said, taking the amphibious route across the canal seemed to have been the correct decision. Cary had charted a course across the sluggish water that paralleled the concrete pilings supporting the bridge in an effort to avoid drawing the attention of the motorists on the Dongbu Expressway. The busy highway mirrored the canal's western shore, and a steady stream of cars still rumbled across the bridge, ignoring the shelter-in-place edict. As such, the two men employed a slow and steady stroke designed to minimize splashing or water churn. Pausing to rest while holding on to a concrete piling midway through the swim, Cary had heard voices drifting down from the bridge. His prediction had proven correct.

The police had erected a blockade on the bridge. Unfortunately, the Green Berets may have traded one barrier to entry for another. The South Koreans he'd met thus far had all been unfailingly polite, but Cary couldn't imagine a scenario in which the doorman allowed two half-drowned river rats to drip puddles of brown, oily water onto his polished marble floor.

"Remember, we belong here," Cary said, more to bolster his own flagging confidence.

"Then somebody better tell that guy," Jad said. "We're going to need a miracle to get past him."

Cary knew Jad was right. In the minute or two the commandos had been standing outside, the doorman had drifted closer to the entrance, no doubt preparing to interdict the ne'er-do-wells before they could tarnish his hotel's sterling reputation.

A miracle indeed.

And then the divinity took the form of a trio of police officers.

The three men materialized from the busy street to the west. Cary and Jad were standing amid clumps of trees bordered by beautifully landscaped flower beds. The foliage provided a natural barrier between the hotel and the busy intersection to the northeast, and the law enforcement officers passed by the Green Berets without noticing them. The men entered the lobby, and the doorman moved to intercept them. The black-clad man offered a bow, but the lead officer didn't reciprocate.

Instead, he drew his pistol and shot the doorman in the torso.

"Shit fire," Jad said as the man crumpled to the floor. "What now?"

The policeman who'd fired the initial shot stepped over the doorman's body and casually put another round into the man's prone form. Then the trio headed for the stairs and presumably the second floor.

The floor housing a bar packed with Americans.

"Cowboy up, brother," Cary said, pulling the waterlogged K7 from his belt. "It's time to save the day."

24

SEOUL, SOUTH KOREA

ISABEL'S PHONE RANG WITH A MULTITONE ENSEMBLE reminiscent of the soundtrack to an old video game.

"What?" Isabel said in answer to Jack's frown. "Your buddy picked the ringtone."

She had a point. Gavin had cloned Jack's and Isabel's old phones onto the new burners in an effort to further mask their digital trail. If the pudgy keyboard warrior had been responsible for configuring the cell's settings, there was a good chance the ringtone had been lifted from an Atari classic.

Or worse.

The theme song to an eighties cartoon series.

"Who is it?" Jack said.

"Kira. Want me to take it?"

Jack glanced at their surroundings, considering. After he'd finished with Clark, Jack had needed to make a decision. Rustling up a safe house was going to take a bit of doing, even for the intrepid Campus logistic folks. These were the moments when the limitations associated with working for a small-time, off-the-books intelligence organization were highlighted in stark relief. Unlike the Central Intelligence Agency, which had offices that were termed **station** or **base,** depending on their size, The Campus had no permanent employees stationed overseas. This meant that there was no local liaison in South Korea, much less Seoul, who could utilize previously established relationships to procure lodging behind the impenetrable veil of front companies. Or, in all likelihood, simply pass Jack the keys to an already rented and vetted property that existed for in extremis situations like this one.

This was not to say that The Campus's administrative folks weren't competent. Just that the procurement would take time. Time that Jack needed to burn while staying under the radar with Isabel in tow. It was this more than anything else that drove Jack's decision to move to the pair's current location. Evading surveillance as a single trained operative was trying. Doing so while hand-holding a civilian was a recipe for disaster. Jack needed more manpower.

Or in this case, womanpower.

"Yeah, go ahead and answer," Jack said.

He and Isabel were seated in a dark corner of the hotel's music-themed bar.

Vinyl records packed the floor-to-ceiling wood shelves while turntables, analog amplifiers, and massive seventies-era speakers added to the bar's ambience. The décor was, in a word, **cool,** but the establishment's hipness was of a secondary concern. Jack cared more about the establishment's dim lighting, plentiful Americans, and proximity to Lisanne.

Isabel thumbed the answer button and held the phone to her ear.

"Kira?" Isabel said.

Jack snuck a glance at his watch. Lisanne should be down from her room any minute. As soon as they linked up, he intended to be back on the street. Riots were springing up across Seoul and growing in intensity. No additional bombings had been reported, but Jack thought the crowds of citizens defying the government-ordered lockdown seemed like lucrative targets. The police guarding the hotel had pulled off station about thirty minutes ago, and Jack had made the snap decision to grab Lisanne in person. Now that he was here, Jack realized that the hotel could quickly become a prison.

"What?" Isabel said, her face twisting into a look of confusion.

A patron seated on the other side of the room got to unsteady feet. The man let his index finger glide across the shelved records before seemingly choosing one at random. He removed the jacket and placed the disk on the turntable. A moment later, Steve Perry's unmistakable tenor cut through the air. Jack was more of a Fleetwood Mac fan, but as eighties bands went, Journey wasn't terrible.

"She wants to talk to you," Isabel said, holding the handset against her chest.

"Me specifically?" Jack said.

"No. She asked me to go to the U.S. embassy and deliver a message to the CIA. That's the same as talking to you, right?"

"Close enough," Jack said, accepting the handset. "Hello? Kira?"

"Hello, yes, I—"

Shuffling noises sounded from the cell as the voice cut off midsentence.

"Hello?" Jack said, sticking a finger in his ear to block out the room's ambient noise. "Kira—can you hear me?"

"This is not Kira. But I can hear you. Perfectly. With whom am I speaking?"

Jack jerked in surprise. The voice was a new one. Still female, but decidedly not Russian. The accent was hard to place, but Jack sensed an Asian flavor to the syllables.

"This is Bill," Jack said. "Bill Jones. Where's Kira?"

"Right beside me. She's safe. For now. How long we stay that way is up to you."

Shuffling the phone from one hand to the other, Jack found and activated the record feature.

Then he put the device back to his ear.

"What are you talking about?" Jack said.

"Are you in Seoul?"

Jack paused, considering his answer. He wasn't in the habit of revealing his whereabouts to anonymous callers. Then again, the woman was using Kira's phone, and Kira knew that Isabel was in Seoul.

"Yes," Jack said.

"Then you most certainly know what I'm talking about. The bombing."

"What about it?" Jack said.

"There will be more."

"Why?"

"This is the work of a nation-state, Mr. Jones. A prelude to war."

Across the room, a second man made a selection from the record library. Neal Schon broke off mid guitar solo, replaced by a riff that had mesmerized countless eighties aficionados as a haunting baritone confessed an obsession with his best friend's girlfriend. Jack was on the phone talking about war and Rick Springfield was singing about Jessie's girl.

Only in Korea.

"How do you know?" Jack said.

This was the question every intelligence officer

was trained to ask when presented with tantalizing reporting. A question that was too often ignored, especially when the reporting in question was particularly spectacular. Like their journalist cousins, case officers were often seduced by a story's implications. The juicier the reporting, the greater the temptation to sidestep the need to verify its veracity in favor of focusing on the lurid details.

Jack was determined not to fall into this trap.

"First my terms, Mr. Jones. Then the information."

"Nope," Jack said. "Tell me what you know and how you know it. Then we discuss terms. Otherwise, we're done."

"Are all Americans this stupid?"

"Not stupid," Jack said, "just stubborn. Mom made sure I knew the difference. What's it gonna be?"

The woman hissed in frustration.

For a moment, Jack was convinced she was going to hang up.

Then she began to speak.

"The next attack will occur at the Port of Busan. In four hours' time, I will check the location of this phone. If it is in the vicinity of Busan, I will call. If you are the one who answers, I will provide the necessary information to stop the attack. If these conditions are not met, I will conclude our relationship. Is that specific enough?"

"Almost," Jack said. "You're still missing the second part of the question. How do you know about the pending attack?"

"Do you often receive calls of this kind?"

"Actions speak louder than words, ma'am," Jack said.

"Indeed they do, Mr. Jones. I believe you Americans have another expression that also fits—a picture is worth a thousand words."

The phone vibrated in Jack's hand as the woman spoke. Jack flipped the device over to see the screen. The woman had texted him a picture. An unconscious Asian man was lying in a hospital bed with swarms of tubes and wires snaking from his body. His arms and neck were wrapped in white bandages, but his face was clearly visible. Despite the purple bruising obscuring his features, the man's face looked familiar.

Jack stared at the image, trying to place the face.

Then he had it.

"Holy shit," Jack said.

"Indeed, Mr. Jones," the woman said. "Talk soon."

The woman hung up.

"Who's that?" Isabel said, looking over Jack's shoulder.

"Not one hundred percent sure," Jack said, zooming in on the man's face, "but if I had to guess, I'd say it's the leader of North Korea."

"What happened to him?" Isabel said.

"Hell if I know," Jack said.

Even though Isabel had asked a valid question, Jack had already moved on from the disturbing photo and its unspoken implications to something else.

The trio of men standing at the entrance to the bar. Men with guns.

25

CARY MOVED ACROSS THE SMALL COURTYARD AT A PACE somewhere between a fast walk and a slow run. Though he knew that every moment the three pseudo-policemen were allowed to roam through the hotel unchallenged was another opportunity for an innocent bystander to end up like the doorman, Cary did not sprint. Shooting accurately from a run was almost impossible. With a hotel full of people and a trio of armed killers, Cary knew his marksmanship abilities were about to be put to the test.

Cary paused at the glass door until he felt Jad squeeze his shoulder. Then he flowed inside, leading with the K7's muzzle. Much like a Glock pistol, the K7 had a much-deserved reputation for ruggedness. While taking the submachine gun for a swim wasn't the preferred way to clean the weapon, a K7 that had been soaked in water would still fire.

The ammunition cartridges were airtight, meaning the powder inside would still be dry and therefore combustible. Moisture in the barrel could affect the bullets' trajectory, but more so for distance shots than the close-in work Cary was expecting.

Cary entered the lobby, viewing everything through the K7's circular front sight. The doorman lay in a crumpled heap, blood seeping from his body across the white marble floor. The lobby was oddly situated in that it sat squarely between the outside entrance to the northwest and the parking garage to the southeast. To the left, a hallway led to what Cary assumed were the check-in desks, while an elevator and the flight of stairs sat to the right. No one had responded to the gunshots, leading Cary to believe that the hallway to the left went some distance. Either that or the workers at the other end were still cowering in fear. In any case, one look at the sprawled form confirmed Cary's initial impression.

The doorman was beyond help.

Cary moved past the body to the stairwell, again waiting for Jad's shoulder squeeze before starting up. Clearing a stairwell that proceeded both up and down was best done with a team of six to eight assaulters. Cary had two. So rather than the deliberate method he'd practiced countless times in the shoot houses back at Fort Campbell, he sped up the stairs, ignoring the lower floor as Jad kept pace. The double set of stairs got Cary's heart pounding even as he worked to control his respiration in anticipation for the shots he knew were coming. His breathing and racing pulse seemed impossibly loud. He placed each foot softly on the steps in order to mask the sound of his approach.

The Korean shooters had no reason to suspect that anyone would be coming up the stairwell behind them. With a bit of luck, Cary thought he and Jad might be able to get the drop on the shooters before they killed again.

Until he heard the screams.

26

IN WHAT SEEMED LIKE A FIRST IN JACK'S KOREAN adventure thus far, the guns in question were currently holstered, as was befitting members of the Korean National Police. Even better, the trio of officers didn't at all seem interested in him or Isabel. Unfortunately, Lisanne chose this exact moment to make her entrance. Everyone in the bar seemed to be interested in her.

Including the three policemen.

Jack understood their fascination.

Lisanne breezed through the door opposite the police, wearing boots, tight-fitting jeans, and a sleeveless blouse. Her dark hair hung loose about her shoulders in a raven curtain, and Lisanne paused in the entranceway to brush it from her eyes one-handed. Though undoubtedly done to provide her with a chance to survey the room, the gesture only drew more attention to the Campus operative. Not only was Lisanne strikingly beautiful, she was also missing one arm below the elbow. She couldn't have been more the center of attention if a spotlight had shone down from the heavens.

Or perhaps not.

The clearly inebriated businessman who was manning the turntable reached for his drink while staring at Lisanne. He missed the glass of rum and Coke but managed to hit the turntable, producing an ear-piercing screech as the needle plowed across the record.

Lisanne's olive skin flushed. Then her dark eyes found Jack, and her full lips formed a relieved smile.

Jack found himself smiling in return as he got to his feet.

Until the Korean police moved to intercept Lisanne.

Though he couldn't hear what was said over the blasting guitar solo, Jack watched the happy expression fade from Lisanne's face. She nodded once, lips compressed into a thin line. Then the cop closest to her placed a hand on Lisanne's shoulder, transforming a polite conversation into something decidedly less so.

Jack gritted his teeth as he fought the urge to go to his fellow Campus operative's aid. The two policemen standing beside the officer focused on Lisanne were watching the bar's crowd like . . . well . . . policemen. Fortunately, for once Jack's discretion paid off. After a final exchange, the cop gestured for Lisanne to enter the bar. She smiled her thanks, white teeth sparkling against brown skin.

Then she was walking toward Jack wearing a different smile.

A smile Jack didn't return.

He was too focused on the policeman behind her.

The one drawing his pistol.

A pistol now pointing at the back of Lisanne's head.

Jack came out of the chair in a blur of motion, a lightning bolt of seething fury. The joy on Lisanne's face changed to surprise and then something that looked like comprehension. A woman seated next to the entrance screamed, the sound foreshadowing what was to come. Jack raced toward Lisanne, but events were now unfolding in slow motion.

Lisanne slowly turned toward the sound of the scream.

The muscles on the policeman's forearm tightened.

More shrieks.

Then gunfire.

Jack howled, but Lisanne was still standing.

The policemen behind her were not.

The officers' uniform-clad bodies fell to the carpet as bullet after bullet tore into them, sending geysers of blood arcing skyward. Two men flowed into the room, one Caucasian, one Middle Eastern. The pair were the embodiment of the old maxim

slow is smooth, smooth is fast, fast is deadly. With a rolling walk that spoke of countless hours spent on a range shooting tens of thousands of rounds, the men swept across the entryway, peppering the fallen Koreans with constant aimed fire until the bodies ceased moving.

Then the men turned toward Jack.

Grabbing Lisanne, Jack pulled her behind him even as he stood to his full height and stretched out his arms, shielding his fellow operative. The men carried K7 submachine guns and certainly knew how to employ the weapons, but their clothes and hair were sopping wet. For the life of him, Jack couldn't decide what to make of the shooters.

Apparently the sentiment was mutual.

With practiced motions, the men panned their K7s across the surging crowd of screaming patrons, searching for additional threats.

Then both muzzles centered on Jack.

"Hey, boss," the dark-complexioned man said. "Is it just me or does this dude look familiar?"

"Familiar how?" the second man said.

"I don't think we've met," Jack said, raising his hands to shoulder level.

"Not formally," the dark-complexioned man said. "You were too busy getting nailed to a cross at the time."

"Hells bells," the second man said. "He's the one?"

"You never forget your first crucifixion," the dark-complexioned one said.

"You're one crazy fucker," the second man said, looking at Jack.

"Heard that before," Jack said, slowly lowering his hands.

"You guys know each other?" Lisanne said.

"No," Jack said, "but I think we've got some catching up to do."

"Agreed," the first man said. "Let's talk somewhere private. We're kind of on the run."

"Kind of?" Jack said.

"It's a long story."

"You're going to fit right in," Isabel said.

27

"HOW DO YOU GUYS KNOW EACH OTHER?" ISABEL SAID.

The three men and two women were now crammed into an elevator shooting upward. They'd exchanged names but little else in their hurry to leave the chaos enveloping the bar behind before more men with guns, real police or otherwise, arrived.

"It's complicated," Jack said, willing the red LED floor numbers to change faster.

"Not really," Cary said. "Jad and I were in a hide site observing an apocalyptic cult in Syria when old Jack here tried to get himself nailed to a cross."

"Not so much **tried** as **did**," Jad said. "The crazies put at least one nail into him."

"You were nailed," Lisanne said, her dark eyes widening, "to a cross?"

"I told you about Syria," Jack said, his face flushing.

"I think you left out a couple things," Lisanne said.

"He didn't mention my shot?" Jad said.

"Wait," Isabel said, turning to Jad. "You shot someone?"

"No, sweetheart," Jad said, eyes twinkling. "I took out three bad guys at almost a thousand meters with a fifteen-knot crosswind. That's the sniper equivalent of painting the **Mona Lisa** hanging upside down while blindfolded."

"So dramatic," Cary said. "It was only nine hundred meters and the crosswind wasn't over twelve knots."

"That's jealousy talking right there," Jad said. "Besides, you have to admit that old Jack certainly wasn't making things easy on me."

"I was busy," Jack said, the answer sounding defensive to his own ears.

"Lying on a cross?" Lisanne said.

"Hell, no," Jad said, his grin growing wider. "Your boy wasn't just lying there. This mofo went after the bad guys with a hammer. You should have seen the way—"

"They get the picture," Cary said.

"Actually—" Lisanne said.

"Look, it's our floor," Jack said, as the elevator came to a stop. He charged through the open doors like he was the number-one man in a tactical stack. At that moment, Jack would have rather faced just about anything than endure another moment in the elevator.

Even crucifixion.

Near-death experiences aside, Jack's discomfort had more to do with his current situation than it did with reliving Syria. When he'd asked Clark for permission to helm a Campus operation, Jack hadn't envisioned his team consisting of two Green Berets, a civilian with a Russian scientist for a pen pal, and the only Campus operative who lacked both hands.

The 1995 Chicago Bulls they were not.

Not to mention that while Jack was deeply grateful to Cary and Jad, two Americans gunning down a gaggle of Korean police officers in front of a crowd of witnesses presented its own problems. As did the wail of police sirens that was steadily growing closer. Jack was done with Korean police. Until he better understood who was running the show, Jack no longer trusted that the next uniformed man or woman wasn't a mass murderer in disguise. With the cell-phone network once again down, Jack had made the decision to take the elevator to Lisanne's room in order to retrieve her satellite phone. From there he reasoned they could hide in the hotel until the ruckus died down or use one of the many exits to try their hand on Seoul's streets. Either way, Jack wasn't going anywhere until he had a means of communication separate from the Korean cell or Wi-Fi networks.

The elevator's doors swished shut as the rest of his ragtag team followed Jack into the hallway.

With five Americans crowded into its narrow confines, the corridor suddenly felt cramped, and the looming walls oppressive.

Lisanne's modest room would be even more so.

"Grab your phone," Jack said to Lisanne. "We'll keep watch on the elevators."

"I thought we were hunkering down?" Lisanne said.

Jack shook his head. "Change of plans. I don't like the idea of all of us holed up in one place. Feels too much like the Alamo. Besides, we need open sky for the phone to work. Take Isabel to help."

Lisanne nodded, and for once Isabel didn't argue. Perhaps she was starting to trust Jack. Or maybe she was too tired to protest. At this point, either answer was fine. Lisanne and Isabel took off down the hall at a run while Cary and Jad spread apart, one commando focusing on the elevator while the other covered the door leading to the stairwell.

"What agency did you say you were with again?" Cary said.

"I didn't," Jack answered.

"I know," Cary said. "That was me trying to be polite."

"What my team sergeant is trying to say," Jad said, "is that our last interaction with a CIA case officer was less than satisfactory."

"He was a lying SOB," Cary said.

"As I said," Jad said, "less than satisfactory."

Jack chuckled. "I'm not with the CIA."

"Then who?" Cary said.

"Technically, we don't exist," Jack said.

"Shocker," Cary said. "Next you're going to tell me that Santa Claus isn't real."

"Wait a minute," Jad said. "Did you just say—"

"Got it," Lisanne said, racing back down the hall with the satellite phone in her hand and Isabel in tow.

"Hallelujah," Jack said.

"Who do you guys work for?" Cary said to Lisanne.

"I think they're CIA," Isabel said.

"Technically, we don't exist," Lisanne said.

Both elevators dinged, and Jack watched as the floor numbers ticked down.

Someone was calling the cars to the lobby.

"As much fun as the conversation has been," Jack said, "I think that's our cue to hit the stairs."

28

FIFTEEN SWEATY MINUTES LATER, JACK STOOD ON THE
building's roof.

Other than the distinctive Seoul skyline glittering back at him, there was nothing particularly
unique about the view. The roof had a single access
point in the form of a service door and was covered in pea gravel. Though hulking HVAC units
took up most of the real estate, there was about
fifty square meters of open space just off the door.
Judging by the collection of cigarette butts next to
a pair of rusted reclining pool chaise longue chairs,
the open space also served as an unofficial gathering place for the hotel's staff.

Hopefully no one would be coming up for a
smoke break anytime soon.

"Anyone have cell service?" Jack said as he extended the antenna on the Iridium 9575 Lisanne
had passed him.

While he was certain the satphone offered connectivity, Jack also knew it came with none of
the Gavin-engineered encryption functionality of
their smartphones. Compared to the latest Apple
or Android offering, satphones were decidedly low
tech in the app department. To Jack's eye, the contraption more resembled a turn-of-the-century flip
phone, a device in which texting required hunting and pecking through the three available letters
assigned to each digit. There would be no implementation of the Eye of Sauron or any of the other
similarly named security applications Gavin was
famous for developing. With this in mind, Jack
wanted to ensure that no other means of communication were available before he lit up the Iridium.

Unfortunately, four shaking heads confirmed
his fears.

It was the satphone or nothing.

Dialing, Jack put the handset to his ear even
as he rehearsed how his second conversation with
Mr. Clark would go. The last time they'd talked,
Jack had hung up feeling optimistic. He'd laid out
the progress he'd made in a straightforward manner while making the case for operational control. Mr. C. had agreed. Jack had a feeling things
wouldn't be quite so smooth this time.

"Lisanne?"

"Ding?" Jack said with surprise.

"Hey, Jack. Yep, it's me. Where's Lisanne?"

"Standing right next to me. Hang on."

Jack activated the phone's speaker mode.

"Can you still hear me?" Jack said.

"Yep. Where are you?"

"On a rooftop."

"Interesting," Ding said. "Should I ask why or would it be quicker for you to just tell me?"

"I'll give you the scoop," Jack said. "But you're talking to an audience. Besides Lisanne and me, we've got two Green Berets and a potential Campus helper. Maybe you should get Mr. C. on the line. This one's a doozy."

"No can do, kid. Clark gave me marching orders, too. He said when you called, I was supposed to handle it."

There were several aspects to Ding's answer that Jack found interesting. For one, Mr. C. had automatically assumed Jack would be calling for help. That his boss had been correct only rubbed salt in Jack's wounds. But Jack would have to deal with his hurt feelings later. His current situation gave new meaning to the phrase **under the gun.** If the anonymous caller was to be believed, an attack against the Port of Busan was looming. Not to mention that he and his teammates were trapped in a hotel and probably wanted by the Korean National Police.

Time to swallow his pride and ask for help.

He seemed to be doing a lot of that lately.

Maybe that's what being in charge was all about.

"Okay," Jack said, "here's the short version—

I need to get to the Port of Busan in the next four hours to stop another spectacular attack. One on the same level of magnitude as this morning's bombing. I'm currently on the roof of a luxury hotel, hiding from the Korean National Police, who may or may not want to talk to me about the shooting deaths of several men who may or may not be their fellow officers. Also, Seoul is currently under a state of emergency, so all cellular and Wi-Fi communications are locked down, and the police are manning checkpoints for both foot and vehicular traffic."

"Holy crap, Junior. Is that all?"

Jack thought for a moment.

"Not quite," Jack said. "I could also use kit for three shooters."

"Four," Lisanne said, interjecting.

"Okay, maybe four," Jack said. "And two of the shooters are snipers, so if you could throw in some long guns, that would be perfect."

"SCAR heavy rifles with SIG Tango6T optics," Cary said.

"With an M151 spotting scope," Jad added.

"Other than that, I think we're set," Jack said, girding himself for Ding's response.

"That was supposed to be a rhetorical question," Ding said. "Good night, Jack. I can already tell we're going to get there too late."

"Get where?" Jack said.

"Seoul. You asked Mr. C. for muscle. Me, Midas,

and Adara are headed your way on the Gulfstream with a cargo hold full of kit, but we're still a good twelve hours out. I've got some pull, but I'm not God. Let me see what I can do."

"Sorry to interrupt," Cary said, edging close to the phone, "but how much pull?"

"Who's this?" Ding said.

"Master Sergeant Cary Marks, sir. Fifth Special Forces Group. I think I can get us off this roof, but it's gonna take more rank than I can muster."

"Lay it on me, Cary," Ding said. "If there's one thing we've got no shortage of in this organization, it's rank."

29

MAN-MADE THUNDER REVERBERATED AMID THE STEEL canyon to either side of the skyscraper. One moment Jack was eyeing the metal fire door that led to the roof, wondering how much longer the makeshift barricade they'd constructed would keep whoever was pounding on the other side contained. The next, thunder seemed to be echoing from everywhere.

"What's that?" Isabel said.

"The sound of freedom," Cary said.

"Or doom," Jad said. "Those two things sound a lot alike."

"You guys should take your act on the road," Jack said, craning his head over the building's edge.

"That's what I keep saying," Jad said, "but he thinks we already spend too much time together."

"This side," Lisanne said, screaming over the ruckus.

Jack turned just in time to see a pair of black helicopters rocket over the side of the building, only to nose into a dive that planted their skids dead center in the open space on the hotel's roof. The rotor wash launched one of the lounge chairs into the air, sending it tumbling into the access door.

"Night Stalkers are some strange dudes," Jad said, shaking his head. "But those flyboys sure know how to make an entrance."

The aircraft reminded Jack of the famous helicopter on the eighties show **Magnum P.I.,** but with a few not-so-subtle differences. For starters, these variants were employed by the Army's vaunted 160th Special Operations Aviation Regiment and known as the MH-6 Little Birds. Accordingly, the airframes sported dark paint schemes and were crewed by two pilots flying the helicopter in the doors-off configuration. Sensor pods, antennas, and various other not-so-easily-identifiable aftermarket add-ons protruded from the egg-shaped fuselages in clusters. The purpose of the bench seats fastened to the outside of the aircraft and stretching from just behind the pilots to the small passenger compartment was much easier to deduce. Iconic pictures of kitted-up, bearded operators riding into battle on those very benches were all over the Internet.

Now it was Jack's turn.

"Take the rear bird," Jack said to the two Green Berets. "We'll jump in lead."

Cary flashed a thumbs-up rather than attempt to compete with the howling turbine engines.

Lisanne nodded and headed for the first helicopter. Not Isabel.

"I have to ride in that?" Isabel screamed. "I have a thing about helicopters."

"Nope," Jack said. "You can stay here."

The stairwell burst open, and a scrum of Korean police spilled onto the roof.

They didn't look happy.

"Maybe helicopters aren't so bad," Isabel said.

Isabel piled into the open passenger cabin, taking a seat alongside Lisanne, while Jack jumped on the bench seat mounted behind the pilot.

"Go, go," Jack shouted, slapping the fuselage.

The gesture felt a bit ridiculous, but without a headset, he had no way to communicate with the flight crew. Jack locked his belt harness and then reached for the pilot's leg, thinking the aviator hadn't heard him.

He thought wrong.

In a blast of wind that felt like the eyewall of a hurricane, the nimble helicopter lurched skyward. Torrents of air clawed at Jack's clothes and hair, scouring him with grit. The abrupt maneuver dropped his stomach to his shoes.

Jack half thought the pilots were showboating.

Then he saw the muzzle flashes from the police's drawn weapons.

As soon as the tips of the Little Bird's skids

crested the roof's edge, the pilot tipped the MH-6's nose into a near-vertical dive. Jack had about half a second to wish that he'd secured his lap belt a bit tighter before the pilot arrested the free fall, leveling the aircraft out about fifty feet above the street. Jack found himself eye level with an office worker in an adjacent building. As the helicopter hurtled by at better than one hundred knots, the cubicle dweller slowly waved.

Jad was right about one thing—Night Stalkers were some strange dudes.

30

"WE'VE GOT A PROBLEM," THE HELICOPTER PILOT YELLED, HIS, voice barely carrying over the rushing wind and screaming engine.

Jack wasn't surprised. That statement could serve as the motto for this entire operation. Though to be fair, the availability of a pair of 160th helicopters able to whisk his makeshift team from the top of a Seoul skyscraper was nothing short of miraculous. Like Cary and Jad's ODA team, the 160th was also conducting urban training in Seoul. In fact, Triple Nickel had been slated to participate in a culmination exercise with the Army aviators the following evening. Cary had provided Ding with the satcom frequency for the 160th TOC. Then it was just a matter of persuading the Night Stalkers to abandon their training flights in favor of a real-world mission.

Jack didn't imagine that had been a hard sell.

Pilots volunteered for the Regiment's grueling selection regimen for the same reason that SEAL candidates endured BUD/S—because they wanted to serve with the very best. As Cary had guessed, as long as they had someone of sufficiently high rank make the request, the nation's premier aviators were only too happy to put their aviating skills to use. Busan was about a two-hour helicopter flight from Seoul. Not enough time to lollygag, but more than enough margin to get on the ground, talk to the mystery caller, and formulate a plan.

Unless of course the helicopters broke down.

"What?" Jack yelled back.

"Mechanical issue," the pilot said, enunciating each word. "Need to land."

Jack nodded as if giving his assent, knowing full well that he had zero say in the matter. His experience with helicopters and their pilots, while not extensive, was enough for him to know that rotary wing aviators were a different breed. Unlike an airplane, which actually wanted to fly, a helicopter, if left to its own devices, would spin about its transmission and auger into the earth. Helicopter pilots tended to be . . . well . . . a bit more **independent.** Jack thought this attitude was a by-product of the hours they spent at the controls of a machine that wanted to kill them.

In this case, the pilot seemed to be conspiring with the homicidal machine.

One moment the Little Bird was flying straight and level.

The next, it was streaking toward the earth like a lawn dart.

Jack grabbed his lap belt as an updraft buffeted the tiny helicopter even as the field below grew rapidly larger.

Like most things involving aviation, riding on the exterior bench looked a whole lot more fun than it actually was. The constant pummeling from both the wind and the occasional bug convinced Jack that life was much better inside the aircraft. Especially when the ground was rushing upward. With a chuffing of rotor blades, the pilot landed the aircraft with a surprisingly light touch.

Perhaps the rapid descent hadn't been a controlled crash after all.

The engine noise died, and the blades began to slow.

Or perhaps it had.

"What gives?" Jack said.

"Losing transmission fluid," the pilot said, pointing a gloved finger at the rotor. "Bad things happen when the big fan stops spinning."

"Can you fix it?"

The pilot shook his head. "A crew chief'll have to take a look. Those guys are pretty good at field-expedient patches, but it depends on the damage. We probably took some rounds during takeoff. One of them must have ruptured a line or punctured

the reservoir. Won't know for sure until the maintenance team arrives."

"How long for that?" Jack said.

"Probably an hour or so," the pilot said. "They'll
need to round up spare parts and fly everything
out here along with a mechanic or two. If the re-
pair goes smoothly, they'll have the part replaced
in an hour. You're probably looking at a two-hour
delay, best case."

"Worst case?" Jack said.

"Replacing the entire reservoir is a bitch," the
pilot said. "That could take the better part of a day.
If they have to drive out any special tools or equipment, it will be even longer."

The two helos were perched on a bed of loose
stone. To Jack's right, a shallow river meandered
past the landing site, while in his view to the left
a series of rice paddies led to a distant farm road.
Jack guessed that they were on the equivalent of a
sandbar that stayed dry when the water was low
and submerged when the river flooded. Hopefully
that wouldn't happen anytime soon. Either way,
time was not Jack's friend. He needed to get to
Busan in the next ninety minutes.

He had to get back in the air.

"What about the other bird," Jack said, pointing
at the helicopter behind them. "Can it fly?"

"Yep," the pilot said. "But not all of you."

"How many?"

The pilot shrugged. "Depends how froggy Jeff's

feeling and how much kit you offload. He's got an armory's worth of Pelican cases in the backseats."

Jack knew he was to blame for the extra cargo the helicopter was carrying. He'd put in a pretty large kit order during his phone call with Ding. The Campus's second-in-command had probably insisted that the aviators scrounge up every last piece.

Unbuckling his seatbelt, Jack trotted toward the trail helicopter.

Lisanne fell in behind him.

"I know what you're thinking," Lisanne said.

"That would make exactly one of us," Jack said.

"You're leaving me behind," Lisanne said, ignoring his attempt at humor. "Aren't you?"

Jack sighed.

This was a discussion he'd been hoping to avoid. Frankly, one that he thought Clark and Ding were still mulling over. There was no getting around the fact that Lisanne's injury had altered her role in The Campus. She had only one arm, and contrary to the movies, people who shoot with one hand don't last long in a gunfight. Until this instant, everyone had tap-danced around Lisanne's injury. Not so much pretending it didn't exist as kicking the decision about her status as a Campus operative down the road. The trip to South Korea had been an opportunity to do two things—give Lisanne a chance to stick her toes back in the water and allow the Campus leadership team to assess how her new physical limitations affected her performance. **Milk run** were the exact words Ding had used when laying out the mission's parameters.

Not anymore.

"Yes, I am," Jack said, looking over his shoulder at the raven-haired beauty. "I'm sorry, Lisanne."

A number of emotions played across her face—anger, disappointment, and a few Jack couldn't name.

He understood.

He'd feel the same way in her position.

But Jack wasn't in her position.

"I get it," Lisanne said, her voice heavy. "Really, I do. But I don't like it."

"I wouldn't, either," Jack said.

"But what I want doesn't change things, though, does it?"

Jack abruptly stopped, and Lisanne crashed into his chest.

It wasn't an unpleasant feeling.

Lisanne pushed away and looked up, her gaze meeting his. Jack swallowed, his mouth suddenly dry. He felt dangerously close to drowning in Lisanne's luminous eyes.

"I know this isn't the place or time," Jack said, rushing out the words, "but I need you to hear something. What you want changes everything for me. Absolutely everything."

Lisanne looked back at him in silence for a beat.

Then she traced his jaw with her finger.

"This is exactly the right time and place," Lisanne said. Stepping onto her tiptoes, she brushed her lips across his cheek. "This conversation isn't over, Jack Ryan. Get back to me in one piece so we can finish it."

"Yes, ma'am," Jack said, his lips twisting into a goofy grin.

It must not have been too goofy, because Lisanne smiled in return. Then her expression turned serious. Jack swallowed, searching for the right words to say.

Here again Lisanne saved him.

"Later," Lisanne said, pressing her index finger to his lips. "Later."

Then she was gone.

"Hey," the pilot said, screaming over the helicopter's idling engine. "You coming?"

"Yep," Jack said, sprinting for the Little Bird.

But for the first time in his life, he wanted to answer differently.

31

PORT OF BUSAN, SOUTH KOREA

THE BUILDING WAS NONDESCRIPT AND SMALL. A forgotten structure tucked away in a forgotten corner of a sleepy military installation. The brick façade was a lackluster brown devoid of any signage or labels. The building's architecture was similarly uninspiring. The type of boxy form normally associated with warehouses or prisons, though the structure was neither. But the barbed wire that ringed the building's perimeter and the lack of windows suggested a sinister purpose all the same. The majority of South Koreans who called Busan home agreed with this assessment.

The building was a laboratory.

A bioweapons laboratory.

The U.S. and South Korean governments had spent years trying to convince the local populace that the work done in the lab was both safe and benign, but the citizens of Busan were not assuaged. Rather than a forgotten structure in a sleepy installation, they saw a high-security facility purposely located on a plot of land surrounded on three sides by water and the fourth by triple-strand concertina wire. Their fears were further validated when the U.S. government was forced to acknowledge that a live biological agent had once been mistakenly sent to the weapons laboratory.

America was conducting potentially deadly research on the outskirts of a city of 3.5 million inhabitants in a building located less than a kilometer from several South Korean schools. Busan's citizens expressed their displeasure with their American guests Korean-style with massive protests held outside Pier 8's gates. Years later, the size of the protests had diminished, but the local populace's ardor had not. At least twice a month, a crowd of placard-bearing residents conducted a mostly peaceful protest outside the installation. The protest organizers had taken to publishing the dates and times of each event on an open Facebook page for all of Busan's residents to see.

The next protest was scheduled to begin shortly.

"Ready?" Min-jun said.

Kwang-ho finished the final steps of his preflight.

Then the commando nodded.

"Send it," Min-jun said.

The drone leapt skyward, accompanied by the high-pitched whine of four propellers. Like all of the best hobby UAVs, this one came from China. The UAV was readily available on the commercial market with a standard payload of sensor packages unimaginable a decade earlier. Digital zooms, low-light capabilities, infrared cameras, and GPS-synced flight were all factory-standard specifications. But Min-jun hadn't selected the UAV based on its sensor suite, impressive though it was. He cared about cargo capacity. Even though it folded down to a configuration small enough to fit into a backpack, the drone could still lift more than two kilograms. This made the aircraft perfect for the mission, which had brought Min-jun and his team thousands of kilometers and required them to navigate turbulent surf, duplicitous assets, and corrupt police officers.

This was the moment Min-jun had prepared for his entire adult life. Now his success or failure was in the hands of a Chinese toy.

Not exactly an encouraging feeling.

Min-jun had pored over imagery of the port for hours during the mission's planning phase, trying to determine the best possible place to base his team during this critical juncture. The next several minutes would be even more precarious than the treacherous currents that had cost him Gi-ung. Risk of discovery had to be balanced against the drone's constraints. Ultimately, Min-jun had decided to make use of the same geography that lent the laboratory its sense of security.

Pier 8 was a rectangle-shaped land mass arrayed on a southwest-to-northeast running axis. Harbor water surrounded the land mass on three of its four sides, allowing the installation's occupants to focus the majority of their security efforts on the landlocked northeastern side.

This was why the drone was approaching from the southwest.

But Min-jun's strategy was not without risk.

The drone was now traversing open sea, and the aircraft's cargo was close to exceeding its max load. If any of the craft's four engines malfunctioned, the UAV would plummet into the sea along with its precious payload. Not to mention that the two kilometers separating the commandos from the laboratory rendered the UAV invisible to the men controlling it.

To mask the drone's telltale acoustic signature, Kwang-ho had programmed the UAV to traverse the ocean at an altitude of two hundred meters. This distance, coupled with the fact that Kwang-ho had disabled the drone's LED position lights, transformed the aircraft into nothing more than a shadow in the night sky. Fortunately, the drone's GPS system allowed the craft to navigate this leg of the flight without human assistance.

But the hands-free flight mode would cease the moment the aircraft arrived over land. In a nod to the installation's importance, the American government had ensured that the target building's

GPS coordinates were not commercially available. With this in mind, Min-jun had mercilessly drilled Kwang-ho for this phase of the mission. The team's sniper had practiced piloting the same model drone a similar distance under similar environmental conditions just in case the UAV's GPS signal was blocked or satellite reception was unexpectedly poor on the day of the mission. If there was one thing Min-jun learned during his years of service, it was the importance of hard, realistic training. If the pre-mission training regimen was properly constructed, the actual operation should seem easy in comparison.

So far, that adage was proving true.

"GPS fix is holding," Kwang-ho said. "Feet dry in thirty seconds."

The commando stared at his cell, engrossed in the now tiny-seeming screen.

Though the drone came with a much larger controller, Min-jun had left it behind in favor of the smartphone app. While the aircraft collapsed into a nondescript, easily hidden form, the controller and its multiple antennas and plethora of switches and joysticks were impossible to disguise. As such, Kwang-ho's cell phone was now Bluetooth-linked to a satellite radio secured in a hidden compartment of his backpack. Piloting the UAV using the app obscured the men's true purpose in the event they were compromised while the aircraft was over its target.

But these benefits came with a trade-off.

During the most difficult phase of the flight profile, Kwang-ho would have to pilot the drone using video from the device's onboard sensor package and virtual controls, which were both displayed on the cell phone's fifteen-centimeter screen. While rehearsing the operation, the team sniper had crashed more than one drone as he'd slowly acclimated to the app's difficult user interface.

"Feet dry," Kwang-ho said, hissing the words through clenched teeth.

Chi-won's shoulders tensed, and Min-jun felt his own heart rate accelerate. The transit over the channel had proven uneventful, but now the fate of the entire operation rested with Kwang-ho's nimble fingers.

"We have company," Chi-won murmured.

Min-jun looked from the black-and-white infrared imagery displayed on the cell phone to his team sergeant.

Then he swore.

Min-jun had chosen the team's current location with an eye toward balancing the need to maintain line-of-sight communications with the drone and his desire for seclusion. He wanted a sparsely populated location, but one that saw enough traffic that he and his men would not look out of place. These seemingly divergent criteria had made the selection process difficult. The busy harbor offered many locations that met one of his requirements, but not both. After ruling out everything from shipping container lots to coffee shops, Min-jun stumbled on the perfect location after clicking on a social media post about the port.

The Busan Harbor Bridge was an iconic structure that offered an unparalleled view of the shipping traffic transiting the port. Its distinctive cable construction and beautiful nighttime lighting drew visitors at all hours. More important to Min-jun, the bridge was southwest of Pier 8 and only one and a half kilometers as the crow flew. As Min-jun had scrolled through images, he'd noticed a peculiar circular structure formed by a spiraling onramp leading to the bridge from a nearby side street. The structure was supported by a series of concrete columns that bounded a grassy park crisscrossed with walking trails. With no barriers or enclosures, the little plot of land was open twenty-four hours a day. That said, from what Min-jun could glean from social media, visitors usually frequented the park only during daylight hours, with the exception of the occasional fisherman.

Fishermen and whoever was currently pulling into the gravel parking lot.

As Min-jun watched, a Hyundai minivan slowed to a stop. A moment later, the engine died and a metallic **pop** sounded. The driver's-side door opened and a man exited the vehicle. Walking to the front, he raised the minivan's hood. He made eye contact with Min-jun, staring at the commando for a long moment before climbing back into the vehicle.

At first Min-jun didn't know what to think.

Then he understood.

The park's easy access and somewhat remote location must appeal to more than just North Korean commandos.

"What do you think?" Chi-won said.

"Our friend is waiting for someone," Min-jun said, "and he doesn't know what they look like."

"Should we be that someone?" Chi-won said.

Min-jun had been pondering the same question. If he was right and the man in the minivan was here for nefarious reasons, things weren't going to go well when his partners arrived. A person chose a remote location because they didn't want to be seen. Once the park's other visitors realized that their anonymity was compromised, they would have to decide how far they were prepared to go to get it back.

A subject Min-jun was also contemplating.

At this moment, Min-jun and his commandos held both the numerical advantage and the element of surprise. Once the minivan's friends arrived, he'd lose both.

Assuming he was reading the situation correctly.

Min-jun turned back to Kwang-ho, watching the UAV's video feed. The team sniper had identified the correct building and was now hand-flying the drone to its target. As Min-jun watched, an errant gust of wind buffeted the aircraft, causing the video to shake as the quadcopter drifted uncomfortably close to a cluster of antennas budding from the building's roof. Kwang-ho sucked in a breath as he routed the aircraft and its precious cargo past the aerials' jagged, reaching edges.

The near miss clenched Min-jun's decision. As tempting as it was to deal with the minivan's driver now, he would do nothing to distract the sniper until the flight was complete. In this case, patience was the better course of action.

And then another car pulled into the lot.

32

THE CAR WAS LARGE. A SPORT UTILITY VEHICLE WITH four doors, a hatchback, and tinted windows. The SUV was painted a dark muted color. The model wasn't new, but it was in good shape, with none of the obvious dings or dents often borne by South Korean vehicles. A vehicle that looked good enough to be on the road, but not flashy enough to be remembered.

The ideal conveyance for transporting something illegal.

"What now?" Chi-won said.

"We wait," Min-jun said. "Kwang-ho is almost done. Whether or not this turns into something more is up to them."

The team sergeant gave a quick nod and went back to fiddling with the jack mounted next to a perfectly good tire. He'd angled the car so that the side with the pretend flat faced the ocean, away from prying eyes. He peered over the bumper as he worked. Min-jun squatted down to help, even as he thought through a contingency plan. Gun violence was exceedingly rare in South Korea, which meant that Min-jun and his fellow commandos were probably better armed than the park's other inhabitants.

Or perhaps not.

Factoring in the proximity to the port and the two large vehicles, Min-jun thought the visitors were likely smuggling contraband. Probably drugs. The South Korean criminal code took a draconian view of drug-related offenses and reserved the death penalty for traffickers. Men risking execution didn't heed firearms restrictions, and weapons could be smuggled into the country as easily as drugs.

Then there were the practical considerations of engaging yet another gunfight. While the traffic on the bridge overhead was minimal, each passing moment brought Min-jun closer to Busan's rush hour. The park was isolated, but it was also located right at the sea's edge. A pistol's muzzle flash would be easily seen against the black backdrop, and the gun's report would carry a great distance over the water.

If possible, Min-jun wanted to leave this site without shedding more blood.

"I'm down," Kwang-ho said. "Cargo is in place. What do I do with the aircraft?"

That was an excellent question. Originally, the plan had been for Kwang-ho to pilot the drone back to the park so that the commandos could recover it, but the visitors made this unfeasible. Min-jun wanted there to be no reason for the occupants of the two vehicles to remember his team.

The drone needed to disappear.

"Can you ditch it?" Min-jun said.

Kwang-ho nodded. "I can drop a GPS point several kilometers out to sea and command the drone to loiter there until the batteries run dry. But it might float for a bit, depending on how hard it hits the water. Better if I fly it into the ocean at full speed."

"Do it," Min-jun said, before turning to Chi-won. "Pack up. We're leaving."

The team sergeant nodded and began gathering the jack and spare tire. Min-jun edged his head around the bumper for a look just in time to see four men spill out of the SUV. Definitely criminals. Their muscular builds, hair worn shaved on the sides and long on top, and heavily tattooed forearms screamed "gangster."

The minivan driver joined them.

Then the group headed toward Min-jun.

Min-jun didn't think they were coming to say hello.

"Ditch now," Min-jun said to Kwang-ho. "We're out of time."

The team sniper looked up from his phone, eyes narrowing as he saw the approaching men.

"Ne," Kwang-ho said, his fingers playing across the phone. Then, with a final sigh, he slipped the device in his pocket. "It's done."

The comment represented the culmination of months of preparation. Min-jun should have felt a sense of relief. He didn't. All he could think about was how easily the entire endeavor could still be undone by the approaching ruffians.

"Take them?" Chi-won whispered.

The squat team sergeant was still crouched next to the tire, the disconnected jack at his feet. Min-jun understood his hesitation. Once he picked up the tire-changing equipment, Chi-won would no longer be able to draw the weapon holstered at his back. Not to mention that the protection offered by the wheel well provided the ideal spot to wage a gunfight if an armed confrontation was inevitable.

"Stow the gear," Min-jun said. "They don't want a fight any more than we do. Let's not give them a reason."

Min-jun could tell Chi-won didn't like the decision, but the commando nodded all the same. The grizzled warrior had been a Special Operations operative for decades. He understood the deadly nature of indecision. Right or wrong, his team leader had made a decision. Chi-won would execute it.

"What are you doing here?"

The question came from the lead gangster, a stocky man whose T-shirt did little to conceal his bulging biceps and heavy shoulders.

"Changing a tire," Min-jun said. "Is there a problem?"

He kept his tone unprovocative but firm, locking gazes with the gangster. From the corner of his eye, Min-jun saw Chi-won open the trunk and begin to stow the disassembled jack and lug nut wrench. To the casual observer the gray-haired commando looked oblivious to the entire encounter. To Min-jun, his team sergeant's posture was a dead giveaway. Chi-won stood with his body slightly bladed to the left to obscure the movement of his right hand, should he need to draw his concealed pistol.

The passenger-side door opened on the opposite side of the car, revealing Kwang-ho. The team sniper faced the approaching men, hands hidden behind the car's frame. Like Min-jun, the drone operator's stance conveyed strength without provocation, an essential combination for interactions with thugs. Predators were the same, regardless of whether they walked on four legs or two. People who acted like prey were treated as such. If they saw backbone instead of weakness, scavengers often went in search of easier takings.

"You tell me," the lead thug said. He rolled up the sleeve on his shirt, exposing an intricate tattoo that encircled his upper arm and shoulder.

Min-jun had dedicated much of his career to

studying his future battlefield—South Korea. His training had covered a variety of subjects, everything from dialect and slang to tips for navigating Seoul's subway system. Since operatives like Min-jun were expected to survive behind enemy lines until the victorious northern armies reunited the peninsula, a portion of this instruction included South Korean gangs and other organized criminal elements. This was partly because DPRK military strategists had entertained the idea of buying the cooperation of some of the larger criminal entities in the same manner in which the Chinese Communist Party had an alliance with some of the triads active in Taiwan. But situations like this one were the more practical reason for the instruction.

Given the similarities between their operating profiles, it was not unreasonable to assume that someone like Min-jun might cross paths with criminals while hiding from the Korean National Police. If that happened, determining the difference between two-bit hustlers and connected gangsters would be essential. Tattoos were an easy way to make that distinction. Korean organized criminals wore their affiliation in ink, and the lead thug had just exposed his résumé.

"We had a flat tire," Min-jun said. "That's it."

Min-jun squared his shoulders as he spoke, matching the lead thug glare for glare. Min-jun knew he was walking a fine line. He needed to convey a sense of strength while still giving the gangster a way to de-escalate the situation without losing face.

"Check the trunk," the thug barked at one of his men.

His subordinate, a thin man with ropy muscles and a receding hairline, started toward the car with his fists clenched. Chi-won glanced from the man to Min-jun, the question in the team sergeant's eyes easy to see.

"Let him," Min-jun said.

Chi-won obediently stepped to the side as the slim man shouldered past. Min-jun was on dangerous ground, but he felt the risk was worth the reward. There was still a chance to resolve the situation without violence and the complications going kinetic would bring.

"Tire-changing things," the thin man said, poking his head back above the open trunk. "Nothing else."

"I guess that's that," the stocky man said.

"Maybe not," the slim man said.

"What do you mean?" the stocky man said with a frown.

"If they're changing a tire, where's the flat?"

Another decision point.

Try to explain away the contradiction or accept that violence was inevitable. Min-jun hesitated for a fraction of a second, still hoping for the impossible. Then he watched as realization dawned on the lead gangster's face.

Violence it was.

Min-jun nodded at Chi-won.

The team sergeant fired a blow into the thin man's kidney, driving from his waist and snapping his shoulder into the punch. The thin man folded, gurgling a prolonged groan. One Chi-won truncated by slamming the trunk on the gangster's head.

Min-jun drew his pistol even as he saw Kwang-ho doing the same.

This was the moment that separated a trained operative from a common thug. While the gangsters were still fumbling with their waistbands, Min-jun cleared his holster and acquired his first target. Finding center mass on the lead gangster with his pistol's stubby front sight post, Min-jun aligned the slender bit of metal in the notch offered by his rear sight.

Then he smoothly pressed the trigger.

The gun barked.

Min-jun repeated the sequence.

His target fell to the ground.

Panning the front sight post to the left, Min-jun acquired his next target.

In spite of the chaos unfolding around him, Min-jun felt as if he were standing in the eye of a storm. All the second-guessing and strategizing of the last several moments was gone, replaced by something that felt infinitely more familiar and therefore calming.

A close-quarters gunfight.

A scenario for which Min-jun had incessantly trained his entire adult life.

And the training showed.

Min-jun's second target crumpled to the ground. He panned his front sight post across the clearing, searching for additional threats. He found none. In the space of a few seconds, Min-jun and his teammates had reduced a numerically superior enemy to a pile of corpses.

They were very, very good.

But not infallible.

A wet cough gurgled from Min-jun's left. Turning, he found its source and swore. Chi-won swayed on his feet, keeping himself upright through pure willpower. One hand grasped the trunk in a white-knuckled death grip while the other was pressed to his chest, doing little to stanch the rapidly expanding circle of blood.

"I've got you," Min-jun said, rounding the trunk, but the commando shook his head and stepped out of reach.

"I'm done," the grizzled veteran said, swaying before slowly sinking to his knees. "Hand me one of their pistols. Then leave."

"No," Min-jun said, rage coloring his voice.

"Yes," Chi-won said, his voice breathy. "Do not dishonor me by making my sacrifice in vain. We have come far together. Farther than I ever would have dreamed. I will die having done my duty. A soldier cannot ask for more."

As much as he wanted to believe otherwise, Min-jun knew that his team sergeant was right. Chi-won's lips were flecked with blood and a thin stream of crimson drool was leaking from the side of his mouth. The killing bullet had gone through his lungs and probably nicked an artery. Even in the hands of a gifted trauma surgeon with the resources of a state-of-the-art hospital at his disposal the man's survival would have been uncertain.

Min-jun had access to neither of these things.

Grabbing the still-breathing thin man from where he was sprawled half in and half out of the trunk, Min-jun removed the gangster's pistol before shoving the man to the salt-stained concrete.

Then he placed the gangster's weapon into his mentor's hands.

"You will have to help me," Chi-won said, rasping out the words. "My time is short."

Not trusting himself to reply, Min-jun only nodded. Putting his own hand on top of the fingers of the man he loved like a father, Min-jun steadied the pistol and helped Chi-won press the trigger. The pistol's **crack** assaulted Min-jun's already tender eardrums, the report echoing across the water.

The crumpled form twitched and lay motionless.

Though his eyes were now closed, Chi-won

seemed to somehow understand that his final task was complete. He wheezed once more.

Then he was still.

Min-jun let his mentor collapse to the concrete, resisting the urge to arrange the body in a pose more befitting a warrior. Chi-won had a final role to play.

With luck the puppets would believe this to be a disagreement between criminals.

Turning, Min-jun caught Kwang-ho's eye and jerked his head toward the car.

There was still work to be done.

33

BUSAN, SOUTH KOREA

CAPTAIN SEOK KO OF THE DPRK'S KOREAN PEOPLE'S Navy sucked the thick, fetid air in through his mouth. The dehumidifiers had quit functioning an hour ago, and the atmosphere inside the cramped Yono-class midget submarine had already taken a turn for the worse. Condensation had begun to gather on the ceiling, dribbling downward in fat droplets. Ko would have found the artificial rain annoying if he wasn't already soaked. At this point it didn't matter whether the dark splotches in his uniform were from sweat, humidity, or spills from his ever-present cup of **cha.**

As long as the liquid wasn't salt water, he didn't care.

"I've got a track, Captain."

"Range and bearing to target," Ko said.

Ko kept the sense of relief from his voice, but it

wasn't easy. The midget sub's small crew occupied an even smaller living space. The entire submarine was only twenty meters long and less than three wide. Most commercial passenger airplanes were larger. In quarters this tight, every crew member was acutely aware of the man seated to his left and right, and that went double for Ko, the tiny vessel's captain. Ko set the tone for his men. If he was anxious, they were doubly so. But if he acted as if this was just another mission, they would follow his example.

Even though this was far from just another mission.

"Track is bearing 285. Range one thousand meters. Based on the engine noise, I believe this is our target."

"Excellent," Ko said, his response still deadpan even though his heart was thundering.

Shuffling to the sonar technician's station, Ko watched the squiggly lines forming the visual rendering of the surface ship's acoustic signature crawl across the computer screen. Though the sparsely furnished bridge suggested otherwise, the midget submarine's unassuming exterior concealed a good deal of cutting-edge technology. The sub's battery packs were imported from China and represented top-of-the-line electrical storage technology stolen from an American car company and reverse-engineered. Likewise, the passive sonar array feeding information to the audio technician was based on a Russian system that had originated with a disaffected American acoustic scientist.

While the U.S. still led the world in submarine technology, her enemies had become adept at closing the gap through espionage and outright theft. Unfortunately, the Korean People's Navy hadn't been nearly as interested in the many innovations geared toward crew comfort. So while the minisub boasted a retrofitted sensor suite and a silent propulsion system worthy of its Western cousins, living conditions were still reminiscent of the World War II–era boats.

But that was fine.

Submariners were odd individuals by nature. Ko had spent his career thwarting death, whether in the form of the ocean's crushing fists or adversarial mariners. Given the choice, he would take sensors and weapons over creature comforts any day, though the last twelve hours had put his cavalier attitude to the test. Even so, a single look at his technician's display made the hardships worthwhile.

The acoustic signature matched.

His target had just entered the harbor.

34

BUSAN, SOUTH KOREA

"WHAT DO YOU THINK?" KWANG-HO SAID.

Min-jun eyed the red and blue lights flashing in the distance, trying to settle on a reply. What he thought and what he should say were two different things. The team's sniper had held up well considering the hardships the team had endured thus far, but every man had his breaking point.

When the commandos had boarded the tiny midget ship days ago, Min-jun had taken great care to ensure each of his men understood that their trip was one-way. Either their comrades-in-arms would successfully overthrow the southern puppets, and thereby pave the way for a joyful reunion with the Korean People's Army mechanized and armored formations, or Min-jun and his men would be captured and executed. Either way, Min-jun had looked each commando in the eye when he'd told them there would be no clandestine exfiltration route home. Even so, nothing could prepare a man for the moment when he realized the end of his life was near. Judging by the slew of flashing lights spreading through the evening darkness, Min-jun and Kwang-ho were approaching that moment.

"We need to be ready," Min-jun said, forcing himself to look from the flashing red and blue lights to the stretch of road leading to Pier 8. "The trigger should occur any moment."

Should was definitely the operative word. If there was one thing his years as a special operator had taught Min-jun, it was that operations seldom went according to plan. This was doubly so for synchronized operations. This mission at hand was both synchronized and incredibly complex. As the team leader, Min-jun knew about the multiple critical elements that had to come together at exactly the correct moment for the overarching operation to succeed. Kwang-ho did not. Normally Min-jun was of the opinion that information equated to morale, and he tried to keep his subordinates as informed as possible.

Not this time.

The young operative was already smarting from the loss of two team members. Min-jun was afraid the full scope of the mission might very well overwhelm the commando or at the very least distract him.

"What is the trigger event?" Kwang-ho said, his spotting scope trained on the Pier 8 facility.

"Keep your eyes on the road," Min-jun said. "You'll know it when you see it."

The men were across the bay from their earlier location, their car nosed into a parking lot housing the vehicles of hundreds of dockworkers. Min-jun could just make out the laboratory building on which they'd landed the drone off to the east, while the blue and red lights continued to strobe to the southeast. The Busan Harbor Bridge, its structure lit with multicolored lights, seemed to span the points of interest even though the target area was another kilometer or so beyond the northwestern corner of the bridge. But Min-jun hadn't chosen the parking lot for its view of the bridge, the park, or the target building. No, the commando was interested in something else entirely—the four shipping lanes that led from the harbor's eastern entrance and passed under the bridge before terminating in the Port of Busan's international terminal.

Or, more specifically, the ships transiting those lanes.

As Min-jun watched, a U.S.-flagged tanker sailed beneath Busan Harbor Bridge before making a turn to the north. Pressing a pair of binoculars to his eyes, Min-jun scanned the vessel, looking for a name. Panning along the waterline, the commando centered his search on where he expected to find the large block letters that would confirm his suspicions.

He was not successful.

No sooner had Min-jun found the string of English than his view was obstructed. The blurry image was impossible to interpret. Lowering the binoculars, Min-jun looked over their plastic edge and began to swear. The object fouling his line of sight was another watercraft.

But not just any boat.

The English and Korean word POLICE made recognition a foregone conclusion. But just in case he had any questions, the light bar atop the boat activated, sending strobes of red and blue light dancing across the waves.

Harbor security.

"Are they looking for us?" Kwang-ho said.

Min-jun couldn't imagine this to be the case. After all, Busan Harbor was South Korea's largest and most important port. It was home to a mind-boggling amount of commerce, both of the legal and illegal varieties. Min-jun's team had certainly experienced more than their share of poor luck thus far, but there were other bad things happening in a port that handled over one hundred and thirty vessels per day, as evidenced by the drug dealers they'd encountered earlier. The key to surviving in a hostile environment was to acknowledge each potential threat without letting it consume you. Yes, the patrol boat was nosing around in the shallows just one hundred meters away from where he and Kwang-ho sat, but that didn't mean the sailors manning the craft were looking for the commandos.

Min-jun opened his mouth to say as much. Before he could, a fifteen-thousand-lumen xenon searchlight speared through the darkness, lancing the inside of his car.

A searchlight originating from the patrol boat.

35

PRIVATE FIRST CLASS KELSEY SMITH EYED THE GATHERING crowd and swallowed. His apprehension wasn't a response to the number of men, women, and children coalescing outside Pier 8's front gate, though the protest's size wasn't insubstantial. No, Private First Class Smith was forcing saliva down his throat for another reason. In direct opposition to his squad leader's instructions, Kelsey had reported for guard duty with a wad of Skoal tobacco in his lip.

Not a small wad.

In the murky decision-making process typical of Army privates, Kelsey had reasoned that the punishment he'd receive for appearing sleepy while guarding the front gate far outweighed the infraction that would be leveled against him for using smokeless tobacco. His roommate, Private First Class Johann Van Lierop, had cemented Kelsey's decision. The eighteen-year-old Florida boy had spent a good portion of his guard shift running wind sprints after a surprise inspection by Sergeant Chad Stover, Johann and Kelsey's squad leader, had caught Private Van Lierop napping on duty.

A single glance at his battle buddy's sweat-drenched form as Johann stumbled into their barracks room had been all the confirmation Kelsey needed. Besides, Kelsey had a plan. He intended to strategically spit the tobacco juice into the shrubbery lining the gate. Unfortunately, Kelsey had devised this brilliant plan before a crowd of two hundred or so raucous demonstrators had formed mere feet from the aforementioned foliage. Now Kelsey was swallowing the tobacco juice even as he willed his heaving stomach not to further embarrass him. He intended to discuss this miserable turn of events with Johann after his fellow military policeman relieved him in six hours' time.

Assuming Kelsey hadn't vomited all over his freshly shined boots by then.

"What's going on?"

The question came from PV2 Shannon Way, Kelsey's fellow sufferer. Though he technically outranked his comrade, authority among privates was fickle. Besides, Shannon's auburn hair, porcelain skin, and green eyes made Kelsey's shifts with the Midwestern girl rather enjoyable. He hadn't worked up the courage to ask her for coffee yet, but today was a new opportunity.

As long as his stomach cooperated.

"The Koreans protest outside the gate a couple times a month," Kelsey said, his answer carrying with it the iron confidence of a soldier who had been in country exactly two months longer than his companion.

"Why?" Shannon said.

Kelsey shrugged. "Can't say I've ever asked them. But I think it's about the lab."

"Lab?" Shannon said.

Kelsey nodded. "Yep. There's some kind of secret weapons lab back by the harbor. They grow anthrax and shit."

Kelsey responded with the authority of someone who'd been there and done that even though the source of his information came from none other than Private Van Lierop. Johann had heard about the secret lab from a private in their sister platoon who had it on good authority from a corporal friend of his that the eggheads in the lab were working on a gas that turned soldiers into zombies. Kelsey didn't want to scare Shannon, so he made the work about anthrax instead.

Truthfully, he hadn't a clue what the scientists did at the innocuous-looking building situated behind the triple-strand concertina wire. That entire area of the installation was off-limits. In fact, Kelsey might have dismissed Johann's story completely were it not for an article about the laboratory he'd seen in the **Stars and Stripes** newspaper.

The article didn't mention anything about zombies or anthrax, but Kelsey figured a military newspaper would never tell the whole story anyway. Besides, Kelsey viewed rumors about the mystery lab with a sense of pride. No longer was he just a simple MP checking IDs at a backwater installation in a forgotten part of South Korea.

No, sir.

Private First Class Kelsey Smith was single-handedly guarding the most important research installation in the entire American offensive bio-weapons program. That no such program existed mattered little to Private Smith or the demonstrators.

Both had a job to do and both were determined to do it.

The crowd shuffled mindlessly for several minutes, permitting Kelsey a single visit behind the squat brick building that made up the gatehouse. With a practiced flick, he rid his lip of the tobacco, not caring that the brown, soggy mess landed on concrete rather than grass. In the hierarchy of sins, Kelsey judged that leaving his post for the longer duration it would have taken to empty his lip in a less obtrusive place rated much higher than desecrating the white concrete with a dried-up husk of tobacco. With any luck, the previous guard shift would share in the blame. Dubbed the hillbilly duo by Sergeant Stover, since both privates hailed from Kentucky, the two farm boys dipped like they'd been born with tobacco in their lips.

Kelsey had taken punishment meant for them at least once already.

Turnabout was fair play.

But thoughts of the creative punishment Sergeant Stover would delve out quickly faded as the crowd morphed from a collection of bodies into a mass of protesters, thanks to the appearance of several agitators equipped with bullhorns. While Kelsey couldn't understand the shouted instructions, the results were plain to see. One moment the crowd was milling aimlessly on the other side of the two-lane road leading to the guard shack. The next, they'd coalesced into a single organism. Placards were distributed and people arranged.

Then the crowd began to chant.

"American go home. American go home. No chemical weapons. No chemical weapons."

"What do you think?" Shannon said, her earlier wit replaced by worry.

"As long as they stay on that side of the road, they can chant all they want," Kelsey said with a nonchalance he didn't feel. "It's a free country."

"Is it?" Shannon said.

"What?"

"A free country. I thought South Korea had a military government."

"Hell if I know, Shannon," Kelsey said. "I'm just saying it's their country. They can damn well do what they want, as long as they do it over yonder."

Kelsey figured this was a true enough sentiment

regardless of the type of government the South Korean people enjoyed. The only problem with Kelsey's newly stated doctrine was that the crowd no longer seemed content to demonstrate **over yonder.** In response to another command shouted from the little man with the bullhorn, the mass of bodies surged across the double yellow line in the center of the road, heading straight for the guard shack and two unprepared privates.

"What do we do?" Shannon said, her voice quavering as she fingered the 9-millimeter SIG Sauer holstered at her belt.

"No clue," Kelsey said, picking up the phone affixed to the guard station's wall, "but I reckon Sergeant Stover's got an idea or two."

Maybe Sergeant Stover wasn't such a bad guy after all.

36

BUSAN, SOUTH KOREA

JACK RYAN SMELLED THE PORT OF BUSAN LONG BEFORE he saw it. The cool air carried with it the odors of salt water and decaying fish, and the underlying scent of exhaust as it billowed past his body. He'd convinced the Little Bird pilots to fly into the harbor, reasoning that the port facilities offered the most lucrative target, but even Jack was starting to feel less assured about what they'd find.

Assuming there was something to find in the first place.

Either way, the 160th aviators were doing their damnedest to stay off the radar, both literally and figuratively. Like that national lockdown in Seoul and the disruption of the national cell network and corresponding Wi-Fi, all general aviation was currently grounded in response to the national emergency. As such, the tiny helicopter was flying with its transponder off and position lights extinguished.

Night Stalkers conducted most of their missions blacked-out while trying to stay invisible. The low altitudes and nap of the earth flight profiles the aviators were employing made Jack reasonably certain that they weren't appearing on anyone's radar. But his sense of unease went beyond just hiding from the South Koreans. He felt like a puppet dancing at the end of a string. He still didn't know the motivations or identity of the mysterious caller. And while he still stood behind his decision to fly to the port, doubt was building with every second.

"Port of Busan is dead ahead. Five miles."

"Roger," Jack said after thumbing the transmit button on his intercom system.

After saying his good-byes to Lisanne and Isabel, Jack had taken a few precious moments to better prepare himself and the two Green Berets for whatever came next. In Jack's case, this meant availing himself of a headset and mic so he could talk with both the pilots and the commandos. While Jack was riding on the starboard side of the helicopter behind the pilot in command, the two commandos were on the port side. The Little Bird was little in every sense of the word, and the weight of the three passengers needed to be evenly distributed.

Not to mention that the two Special Forces operatives had broken into the multiple Pelican cases the 160th aviators had brought per Ding's guidance and kitted themselves out accordingly. Both men had climbed aboard the benches carrying SCAR heavy rifles, chest rigs, sidearms, and who knew what else. Which just went to prove that Green Berets wholeheartedly subscribed to the belief that you could never have too many guns or bullets.

For his part, Jack had made do with an MP5K submachine gun equipped with a red-dot optic. The weapon certainly wasn't zeroed to his eye, but as per most military weapons, Jack figured it was sighted in at fifty meters, which was good enough for him. As far as Jack was concerned, the two snipers could have any shots beyond that. Assuming he ever figured out what exactly they were doing here and who, if anyone, needed to be shot.

"Hey, sir," the lead pilot said, breaking into Jack's thoughts, "what do you want us to do once we reach the port? We've masked our flight so far, but we're about to run out of cover. That harbor is South Korea's largest. Hell, it's one of the biggest in the world. A single black helicopter isn't going to go unnoticed."

These were the same thoughts that had been banging around inside of Jack's head. The Little Bird crested the final bit of terrain and the port opened up before him. They were approaching from the east and were already transiting across the high-population area ringing the harbor.

A constellation of lights sat beneath him, illuminating apartment buildings, houses, and industrial areas. To the north, Jack could just make out the rotating beacon marking the presence of Gimhae International Airport. Since the helicopter was barely one hundred feet above the ground and the transponder was off, Jack wasn't worried about air traffic control spotting them. But the pulsing light drove home the reality of his current situation with every flash. He was transitioning into some pretty crowded real estate at a moment in time when the fabric binding South Korea together was under enormous strain.

This wasn't the moment to surprise anyone.

But that's exactly what they were about to do.

"Roger that," Jack said. "Can you come out over the water? Stay to the east of the bridge, but maybe pick up a bit of altitude? That will give me a chance to see what's what."

"Yep," the pilot said. "But I can only give you an orbit or two. More than that and we'll have company. Lots of it."

"Tracking," Jack said, after checking his watch. "Two orbits. If I don't see anything by then, we'll beat feet."

The mystery woman should be calling in less than two minutes. If she didn't, there was no sense burning holes in the South Korean sky.

"Roger all," the pilot said.

Left unsaid was the obvious question: **Beat feet to where?**

Jack didn't have an answer.

37

"VERIFY RANGE TO TARGET," CAPTAIN KO SAID.

He kept his voice steady, as much for his crew's benefit as his own. The minisub had entered the port earlier in the day, trudging along in a cargo container ship's substantial wake. To hide from the plethora of acoustic sensors ringing the harbor, Ko and his crew had intercepted the tanker more than forty kilometers and four hours before the container ship had trudged into port at a stately fourteen knots.

While still in the open sea, Ko had maintained a kilometer of separation between the two ships. But once the vessel had turned into the port, he'd tightened the range to less than one hundred meters. For all intents and purposes, the two ships presented a single acoustic signature. The technique worked, but the strain on his helmsman had been immense. The poor man had sweated through his uniform and now his seat was ringed with pools of moisture. Even so, the sailor had done his duty. As the freighter steamed into port, the minisub had flooded its ballast tanks and drifted to the harbor's floor.

Then came the waiting.

For the next several hours, the operational spotlight had shifted from the exhausted helmsman to the sonar technician seated next to him. Every sound was analyzed and each engine categorized as the crew remained alert for their target as well as the dreaded signature of an approaching South Korean frigate. While the minisub made almost no noise resting on the sandy soil, there was another variable that threatened their existence—the sun.

The depression in which the minisub sought refuge was a perfect place to hide in plain sight, but the harbor was only sixteen meters deep. Ko was fairly certain his tiny vessel was safe from visual detection, but he couldn't be sure. Submariners operated in a clandestine world in which discovery almost always carried with it death. Usually this discovery was acoustical in nature—a bearing squeaking at an inopportune time or an unsecured tool clattering against the deck floor. In this case, Ko was worried about aerial discovery. A hated P-3 Orion sub hunter flying overhead might notice something dark lurking on the harbor's floor. Even a hobbyist drone pilot could spot the midget sub if the conditions were exactly right. In the claustrophobic confines of the gloomy bridge, Ko had been forced to watch the time tick by minute by minute as he calculated the sun's location and guessed at what it might reveal. Only after the sun slid below the horizon did Ko feel as if he could breathe again. Now the tension returned to the base of his neck as the hunt began.

"One kilometer and closing," the sonar operator said, his voice a whisper.

Unlike a traditional submarine outfitted with dozens of torpedoes for multiple launchers, Ko's Yono-class submarine was not an armed marauder. His boat was an intelligence-gathering platform designed for sabotage. It had a single torpedo tube for defense, but a torpedo was not the munition Ko intended to employ.

"Ready the weapon," Ko said, his voice rising in pitch despite his best efforts.

Projecting calm to the crew was necessary, but there was something amiss with a submariner whose heart didn't beat faster while readying for the kill.

"Weapon is powered. Self-test complete. Ready for target data."

The torpedo officer's announcements were crisp and professional, but his cadence was faster than normal. This was no longer a drill, and the crew knew it.

They were going to war.

"Load target data," Ko said.

"Aye, Captain. Loading target data."

In another novel piece of Chinese engineering, this weapon was neither a torpedo nor a traditional antiship mine. As per the unconventional nature of the minisub, the munition was more of an undersea drone designed to clandestinely scoot across an enemy harbor at a handful of undetectable knots before affixing itself to a target and detonating. The drone's sophisticated guidance system included a passive sonar array capable of identifying a specific acoustic signature in a crowded harbor full of ships. This was why the midget sub's sonarman station was digitally linked to the weapons station. With the click of a few buttons, the sub's weapons officer loaded the target's profile into the drone's guidance system.

Ko looked over the man's shoulder, eyeballing a comparison between the squiggle of lines on the weapons officer's monitor and the reading on the sonarman's display. Ko had no idea if the collection of lines matched. It all looked like abstract art to him, but verifying the target data seemed like an appropriate action for a captain to take.

"Target signature confirmed," the weapons technician said, "weapon standing by."

The drone was now operating on its own internal power supply, which was limited. Even so, Ko still peered at the range and bearing a final time. Because it lacked the frightening speed of a traditional torpedo, the drone would intercept the target vessel by tracking on a course ahead of and perpendicular to the approaching freighter. Then the drone would turn, swimming on a reciprocal heading to the freighter's course until predator and prey collided. The interdiction was supposed to occur at nearly the drone's maximum range in order to give the minisub as much time to clear the engagement area as possible, but Ko decided to alter the plan. There was no honor in returning home safe but without achieving his goal.

Glancing at the digital clock mounted to the sub's bulkhead, Ko announced his decision.

"Mark thirty seconds," Ko said.

"Thirty seconds, aye," the torpedo officer said.

The first officer briefly caught Ko's eye from behind the helmsman's shoulder, but he did not speak. Submariners were an independent bunch, and the officers who manned minisubs even more so, but a captain's orders were still sacrosanct. This was especially true during a tactical engagement. The first officer had communicated his question with a look. Ko had answered the same way.

Nothing else was expected or needed.

The thirty-second delay would move the engagement farther inside the drone's operational envelope, providing a buffer in the event the freighter unexpectedly altered course. But this margin for error would come at the expense of the minisub's safety. Since the attack would now occur much closer, the midget sub would have less of a head start before enemy vessels began to flood the harbor, looking for the explosion's source. So be it. Commanding a warship was not a vocation for the timid.

The red digits crept down with a painful slowness, even as the tactical display showed the freighter moving ever closer.

After an eternity, the thirty-second timer reached zero.

"Fire the weapon," Ko said.

"Fire the weapon, aye," the torpedo officer said.

His slender fingers pressed several buttons.

A moment later an indicator on his screen changed from red to green.

It was done.

"Weapon away," the torpedo officer said.

Unlike with a conventional torpedo tube, the drone wasn't sent streaking toward its target with a blast of compressed air. Instead, the munition detached from the submarine's hull and motored toward the intercept point, its whisper-quiet transmission propelling it to a sprint speed of twenty knots.

"Ninety seconds' time to impact," the weapons technician said.

"Break station, sir?" the first officer said.

Ko looked from his second-in-command's questioning eyes to the tactical display. He'd originally planned to evacuate the harbor the moment the weapon launched. Now he was reassessing this course of action. The minisub was deathly silent, but there was a chance that a passive sonar array might detect the noise the minisub would make as it unbeached from the harbor's bottom. Better to wait and use the cover of the weapon's detonation to egress.

"Break station after impact," Ko said.

"Understood," the XO said, even as he confirmed the egress bearing and speed with the helmsman.

Then he, like the captain, watched the countdown on the torpedo officer's display.

38

FRANK ANDERSON STOOD SEVERAL STORIES ABOVE THE
ocean on the external walkway adjacent to the
bridge with a steaming cup of Mural City Coffee
Company's Aviator's Blend in his chipped mug.
Though his wife and daughters lived in Ohio,
Frank was a mariner through and through. After
stumbling upon his first oceangoing gig at age
nineteen, he'd fallen in love with the sailor's life.
Over the ensuing thirty-odd years, Frank had tried
to make his long and frequent absences bearable by
locating his wife and children near family, but he
knew his girls lived a hard life.

Frank had often second-guessed his choice
of vocation. While his landlocked friends never
missed birthdays or anniversaries, Frank had
been gone more than he'd been present. Instead,
he spent his time monitoring the fickle dials and
gauges that showed the health or illness of the

one-hundred-and-thirty-ton container ship he called home. More than once he'd fielded long-distance satellite calls from his wife at her wits' end or his daughters in tears. The thousands of miles separating them permitted Frank to do little but listen and sympathize. The advent of broadband Internet had turned once scratchy conversations into high-definition video calls, but a two-dimensional image was no substitute for a father's hug or a husband's tender embrace.

Frank had tried to give up the sea more than once, but it usually took no more than a month for his wife to gently prod him back toward his calling. Just as an eagle was created to soar, Frank was born to navigate the world's oceans. It was not the life for everyone, but it was undoubtedly the existence for him. Frank was never more certain of this truth than at moments like this.

For the last few days the weather had been iffy. An unseasonable squall had set upon the tanker, harassing the vessel with pounding waves and driving rain. Conditions had been nowhere near dire enough to cause Frank to circumvent the storm, but the inclement weather had been an inconvenience, to be certain. The galley had even closed for a spell in deference to the rough seas, forcing Frank to break into his emergency store of beef jerky and pistachios. But now the earlier turbulence was all but forgotten. The cloudless night sky showcased a brilliant collection of stars that Frank was convinced existed only above the ocean. His monster ship had begun the final run into port on water calm enough to water-ski.

Technically, Frank was on duty, which meant he should have been inside the bridge. Technically. But Frank was the vessel's captain, and captains were afforded certain privileges, chief of those being the right to stand on the balcony with a salty breeze in his face, a good cup of coffee in his hand, and a sea of glass beneath him.

After taking a final breath of ocean air, Frank prepared to go back inside.

Something stopped him cold.

Something in the water.

For an instant, the harbor's ambient light had hit the sea's still surface at just the right angle. A dark, foreboding shape was skimming just below the surface. For reasons he couldn't articulate, Frank was filled with dread. Though it wasn't uncommon to encounter debris in a harbor this size, there was something about the shape's angular form and purpose of movement that Frank found unsettling. But he couldn't for the life of him put a finger on why.

Then he knew.

The bow wave generated by his ship's tremendous bulk was substantial even at low speeds. The subsurface turbulence was strong enough to buffet even the most persistent flotsam. The shape Frank had seen should have been riding this man-made current away from the hull.

But it wasn't.

This could only mean one thing.

The shape was powered.

Turning, Frank reached for the hatch leading to the bridge. He was unsure what command if any he would give once he arrived at his station, but that didn't matter. His sailor's intuition said that he needed to be at his ship's nerve center, and Frank had long ago learned to heed his maritime sixth sense. A rumbling swept the length of the steel structure as his fingers closed around the hatch's handle. At first Frank thought that they'd somehow run aground. Then the answer became clear as the ship began to decelerate.

Something had fouled the freighter's propeller.

"Report," Frank yelled as he yanked open the hatch and strode onto the bridge.

"Engine RPMs were high-siding," the watch officer said. "We took the transmission offline, but the spike was so sudden I'm afraid we might have damaged the drive shaft."

"Rudder's not responsive," the helmsman said. "I have no directional control."

"Engineering, bridge," Frank said, using the ship's intercom system, "report."

"Bridge, engineering, both mains are offline. RPMs spiked before the emergency clutch engaged.

Number-one engine redlined. Probable damage to both the engine and the transmission."

"Understood," Frank said, "but I'm going to need you to reengage the least-damaged engine. I've got no steerage and rudder is not responding."

"Okay, Captain. Stand by."

Frank gritted his teeth, resisting his inclination to spur his chief engineer to work faster. Like Frank, his chief engineer, Jeff Davis, was a professional. Jeff knew his job and understood the danger an uncontrollable vessel posed in the harbor's tight confines. He was working as fast as he could. Further prodding from his captain would accomplish nothing.

At least that's what Frank's intellect told him. But his gut was telling him that the Busan bridge was growing in the bridge's windscreen at an alarming rate. If he didn't gain control of his ship soon, the results would be catastrophic.

"Bringing number two online now," Jeff said.

Frank felt the deck shudder as the diesel combustion engine delivered almost forty thousand horsepower to its propeller. And just as quickly the low rumbling Frank expected to hear from a functioning transmission morphed into a high-pitched shriek as the engine ran away and the RPMs redlined. If the drive system hadn't been damaged before, it sure as shit was now.

Frank mashed the transmit button to order the engines offline, but Jeff beat him to the punch.

"Disengaged the engines," Jeff said. "Sorry, Captain, but the drive shaft must be split clean through. There's no load on the transmission."

Frank heard the chief engineer's words, but he was arriving at a different conclusion. What Jeff said made sense, and if Frank hadn't seen the dark shape slicing through the water moments before their troubles had begun, he'd agree with his sniper's assessment.

But he had.

"Bridge, aye," Frank said, "stand by."

Dropping the mic so that the winding black cord caught the handset, Frank strode out the back entrance to the bridge, opening the hatch that led to the aft-facing observation post. Again trading the coffee-laced bridge air for the smell of ocean, Frank edged to the railing and peered over the side.

His heart shuddered inside his chest.

The aft end of his ship was missing.

39

"SIR? I THINK THERE'S SOMETHING YOU OUGHT TO SEE."
The pilot's voice jerked Jack's attention from the still-silent phone in his hand to the man sitting within touching distance away.

"Whatcha got?" Jack said.

"I don't know if this is what you're looking for," the pilot said, "but there's something going on in the middle of the harbor. I'm going to kick the nose to the left so you can take a look."

The helicopter yawed as the man spoke, and a hundred-knot headwind smashed Jack in the face. He angled his hand into a kind of makeshift windscreen as he squinted against the blast. At first he couldn't make out much beyond the tears in his eyes.

Then he saw it.

The helicopter had dropped over the port's outlying buildings and was now buzzing above the harbor proper. The Busan Harbor Bridge loomed to Jack's front, reminding him of a similar suspension-type structure he'd once jogged across on a visit to Charleston. But it wasn't the bridge that demanded his attention.

It was the vessel beneath it.

Or, more aptly put, the vessel floundering beneath it.

A massive cargo container ship shuddered, the aft end already listing seaward. But the ship's precarious position was the least of Jack's concerns. For reasons he didn't understand, the massive vessel seemed to be at the mercy of the sea. The container ship was edging ever closer to the bridge's southwesternmost structural support. As Jack watched, the ship's bow made glancing contact with the structure's square-shaped concrete skirt.

He could hear the resulting shriek over the helicopter's roar.

The support structure's skirt seemed to be protecting the pillar itself. Hopefully this meant that the bridge was in no danger of collapsing. But the cargo ship settled even lower in the water as an expanding pool of fuel dumped from its ruptured hull.

Not good.

Jack looked from the support structure to the stricken ship in time to see a man lean over the aft railing, peering into the water. Jack didn't know what he saw, but it must not have been encouraging, based on the way he sprinted back into the bridge. An American flag popped and snapped in the breeze, the Stars and Stripes pointing toward the already damaged piling. Unless a miracle occurred, the wind and current would keep smashing the freighter against the bridge until one of the two structures gave way. With a line of rush-hour traffic snaking across the bridge, Jack hoped the container ship buckled first.

"Want to get closer?" the pilot said.

Jack turned the words over, considering. The voice on the phone had been adamant that he needed to be at the Port of Busan in order to prevent an attack. But surely she hadn't meant this? Other than watch the ship sink, Jack couldn't do anything to stop the titanic-sized forces at work.

Unless he'd somehow been too late?

That thought made his stomach clench.

Jack's telephone buzzed.

Flipping the device over, Jack plugged a dongle from his headset into the cell and answered.

"Hello?"

"Very good," the familiar voice said. "You're both where you're supposed to be and on time. Two important qualities."

"Cut the bullshit," Jack said, as the freighter smashed against the concrete, opening a visible gash along its side. "I followed your instructions and the attack still happened."

"What do you mean?" the voice said, all earlier traces of levity gone.

"The freighter. It's already dead in the water. I'm too late."

A long pause greeted Jack's response. When the woman spoke again, her tone was tinged with anger.

"I don't know what you're talking about. Their plan has more facets than even I realized."

"Whose plan?" Jack said.

"I'll tell you everything I know about the attack as a show of good faith," the voice said. "Then I will call back in one hour's time to discuss the rest. One hour. Understand?"

"What do you want?"

"My safety in exchange for stopping a war."

"What war?" Jack said, not bothering to hide his exasperation.

"The one about to engulf the Korean peninsula. More on that later. First, stop the attack."

"What attack?" Jack screamed.

Then she told him.

40

"WHAT DO WE DO?" KWANG-HO SAID.

What indeed.

The patrol boat's eye-searing searching transformed the car's interior from night to day. The watercraft was motoring closer. Min-jun shielded his eyes from the glare to see that the shouted commands echoing from the boat were emanating from a loudspeaker mounted to its superstructure. Min-jun checked his watch, ignoring the chaos around him. He'd set the digital alarm for the exact moment he was supposed to initiate the attack, but he checked the time anyway.

Close, but still too early to trigger.

"You still have communication with the device?" Min-jun said.

"Yes," Kwang-ho said, eyeing his cell phone.

The scientists and technicians who'd created the

drone's payload had installed a secondary feature after an initial test run had proven unsuccessful. Because the two commandos would be actioning the device at a significant distance, there was no easy way to tell if the command to initiate was successful. Or, perhaps even more important, whether or not the device and its controller were still in radio contact. As such, the designers had engineered a simple add-on. Once a minute, Kwang-ho's cell transmitted a single pulse on the high-frequency radio band, and the device answered. If the communication's check functioned properly, the app's status remained green. If it didn't, the indicator turned red, alerting the commandos to the need to reestablish a sync between phone and device.

In theory this wasn't necessary, as both devices communicated via satellite, but theories tended to fall short in the face of operational challenges. As any operative knows, satcom radios could be finicky under the best of conditions. Inclement weather, obstacles, or even atmospheric noise played a factor in the transmission's quality. With this in mind, Min-jun had made the executive decision to remain in place for the operation's final phase. If Kwang-ho had indicated that his smartphone no longer had communication with the device, Min-jun would have entertained the idea of potentially relocating to hide from the glaring searchlight. But one look at the green indicator next to his sniper's right thumb let the commando know this was not the case. The men had reached the end of their operational road.

One way or another, the mission would conclude here.

"I'm going to draw their attention," Min-jun said, sliding his pistol into his lap. "Trigger the device exactly on schedule. Not a moment before. Then make your escape."

"Wait," Kwang-ho said, reaching across the car. "Let's just trigger it now. What difference does sixty seconds make?"

"I don't know," Min-jun said, "and that's the point. We've come too far and sacrificed too much to second-guess our instructions now. Trigger on schedule. Understood?"

"Yes," Kwang-ho said, the cell quivering in his hand.

"Remain strong," Min-jun said with a heartfelt smile. "We've done what few thought were possible. We will strike a decisive blow for the Fatherland. There is no greater honor."

Kwang-ho nodded.

The man didn't speak, but his hand no longer shook.

Press-checking his pistol, Min-jun opened the car door and took off at a dead sprint.

As expected, the spotlight followed, bathing him in its sterile light. He counted as he ran, legs pumping, arms swinging. After reaching fifteen,

Min-jun turned, centered his pistol sights on the glaring artificial sun, and pulled the trigger. The shots went wide, or at least Min-jun assumed they did. The searchlight's blinding glare made the commando squint. That was okay. Min-jun wasn't trying to shoot out the glass, even if such a shot were possible at this distance. His intent was to get noticed.

He succeeded.

A cacophony of small-arms fire answered his shots. Rounds snapped by his head, pinging off shipping containers in violent sparks. Tucking his head to his chin, Min-jun ran toward a rectangular container twenty meters distant. There was nothing particularly compelling about its rusted-out skin and flaking paint, but Min-jun hurtled toward it all the same. He hadn't picked the metal box for tactical reasons. In the last several minutes, Min-jun's priorities had undergone a drastic change. He was no longer trying to survive. His death was inevitable. No, the commando was now attempting something soldiers on battlefields far from home had aspired to since the beginning of warfare.

Min-jun wanted to make his sacrifice count.

The container was close enough that he stood a chance of reaching it and far enough away that his attempt would help him to combat the real enemy in this engagement—time. An invisible hammer pummeled Min-jun's calf, the impact forcing him to lose a step. Equal parts shock and adrenaline kept the pain from taking hold, but Min-jun understood the wound's significance all the same.

His running days were over.

Min-jun pitched forward against the dirty concrete. A dull throbbing pushed past his overloaded nervous system, suggesting that the gunshot wasn't a ricochet, as he'd hoped. Min-jun checked his leg and immediately wished he hadn't. A length of pale bone protruded from his calf as blood poured from the grievous wound in a crimson flood. Gritting his teeth, Min-jun settled into a crouch even as small-arms fire impacted the ground, filling the air with stinging concrete slivers. Though he'd long since made the decision to die, facing his mortality in such stark terms was still a daunting matter.

A glance at his watch showed the commando that he still had time to burn.

With a soldier's smooth, practiced motions, Min-jun ejected his pistol's magazine and reloaded. Then he extended the weapon in a two-handed grip, sighting along the barrel even as his exhausted leg and core muscles struggled to provide him with a stable shooting platform. Min-jun had always thought that his last moments on earth would be spent contemplating his life. The choices he'd made and the sacrifices he'd willingly embraced. He'd even wondered if perhaps a calm would settle on him as he reflected upon his nation or the love that burned for his wife and child.

But Min-jun did not have the mental capacity for any such thoughts. Instead, he concentrated on the shooting drill he'd practiced so many times. Align the three stubby sight posts and press the trigger in a single, smooth motion.

The shot broke just as a flurry of rifle fire caught Min-jun in the chest. He flopped onto his back and stared at the starry night sky. He wondered if his porcelain-skinned wife and chubby-cheeked son saw the same stars from the bay window of their tiny flat.

Then Min-jun was gone.

A moment later, the watch on his already cooling arm began to chime.

41

"WHAT IS THAT?" SHANNON SAID.

Kelsey looked away from the swirling crowd for the first time since he'd called Sergeant Stover for instructions. Though the demonstrators had yet to attempt to breach the security checkpoint, they'd grown increasingly rowdy. Men with bullhorns were leading them in chants, and several crowd members were beating their placards against the pedestrian barriers erected in front of the checkpoint. Kelsey might be new to the Army, but he knew a riot when he saw one. The crowd's energy was escalating. Before long the protesters would transition from beating on the barriers to beating on the MPs guarding the gate.

If that happened, all bets were off.

"What?" Kelsey said, shouting to be heard.

"That. Above the building."

Kelsey looked where Shannon was pointing

and swallowed. A purple-tinged cloud was swirling skyward from a building adjacent to the guard post. As Kelsey watched, an errant breeze snared the smoky air, pushing it toward the crowd.

The results were instantaneous.

As the purple tendrils snaked into the demonstrators, people began to cough and gag. A woman dropped to her knees while clutching her throat. The man standing beside her pitched headlong onto the ground, his body collapsing in a tangle of limbs.

"What do we do?" Shannon said.

Kelsey stared at the thrashing woman, dumbfounded. His instructions from Sergeant Stover had been clear: **Remain at your post and stay calm until I arrive.** But for the first time in his Army career, the words of Kelsey's squad leader didn't carry their usual weight. If Sergeant Stover drove, he'd be at the gate in ten minutes. If he walked from the barracks, Stover's trip would take closer to twenty.

In the meantime, protesters would continue to die.

As if to punctuate Kelsey's thought, another person fell to the ground, thrashing. This time the victim was a teenage girl, about the age of Kelsey's high school sister. What would he do if it was Thelma spasming on the ground instead of an unknown Korean?

The answer came in a flash.

He would act.

"Get inside the building and wait for Sergeant Stover," Kelsey said, the steel in his voice emphasizing the difference in their ranks for the first time. "Keep the doors and windows closed. If you can find a gas mask, put it on. Got it?"

Shannon nodded, her blue eyes as wide as saucers.

"Then git," Kelsey said, pointing at the guard shack.

Shannon bobbed her head and ran.

Kelsey knew how she felt. He wasn't Captain America, but he'd been a volunteer firefighter in his hometown of Bellevue, Washington, before enlisting. He'd never gone toe-to-toe with another man bent on killing him, but he'd followed his teammates into the teeth of a rampaging fire more than once. Up until this moment he'd thought that he was pretty good at managing fear.

But the purple-tinged death changed everything.

It was one thing to run into a building side by side with brother firefighters kitted up, adrenaline pumping and hose water splashing. This was something else. The lavender tentacles reaching into the crowd carried death. Kelsey was no better equipped to deal with the situation than the demonstrators were.

No matter.

Kelsey hadn't joined the Army to be a paper pusher. He'd told the recruiter he wanted a job that would put him in the thick of the action. Time to step up to the plate. Abandoning the relative safety of his guard post, Kelsey rushed toward the crowd.

While he could do nothing to stop the source of the toxic fumes, and probably little to help its victims, he might do something to keep more demonstrators from becoming exposed. Though the edges of the crowd closest to the gate were attempting to get away, the press of bodies extended up the street were preventing them from doing so. Kelsey needed to somehow disperse the crowd. But the chances of them listening to instructions from an English speaker over the chanting in Korean and exhortations from the bullhorn-waving leaders was basically nil.

He needed to get the crowd's attention.

Fast.

Taking a deep breath, Kelsey strode into the middle of the pandemonium. While he didn't claim to understand Korean culture and his knowledge of the language was minuscule, Kelsey had encountered quite a few frightened people. Next to a fire, there was just one other stimulus that universally commanded attention. Unholstering his SIG Sauer, Kelsey pointed the pistol into the air and squeezed the trigger.

The sharp **crack** echoed from the surrounding buildings. For an instant hundreds of eyes turned his way. Expelling his held breath in a rush, Kelsey uttered the one Korean word he knew.

"**Wiheommul.**"

Danger.

Then he fired the pistol twice more.

Like a herd of startled cattle, the crowd ran back down the street, vacating the area in front of the gate. Kelsey wondered what old Sergeant Stover was going to say about his unorthodox employment of his sidearm. Then he decided that he had more important things to worry about.

Like dying.

Even though Kelsey had yet to draw a breath, the world was already beginning to waver. He stumbled to his right, trying to find a pocket of clear air. His legs betrayed him. Sinking to the ground in a controlled fall, Kelsey had just one final thought.

He sure hoped Sergeant Stover had decided to drive.

42

"HEAD TOWARD PIER EIGHT," JACK SAID, CLICKING OVER
to the helicopter's intercom channel.

"Where?" the pilot said.

"Pier Eight. It's the U.S. installation on the
northeastern side of the harbor."

"What's there?"

"A weapon of mass destruction. It's about to be
turned loose on a crowd of demonstrators."

The helicopter's nose dipped and the engine's
roar changed pitch as the pilot increased power.
Jack hadn't been working with Night Stalker aviators long, but he could already tell they knew when
to ask questions and when to just get shit done.
But even if the pilots had voiced questions, Jack
wouldn't have been able to answer them. After
telling Jack about the looming attack, the woman
had rushed off the phone. This was the third time
the mystery woman had dictated the terms of their

relationship. Putting aside his annoyance with the one-sided calls, Jack believed that their timing and the odd intervals between them were significant. But further analysis would have to wait for later.

He had an attack to stop.

"Google says the little jut of land at our one o'clock is Pier Eight," the pilot said, breaking into Jack's thoughts. "What are we looking for?"

Jack was unsure how to answer. The mystery caller had vomited out a stream of information. The rapidness of her speech and her refusal to answer Jack's clarifying questions reinforced his notion that she couldn't communicate freely. Even so, the information dump she'd provided was compelling. A team of North Korean commandos had placed a device on the roof of a building located in the Pier 8 complex. Once activated, the device would dispense an airborne variant of the nerve agent that had become the weapon of choice for North Korean assassins.

"Hey, boss, this is Jad, I think I've got something."

The unfamiliar voice startled Jack. In all the confusion, he'd completely forgotten about the two Green Berets seated on the opposite side of the helicopter.

"Go ahead, Jad," Jack said.

"Yeah, roger. Looks like we've got a crowd of protesters at the entrance to Pier Eight. I see at least half a dozen prone bodies along with a cloud of some seriously sketchy-looking purple shit, over."

"Tally purple cloud," the pilot said. "It's originating from the roof of the northeasternmost building. Is that our target?"

"It is now," Jack said. "Head that way."

"Roger that. Winds are from the southwest at five to ten knots. We'll try approaching upwind from the cloud of nastiness."

From the tenor of the pilot's voice, they might have been discussing the Ravens' Super Bowl chances. The 160th aviators brought new meaning to the term **cool customer.** Even so, pilots with ice in their veins were all well and good, but Jack still needed to understand what they were up against. Straining against his lap belt, he tried to edge around the cockpit for a better look.

No joy.

Between the wind battering his face and the helicopter's protruding nose, Jack couldn't see much of anything. He needed to put eyes on the target. Fortunately, the two Green Berets were positioned to do just that.

"Jad and Cary, can one of you glass the cloud's source and talk us through what you see?"

"I got you," Jad said. "There's a square-shaped object at the edge of the building's roof. It's about the size of a case of MREs, and it's spewing purple haze."

"This is Cary," the second Green Beret said. "I'm no expert, but this doesn't seem right. We received an extensive WMD briefing before deploying to

Syria. Nobody mentioned an agent or bioweapon that manifests as purple smoke. Sometimes exploding shells containing blister agents produce yellow smoke, but that quickly fades. It's almost like someone's drawing attention to the box."

Something about what Cary had just said sent a **ping** through Jack's mind. He knew the Green Beret was on the right track, but Jack couldn't quite nail it down.

"Can you guys confirm that the purple haze is what's incapacitating people?" Jack said. "Or is the smoke a ruse?"

"We're going to be on top of that building in about thirty seconds," the pilot said. "I need a plan before then."

"Tracking," Jack said. "Jad and Cary—talk to me about the smoke."

"Like the boss man said," Jad said, "all the casualties seem to be within the vicinity of the purple haze."

"Agreed," Cary said. "The agent could be coming from somewhere else, but the casualties suggest otherwise. Those bodies are pointing toward the building."

"Several buses heading down the road toward the installation's front gate," Jad said. "Probably more demonstrators."

Demonstrators. The initiation time for the device must have been somehow tied to the demonstration. Perhaps when it was scheduled to start?

Either way, that didn't matter now. The device had been triggered and more people were going to die.

Unless someone did something.

Unless Jack did something.

"Hey, pilots," Jack said, "that thing on top of our helicopter is just a big fan, right?"

"In a manner of speaking."

"Then let's use it."

Two minutes later, Jack was orbiting upwind of the target building while explaining his plan for what seemed like the tenth time.

"So you want us to try and blow the smoke upwind—" the pilot said.

"While we shoot the box and hopefully knock it into the ocean—" Jad said.

"Where it will theoretically sink like a stone," Cary said.

"Exactly," Jack said. "Questions?"

"Seems pretty sketch," the pilot said.

"The best plans usually are," Jad said.

"Either we do this or more people are going to die," Jack said.

"Fuck it," the pilot said. "It's been a slow day. I'm in."

"Excellent," Jack said. "The snipers will cue off you. Call it."

As they'd briefed, the pilots maneuvered the Little Bird into a wide, descending turn, the rotors making a strange huffing sound as the composite blades took ever-larger bites of the humid air.

The helicopter was oriented to provide the snipers with a broadside shot at the device dispensing the purple haze. Since Jack was on the opposite side of the bird, he couldn't see what the aircraft's downdraft was accomplishing, but he could witness the effect the helicopter's downdraft was having on the purple-tinged air. The gusts of artificial wind slowed the haze's progress but couldn't stop the toxin's drift completely. Tendrils of purple death crept along the ground and flowed down the sides of the building, attempting to circumvent the barrier created by the Little Bird's rotor wash.

"That's about as good as we're going to get," the pilot said, the strain of holding the helicopter in place evident in his voice. "Any lower and we'll generate vortices along the ground."

Much of the thirty-second aerodynamics class the pilot had given while jockeying the helicopter into place had gone over Jack's head, but he did understand the basics. In the same way that a river's current diverged into whirlpools and eddies while flowing around obstacles, the Little Bird's rotor wash was unpredictable. In a worst-case scenario, one of the surrounding structures might serve as a trampoline, bouncing the haze skyward, where it could envelop the helicopter.

That was undesirable.

Accordingly, Jack had instructed the pilots to use their best judgment, but to play it conservatively. As much as he wanted to save the demonstrators, Jack couldn't help anyone if the helicopter crashed.

"All right, Jad and Cary," Jack said, "it's your show."

"Tracking," Jad said. "Prepare to be amazed."

The sniper's light tone belied the situation's seriousness. While both Green Berets had agreed that Jack's concept of pushing the dispenser off the roof with successive shots stood a chance of working, Jad had been quick to point out the alternative. It wasn't nearly as rosy. The high-powered sniper round could rupture the device, spraying its contents across the roof, or, worse yet, send the box lurching skyward.

With this in mind, Cary had suggested that they try firing just in front of the dispenser in the hopes that the bullets would fragment against the stone roof, pushing the device with metal splinters and other bits of debris.

"Here we go," Cary said.

The commandos were armed with SCAR heavy rifles. Like most firearms employed by special operators, the long guns featured suppressors. While this modification did nothing to mask the telltale **crack** a rifle bullet made while transiting the sound barrier, the suppressor did seriously reduce the muzzle blast. Accordingly, Jack could hear nothing of the Green Berets' efforts over the sound of the howling engine, the thumping rotor blades, and his noise-canceling headset.

The Little Bird danced back and forth as the pilot worked to keep the aircraft steady despite the unstable aerodynamics that came with hovering over a concrete mountain range. The helicopter's yawing nose offered Jack glimpses of the stricken freighter and what looked like a cargo container holding area on the western side of the harbor.

The floundering ship seemed to be drawing the majority of the harbor police's attention. Though the vessel hadn't sunk, it was riding dangerously low in the water and had begun to roll from side to side. Each rotation to the vessel's starboard side crushed the hull against the bridge's support structure, producing the agonizing wail of concrete against steel.

A flotilla of harbor patrol speedboats and other assorted craft ringed the ship, frantically offloading crew members, but the freighter was clearly on borrowed time. Sooner or later it would rotate too far and the vessel would go under. But as horrible as that scene was to watch, something in the container lot grabbed Jack's eye. Though he was too far away to hear anything, he could see one of the patrol boats racing along the shore's edge. The massive searchlight mounted to the watercraft's roof was angled toward land. From the way the beam hopped from container to container, Jack guessed they were hunting someone.

"It's working," Jad said, breaking into Jack's thoughts. "The device is almost to the roof's edge."

Jack was too busy watching what was unfolding on the other side of the harbor to reply. A series of sharp cracks echoed across the bay as a marksman aboard the patrol craft unloaded on the person framed in the spotlight's overpowering glare. The armed response was sobering. With all the chaos enveloping the port, Jack figured there was a finite amount of time that their helicopter could hover over a smoking building without attracting the wrong kind of attention.

"How's it looking?" Jack said.

Or at least that's what he meant to say.

Unfortunately, his question came out more like a sustained **haaahhh** because the moment he depressed the transmit button, the helicopter dropped out of the sky.

And it didn't stop.

43

KWANG-HO SUCKED IN A BREATH AS HE WATCHED THE torn body of his commander tumble to the ground. Though death was something every commando faced, it was not a topic Kwang-ho had spent much time considering. For one, he was young, and with youth came a feeling of invincibility. For another, Min-jun and Chi-won were his team leader and team sergeant. Even among the storied ranks of the KPASOF, these two operatives were legends. Both men had worked operationally in the south and returned unscathed. Even if he'd been afforded the opportunity to pick his leaders, Kwan-ho wouldn't have chosen different men.

But that had been before.

Before the seriousness and brutality of this operation had been revealed in a gritty, undeniable fashion. First there had been Gi-ung during the tumultuous exit from the minisub. Then Chi-won had fallen in the skirmish with the gangsters. Now Min-jun to the puppet police.

Only Kwang-ho remained.

It was not the ending Kwang-ho had envisioned when he'd boarded the minisub, but it was an honorable one all the same. The cost had been high, but the operation was a success. Min-jun had drawn the harbor police's focus long enough for Kwang-ho to slip out of the car. He'd slithered between cargo containers, losing himself in the maze until he was certain he wasn't being pursued. At first he'd thought to remain hidden among the rusting hulks of steel. Then pride had decreed otherwise. What if the abundance of metal interfered with the signal or prevented him from achieving a clear line of sight to the orbiting communications satellite?

Too many had sacrificed far too much for Kwang-ho to rely on luck now.

With a bit of a struggle, he'd climbed up a cargo container, positioning himself on the broad, flat top. From this perch he'd activated the device precisely on schedule while witnessing Min-jun's final sacrifice.

Then he'd watched.

Though the commandos had been given secondary targets, Kwang-ho knew his ability to prosecute them as a single shooter was limited. His Type 88-2 rifle was still strapped to his back, but without other team members to serve as spotters, security, or additional shooters, Kwang-ho wouldn't be participating in any complex ambushes. When the attack against the harbor was complete, he would attempt to contact another sleeper cell for instructions. Barring that, he would act as a saboteur and troublemaker, creating chaos wherever possible until he was either killed or reunited with his countrymen when the Korean People's Army victoriously marched through Seoul.

Such was the life of a commando.

But as Kwang-ho tucked against the metal's cold, unforgiving surface to watch the fruit of his labors, he was confronted by something unthinkable.

Failure.

Failure in the form of a tiny helicopter.

At first Kwang-ho had thought that the pilots would simply land next to the device. He'd chuckled, relishing what would come next. But they hadn't. Instead, the aviators hovered above the dispenser, blowing the lethal fumes out to sea even as a pair of shooters tried to displace the box.

This would not do.

Without considering the repercussions, Kwang-ho unslung his rifle and sighted along its narrow barrel. At first, he'd been unsure where to shoot, as helicopters were notoriously hard to down, especially with small-arms fire. Then the answer presented itself in the form of the open cabin doors. The aircraft had redundant systems and armor plating designed to absorb small-arms fire. The same could not be said of its pilots.

Steadying his sight picture, Kwang-ho centered the aiming reticle on the aircraft's open door. He squeezed the trigger. The rifle barked.

A round sparked off the metal fuselage to the left of the pilot's head.

Kwang-ho adjusted his aimpoint down and to the right, waited for the natural pause between breaths, and squeezed the trigger a second time.

The pilot jerked, and blood sprayed across the windshield.

With a feral grin, Kwang-ho squeezed the trigger again and again until the helicopter plummeted toward the building's roof.

44

"TAKING FIRE! TAKING FIRE!"

The words crackled over the intercom to the accompaniment of the kind of gurgled breathing that spelled bad news. Jack reached toward the pilot whose slumped form was leaning outside the cockpit as the helicopter corkscrewed to the right, slamming Jack against his lap belt.

"Anyone see where it's coming from?" Cary said.

"I think I did," Jack answered, replaying the previous seconds as he spoke. "Check the cargo lot to our west."

"Where that harbor police boat is nosing around?" Cary said.

"Affirmative," Jack said.

"Tally," a new voice said. "I've got muzzle flashes at eleven o'clock."

"Give me some right pedal," Cary said. "The angle's too sharp for us to engage."

In another demonstration of why the Night Stalkers were the best pilots in the world, the Little Bird's copilot put the helicopter through a maneuver that a ballerina would have found tricky. While simultaneously spinning on its axis, the helicopter popped up fifty feet in altitude, clearing the treacherous purple haze while presenting its port side and the two Green Beret snipers to the cargo lot.

"Tally target," Cary said. "Taking the shot."

The helicopter jerked again in response to additional incoming fire.

"Missed low," Jad said.

"Adjusting," Cary said.

The two snipers might have been talking about the weather for all the tension displayed in their voices. While Jack would have loved to have just sat back and listened to the professionals work, he had a more pressing matter. Though the Army commandos had done an admirable job scooting the purple haze dispenser to the roof's edge, they hadn't completed the work. Smoke was still pumping from the box in lethal quantities. Purple haze pooled at the building's base before flowing toward the demonstrators. As Jack watched, three buses pulled up to the gates and began disgorging passengers, adding to the pandemonium.

The attack was about to become a massacre.

Jack was no sniper, able to skip ricochets across the roof, but he had to do something. Fitting the

MP5 to his shoulder, Jack centered the EOTech's holographic dot on the container. He was in the middle of his trigger press when the helicopter jumped again, sending his aiming reticle panning across the roof. Swearing, Jack brought the scarlet circle back onto target as he thumbed the rifle's selector switch from semi to three-round burst.

Then he fired.

Rounds tore into the box, flipping the entire contraption into the air. With his heart in his chest, Jack watched as the dispenser tumbled skyward, trailing a thick plume of purple haze. The dispenser shuddered in midflight, broadsided by a gust of wind. Then the contraption tumbled into the ocean with a splash.

Sighting on the now floating dispenser, Jack fired two more bursts into the device.

The second set of rounds did the trick.

With a final belch of purple smoke, the box slid below the water's churning surface.

"Got him," Cary said.

At first Jack thought the sniper was commenting on his own shooting. Then he realized that the Green Beret must be referring to the enemy rifleman.

"Confirmed," Jad said. "Shooter down."

"We done?" the copilot said. "Russ needs a doctor. Fast."

"Clear on my end," Jack said. "Let's get the hell

out of here before someone else starts shooting at us."

As if to emphasize his point, the harbor patrol boat swung away from the pier, pointing its bow at the helicopter as it accelerated across the open water.

"Roger that," the copilot said, as the MH-6's nose dropped. "Hang on."

"You need vectors to a hospital?" Jack said, fishing his smartphone from his pocket.

"Negative," the copilot said. "I've got somewhere else in mind. See to Russ."

"On it," Jack said, releasing his lap belt as he climbed into the cabin.

"Pull him into the rear seat," Jad said. "I'll help."

"Is this over?" Cary said.

Jack wanted to answer yes, but couldn't.

His phone was ringing.

45

JACK EYED HIS CELL, WISHING HE HAD A REASON NOT to answer.

Beside him, Jad and Cary were both frantically working on the fallen pilot. Though the Green Berets' medical expertise wasn't trivial, Jack didn't believe there was much anyone short of a surgeon could do. The pilot was hit at least once in the chest. After seeing the severity of the aviator's wounds, Jack had strapped himself back on the exterior bench so the commandos had more room to work. The men had stopped the bleeding, but the aviator was still fading fast. His skin was white and clammy and his respiration was elevated. If the copilot didn't find a hospital soon, his fellow Night Stalker wasn't going to make it.

The copilot seemed to understand the urgency. He had the Little Bird nosed over, and by the sound of the engine, the aviator was squeezing every last bit of power out of the Allison turbo-shaft engine and then some. The copilot explained his plan in short bursts. The 160th pilots had been doing a naval workup as part of their Korea rotation with a detachment from the U.S. 7th Fleet. The **Ticonderoga**-class guided-missile cruiser on which they'd been practicing landings had a level-one trauma center and a surgeon standing by.

That's where they were headed.

This did nothing for Jack's already foul mood. While he couldn't help the Green Berets save the pilot, or enable the copilot to fly faster, he could get answers from the woman who'd led them down this path.

And Jack intended to.

"What?" Jack snarled, answering his phone.

"Not the greeting I expected," the mystery woman said.

"What did you expect?" Jack said.

"Gratitude."

"Look," Jack said, his anger boiling over as the commandos began CPR, "I'm done playing games. Tell me who you are and how you know what you know or we're through. People are dying."

"As will millions more," the woman said, not at all cowed by Jack's outburst. "The attack on Busan was just a prologue. You still don't understand what is happening."

"Enlighten me," Jack said, "and cut the court-intrigue bullshit."

"Fine," the woman said. "Complete and total war on the Korean peninsula is just hours away. If you don't—"

"No," Jack said. "We're not doing this again. Identify yourself or I'm hanging up."

The fuzzy gray outline of a ship of war appeared out of the haze just off the helicopter's nose even as the Green Berets' efforts intensified. Jad was giving the stricken pilot chest compressions as Cary administered rescue breaths. Jack had never felt so helpless in his entire life, and the voice on the other end of the line was to blame.

"Very well," the woman said. "I'm going to trust you with my life. Hopefully you make better use of this than the other information I've provided."

Jack bit down an acidic reply. Too many people had already died for him to sour this already tenuous relationship with a caustic comment. Besides, the mystery voice was at least partially correct. He bore some of the responsibility for the lives that had been lost.

"I'm listening," Jack said.

The helicopter flared as the copilot brought the Little Bird in over the cruiser's fantail hard and fast. A naval crewman holding brightly lit flashlights was trying to give the pilot instructions, but the Night Stalker wasn't having any of it. Instead, he planted the bird's skids onto the swaying metal deck with a precision that impressed even a non-aviator like Jack. Then again, landing on the cruiser's helipad was probably child's play for pilots who made their living inserting commandos onto the roofs of rickety buildings in the dead of night.

Unless your brother aviator was fighting for his life in the seat behind you.

"My name is Mesun Choi," the woman said, her calm answer at odds with the chaos surrounding Jack. "Do you know it?"

Jack did, but only because Lisanne had insisted he read a Campus-generated primer on the Korean peninsula during their long flight to Seoul. Mesun shared two distinctions that set her apart from the hermit kingdom's twenty-five million inhabitants. One, she was the full-blood sister of the Supreme Leader.

Two, unlike many of her less fortunate relatives, she was still alive.

The importance of the last point couldn't be overstated. The Choi family tree was known to experience sudden and violent pruning. Her assassinated half-brother was just one example. But his death, though brutal, was gentler than most her brother, Ha-guk, doled out. Jack suspected this was largely because her half-brother had been lucky enough to escape North Korea. For those less fortunate, the Supreme Leader had devised countless more colorful execution methods. Since his rise to power, he'd done everything from burn detractors alive to flatten them with steamrollers. In one of his more spectacular executions, the Supreme Leader had used victims as target practice for an anti-aircraft system meant to punch golf ball–sized holes through armored helicopters.

There hadn't been much to bury after that episode.

All of this to say that if the woman was truly who she claimed to be, Jack could understand why she'd been so cautious. An unauthorized conversation with a Westerner by itself was grounds for execution. But if Ha-guk suspected that his sister was engaged in treasonous calls with an American intelligence officer, her death would be both prolonged and horrific.

"I recognize the name," Jack said. "How do I know you're her?"

"What proof do you want?" the woman said, voice raised.

"A picture of your face," Jack said. "Right now. Hold up your middle and index fingers beneath your nose."

"We don't have time for such nonsense," the woman said.

"Which is exactly why I want you to do it," Jack said. "I played it your way before and people are dead. If you want to continue our relationship, convince me you're who you say you are. Picture. Now."

The woman hissed.

For a moment, Jack thought she might just

refuse. If so, he was okay with that decision. A team of Navy corpsmen appeared at the helicopter's side to transfer the pilot's limp body to a rolling stretcher. The two Green Berets were still doing CPR, but Jack could see the resignation on their faces.

The Night Stalker was gone.

"Fine," the woman said, venom dripping from the word. "But no more games. Agreed?"

"Agreed," Jack said.

The Navy medical personnel traded positions with Jad and Cary, continuing lifesaving measures as they wheeled the bed into the ship and the waiting sick bay. The commandos watched the gurney for a moment before turning to look at each other and then at Jack. The question written across their faces was plain enough to see.

Now what?

Great question.

Jack's phone vibrated.

He clicked on the image waiting in the text stream, enlarging the picture. An Asian woman stared back at him. Mid-forties, with a round face and high cheekbones. She was holding two fingers to either side of her nose—the index and middle. Scrolling through the documents on his phone, Jack found The Campus's Korean intelligence summary with the photograph of the Supreme Leader's sister.

It was the same woman.

"I believe you," Jack said, placing the phone back against his ear. "Tell me the rest."

She did.

By the end, Jack wished that she hadn't. She was right. People were still going to die.

Millions of them.

46

MUCH LIKE WAGING A SUCCESSFUL INSURGENCY, THE
key to a good coup was invoking the feeling of
inevitability. The perception that the takeover was
a fait accompli. Unstoppable. That the people staging the coup had already succeeded. Resistance
was futile because there was nothing left to resist. This thinnest of tendrils was what separated
victory and defeat.

Or in Pak's case, life and death.

"The general will see you now."

Pak looked up from the phone he'd been pretending to consult and studied the general's secretary as if seeing the man for the first time. The
secretary was missing an arm, but still wore his
dress uniform with pride. Defying common practice, General Dae-jung Sen, commander of the
Korean People's Army Special Operations Force,

or KPASOF, a contingent of two hundred thousand soldiers, did not use pretty young women as assistants. His orderlies were always former SOF soldiers, usually ones who'd suffered career-ending injuries on training or operational assignments.

General Sen was tough but loyal, and his men loved him.

This was why Pak had made the trek to the 11th Corps headquarters in Tokchon instead of requesting the general's presence, as was befitting Pak's station. Pak also wanted no record of the conversation that was about to take place. He knew that if Sen gave the order, the general's subordinates would go to their graves before revealing anything their leader wanted kept secret.

But that didn't mean Pak came here to grovel.

"Do you know who I am?" Pak said, his emotionless words evenly spaced.

"Yes," the orderly said.

"Good," Pak said. "If you ever force me to wait again, I'll have your other arm cut off and fed to the dogs while you watch."

"Yes, comrade," the orderly said.

The man's response was respectful, but without the terror Pak had expected. Yet another reminder of the advantages Pak had ceded by holding the meeting in the general's sanctuary.

Hopefully Pak had gambled correctly.

"COMRADE PAK, YOU HONOR ME WITH YOUR PRESENCE."

The man sitting behind the sparse desk said the appropriate words, but his grimace belied their meaning. Clearly Pak's intuition was correct. This meeting needed to be held face-to-face.

"Not at all," Pak said, treating the general's reply as if it were a reflection of his true feelings. "Some conversations are best conducted in person."

"Of course," the general said, clambering to his feet. "Would you care to join me for **cha**? My pot has grown cold, but I'm certain my orderly has just made some."

"You're very kind," Pak said, "but I wouldn't want to impose. Let's enjoy cold tea together much like our forefathers did during the Fatherland Liberation War."

The general gave a brisk nod and gestured to the simple table in the corner of his office. Though Pak was certain the old war dog understood the implication behind Pak's reference, he gave no sign. Instead, the general crossed the room in four strides, his brisk pace unaffected by his ever-present limp.

In the treacherous hierarchy of violence and entitlement that formed North Korea's ruling class, General Dae-jung Sen was a rarity. The battle-wagon hadn't risen to his rank through curried favors or backroom dealings. Sen was something much of the elite were not—competent. Under his tutelage, North Korea's cadre of SOF warriors had proven capable of carrying out dangerous and daring raids to the south. Unlike the rest of the Korean People's Army, Sen's soldiers were battle-tested in the sense that every SOF operator faced a culminating exercise in which they were inserted in South Korea. More often than not, their assignments were nonkinetic, in that they met with assets, took pictures, and generally familiarized themselves with the country that would one day be their battlefield.

After a week to ten days, Sen's operatives either made their way north via established ratlines or were repatriated via minisubs or other clandestine extraction methods. While these exercises didn't yield much in the way of intelligence, they fulfilled their purpose in other ways. For daring to operate on the puppets' own turf, Sen's men were respected and their leader idolized. But Sen had never tried to convert his popularity into political currency. In yet another novelty, the soldier had no aspirations beyond his current role. He wanted nothing more than to forge his men into effective weapons.

Until now.

The general pulled out a chair for Pak and poured him a cup of tea, as was appropriate. Only once Pak was seated and comfortable did Sen lower himself into an adjoining chair. Pak poured Sen a cup as the general was situating himself, obligating the soldier to offer the first toast.

"To the Supreme Leader," Sen said.

Pak nodded and took a swallow of the lukewarm

liquid. Barley tea by the taste, though it was weak enough to make a definitive identification challenging. A man in Sen's position could have had the finest leaves the black market had to offer. Instead, he drank the same brew available to his men in the mess hall.

The legend lived on.

"I assume your visit has significance," Sen said.

The words weren't so much a question as a statement. Pak treated them as such.

"Yes," Pak said.

He'd taken the measure of the man across from him on countless occasions, arriving at the same conclusion each time. Sen was a patriot who would do the right thing for the soldiers he cared for like his own children. Though Pak still believed this sentiment to be true, his tongue suddenly felt thick and unwieldy. Up until this point, the steps Pak had taken were explainable, deniable, or both.

That was about to change.

"Our nation is at a crossroads," Pak said, arranging the teacup so it sat directly in front of him. "You will be the one who chooses which path we take."

"Me?" Sen said. "Why?"

The limp that plagued the general's walk was the result of a training accident. At least that was the official story. This was true, but only partially. The actual account of what had occurred eight years ago was much more visceral. While supervising a maritime operation, the engine of the Kong Bang II hovercraft Sen was riding in had exploded, engulfing the craft in flames.

The reason?

Poor construction—a common root cause of the catastrophic failures that frequently befell equipment and arms produced by the regime. From his position at the bow of the craft, Sen could have escaped without injury.

He didn't.

With a complete disregard for his own life, Sen rushed into the inferno, rescuing crewman after crewman. Five soldiers perished in the incident, but another six didn't because of one man—General Sen. But Sen didn't come out unscathed, either. A collapsing bulkhead crushed his leg, requiring amputation of the mangled limb below the knee. In a normal military, Sen would have retired with a healthy pension and his nation's thanks.

The Korean People's Army was not a normal military.

Disasters of this magnitude were impossible to hide. Disasters caused by the shoddy workmanship and poor materials endemic to DPRK manufacturing were both impossible to hide and reflected poorly on the regime. The Supreme Leader normally rectified this shortcoming by executing the survivors and transferring any witnesses to guard duty at the regime's reeducation camps.

Not this time.

Sen might not have an appetite for politics, but he certainly had the aptitude. Before the propaganda machine could even begin to churn, he put out his own statement **praising** the nation's manufacturing prowess. According to the general, only superior DPRK workmanship kept the vessel afloat long enough for the survivors to escape. The disaster had clearly been caused by faulty fuel imported from China.

The ruse had worked.

Sen lost his leg but gained the lives of his officers and men. That his own was also spared in the process hadn't seemed to enter into the general's calculus. Sen had been popular with his men before the incident. Once word of what he'd done to both rescue his subordinates during the fire and safeguard them from the vindictive regime afterward began to circulate, his name became legend. Pak had watched the general with interest, convinced that the Supreme Leader would yet engineer Sen's fall from grace rather than risk a rival to power.

But Sen had been fortunate. Eschewing the fame that came with tales of his exploits, he instead devoted his time to training his special operators. He turned down invitations to Party functions and refused to participate in palace intrigue. Instead, he kept his head down and did his job. After several years, the lickspittles and power-hungry bureaucrats gave up trying to subvert Sen. In the game of politics, the military commander was but a simpleton.

Pak didn't buy it.

A man with the courage to charge into a raging inferno and the cunning to keep those he led from the disastrous aftermath was no simpleton. Sen was a fox posing as a chicken. At least that was the theory on which Pak was now betting his life.

It was time to put that theory to the test.

"You will choose the path," Pak said, "because the fate of your men and our nation depends on you."

Sen's teacup froze midway between his mouth and the table. His eyes narrowed, deepening the crow's-feet in his weather-beaten face. After a moment of silence, the general set the cup on the table, delicately, as if afraid the porcelain would shatter.

"Comrade Pak," Sen said, his words coming slowly, "I am a soldier, not a politician. An ordinary man."

"We both know that isn't true," Pak said. "Even if it once was, it is no longer. I am not a soldier, but my father was. He once explained to me that for all the planning and rehearsing that occurred prior to a battle, victory often went to the warrior who recognized an opportunity and wasn't afraid to seize it. Such an opportunity now lies before us. Whether you asked for it or not is immaterial."

"Speak plainly," Sen said, not bothering to mask his irritation.

"You know about the weapons test?" Pak said.

He didn't specify which weapons test. There was no need. In a country that revolved around the whims of a single man, the only weapons test that mattered was the one the Supreme Leader had attended.

Sen slowly nodded.

"And the ensuing disaster?"

Another cautious nod.

"I thought as much," Pak said as he slid back in his seat. "Hiding a catastrophe of that scale would be a struggle for anyone. Here is the rest of the story. The Supreme Leader has been incapacitated for the last week."

This time it was Sen who sat back in his seat, his teacup long forgotten. Pak agreed with the cautious general on at least one point—the man had no future in politics. A series of emotions flitted across the soldier's drawn features: confusion, suspicion, fear, and then the one Pak had been hoping for—anger.

"That is impossible," Sen said, folding his arms across his chest.

"Why?" Pak said. "Because you received orders from the Supreme Leader to initiate the first phase of Op Plan Dragon Fire?"

Op Plan Dragon Fire was known by name to

only a select few. It was the predicate for a full-scale invasion of South Korea. A select number of SOF teams would be inserted as pathfinders. The majority of KPASOF would follow in the next wave as part of phase two, flowing into South Korea by air, land, and sea. The pathfinders in phase one were charged with setting the conditions for the follow-on forces. Their missions included acts of sabotage, assassinations of high-ranking governmental officials, and a series of activities designed to sow mistrust between the South Korean people and their government. Added to this was one very specific operation that was solely Pak's brainchild. Based on the events unfolding in Busan, this operation had been successfully accomplished.

From Pak's perspective, phase one had been a complete success. Phase two of Dragon Fire was much broader in scope and involved almost the entirety of the two-hundred-thousand-strong SOF contingent. In a bid to overwhelm South Korean defenses, the remaining SOF operatives would infiltrate the southern peninsula by parachuting from An-2 Colt aircraft and zipping past coastal defenses on an assortment of fast and stealthy waterborne craft like the general's ill-fated Kong Bang II hovercraft. The second wave of SOF troopers would build on the success of the pathfinders, paving the way for North Korean conventional mechanized forces to sprint across the DMZ and quickly capture Seoul. Dragon Fire was a magnificent plan, but there was a catch. Only one man could initiate the next phase of the campaign—General Dae-jung Sen.

General Sen stared back at Pak with hard eyes, not answering.

Pak understood the soldier's reticence. Charging into a blazing inferno took courage, but fire, while a terrible adversary, was something that could be seen and felt. Something that could be understood. The political quagmire Sen now faced was more akin to wading into a pit full of writhing vipers blindfolded. Removing his phone from his pocket, Pak scrolled through the encrypted images stored in an unnamed folder until he found the one he sought.

The one he'd instructed a certain doctor to take.

"This is our Supreme Leader," Pak said, sliding the phone across the table. "As you can see by the **Workers' Newspaper** at his side, the photo was taken today. This morning, in fact. He has been incapacitated since the accident. He did not give the orders you executed."

Sen accepted the phone gingerly, as if its edges were made of razor blades. He stared at the image, enlarging it and panning around in an effort to disprove what his eyes were seeing. With a long sigh, he set the device back on the table.

"How?" Sen said.

"Simple," Pak said. "After assuming power, the Supreme Leader drafted a series of secret standing orders to be executed in the event of his untimely passing. A dead man's switch, if you will. The Supreme Leader came to power via a coup, and he feared being deposed in the same manner. His incapacitation inadvertently triggered phase one of Dragon Fire. The Supreme Leader's greatest wish was to see the peninsula reunited in his lifetime. He was determined to follow through on this wish even in death. Unfortunately, this will never come to pass."

"What do you mean?" Sen said.

Pak gave an elaborate shrug.

"His prognosis is not good. I spoke with the physician in charge of his care this morning. The Supreme Leader's condition continues to deteriorate. He is expected to join his ancestors in the next forty-eight hours."

"You are certain?" Sen said.

Pak nodded. "I can make his doctor available for questioning if you like. But if I were you, I would speak to the man quickly."

"The struggle for succession has already begun?" Sen said, shaking his head.

"It began immediately after the accident. At this point, I'd say that it's almost assured that the Supreme Leader's sister will take control. She has no appetite for the coming war and has counseled her brother against antagonizing the Americans in the past. You know this to be true. She will seek an accommodation with the South in exchange for their acceptance of her rule."

"Even if you are correct," Sen said, "I don't see what this has to do with me."

"That is because you are a soldier, not a politician," Pak said, "and an honorable one at that. Our Supreme Leader's sister is wise in the ways of the world. She knows that to win the puppets' support she must offer them something. A sacrifice."

"My men," Sen said, color fading from his face.

"Exactly," Pak said. "She will secure her position by trading away the lives of your men. Her first act after assuming power will be to provide the Americans with the size and location of every pathfinder team operating in the South, along with their intended targets. Check with your plans officer. I'll bet he's already received a request for this information from the Supreme Leader."

Pak knew this request had been placed, because his own spies had reported to him the moment Mesun had made it. The sister, though unpredictable, was Pak's insurance policy. If his coup succeeded, she became expendable. If it faltered, the sister was a convenient scapegoat. As her half-brother's assassination had demonstrated, familial ties to the Supreme Leader did not insulate a person from his wrath. Keeping Mesun alive and allowing her a few controlled opportunities to meddle was dangerous, but in the Democratic People's Republic of Korea, so was breathing.

Pak waited in silence, allowing the weight of his words to hang in the air. Sen was a good man. A man of conscience. Like all good men, the general had a singular weakness—honor. He would feel compelled to do the right thing, no matter the cost.

Pak fervently hoped that he never became such a man.

"What can I do?" Sen said, his voice haunted.

"Sometimes those hovering on the brink of a cowardly decision can be fortified into making the courageous choice. Especially when they find it is the only option left to them. Activate Dragon Fire's second wave. Now. Once your men hit their targets, our feet will be irrevocably placed on the path the Supreme Leader has chosen."

"What about his sister?"

"Political problems have political solutions," Pak said. "Leave her to me. Give me your word that you will activate phase two. I will handle the rest."

Sen stared at Pak, his expression unreadable. For a long moment, nothing was said.

Then the general nodded.

"I will do as you say," Sen said, his voice finding its footing.

"Excellent," Pak said, getting to his feet. "I will leave you to it."

"Wait," Sen said, rising as well. "You don't want to hear me give the order?"

"You're a man of honor," Pak said, "as am I. Such men are rare. If we can't trust each other, the puppets have already won."

Turning, Pak strode from the room without waiting for the general's reply. At least one thing that he'd told the general was true—in life, honorable men were rare.

But the graveyards were full of them.

47

POHANG, SOUTH KOREA

"YOU READY UP THERE, SIR?"

Second Lieutenant Mike Reese looked from his kneeboard to the string of letters and numbers listed on the navigational page of the large multipurpose display mounted on the right side of his crammed cockpit. At least one of the route's waypoints had been stored incorrectly on the data-transfer cartridge Mike had just loaded into the helicopter's flight computer. Now he was double-checking the remainder of the eight-digit coordinates at a manic pace.

But not quickly enough.

Time and AH-64E Apache helicopters waited for no man. The bird's engines were at one hundred percent, and the mission window was open. It was time to ask ground control for clearance to taxi. They were ready.

Or at least they had been ready.

"Roger that," Mike said, pressing the enter key on the miniature keyboard to the left side of the cockpit while hoping for the best. "All set, Miss Shaw."

"It's Kassi, sir. Just Kassi. I know in flight school they tell you to address warrant officers as Miss or Mister. That's just schoolhouse shit. We're your warrant officers. Use our first names. Trust me on this."

"I do trust you, Kassi," Mike said, smiling in spite of the mission butterflies bouncing around in his stomach.

He looked in the mirror hanging from the top-left corner of the canopy and was relieved to see an answering smile on Kassi's pretty face. In Apache gunships, the pilots sat one behind the other, with the less experienced crew member normally occupying the front seat, as was the case with Mike. In a thirty-million-dollar-plus helicopter, pilots could only look each other in the eye by using a two-dollar mirror.

"Glad that's settled," Kassi said. "Is my route active?"

"Yes, Miss . . . I mean Kassi," Mike said, double-checking the navigation page.

"Then why is the fourth waypoint taking us halfway to North Korea?"

"Shit," Mike said, punching back into the co-ordinate list. "Sorry."

"Not your fault," Kassi said. "At least not entirely. Ben is lazy, and his attention to detail is shit. I'm going to have words with him, warrant officer to warrant officer, once we get back to the tactical operations center. Life lesson for you, sir, always spot-check the route if a pilot not flying the mission is the one who built it."

"Noted," Mike said. He pulled the coordinates for the waypoint in question from his map and found the error. Two of the numbers had been reversed. Mike made the correction. "Correct waypoint's entered."

"You sure?" Kassi said.

"Positive."

"Great. 'Cause you're about to get some brownie points. Key the radio and tell the flight that you found an error in the ingress route. Then blast them the updated version."

Mike recognized the request for what it was—a test. In addition to being his assigned back-seater, Chief Warrant Officer Three Kassi Shaw was also the troop's senior instructor pilot. This was part of the reason why she was crewed with Mike, who was the junior-most pilot not just in Charlie Troop, but in the entire squadron. He'd arrived in South Korea barely a month ago, and it was safe to say that Kassi had forgotten more about the AH-64E Apache Guardian helicopter than Mike had ever known. Mike's relative inexperience was par for the course for new platoon leaders, but he was still expected to set the example for the warrant officers he led by studying his ass off. He couldn't magically accumulate flight hours any faster, but Mike could keep his nose in the books night and day until he became an expert on the gunship's systems. If he had the required motivation, that is.

Not all platoon leaders did.

This was what Kassi was now testing. She didn't expect her green platoon leader to be able to fly fifty feet off the deck under a night-vision system three weeks out of flight school. But a leader in the troop should be burning the midnight oil when it came to the academics portion of the job. Now she was checking to see how her new front-seater measured up.

Mike intended to rise to the challenge.

Selecting the ingress route on his multipurpose display, Mike went through the keystrokes necessary to blast the changes to his troop via the Apache's secure UHF radio. A moment later a warbling tone indicated that the updated file had gone through.

Success.

"Not bad, sir," Kassi said. "Not bad at all. All right, let's get this show on the road. You handle the flight internal radio calls and I'll take care of air traffic control. Ready?"

"Absolutely," Mike said.

"Great. Let's turn some jet fuel into noise."

FIVE MINUTES LATER, MIKE HAD CLEARED POHANG
airspace and was winging across the East Sea at
one hundred feet off the deck and a steady one
hundred and twenty knots. Though he'd known
that his aviating skills had a long way to go before
he'd attain the rating of readiness level one, Mike
still hadn't realized just how demanding flying the
Apache in an actual mission profile would be.

He did now.

With a new moon and an overcast sky mask-
ing the starlight, Mike had no way to differentiate the hazy visible horizon from the ocean.
From his vantage point, the sky and water were
indistinguishable.

At least with his left eye.

Like all Apache aviators, Mike's right eye was
augmented by the helmet display unit, or HDU,
resting against his cheekbone. Rather than a
heads-up display, Apache pilots received critical
flight and targeting data through the monocular
HDU. At this moment, Mike had the aircraft's
forward-looking infrared, or FLIR, targeting pod
slaved to his right eye. The sensor followed Mike's
head movement, providing video that rendered
the night sky into shades of green and white in
whichever direction Mike looked. But even with
the technological marvel of "seeing" without a visible light source and the assistance provided by

the flight symbology detailing Mike's heading, altitude, airspeed, and a plethora of other data overlaid on top of the FLIR video, flying the Apache wasn't easy.

"Watch your altitude, sir," Kassi said, as if hearing Mike's thoughts. "You're edging closer to ninety feet."

Mike transferred his attention from the rolling ocean to the carrot-shaped arrow known as the vertical speed indicator, or VSI, on the right side of his display. The arrow was below the neutral mark and sinking fast, indicating that Mike was descending. If he were thousands of feet above the earth, the slight altitude deviation wouldn't be cause for concern. But at less than one hundred feet above an unforgiving sea, a lapse in attention could prove deadly.

"Got it," Mike said, adding power as he inched the collective stick in his left hand upward.

Though the change in descent wasn't something Mike could feel, the VSI ticked obediently up, popping past the neutral mark until the aircraft was in a slight climb. Only after his radar altimeter showed him at exactly one hundred feet above ground level did Mike ease the collective back down and apply friction with a twist of his wrist to keep the control locked in place. The Echo-model Apache offered much in the way of digital wizardry, including both airspeed and altitude holds designed to offload some of the crew's workload with autopilot-like functions. Kassi wasn't letting Mike use either. Most instructor pilots subscribed to the notion that new pilots needed to "earn" the right to use the aids by first demonstrating the ability to fly without them.

Kassi was no exception.

Mike didn't fault his back-seater's logic, but he still longed for the assistance the hold functions would provide. Despite the Apache's stellar climate-control system, Mike's flight suit was drenched with perspiration from the mental effort of keeping the helicopter from the sea's clutches.

"Blackjack 16, this is Talon 23, over."

"This is Blackjack 16," Mike said, thumbing the radio transmit button on the cyclic control stick he held in his right hand.

"Roger, Blackjack. Talon 23 has a change of mission, over."

Interesting.

Though Mike and his wingman were both loaded with live 30-millimeter ammunition, they were on a training mission. As training missions went, this was one for the books. The two Apaches were slated to practice overwater gunnery skills by shooting up a target towed behind the USS **Lake Champlain,** a **Ticonderoga**-class guided-missile cruiser. As part of the exercise, the gunships would be vectored onto target by an orbiting P-3 Orion outfitted with a digital multimode radar system.

Doctrinally, the exercise was about more than just filling a floating Mylar target with 30-millimeter holes from the Apache's devastating chain gun. In the days leading up to hostilities on the Korean peninsula, North Korea was expected to flood its southern neighbor with Special Operations assassination teams using boats that were both stealthy and highly maneuverable. Boats that the Apache helicopter was uniquely suited to interdict. As such, Charlie Troop, 1-6th Cavalry, was gaining real-world experience by flying over water under naval control while doing what every gun pilot loves—putting steel on target.

But the P-3's radio call changed things.

According to the pre-mission brief, Mike wasn't supposed to make contact with Talon until his flight reached the Bullseye loitering zone another twenty minutes distant. If Navy aircraft was reaching out now, something was up. Something that would require Mike to exchange his role as pilot of a single aircraft for his responsibility as air mission commander.

"Kassi, can you take the controls?" Mike said.

"I have the controls," Kassi said.

"You have the controls," Mike said.

"I have the controls," Kassi said, formalizing the transfer of responsibility for the aircraft. "Good decision, sir. Let me fly the aircraft. You fight her."

"That'll keep us from getting wet," Mike said.

Mike took Kassi's ensuing chuckle as a good

sign. After verifying that he had the correct radio selected, Mike spoke.

"Talon 23, Blackjack 16," Mike said. "Send the change of mission, over."

Mike had keyed the transmit button on the floor with his left foot instead of using the one on the cyclic, since Kassi was now flying. Having too many hands on the helicopter's controls was only slightly worse than having too few.

"Roger that, Blackjack. We're picking up a series of waterborne targets approximately thirty miles from your location in the vicinity of Bullseye Charlie. Targets are intermittent on my scope, but appear to be heading south at a high rate of speed. Request you take a look, over."

Mike triggered the lip light attached to his microphone and directed the soft, red glow toward the map strapped to his kneeboard. The Bullseye was a graphical symbol tied to a specific location on the ocean. It was used as a navigational reference point, since the flat water provided no topographical features. Each Bullseye was tied to a GPS location, but Bullseye Charlie was significant. Unlike the Northern Limit Line that existed in the Yellow Sea on the western side of the Korean peninsula, there was no firm maritime boundary between North and South Korean waters in the East Sea. With this in mind, Bullseye Charlie had been designated as the northernmost limit of advance for the training exercise. If the fast boats Talon was seeing on his radar were of North Korean origin, they were well south of traditional North Korean waters.

Mike's mission brief had specifically stated that he was to stay clear of Bullseye Charlie, and he readily understood the reason. No one wanted an accidental incursion into North Korean airspace. In fact, the last time a helicopter had mistakenly strayed across the demilitarized zone, or DMZ, North Korean gunners had shot the aircraft down, killing the helicopter's passenger and wounding the pilot. Even so, Mike was a cavalry trooper serving as the ground force commander's eyes and ears. Mike's job was to find and fix the enemy in order to keep the bad guys from surprising the good guys. Investigating the boats nosing around Bullseye Charlie seemed to be a pretty clear-cut cavalry mission.

"Talon 23, Blackjack 16," Mike said. "Can you plot an intercept point and provide the range and bearing? Also, please send a grid to the center mass of the contact's current position."

"Roger that, 16. We'll send both via Link 16. Stand by."

Link 16 was a tactical network that digitally connected friendly forces on the battlefield. Just as Mike could see an icon for the orbiting P-3 on his tactical situation display, or TSD, he'd soon have an icon for the approaching fast boats as well as the intercept point. The information would be updated in real time and shared among Mike, his wingman, and the Navy fixed-wing aircraft.

"What are you thinking, sir?" Kassi said.

"I'm thinking we're going to head toward the intercept point to take a look. I'll call the commander with a sitrep en route. If he doesn't think this is worth our time, we'll go back to filling Mylar balloons with holes. But my gut says differently."

Mike regretted the words almost the moment they left his mouth. He was straight out of flight school with a whopping three weeks in-country. Kassi would be well within her rights to say that Mike's gut wasn't qualified to say much of anything.

"Roger that, sir," Kassi said. "Sounds like a plan."

Mike thumbed his radio selector switch, moving the transmission indicator from the UHF radio he'd been using to communicate with the P-3 to the high-frequency radio.

Then he stomped on the transmit button.

48

"BLACKJACK 6, THIS IS BLACKJACK 16, OVER," MIKE SAID.
Mike had essentially no experience with his troop commander. In a turn of events that would seem absurd for an outside entity, but par for the course for the Army, Mike had arrived in South Korea only to find no one from his command to greet him. His sponsor and sister platoon leader, John Broam, was out of the country on mid-tour leave and his commander, Captain Tom Tucker, had been tasked to conduct an external evaluation of another aviation unit. As such, Mike had spent his first two weeks getting acquainted with the troop's warrant officers and enlisted troopers, using his first sergeant and senior warrants like Kassi as his guides.

After returning from his tasking, Captain Tucker had conducted a brief interview with Mike before disappearing on a three-day pass. It was fair to say that neither man had been all that impressed with the other. A day into Captain Tucker's pass, a last-minute opportunity to shoot an overwater aerial gunnery with the Navy had surfaced. Charlie Troop had been in the hopper, but the squadron S3, or operations officer, had been poised to give Alpha Troop the slot instead, since Captain Tucker was gone and Mike was very new to the ball game.

Mike, Kassi, and Mike's first sergeant, Jeff Marlow, had all jointly intervened. The meeting with the S3 had been Mike's first indication that his absent commander wasn't all that highly regarded. After hearing his plea that Charlie Troop be allowed to conduct the highly sought-after gunnery, the S3 had eyed Mike with a skeptical glance, but shrugged all the same.

"I guess you couldn't screw this up any more than Captain Tucker. If you want the gig, it's yours, Lieutenant. But I can't cut you any slack just because you're the new guy."

"Wouldn't have it any other way, sir," Mike said.

Now Mike was beginning to wonder if he'd end up regretting his audacity. Upon hearing that his troop was deploying to a gunnery without him, Captain Tucker had cut short his pass and descended on the troop with a vengeance. Apparently junior officers who showed initiative weren't highly regarded by Blackjack 6.

In any case, the troop had deployed to Pohang.

Rather than travel together, Captain Tucker had sent Mike ahead with the first four aircraft, stating that he would follow along with the remaining four in three hours' time. Mike had a feeling that this was further retribution. Mike would have to set up the troop area on his own, allowing Captain Tucker to arrive after the hard work was done.

Either way, the change of mission Talon 23 was proposing was above Mike's pay grade. He needed to check in with his boss, even if the officer had prioritized a last-minute beach trip to Jeju Island over helping his new officer learn the ropes.

"Blackjack 16, this is 6. What didn't you understand about the order I gave you to keep this frequency clear, over."

Condescension dripped from Captain Tucker's voice, and Mike ground his teeth as he formulated a reply. Not only had Blackjack 6 decided to give his newest lieutenant a dressing-down, but he'd done so over the Blackjack internal frequency so that every pilot in the troop could listen.

"He's an asshole, sir," Kassi said, interrupting Mike's thoughts. "No two ways about it. But he's also the commander, and there's no regulation against being a jackass. Be professional. Don't take the bait."

Mike flashed his back-seater a thumbs-up in the mirror and pressed the transmit button.

"Blackjack 6, this is 16. Talon 23 is requesting a change of mission. They have a series of unidentified surface contacts in the vicinity of Bullseye Charlie. They've asked us to take a look. Our ETA is one zero mikes, over."

"One six, this is 6. You're already en route?"

"That's affirm, 6."

"That's not part of your mission brief."

"Understood, sir. That's why I'm calling you, over."

"Why in the hell did you deviate from your mission brief?"

Mike shook his head, feeling like he was in bizzarro world.

"Talon 23 has a real-world scenario," Mike said, trying again. "Since we are the closest assets, I thought we should take a look. If you want us to turn around, say the word, sir."

The ensuing silence was deafening. After several long moments, during which Mike contemplated what his mess-hall office would look like once Blackjack 6 fired him, his boss's voice crackled over the airwaves.

"Blackjack 16, this is 6. I'll call Squadron for instructions. Stand by."

"Six, 16, roger that. Standing by."

"Well, that was fun," Kassi said. "So we're supposed to stand by. What does that mean?"

"Excellent question, Chief Warrant Officer Three Shaw," Mike said. "As the term **stand by** has no doctrinal meaning, I guess we're in a bit of a quandary. Fortunately, we are air cavalry officers. Last time I checked, the first fundamental of the cavalry is to gain and maintain contact with the enemy. Since that's kind of hard to do from the middle of the ocean, I guess we're going to just press on to our objective while we await further orders."

"You sure about this, sir?" Kassi said.

"Yep," Mike said. "What's the worst that can happen? It's not like they can make me fly Black Hawks."

Kassi's laugh boomed through the intercom.

"You've got guts, sir," Kassi said. "I'll give you that. I hope you know what you're doing."

So did Mike.

49

"TALON 23, BLACKJACK 16," MIKE SAID. "NEGATIVE radar contact on surface tracks. Please confirm range and bearing, over."

The minutes following Mike's decision to press on toward the unknown surface contacts had passed swiftly.

Perhaps too swiftly.

After announcing his choice to Kassi, Mike had bumped frequencies to the air-to-air channel and given his wingman, Blackjack 19, an info dump. Seeing how Mike didn't really know much, that conversation hadn't taken long.

The two Apaches would proceed along the intercept course plotted by the Navy P-3 Orion. At about four kilometers from the intercept point, the pair of aircraft would begin scanning for surface targets. The P-3 was already linked to each Apache's FLIR targeting system, so the Navy crew members would also be able to see the helicopter's video in real time. If the unknown craft turned out to be benign surface contact, the Apaches would return to the gunnery exercise.

If they weren't, Mike and Blackjack 19 would continue to develop the situation.

Mike knew the plan was vague, to put it kindly, but that was okay. As a cavalry trooper, vague came with the territory. Now he was putting that notion to the test. As he'd learned in the aviation officer basic course, any reconnaissance needed to have a limit of advance. A point at which friendly forces would not continue forward, in order to keep from blindly stumbling into the enemy. As another famous cavalry trooper named George Custer could attest, meeting engagements rarely favored the scouts. With this in mind, Mike had chosen a point two kilometers southeast of the computed intercept point and dropped a graphical symbol denoting limiting advance into his TSD. After data-bursting the info to his wingman, Mike had slaved the Apache's millimeter-band fire control radar, or FCR, along the intercept heading and begun to scan for targets. So far he hadn't had any luck.

"Blackjack 16, Talon 23, lead target is bearing 315 degrees, range four-point-five kilometers, over."

Mike verified the azimuth on which he'd aimed the radar and triggered another scan. The electronically generated green windshield wiper

passed across his pie-shaped screen and returned . . . nothing.

"Blackjack 19, this is Blackjack 16," Mike said,
switching to the flight internal frequency. "Does
your radar register anything on that azimuth?"

"One six, 19. That's a negative. No joy with either radar or thermal, over."

"Roger that, 19," Mike said. "We're two klicks
from the limit of advance. Once we hit, we're
going to begin a right outboard turn and set up
for T-bone tactics."

"One nine copies all."

Mike was about to ask Kassi for her thoughts
when he had an idea. Bumping back to the P-3's
frequency, he began to transmit.

"Talon 23, Blackjack. Can you characterize the
nature of the radar returns, over?"

"Blackjack, Talon. Please explain."

"Roger, can you describe the radar returns. Are
the surface contacts steady or intermittent? Over."

"Blackjack, Talon. I am getting a bit of ghosting
on my scope. The software's able to burn through
the distortion so the returns are fairly steady. But
I'm at thirty thousand feet, over."

Mike turned the P-3's answer over in his mind.
The four-engine airplane was designed to serve
as the eyes and ears for the surface vessels it was
charged with protecting. As such, its search radar
was much more powerful than the Apache's

targeting system. But in today's world, transmitting power was not nearly as important as it once had been. The efficacy of a radar system had once been subject to its height above ground level, or AGL, and the amount of energy it could direct at its target. Now the computer algorithms that analyzed the radar returns were proving to be more and more important.

Case in point, many of the older radar systems that had been on the verge of obsolescence were being granted new life courtesy of an infusion of software rather than changes to their hardware. These new algorithms were guided by artificial intelligence routines leveraging the latest breakthroughs in machine learning. Computers interpreted data in novel ways, breathing life into radar returns formerly considered unusable.

Returns like the ones Mike was now seeing.

"Blackjack 19, this is 16," Mike said. "I'm going to be heads down, fiddling with our radar. Take lead while I work and start a visual sweep along the range and bearing Talon gave us. If I get something, I'll data-link it to you."

"One nine copies all. Taking lead."

"Whacha up to, sir?"

With a start, Mike realized he hadn't coordinated his plan with his own crew member. But like the true professional she was, Kassi had already eased back on the power, slowing the helicopter so that

Blackjack 19 could pass on their right. Effective crew pairings were essential for a number of reasons. Unlike every other helicopter in the Army's inventory, Apache pilots couldn't see what the other was doing. Crew coordination was critical, and overcommunicating was the norm until crew members had logged enough flight hours together to begin to anticipate what the other was thinking.

"Sorry about that," Mike said. "I should have run the formation change by you first."

"No worries," Kassi said. "You're the air mission commander, which means you've got a lot going on. Sometimes we'll have time to talk about things beforehand, sometimes not. We'll get better the longer we're crewed together. Now, what are you doing with my radar?"

"Attempting a trick they taught us in flight school," Mike said, stabbing a button on the multipurpose display with his gloved finger. "These radars received a software upgrade from Boeing, but the visual interface hasn't been finished yet. But if you're willing to dive into the Matrix, you can still see the returns."

As Mike spoke, the previously clean wedge-shaped radar page devolved into a series of blurry returns denoted by staticky-looking ghost images. Mike clicked on the flickering image closest to the heading and bearing Talon 23 had suggested, and tightened the radar's signal to a narrow search azimuth. Then he triggered another scan. The green windshield wiper swept across the screen, leaving a cluster of diamond-shaped images in its wake.

"Bingo," Mike said, pushing buttons with reckless abandon. He manually classified the images as potentially hostile waterborne craft, data-burst the return to both his wingman and the P-3, and then slaved the FLIR to the radar's sightline.

"Damn, sir," Kassi said, watching his work on one of her two multipurpose displays. "You've got skills."

"You might want to reserve judgment till we see the video," Mike said, peering at his blurry thermal display. "I may have just discovered a flock of seagulls."

Kassi chuckled, but Mike was only half joking. The downside to adjusting the radar's sensitivity was that the algorithms attacked a much wider range of radar returns. Things like ocean debris, atmospheric distortion, electronic noise, and, yes, even maritime wildlife now registered as potential contacts on his screen.

But that was okay.

Mike had done a bit of filtering on his own, discarding any radar returns not on the bearing and range the Navy P-3 had provided. The Apache's thermal sight had confirmed his hunch, though the objects were too distorted to identify.

"Bounce out a field of view," Kassi said.

Mike obliged, switching the magnification from zoom to wide, realizing his mistake. Always hunt in wide or medium. Zoom provided greater magnification along a much narrower sight picture. As such, going to zoom too soon was an easy way to miss the target.

A moment later, the image of ocean water was replaced with a flotilla of four boats skipping across the waves.

"Hot damn," Kassi said. "Tally targets."

Mike was too busy working the sensor to reply, but his lips twisted into a smile all the same. The boats were really moving out, and he needed the computer's help to keep the lead craft in frame at this distance. Centering his sight over the watercraft's bow, Mike engaged the auto-tracking feature. A white box magically appeared on the screen, corralling the boat as the Apache's fire-control computer calculated a firing solution for the craft.

"Talon 23, Blackjack 16 has eyes on unknown contacts. Streaming imagery now, over."

"One six, this is 19. We have tally on targets as well."

"Roger that, 19," Mike said. "We're bumping up to lead. Keep eyes on the targets and stand by."

"One nine, roger."

"Blackjack 16, this is Talon—"

"Blackjack 16, this is Blackjack 6, over."

Mike swore as he toggled between radios, deciding who to answer first, his boss or the P-3. He decided to split the difference.

"Blackjack 6, this is 16. Stand by, over."

Before he could dwell too long on the consequences of putting his boss on hold, Mike cycled back to the P-3's frequency.

"Talon 23, this is Blackjack 16, you were stepped on. Say again last, over."

"Roger that, Blackjack. I say again, the craft you're observing are—"

"Blackjack 16, this is Blackjack 6, respond immediately, over."

Mike bumped to the air-to-air frequency even as he turned the black knob associated with the high-frequency radio Blackjack 6 was using to communicate counterclockwise, decreasing the volume.

"Blackjack 19, this is 16. Contact Blackjack 6 on HF and give him a sitrep. I'm going to finish with Talon, over."

"Roger that, 16."

Cycling the radio again to the UHF radio, Mike pushed the transmit button.

"Talon 23, Blackjack 16. I apologize for the interruption. Say again your last, over."

"One six, this is 23. Those are North Korean fast boats. I say again, those are North Korean fast boats, and they are—"

Once again Talon 23's transmission was interrupted. But instead of an irate Blackjack 6, this time Mike heard something altogether different echoing though his helmet. The warbling warning tone associated with a fire-control radar.

A fire-control radar locking up his helicopter.

50

FOR A SPLIT SECOND, MIKE FROZE, STARING uncomprehendingly as the lead boat icon on his radar page began to strobe in angry crimson pulses. Then the electronic icon wasn't the only thing flashing. Cannons on the lead boat's stern and bow blossomed as fire shot from their muzzles.

"Taking fire," Mike said. "Break right, break right."

Chaos filled the cockpit as a stream of ping-pong-ball-sized tracers undulated toward his helicopter like grasping crimson tentacles.

"Breaking right," Kassi said, wrenching the helicopter over into a tight bank.

She tried to say something else, but her voice was indecipherable over the clanging sound of metal on metal. The cockpit vibrated like a tuning fork as rounds smashed into the Apache. Warning lights ignited as the helicopter bucked, clawing for airspace. Kassi was screaming something, probably a warning to Blackjack 19, but Mike was no longer listening.

He was fighting his aircraft.

Seemingly on its own accord, his left hand found the aircraft's master arm switch and activated it even as his right squeezed the trigger for the Apache's laser range finder/designator. The laser return came back almost instantaneously, but the numbers jumped up and down, refusing to steady.

Either something was jamming the Apache's laser or atmospheric interference was preventing the receiver from registering a steady return. Regardless of the cause, the result was the same. Without an accurate range, the Apache's fire-control computer couldn't calculate an accurate ballistic solution for the 30-millimeter cannon. Mashing the button that controlled the fire-control computer's range source, Mike changed the setting from laser to auto-range. Then he clicked the weapons-activation switch with his thumb, selecting the gun. This time the numbers on the bottom-right side of his screen steadied as the fire-control computer used a combination of the aircraft's height above the ocean and the sensor's look-down angle to compute the distance to the boat.

The method wasn't nearly as accurate as a laser range, but it was better than nothing.

"Firing," Mike said, as he pulled the trigger on

the left side of the two handgrips framing his center multipurpose display.

The aircraft floor erupted as the 30-millimeter cannon beneath Mike's feet roared to life, spitting out ten bullets at a rate of 625 per second. The rounds began impacting even before the cannon fell silent, throwing up sprays of water as their high-explosive shaped charges detonated.

"Short, damn it," Mike said, moving the crosshairs from the center of the boat to slightly above it. "Firing."

The cannon thundered again.

This time, the rounds impacted the boat with a series of flashes. Pieces of metal flew through the air as thick, dark smoke curled from midship. Squeezing the trigger twice more, Mike sent two more bursts into the damaged ship, walking the crosshairs from bow to stern as he fired. Flashbulbs erupted the length of the vessel as each exploding round sprayed shrapnel across a four-meter burst area. Then the FLIR flared into a supernova of white as at least one of the armor-piercing rounds found something flammable. The image processors compensated for the sudden flash of light and the picture resolved into something every gun pilot longed to see—an unrecognizable mass of flames that moments ago had been a target.

"Nailed him," Mike said. "We fucking nailed him."

"And he nailed us," Kassi said. "We're losing hydraulic pressure. We're ditching."

Kassi's sobering words brought Mike out of the singular focus he'd been devoting to the speeding boats. For the first time he noticed the acrid smell of smoke and the unhealthy-sounding whine coming from the engines.

"Where's Blackjack 19?" Mike said.

"The trailing two boats had interlocking fields of fire. Bill flew right through it. I saw pieces of the main rotor separate from the fuselage, and then a fireball."

"Son of a bitch," Mike said, the euphoria he'd experienced only moments before now tasting bitter. "Can we circle back to check for survivors?"

"Sir, you're not listening. I've got to ditch this thing before the hydraulic reservoir empties. We need to put her down. Now."

"Roger that," Mike said, thumbing the radio selector switch to HF. "Buy me time to make a Mayday call."

"Thirty seconds," Kassi said, the strain coming through in her voice, "maybe less. Controls are starting to bind."

Mike didn't bother to reply.

Time was too precious.

Next to a dual engine failure, loss of hydraulic power was an aviator's most feared emergency. If both engines failed, the pilot could still autorotate to safety if given enough altitude. But when the hydraulics died, the flight controls froze, reducing the crew to passengers as their helicopter plummeted from the sky.

"Mayday, Mayday, any station this net, Blackjack 16 is ditching vicinity Bullseye Alpha. I say again, Blackjack 16 is ditching vicinity Bullseye Alpha."

Mike was preparing to repeat his transmission when Kassi interrupted.

"Controls are frozen," Kassi said, her voice for the first time unsteady. "Come on the cyclic with me, sir. We need to level the wings."

Mike glanced at the flight symbology in his HDU and instantly understood Kassi's request. Like the good pilot she was, his back-seater had already begun a gentle descent toward the churning water so that if she lost control of the collective, the aircraft would settle at a manageable rate.

But the helicopter's attitude, controlled by the cyclic, was a different matter.

At some point, the Apache had entered a left turn, which had to be corrected. The gunship was built to take a beating, and that included less-than-spectacular landings. If Kassi could keep the helicopter level, they stood a good chance of surviving the crash. But the aircraft wasn't structurally designed to impact the ground on its side. If this happened, the fuselage would crumple, and the rotor would probably enter the cockpit, killing one or both pilots.

Not good.

Wrapping both hands around the cyclic, Mike strained to move the control stick to the right, willing the aircraft to lift its left wing. The artificial horizon shifted slightly in response, but the thin green lines representing the helicopter's orientation remained firmly in a bank. Mike grunted as he heaved the cyclic starboard and then gasped as the stick suddenly swung freely in his grip.

"We broke the SPAD pin," Kassi said, each word clipped. "The BUCS should be active."

The BUCS, or backup control system, was one of many fail-safes built into the world's premier attack helicopter. Designed to transfer control from mechanical to fly by wire in the event that the physical controls jammed, the BUCS was meant to give floundering pilots a final electronic lifeline.

But that lifeline came with a rather large caveat.

Since the engineers who'd designed the system envisioned its use only as a last resort, they hadn't built a way to transfer the controls from one pilot to another. In other words, whoever pushed the controls hard enough to snap the SPAD shear pin had permanent control of the helicopter.

And that someone was Mike.

Without the resistance supplied by the control tubes, the cyclic flopped in Mike's hand like a wet noodle. Slamming the stick against his right thigh, Mike willed the green rendering of the aircraft to level its wings.

Nothing.

"Controls aren't responding," Mike screamed.

"Hydraulics reservoir is empty," Kassi said. "We're about to lose directional control of the tail rotor. I'm chopping the engine. Say when ready."

Mike understood.

Without hydraulic power, the direction pedals the pilots employed to counteract the main rotor's torque would cease to function. When that happened, the aircraft would begin to violently spin around its transmission before slamming into the ocean. The only remedy was to negate the torque generated by the main engines by using the electronic chop collar located midway down the length of the collective to bring both engines to idle. Except that once both engines were at idle, the helicopter would no longer have the power to fly. The crew would have to perform an autorotation.

And that was a problem.

Apaches excelled at a good many things. Autorotations weren't on the list. The gunship's combination of low-inertia rotor blades and heavy gross weight meant that the helicopter autorotated about as well as a sack of concrete.

Then there was the matter of where the helicopter would be landing.

This autorotation wouldn't culminate on a runway or even a nice grassy field. No, the Apache would be dropping into a seething ocean like a runaway elevator. Not to mention that for an autorotation to be successful, the pilot needed to level the aircraft and apply collective just before touchdown to cushion the landing.

Both of these things were impossible to accomplish without hydraulic power.

Then there was the elephant in the room—Mike.

Autorotations were tricky maneuvers under the best of conditions, and the frothing sea and gusting winds hardly counted as those. Since Mike was the one who'd activated the BUCS, the lieutenant fresh out of flight school with a whopping hundred or so flight hours to his name would have to pilot the stricken bird, rather than his thousand-plus-hour instructor pilot back-seater.

Not ideal.

Then again, if Mike had wanted an easy life, he'd have branched infantry.

"Ready," Mike said. "Chop them."

"Chopping . . . now."

An ominous silence followed Kassi's proclamation as both GE T700-701D seventeen-hundred-horsepower turboshaft engines idled. It was the equivalent of muzzling a lion mid-roar. One moment the screeching turbines were rattling Mike's fillings, the next they were murmuring.

But the silence didn't last.

"Get ready with the collective, sir," Kassi said. "If we have any hydraulic pressure left, we're not going to waste it. When I give you the mark, pull that sucker all the way to your armpit."

"Got it," Mike said, as the altimeter spooled downward at an alarming rate.

The helicopter was still in a slight left bank, but the turn angle wasn't growing. Not quite the level attitude Mike had been hoping for, but certainly better than the alternative.

The rate of descent was another matter.

The horizontally pointing arrow on the right side of Mike's digital display indicated that the Apache was hurtling toward the ocean at a rate of four hundred feet per minute and increasing. In a crash sequence, the Apache's landing gear would stroke, attenuating the g-forces. But those were under perfect conditions, with the helicopter at level attitude.

In other words, not anywhere near what Mike was facing.

In a startling moment of clarity, Mike realized there was something he could do. The equation that governed crash forces was the same simple mathematical formula that everyone learned in high school physics: Force equals mass multiplied by acceleration. And while Mike couldn't arrest the Apache's downward acceleration, he could reduce the helicopter's mass.

"Jettisoning stores," Mike said as he thumbed the red button in the center of the collective's head.

A nanosecond later four explosive charges simultaneously detonated, sending the gunship's two empty rocket pods, Hellfire missile rack with two training missiles, and two-hundred-and-thirty-gallon external fuel tank into the ocean. All told, the components represented thousands of pounds of weight that would no longer contribute to the force generated by the inevitable crash sequence. The radar altimeter flashed as the Apache rocketed through fifty feet on the way to zero.

"Lock your harness!" Kassi said.

Mike didn't.

Not because he didn't want to follow the instructor pilot's advice, but because less than forty feet separated him from the ocean. There was no way he was releasing his death grip on the flight controls. Mike didn't know whether his control inputs were having any effect, but he did know with one hundred percent certainty that if he wasn't flying the helicopter, no one was.

"Get ready to cushion," Kassi said.

Mike was ready to cushion.

Actually, Mike was at that moment wishing he'd chosen to fly for the Air Force. An ejection seat would have come in quite handy right about now. But in the words of his flight school instructor pilot, helicopter pilots were not quitters. Unlike jet jockeys, they didn't blast out of their stricken fighter at the first sign of trouble.

The radar altimeter's green digits briefly flashed 10.

Ten feet.

Time to . . .

"Cushion!" Kassi shouted.

Mike yanked the collective up with his left hand even as he pulled the cyclic toward his crotch with his right, attempting to flare the crashing helicopter.

The incriminating green VSI arrow danced up for a heartbeat.

Then steel met water at four hundred feet per minute.

Mike registered the sickly sound of rending metal a split second before he headbutted the instrument panel with a violence that would have done Jack Reacher proud.

Stars supernovaed in a series of brilliant flashes.

In the moment before darkness claimed him, Mike had just one thought.

He should have locked his harness.

51

USS LAKE CHAMPLAIN, SOUTH KOREAN WATERS

UNLIKE HIS MARINE FATHER, JACK HAD NEVER CAUGHT the maritime bug. While he'd enjoyed doing the odd bit of sailing growing up, he didn't like the idea of spending hours on a cramped oceangoing vessel. Now that he was seated in the sensitive compartmented information facility, or SCIF, of the USS **Lake Champlain,** he stood by his decision.

Emphatically.

The **Lake Champlain** displaced over nine thousand six hundred tons of water, was five hundred and sixty-seven feet from stern to bow, and just over thirty-four feet at its widest point. As vessels went, it wasn't aircraft carrier–sized, but neither would the warship be termed small. But to Jack, the maze of passages and hatches that made up the ship's inner bowels brought to mind a prairie dog's warren, and the SCIF felt downright claustrophobic.

Though the assortment of multicolored pipes and bundles of wires that ran along the ceilings of most of the ship's spaces was absent in the SCIF, the conference room couldn't be confused for a cruise ship's lounge, either. With a design that favored function over comfort, the conference table was metal and bolted to the deck. The bulkheads and ceilings were covered in off-tone acoustic-dampening foam, and the carpeting was both cheap and thin.

All in all, not the most welcoming of workspaces.

But the SCIF's spartan decorum was a hundred-fold more hospitable than the thundercloud-faced man staring back at Jack from the television taking up the majority of the far bulkhead.

"So let me get this straight," John T. Clark said, kneading his forehead with thick-knuckled fingers. "The sister of North Korea's incapacitated dictator is willing to help us prevent another Korean War if we rescue her from the men staging a coup against her incapacitated brother. Did I get that right?"

"Yes, sir," Jack said. "According to her, the SOF campaign blitzing the coastline is just the warm-up. The KPA's lead echelon mechanized forces are moving into position now. Once they're at their jump-off points, the invasion will commence with an artillery barrage that's like nothing the world's ever seen. She's confident she can stop the invasion up until Zero Hour, assuming the Politburo official behind the coup doesn't kill her first. But once high explosives start falling on Seoul, all bets are off. We know the invasion will take place tonight, under the cover of darkness. Once North Korean forces hit their lines of departure, it will be too late. Our clock is ticking."

"That tracks with what I'm hearing," Clark said. "North Korea has more than six thousand artillery pieces, many of them in hardened shelters. Conservative estimates think civilian casualties will exceed two hundred thousand dead in just the first two hours once North Korean artillery shells begin falling on Seoul. This was why nuclear war on the peninsula has always been a secondary concern. Enough conventional explosives are sitting in North Korean artillery gun barrels to kill more people than the Hiroshima and Nagasaki nuclear bombings combined."

"She said as much," Jack said, eyeing the refreshments platter on the far side of the table.

In true Navy fashion the station featured copious amounts of coffee, along with a token carafe of water. But while his throat was parched, it wasn't either liquid that Jack sought. It was the jar of Motrin sitting next to them. Between the rough-and-tumble events of the last twelve hours, lack of sleep, and jet lag, Jack had half a mind to down a quarter of the bottle. But one did not show weakness when confronting wild animals or John T. Clark.

"You didn't hear it from me," Clark said, "but so far the North Koreans have us chasing our tails. They're working the gray zone like nobody's business."

"What do you mean?" Jack said.

"Sorry," Clark said, leaning back in his chair to reach for something off-screen. When his hand reappeared holding a battered coffee mug, Jack felt safe making a grab for the Motrin. "You probably haven't had time to catch the news, huh?"

"No, sir," Jack said, shaking his head even as he emptied a handful of pills into his palm. He considered going back to the platter for the water carafe, but dry-swallowed the painkillers instead. No sense tempting fate.

"Then let me break things down for you," Clark said. "The riot you were a part of in Seoul was the start of many now gripping the nation. The Internet is rife with cell videos showing the ambulance explode after demonstrators were herded toward it by tear gas. The Korean populace is demanding answers that the government doesn't have, hence the cellular and Wi-Fi blackout."

"Not good," Jack said.

"Agreed. And it gets worse. While your actions at Busan saved lives, that's not the prevailing narrative. From the Korean perspective, a leak from an acknowledged American bioweapons laboratory killed a bunch of protesters. At the same time, a U.S.-flagged freighter ran aground near Busan Harbor Bridge, fouling the water with fuel oil and closing the nation's busiest port."

"That's not what happened," Jack said, sitting up in his chair.

"Relax, kid," Clark said, waving away Jack's concerns. "I know that, but the rest of South Korea isn't so sure. The communications blackout conveniently lifted just long enough for more incriminating videos featuring the protest, dead kids, eye-catching purple clouds, a stricken freighter, and a gunfight from a black American helicopter to make the social media rounds. The North Korean influencing campaign has been nothing short of masterful. All of South Korea is looking for an American to punch right about now. And while South Korea has been pissed off at us, North Korea's been sending their SOF racing down both sides of the peninsula in fast boats. The Navy took a shit ton of them out with some help from Army gunships, but many still got through. That means more fanatical North Korean operatives are in the South, looking for targets to prosecute."

"Unreal," Jack said. "I always thought North Korea was the JV team."

"As did many of us," Clark said. "Between you and me, I'm not ready to backtrack on that assessment. As you can imagine, Mary Pat has been running around like a chicken with her head cut off. Between keeping your dad abreast of what's happening and trying to sort out the ground truth from cyberpropaganda, I don't think that woman's had an hour of sleep in the last twenty-four. That aside, I did get a couple minutes with her before you called. She didn't come right out and say it, but my sense is that the intelligence community thinks the North Koreans had help. Major help."

"Russia or China?" Jack said.

Clark shrugged. "No proof yet, but my money's on Russia. China isn't a fan of instability in the peninsula, either. If I'm right, this is worse than it seems. The Russians are crafty bastards. They've got us focused on the Koreas for a reason. We need to figure out what they're trying to hide."

Jack sighed, feeling the exhaustion of the last twenty-four hours. Just once he'd love to be on the offensive instead of always playing catch-up with the bad guys. The hammer instead of the nail. That particular metaphor brought with it a much more unpleasant image. A flashback to the Syrian desert and a compound of fanatical cultists.

"What's next?" Jack said, trying to hide a shiver.

Clark gave a sigh of his own.

For the first time in a long time, Jack thought his boss looked his age. Dark circles ringed Clark's eyes, and his Irish features reflected equal parts resignation and frustration. With a start, Jack realized how The Campus's director of operations must be feeling. Sure, Jack was pissed, but at least he was still at the pointy end of the spear. Clark, on the other hand, was helming things from an office in Alexandria, Virginia, leading a quasi-legal organization that was supposed to help prevent the exact cluster now occurring. Operating in places that traditional members of the intelligence community couldn't was part of The Campus's charter.

But this wasn't some paramilitary operation to take down a high-value target in Pakistan. This was the Korean peninsula and a full-blown conventional war. Though Jack certainly wasn't privy to the contingencies his father and Gerry Hendley had been considering when they'd formed The Campus, he had to believe that fighting a war hadn't made the list.

"Junior, it pains me to say this," Clark said, "but I don't know. The entire Korean peninsula is a powder keg. Teams of what we assume are North Korean SOF are still causing mayhem across the major South Korean metropolitan areas. The populace is scared shitless and pissed off at their government, and their elected officials don't know who they should be picking a fight with—us or the North Koreans. Oh, and by the way, we're trying to figure out if we should launch a preemptive conventional strike to take out the KPA's lead echelon formations before they get into position. Or maybe something more than conventional."

My father is considering a nuclear first strike against North Korea?

At first Jack rejected the idea out of hand. But

the more he turned Clark's words over in his mind, the more the notion made sense. Two hundred thousand South Korean civilian casualties in the first two hours. What about hours three and four? Faced with that kind of devastation, Jack could see how a nuclear first strike would enter the battlefield calculus pretty quickly. He pushed the terrifying notion away in favor of focusing on something he could control—the here and now.

"What about the rest of the Campus crew?" Jack said. "I thought Ding and company were heading this way?"

"They are," Clark said, "or were. South Korea has locked down their airspace and all ports of entry. No one in or out. The Gulfstream landed at Incheon International Airport in Seoul, but our crew is still on the tarmac. As of now, South Korea's under martial law. I don't see that changing anytime soon."

Jack nodded as he absorbed the damning information, trying to think. He had a ticking time bomb sitting in front of him and no one to disarm it.

No one but him.

"How about I take a crack at this?" Jack said.

"What?" Clark said, looking at Jack as if he'd lost his mind.

Which was fair, because Jack wasn't at all sure he hadn't.

"Come on, Mr. C.," Jack said. "You said it

yourself—the entire peninsula's a shitshow. I'm sure Dad and his crew are going at the South Korean president like gangbusters, but we don't have time for a diplomatic breakthrough. Mesun was pretty unambiguous in her last call. We've got a window, but it's rapidly closing. Let me see what I can shake loose."

"Don't take this the wrong way, son," Clark said, "but stopping a second Korean war is a bit outside your wheelhouse."

"Completely agree, sir," Jack said. "I'm not planning on saving the world. Just rescuing one woman. Besides, I'm not going it alone. I've got two Green Berets."

"Well, why the hell didn't you say so," Clark said. "Two whole Green Berets? That changes everything."

"Look," Jack said, determined not to bow to John Clark's legendary temper, "there's a ton of stuff we can't do anything about. I get it. But there's one part of this puzzle we can work—Mesun. She said she can stop the march to war. Is rescuing her risky? Sure. But at this point, what do we have to lose? The peninsula's a runaway train and it's about out of track. You and Hendley kept The Campus small so that we could stay agile. Agile enough to take on the missions that make the CIA think twice. If this doesn't fall into that category, I don't know what does."

Clark stared at Jack in silence for a long moment, his thundercloud of a face unreadable.

"Just for the sake of argument," Clark said, "how in the hell would you get into North Korea?"

"I've got some ideas," Jack said, "but I'm also sitting on a **Ticonderoga**-class cruiser that's part of the Seventh Fleet. Something tells me there's a person or two nearby who can help with the planning."

"And if by some miracle you infil into North Korea undetected, what are you going to do?"

"My job, sir," Jack said. "Make contact with Mesun, assess the situation, and provide you with options and intelligence to take to the National Command Authority."

"What if the whole thing's a trap?" Clark said.

"For who?" Jack said. "Mesun doesn't even know my name. Is it risky? Sure. But what's the alternative? If North Korea invades South Korea, the cost in lives will be catastrophic. And not just Korean lives. I've read up on the U.S. OPLAN, too. Even the conservative estimates have us sustaining casualties at a rate we haven't seen since Vietnam or maybe even the first Korean War. I know this is the majors, Mr. C., but I signed up to play in the big show. Don't keep me sitting on the bench on this boat."

Clark looked back at him, stone-faced. Then he shook his head.

"Ships, Jack," Clark said. "Cruisers are called

ships. Okay, you have my permission to pull together a plan. I'm going to get on the horn with Mary Pat, run her through this whole thing, and get her thoughts on the sister. If MP agrees, I'll work on getting you some Navy help, but you're on your own when it comes to recruiting those two Green Berets."

"No sweat, sir," Jack said. "I'm sure they're as ready to get off this ship as I am."

"This is planning only, unless we get National Command Authority authorization, Junior," Clark said, the thunderstorm back in place.

"Tracking, Mr. C."

"That's what I'm afraid of. Out here."

Jack took another long look at the refreshments tray, but decided the coffee could wait.

He had a team to put together.

52

"ALL RIGHT, GENTLEMEN, LET'S GET STARTED. FOR THOSE of you who don't know me, my name is Lieutenant Brandon Cates. I am the SEAL ground force commander for this . . . endeavor."

A mind reader Jack was not, but he was pretty sure that the rugged SEAL standing behind the lectern at the front of the briefing room had been about to describe the proposed operation in significantly less charitable terms. Judging by the scattering of laughs that accompanied the man's comment, Jack was not alone in his assessment.

"Okay," Brandon said, smiling through his beard, "the clock is ticking, and we are significantly behind the eight ball. Bottom line up front, the lead echelon forces of four North Korean infantry corps are moving to their lines of departure in preparation for what we believe to be a full ground invasion of South Korea. Based on the reporting from an asset with access to the North Korean leadership structure, we believe this invasion will occur sometime during this cycle of darkness. The people in this room are going to prevent that from happening."

The people in this room, as the SEAL had termed them, included Jack, the two Green Berets, a platoon of SEALs, and a collection of Army 160th pilots. At least those were the ones going into harm's way. The briefing room also included a number of intelligence, planning, and logistics folks, but to Jack it was the operators who mattered.

"Before we get into the concept of the operation," Brandon said, "Lieutenant Hayley Wilson is going to give an update on our area of operations. Lieutenant Wilson, this is your show."

The SEAL yielded the floor to a slightly built woman with short blond hair and blue eyes. In a room full of operators in faded fatigues and aviators in worn flight suits, her pressed and spotless khaki uniform stood out.

Even so, the woman exuded confidence.

"Good evening, gentlemen," Hayley said. "The Korean peninsula is currently in a state of limited war. DPRK SOF and sleeper cells are wreaking havoc across Seoul and several other metropolitan areas. South Korean digital infrastructure has been hit by a series of cyberattacks, and their national cell networks are offline. Citizens are rioting and the South Korean government is partially convinced that a U.S. bioweapons laboratory in Busan might have leaked a nerve agent that resulted in a number of civilian deaths. U.S. and South Korean relations are quite tenuous. South Korea is under a state of martial law. All ports of entry are closed, and their national airspace is locked down. That said, South Korea does not want a war with North Korea. If you gentlemen can prevent a DPRK invasion, we might still be able to keep the peninsula from going up in flames."

"Thank you for the summary, Lieutenant," Brandon said, "stark though it may be. This entire operation hinges on just one person—our HUMINT operative from . . . Who do you work for, exactly?"

Brandon looked at Jack, and Jack found himself considering how to answer.

The Campus's existence was known to only a select few. Though he had no doubt about the loyalty and discretion of the people he was sharing the room with, Jack also understood a fundamental truth—military folks swapped stories. That was the reason why Delta Force and SEAL Team Six would never remain secret organizations despite the number of clever cover names they employed.

Which gave Jack another idea.

"I'm with OGA," Jack said, falling back on the acronym first invented by the CIA and then parroted by a slew of other three-letter organizations. **Other Government Agency** was now a catchall phrase that basically meant **Don't ask me any more questions.**

"Perfect," Cates said, his smile now looking a bit forced. "What do we call you?"

Another treacherous question. Jack gave his true name most of the time, but in an audience of military folks, bearing the same name as the sitting President of the United States wouldn't go unnoticed. Not to mention that Jack liked to believe there was at least a passing resemblance between him and his old man.

"My name is Jack," Jack said, as he searched for an alias. "Jack—"

"Doe," Jad said. "The Smiths were all taken."

The Green Beret's joke did much to defuse the room's tension, and Jack chuckled along with the rest of the group.

"Lovely," Cates said, his smile now a grimace. "So, Mr. Doe, why don't you tell us why we're here."

"Sure," Jack said, getting to his feet.

Everyone could probably have still heard him if he'd remained seated, but it seemed disrespectful. Men were about to go into harm's way on his behalf. Standing was the least Jack could do.

"Our reporting suggests that everything we're seeing is really just the by-product of a power structure within North Korea," Jack said.

"How so?" Brandon asked.

"I've got that one," Hayley said. Keying the

remote in her hand, she brought the television behind her to life. The image resolved into a familiar image—the picture the mystery woman had texted Jack during their last call.

"This is the sister of North Korea's Supreme Leader," Hayley said. "For the purposes of this operation, she's been assigned the code name TINKER BELL."

"How about just TINK?" Jad said. "Three syllables and two words makes radio comms tricky."

Hayley looked at Brandon, who shrugged.

"Okay," Hayley said. "TINK it is. According to TINK's reporting, the entire North Korean buildup is cover for an ongoing coup."

"What happened to her brother?" Brandon said.

"This," Hayley said.

Now the TV showed an overhead shot of a flat concrete structure. The picture appeared to have been taken from a great height, but Jack could still see what looked like blast marks around the site. Several vehicles were turned on their sides, and the nearest building looked like it had been smashed with a giant fist. Were it not for the clouds of smoke and open fires ringing the picture, Jack would have thought he was looking at the results of a natural disaster.

"This is satellite imagery of the rocket engine test stand at the Musudan-ri test facility," Hayley said. "Or what's left of it, anyway. Seven days ago, a test went catastrophically wrong. The Supreme Leader was in attendance. He hasn't made a public appearance since."

"What the hell kind of rocket engine does that kind of damage?" Brandon said.

"Great question," Hayley said. "The intelligence community's initial hypothesis was that the Koreans were working on novel rocket fuel. Something with greater energy density to increase the range of their ballistic missiles. We were wrong."

The slide changed again, this time showing the schematic for a missile. The rear half was cut away, showing an enlarged rendering of the propulsion system.

"This is a representation of a prototype Russian weapon designated as Skyfall," Hayley said. "It's a nuclear-powered, nuclear-armed weapon."

"Nuclear-powered?" Cary said. "What does that mean?"

"It means that it will never run out of fuel," Hayley said. "Traditional ballistic missiles can fly intercontinental distances, but they follow predictable flight paths. It's this predictability that permits our missile defense systems to intercept their warheads. By comparison, cruise missiles are hard to detect and can conduct evasive maneuvers, but their range is limited to about fifteen hundred miles. Skyfall is the best of both worlds. A missile that can fly at wavetop level along routes designed to evade radar with no restrictions on range. A nearly impossible-to-detect munition capable of devastating a city anywhere on the globe. This system would render worthless the billions we've poured into missile defense over the last forty years."

"A game changer," Cary said.

"Yes," Hayley said with a short nod. "If Skyfall actually works. The explosion that incapacitated the Supreme Leader seems to suggest otherwise. The design is fairly simple in theory—ram air is superheated by the reactor and ejected out the exhaust port. But this is the second prototype to fail. The first one's nuclear reactor went critical off the coast of Nyonoksa, Russia, a number of years ago. The resulting explosion registered on the Richter scale. The North Korean failure wasn't on the same magnitude, but I'd say Skyfall still has a design kink or two."

"Why is North Korea testing a Russian weapon?" Cary said.

Hayley shook her head. "We don't know. Maybe they'd rather have disasters like this on North Korean instead of Russian soil. Our ISR assets have confirmed isotope radiation at the test site that matches trace signatures collected from the Nyonoksa disaster. Fallout isn't anywhere near as severe, but it's there all the same. We assume that the Russians have structured some sort of agreement to test Skyfall in North Korea, but we don't know the details. Can you help with that, Mr. OGA?"

"Nope," Jack said. "That's one of the questions I intend to ask my asset when we're face-to-face."

"Which brings us to the concept of the operation," Brandon said, reassuming control of the briefing. "The Musudan-ri Missile Test Facility is located on the eastern coast of North Korea, about a kilometer inland from the East Sea. It's in the North Hamgyong province just over forty-five kilometers from Kimchaek, the nearest port city. The facility is actually a collection of four major installations covering around five square kilometers. Each installation is self-contained with its own security measures, fencing, and guard force. Arrayed from west to east, the installations are: the missile assembly building, the range control building, the launch tower, and the rocket engine test stand."

The slide changed to a satellite photo showing a large rectangular building surrounded by a fence. Concrete roads branched from either side of the building, while a smaller outbuilding sat in the woods to the west.

"This is the missile assembly complex," Brandon said. "TINK and her brother are being held here." He pointed to the smaller outbuilding.

"Why?" Cary said.

"TINK was with her brother during the accident," Jack said. "They were moved to the structure both to conceal the accident and to treat them for potential radiation exposure. This is when the coup instigators made their move. TINK and the Supreme Leader have been imprisoned in that building for the last week. TINK is communicating with me through a sub-asset who has freedom to maneuver across the site. A Russian doctor. A contingent of Russian scientists and engineers were at the facility to monitor the test. When it failed, the sub-asset was brought in to treat TINK and her brother. She will use her access to bring TINK to us."

"Then what?" Jad said.

Jack paused before answering, but not because he was afraid to give away something sensitive. This was the point in the briefing when his fellow operatives learned just how thin the ice was on which they were skating.

"My contact with TINK has been sporadic and of limited duration," Jack said. "I still don't have a full picture of what's happening. Here's what I do know—the mobilization of the DPRK's conventional and SOF elements has occurred at the behest of the coup conspirators, not the Supreme Leader or TINK. At least one of these coconspirators is a high-ranking general in the Korean People's Army. He has enough pull to get his Corps commanders to their lines of departure, but they will not commence the invasion without hearing the order directly from the Supreme Leader or TINK."

"Like face-to-face?" Jad said.

"Almost," Jack said. "Apparently the Supreme Leader has coups on the mind. I guess that's understandable, seeing that he came to power by one. Prior to his successful takeover, the military staged several that failed. Two KPA Corps commanders came very close to toppling the government back in the nineties. To make sure his career didn't go the way of his predecessor, the Supreme Leader instituted a policy whereby he issues orders to his generals via VTC. The signal carrying the VTC is encrypted with ciphers that change daily."

"Pretty high-tech for North Korea," Jad said.

"The system's from China," Jack said, "which means they probably stole it from us. Anyway, to go forward with the invasion, the coup leader needs to issue the orders to the Corps commanders once their front echelon forces arrive at their lines of departure. In exchange for rescuing her, TINK will countermand those orders and reassume control of the DPRK government."

"How?" Jad said.

"This is more your field of expertise than mine," Jack said, "but apparently the signal uses standard frequencies and waveforms. It's the ciphers that are the deal breaker. The coup leader is using the communication systems installed in the range control building located in the northernmost corner of the Musudan-ri complex to talk with his coconspirators and the military. This is where the ciphers are stored. TINK still has loyalists in the building.

One of them will smuggle her the ciphers, which she in turn will bring to us. We provide the radio and she calls off the generals. Together we end the war."

"And what are the rest of us doing while you meet with TINK?" Cary said.

"You and your spotter will establish a sniper hide site providing overwatch for the meet," Brandon said. "My SEALs and I will be standing by as an extremis assault force. If the sub-asset can't bring TINK out, we will go in and get her."

"And the war's over just like that?" Jad said.

"We're hours away from the entire peninsula going up in smoke," Jack said. "If it does, hundreds of thousands of people are going to die. Possibly more. This thing with TINK is thin, but it's all we've got. Everyone in this room signed up to be a secret squirrel for the chance to one day save the world. Today's our day."

Silence greeted Jack's pronouncement. Not exactly the reaction he'd been hoping for. Then Jad chimed in.

"You've got one hell of a stump speech," Jad said. "Ever thought of running for office?"

"Hell, no," Jack said, which was the exact answer his father had given a lifetime ago. "So, Mr. SEAL, how are we getting into North Korea?"

"You're going to love this," Brandon said with a smile.

53

TURNS OUT THAT WHEN A SEAL SAYS <u>YOU'RE GOING TO</u> Love This, you should run.

Fast.

At least those were Jack's thoughts as he sat shoulder to shoulder with Brandon and four other SEALs in the back of a SEAL delivery vehicle, or SDV, as the dry deck shelter housing the boat slowly flooded. The frigid water poured in from the bottom of the shelter, making an already claustrophobic environment exponentially worse. Brandon had told Jack what to expect, but the SEAL's words had not sufficiently conveyed the terror Jack was now experiencing. As the chamber flooded, Jack closed his eyes and concentrated on his breathing, trying to ignore the fast-rising seawater. Jack Ryan, Sr., loved to tell the story about the time he boarded a submarine by dropping from a hovering helicopter into the roiling surf.

For the first time in his life, Jack thought he had his father beat.

THE PREVIOUS HOURS HAD PASSED IN A WHIRLWIND OF activity. After the briefing's conclusion, the operation's various participants had returned to their organizations to begin the planning process. The 160th pilots disappeared to where their fellow aviators were housed in what was certainly the most luxurious part of the ship to do whatever it was Night Stalkers did while preparing for a mission. Cary and Jad, on the other hand, had a quiet talk with Brandon. After the quick conversation, the naval commando had pointed the two Green Berets toward a naval aviator and that was that.

Which left Jack with Brandon.

"What now?" Jack had said.

"Now we need to catch our ride," Brandon said. "Can you swim?"

"Sure," Jack replied.

"Scuba certified?"

"Of course."

"Then this will be easy."

It was not easy.

Catch our ride actually meant boarding an SH-60 Seahawk for a quick flight out to the middle of nowhere. Except **nowhere** rapidly became **somewhere** when the frothing ocean beneath the Seahawk's wheels parted, revealing the shadowy

hull of an **Ohio**-class submarine. The steel levi-
athan displaced over eighteen thousand tons of
water while submerged. The boat had originally
been commissioned as a boomer—one of the
feared undersea platforms that served as a critical part of America's nuclear triad. Boomers hid
in the ocean with their payload of nuclear-tipped
intercontinental ballistic missiles, ready to rain
down Armageddon on any nation foolish enough
to threaten the U.S. with nuclear destruction.

After the Cold War ran its course, some of the
three-billion-dollar-a-copy marvels of technology
were repurposed to a more practical role—Special
Operations. The metal monsters embodied stealth
long before stealth was cool. Now this heritage was
put to good use slinking into heavily surveilled waters in order to deposit men bent on mischief right
under their enemy's nose.

Men like Brandon and his fellow SEALs.

Unlike his father, Jack had managed to board
his first submarine without making the acquaintance of the swells rocking the boat from side to
side. The naval aviators had hovered the Seahawk
over the sub, allowing Jack and the others to board
without getting wet.

Mostly.

Once aboard, they'd climbed into the conning
tower and descended into cramped but tolerable
living quarters. Not too bad, all things considered.

And then Brandon had explained how they were actually going to get to shore undetected.

After that little gem of a conversation, Jack thought he might just be willing to switch places with his dad after all. Falling into the ocean was one thing. Sitting in a dark metal compartment the size of a car's trunk with four other guys as it flooded was something else entirely.

"How you doing, Mr. Doe?" Brandon said, as the water crested chest level and continued its relentless march upward.

"Since I'm pretty sure we're going to drown," Jack said, speaking around his regulator, "you can call me Jack."

"Nonsense, Jack," Brandon said, squeezing Jack's leg through the wetsuit. "The hard stuff doesn't happen until after we hit the beach. All you gotta do right now is breathe. That's not so bad, right?"

Jack did not agree.

While the SEALs had done their best to prepare Jack for what was coming, there was no readying yourself for the sensation of being buried alive by seawater while wedged in the coffin-tight SDV. Unlike traditional subs, the SDV didn't have atmospheric controls. This meant that Jack had to endure the cold and darkness with zero personal space. Even though the rational part of his mind understood that as long as he had oxygen to breathe, the water swirling around his limbs didn't pose any danger, the animal portion of his brain vehemently disagreed.

Closing his eyes, Jack concentrated on his breathing. He inhaled, paused, then exhaled, even as the ocean's icy fingers transferred their grip from his ankles, to his waist, to his chest. As the frothing torrent of seawater washed over his head, Jack might have lost his shit.

A little.

Though he didn't scream for his mama and try to claw his way out of the metal death chamber, Jack's respiration did increase. Significantly. In the space of about a minute and a half, he sucked almost five hundred pounds of air into his heaving lungs. With claustrophobia about to overtake him, Jack forced himself to concentrate solely on his shallow breaths and pounding heart. For what seemed like an eternity, he wasn't sure he was going to win the battle. Then the fear began to slowly subside as Jack took control of his respiration, not holding his breath, but not giving into the urge to pant uncontrollably, either. After getting his breathing under control, Jack slowly worked to unclench his muscles and relax his shaking limbs.

Then he opened his eyes.

Brandon was staring at him, the SEAL's expression unreadable behind his mask. When he saw Jack's eyes flicker open, the SEAL flashed him the **okay** signal by making a circle of his thumb and forefinger.

Jack answered back the same way.

He wasn't okay, but Jack was controlling his fear instead of the other way around. It wasn't a perfect solution, but he could function, and that would have to be enough. The SEAL seemed to understand. He gave Jack's shoulder a squeeze.

If only Mr. C. could see Jack now.

Check that. Mr. C. was a vintage SEAL—one of the frogmen who hailed back to the origin of naval commandos during the Vietnam War. John T. Clark would offer zero sympathy at this turn of events. In fact, he'd probably geek out on it.

With a flurry of bubbles, the front of the dry dock shelter opened, exposing the SDV to the ocean. The sea's dark expanse felt ominous, a black void waiting to swallow the men whole. The SDV vibrated as its electric motors powered the vehicle away from the submarine and into the gaping chasm. Reaching past Jack, Brandon shut the sliding panel on the side of the boat, plunging the SDV's interior into darkness. The SEAL seated across from Jack cracked open a green chemlight. Then he fished something else from the gear bag attached to his suit.

A magazine.

A magazine with laminated, waterproof pages.

Turning, the commando handed both chemlight and magazine to Jack.

Paging through a magazine was the last thing Jack wanted to do. Then again, Brandon had quoted the transit time from the submarine to the point at which they'd begin their swim to the beach at just under two hours. That was a lot of time to sit in the dark, pondering your poor life choices. Besides, unlike the frogman to his right, Jack wasn't comfortable enough to pass the time sleeping. The magazine it was. Opening the cover, Jack had to restrain a chuckle. It was a surfing magazine.

Of course.

With a sigh that sent a stream of bubbles drifting upward, Jack settled in and began to flip the pages.

54

UNDISCLOSED LOCATION, SOUTH KOREA

"GREAT TO SEE YOU, LIEUTENANT REESE. WHY DON'T you grab a seat up here?"

"Thank you, sir," Mike said with a nod.

If left to his own devices, Mike would have hung out at the back of the tent that served as the TOC. Though crowded, the space wasn't much bigger than a living room, and Mike could both hear the S3's briefing and see the map board and accompanying PowerPoint slides from where he was standing. His dramatic return had already garnered enough attention. At this point, Mike wanted nothing more than to just fade into the background. Unfortunately, the squadron commander had other ideas, and when your boss's boss offered you a seat at the front, you didn't turn it down.

Mike covered the distance to the indicated folding

chair in short, measured strides, aware that all eyes were on him. Which was a problem. Not so much because of the bandage across his forehead covering the row of stitches knitting together the gash he'd sustained in the crash sequence or the nice shiner obscuring his right eye. These were almost badges of honor.

No, the reason behind Mike's careful walk was much more practical.

His bruised body felt like someone had gone at him with a baseball bat.

Even so, there was no way he was sitting out the rest of the war in a hospital bed. Like any good aviator, he'd downplayed the extent of his injuries to the flight surgeon to ensure that he could stay on flight status.

Significantly.

Mike had played rugby in college, and if that experience was any guide, he had at least one rib that was cracked, if not broken. His knee was swollen and tender to the touch, and a newfound sensitivity to light made him think he'd probably sustained a mild concussion. But he also had a platoon to lead and a war to fight. No way he was getting the dreaded down slip.

The Apache's backseat offered significantly more room, or, in aviation speak, crash space. This meant Kassi had come through the hard landing with a couple bumps and bruises but was otherwise no worse for the wear. That his back-seater would continue to fly wasn't in question. This only doubled Mike's resolve. He and Kassi had been in combat together. He'd be damned if some replacement front-seater was going to steal his warrant officer.

Unfortunately, sticking to the bill of goods he'd sold the flight surgeon was a bit more difficult in front of a roomful of pilots. Clenching his fists, Mike made the short journey with minimal limping before settling into the hard metal chair.

"How you feeling, son?"

"Great, sir," Mike said with a smile. "Ready to get back after it."

"Good," Lieutenant Colonel J. D. Jack said, "because you're about to get the chance. Go ahead, Tim."

"Roger that, sir," the S3 said. "Here's where we stand."

The S3 keyed a button on his remote, and the blank television screen mounted to the far wall of the tent sprang to life displaying a map covered with operational graphics. Mike peered at the imagery and saw what he expected—a road that wound along a mountain valley. Like all new lieutenants, Mike had undergone a cursory review of OPLAN 5150 with the squadron S2, or intelligence officer. 5150 was the peninsula go-to-war plan. The playbook U.S. and South Korean forces would follow to beat back a North Korea attack. The OPLAN revolved around terrain. The Korean peninsula's channelizing mountains and narrow valleys were the key to losing or winning the war.

The channelizing terrain would be a nightmare for the North Korean commanders tasked with moving tanks, artillery, and soldiers from their mountain hide sites to potential breach points along the demilitarized zone, or DMZ. Steep mountains and unpassable foothills meant that the hardball, winding roads offered the only high-speed avenues of approach to the front lines. By the same token, the narrow valleys bounded by steep cliffs offered kill zones perfectly suited to the Apache's tank-slaying weapon of choice—the Hellfire missile.

Unfortunately, the helicopters first had to cross the forward line of own troops, or FLOT, to interdict the armored columns. This necessitated passing over the enemy's static frontline positions riddled with integrated air defense systems primed to shoot down unwary American gunships. There was a reason why the peninsula had never returned to all-out war in the more than half a century since the armistice's signing, despite the North's history of provocations and the South's military exercises. This was because interrupting the current stalemate was the equivalent of kicking over an anthill.

In many ways the staggering number of artillery pieces pointing north and south of the demilitarized zone represented a conventional form of the old nuclear trope known as mutually assured destruction. If South Korea crossed the DMZ, North Korean artillery would lay waste to the city of Seoul. By the same token, if North Korean mechanized columns tried to penetrate south, they would have to run a gauntlet of cavalry pilots anxious to try out the next-generation Hellfire and Spike missiles against the ancient Soviet-era North Korean armor. Up until now, neither side had considered the risk worth the reward.

But as the recent naval battle against KPASOF fast boats had demonstrated, old thinking had a way of changing.

"As of 0100 this morning, the lead echelon forces of four DPRK infantry corps moved out of their staging areas and assumed march formations," the S3 said, scrolling through a series of slides. "Ten minutes ago, they began to move south."

"How long until the lead formations reach their jump-off points?" Lieutenant Colonel Jack said.

With a start, Mike realized what he was seeing. Traditionally, Apaches did not take part in the opening stages of the ground fight. Like their cousins to the north, South Korea hadn't spent the years since the signing of the armistice sitting idly by while the North had prepared to invade. While the South Korean military didn't have the means to protect Seoul from an artillery bombardment, they did have considerable resources emplaced in fortifying positions along the DMZ.

In addition to rocket and tube artillery, South Korea had its own mechanized infantry and armor formations prepared to engage advancing North Korean hordes. The battle along the FLOT would be both bloody and violent, but the entrenched forces had no need of Apache air support. Instead, Apaches would be directed hundreds of kilometers beyond the North Korean front lines to conduct deep attacks against North Korean reinforcements. U.S. military planners believed that the North Korean lead echelon forces were much more likely to break and scatter against stubborn South Korean defenses if their reinforcements died fiery deaths far from the battlefield.

No one really knew whether the strategy would work. Massed formations of armored and mechanized infantry were certainly lucrative targets. Then again, each Apache Guardian cost more than thirty-five million dollars. In the ruthless mathematics known as battlefield calculus, losing a squadron of gunships in exchange for one motorized rifle brigade wasn't a winning formula. This was why deep attacks were known as high-risk, high-payoff operations.

But this wasn't a deep attack.

Instead of interdicting second-echelon reinforcements, the S3 was showing the order of the battle for the first wave of North Korean attackers.

Something wasn't right.

"Excuse me, sir," Mike said, raising his hand, "but aren't those brigades the lead echelon forces?"

"Very good, Lieutenant," Lieutenant Colonel Jack said. "Glad to see at least one of my Charlie Troop officers paid attention during the tabletop exercises."

The squadron commander looked at Captain Tucker as he spoke. Mike had arrived at the tactical assembly area, or TAA, less than thirty minutes ago, but that had been more than enough time to hear the scuttlebutt. Apparently Lieutenant Colonel Jack had been less than thrilled with Tucker's handling of the overwater operation. Rumor had it Mike's boss had come within inches of being relieved of command.

While the news did provide him with a certain amount of satisfaction, Mike also understood the ass-chewing wasn't going to make his life any easier. Mike might be a wet-behind-the-ears lieutenant, but he'd been around the block. Just like in the real world, shit still flowed downhill. Once he and Captain Jackass were alone, Mike knew he'd be the recipient of some negative feedback.

"Anyway," Jack said, turning back to Mike, "what you're seeing is a retasking of our mission. The theater commander has decided that we will not execute the war the way we've practiced. National Command Authority isn't keen on seeing Seoul reduced to a pile of rubble while the two

Koreas slug it out via long-range artillery. This mission is our way of showing our Republic of Korea allies we still have their back, the shit in Seoul and Busan notwithstanding. Rather than wait for the artillery battle to play out, we're going to preempt the whole shooting match."

"How?" Mike said.

"By doing what cavalry officers do," Jack said. "We're going to find, fix, and kill those sons of bitches as they uncoil from their mountain lairs. And we're going to fly into North Korean airspace to do it."

"Holy shit," Mike said, eyeing the map.

Even with artillery fire to soften the North Korean defenses, American casualties would be immense. Not to mention that whoever was flying lead would have their hands full. Hit the FLOT too early and they'd run smack into the friendly artillery fire meant to open up a passage point in North Korean lines. Hit it too late and they'd run into a wall of lead from any North Korean air defense sites that had survived the initial artillery barrage. The operation was a nightmare.

Sometimes it paid to be the junior lieutenant.

"Which troop is flying lead?" Mike said, eyeing the air routes.

"Great question," Jack said with a smile. "Since this is an unorthodox mission, I've decided to go with an unorthodox approach. Or maybe not so unorthodox, depending on how you look at it.

Here's the thing—you're the only one with combat experience on this peninsula, so I'm tapping you as squadron lead. Saddle up, Trooper. We're heading into Indian country."

Son of a bitch.

55

**MUSUDAN-RI MISSILE TEST FACILITY,
NORTH KOREA**

KIRA SIDOROVA WAS IN OVER HER HEAD. WAY OVER
her head.

This was not a feeling to which Kira was accustomed. As a doctor who specialized in treating patients suffering from radiation exposure, Kira was used to running the show. The arbitrator between life and death. A tyrant whose word was law and whose edicts were never questioned. Quite simply, Kira was at the very top of her professional game. She had the long list of publications and the international consult requests to prove it. When Kira spoke, people listened. She was the person in charge.

But not here.

Here she had been reduced to a sniveling slip of a girl, scurrying around in the darkness to do another's bidding while constantly looking over her shoulder.

This was unacceptable. It needed to end.

Today.

The current state of affairs wasn't due to a sudden lack of confidence on Kira's part. No, if anything, the situation she found herself in was a result of overconfidence. The surety that came with living a privileged life in a quasi-dictatorship. Early on in her career, Kira had demonstrated a brilliance that was useful to the Russian regime, and she'd reaped the benefits. She studied abroad, lived well, and conducted herself with the impunity of an untouchable, because when her government asked something of her, she dropped everything to do it.

The assignment to North Korea was a perfect example. The weapon test's spectacular failure was a source of embarrassment to the Russian government, and, more specifically, the former KGB operative who ran the Russian government. Though international intrigue was not her area of expertise, Kira suspected that this was the reason the experimental prototype had been tested in North Korea to begin with.

An earlier version had malfunctioned in a catastrophic manner, resulting in a number of deaths and a nuclear disaster that even the Russian propaganda machine could not contain. It didn't take a genius to put two and two together and deduce that further tests would be accomplished at a locale that would offer the KGB operative much greater deniability. When the troublesome engine failed again in a surprise to no one but the North Korean technicians monitoring its performance and the observers unlucky enough to be caught in the blast radius, Kira had received her expected summons to the hermit kingdom.

Unfortunately, that was the very last thing in this entire cursed trip that had gone as predicted.

Squaring her shoulders, Kira marched up to the pair of soldiers guarding the entrance to the unassuming structure in which she spent an increasingly larger percentage of her time. Surrounded by forest on three sides and an open field to the south, the building could have been a barn or perhaps a farmer's rough dwelling but for the significantly larger structure that loomed on the other side of the tree line one hundred meters to the east.

Oriented along a north/south axis with reinforced, hardball roads emanating from each exit and an armed checkpoint guarding the only avenue of approach, this multistory hangarlike structure offered no pretenses of normality. With wide concrete aprons suitable for the transport tractor-trailers that plied their business at the facility and a massive enclosed workspace, the building's purpose was not difficult to discern. Ballistic missiles were assembled in this building. Weapons of war designed to rain down nuclear destruction on

North Korea's enemies. The structure Kira stood before once housed the sentries tasked with guarding this very important building.

No longer.

"Good morning," Kira said, showing the closest guard the identification clipped to her lanyard.

In yet another indication of the compound's value, the guards posted to this building were well fed. Perhaps too well fed. Kira had taken to giving them mental nicknames. With a nod to his thick jowls and slitted eyes, Kira had christened the man studying her ID as Porky. His comrade had a leaner overall build, but his bowling ball–shaped stomach still flopped over his belt in a gelatinous mass.

Neither man was the epitome of soldierly fitness.

Even so, the guards seemed to take their responsibilities seriously. Though Kira was the only member of the Russian delegation who visited the occupants of this building, Porky still dutifully checked her identification each time. Tonight was no exception. Ignoring her salutation, Porky took her badge with stubby fingers, peering at her picture intently, as if this was the first time she'd made an entrance instead of the twentieth.

Kira bore the scrutiny with patience. She knew that attempting to hurry the man was pointless. Then again, Kira supposed that were she in Porky's position, she might also err on the side of caution. The ruthlessness with which the North Korean regime punished those who had disappointed it made her nation's leader seem like a Girl Scout in comparison.

And now she'd aligned her own fate with such people.

Suppressing a shudder, Kira accepted her badge and waited while Porky punched a combination into the cipher lock mounted to the right of the door. Kira's analytical eye had memorized the series of digits long ago, but she still watched the man's sausage fingers pummel the offending numbers. This wasn't so much to see if the combination had changed, though this fact did interest her. No, Kira watched the unlocking with rapt attention because it gave her an excuse not to look at Porky's partner. Unlike his fat comrade, Lanky's eyes were clearly visible, and Kira had long since grown tired of feeling them slide across her figure.

A contingent of Russian paramilitary operatives were housed at the missile complex alongside the cadre of Russian scientists tasked with determining why the weapon had failed. Though the operatives' presence had puzzled Kira at first, she'd quickly come to understand their purpose. Lanky was hardly alone in his fondness for lecherous glances. Kira had a feeling the North Korean soldiers would have quickly progressed to more, were it not for her hulking, bearded countrymen.

The door clicked open, breaking into her rather

unpleasant thoughts. With a nod toward Porky, Kira strode into the barracks trying to ignore the weight of Lanky's hungry eyes on her backside. If she didn't fix her current mess, the soldier's lecherous gaze would be the least of her worries.

56

THE BARRACKS' INTERIOR MIRRORED THE SPARSE
living conditions one would expect of soldiers.
Especially soldiers dispatched to guard a facility
in the middle of nowhere. A combination common area and kitchen dominated the majority of
the space. As with many Asian cultures, Koreans
eschewed Western-style beds in favor of the more
traditional sleeping style. Accordingly, the floor
was empty, but rows of footlockers and rolled-up
mats were stacked neatly against the wall. To her
left sat a sink with a single faucet and a stove consisting of two burners and no oven.

A hallway disappeared to her right.

Kira turned to follow it.

The hallway ended in two rooms and another
pair of soldiers. Unlike the ones guarding the exterior of the building, these men had the hard look
of those who took fitness seriously. Ropy muscles

bulged beneath nondescript uniforms and prominent tendons stood out from their necks like steel
cables. Automatic weapons hung from their shoulders in easily accessible slings.

The men radiated tightly controlled aggres-
sion like coiled springs, and Kira felt the menace
emanating from that section of hallway like a
frigid draft. These soldiers had a similar feel to
the Spetsnaz or Wagner Group operatives that
guarded her countrymen. While their cold eyes
also fastened on Kira as she approached, there was
nothing sexual in their stare. Instead, she felt as if
she were staring into an empty grave.

Perhaps her own.

Again, Kira greeted the men by holding up her
identification for examination. But unlike Lanky
and Porky, neither soldier moved to take it. Instead,
the one closest to her frisked Kira with impersonal
but efficient motions. Like his gaze, the soldier's
hands traveled across her body without the least
bit of sexual intent, but Kira still had to suppress
a shiver. The soldier gestured for Kira to open her
medical bag, which she did. As per her previous
visits, the man sorted through the collection of
medicines, syringes, and tools of her profession.
His agile fingers were thorough but not intrusive.

Only once this ritual was completed did he nod
to his companion.

The second soldier keyed in a passcode, shielding the digits from Kira's watchful eye. The lock

clicked, and the guard opened the door. As she prepared to pass over the threshold, the guard placed a hand on her chest.

"Phone," he said in accented but understandable Russian.

For a moment Kira stared back in shock. This had never happened before. Then, with fingers she hoped weren't trembling, she handed him the device. The soldier accepted it without comment and then ushered her through. The heavy door closed behind Kira as she stepped into the room, the deadbolt slamming home.

The woman seated in a plain chair in the room's center hardly seemed worthy of the multiple layers of security. She was slightly built even by Korean standards, probably no more than forty-five kilos. Her black hair was pulled back into a short ponytail, and she wore little makeup. Her clothes were also unremarkable, trending more toward function than fashion. A plain blouse, dark, loose-fitting slacks, and sturdy shoes. Taken in sum, the woman was altogether unimpressive.

Until you looked in her eyes.

"Good morning," the woman said in flawless Russian.

The woman's countenance was as blank as her clothing, but her eyes burned with unmistakable intelligence. Intelligence and something else. Cunning. Those brown orbs swallowed Kira, seemingly reaching behind her carefully maintained façade of indifference to discover what churned beneath.

Kira felt her resolve begin to waver.

"How are you feeling?" Kira said, the perfunctory words wooden on her tongue. She moved next to the woman as she spoke, her physician's hands already beginning the process of examining her patient.

"As well as can be expected," the woman answered, her tone still carefully neutral.

"Good," Kira said, fishing a stethoscope from her bag. "Let's take a look."

She held the instrument against the woman's fragile chest, but it wasn't the woman's fluttering heart Kira heard. Instead, she bent her ear close to the Korean's lips even as Kira allowed the device's earbuds to slide from her ear canals.

"Is he coming?" the woman hissed, this time in English.

Kira nodded, sliding the stethoscope to another section of skin.

"Deep breath, please," Kira said, again in Russian.

Her patient complied, sucking in a lungful of air.

Then she spoke.

"Just one more thing. That is all."

Kira shook her head, even as she adjusted the stethoscope again.

The words **one more thing** were what had landed her in this untenable position to begin with.

As a pampered member of Russia's upper class, Kira might be naïve to the ways of the world, but she wasn't an idiot. What had begun as an act of kindness had now morphed into a proverbial millstone tied around Kira's neck. She'd spent much of her sleepless hours plotting a way out of this mess. While her plan might not be foolproof, Kira knew one thing for sure.

She was done doing favors for this woman.

"No," Kira said in whispered English. "I brought what you asked, but I won't do anything more. Something has changed. I can feel it. They took my phone."

"I know," the Korean said. "But you must stay strong. This is almost over."

"I've done all I can," Kira whispered. "Please don't ask for more."

"Then you might as well have never helped to begin with," the woman said. "They will kill me. Tonight. The soldiers might be the ones holding the guns, but your finger is on the trigger. Please."

Kira's hard-won resolve crumpled. Like it or not, the slight woman's life was in her hands. She'd come this far. What was a little more?

"What do you need?" Kira said.

The woman told her.

Kira couldn't say no. She'd become a doctor to save lives, not take them. She'd taken an oath to preserve life, and she wouldn't compromise it now.

Even if that life belonged to a dictator's sister.

57

MUSUDAN-RI MISSILE TEST FACILITY, NORTH KOREA

"TRIDENT MAIN, THIS IS TRIDENT 12," CARY SAID. "WE are in position, over."

"Roger that, Trident 12. Say status, over."

"Status," Jad said.

Fortunately, Cary's spotter made the smartass comment as a whispered aside rather than a radio transmission. Still, Cary felt his fellow commando's pain. His fun meter was good and pegged, and the mission had only just begun.

"Trident 12 has eyes on Zeppelin," Cary said. "We are green across the board. Weather is turning rough, but still holding. Fleetwood Mac is ice. I say again, Fleetwood Mac is ice, over."

"Trident Main copies all. Charlie Mike, Trident 12. Trident Main, out."

"Charlie Mike," Jad said in a whisper. "Continue

mission. Thanks for the encouragement, Trident Main."

"Come on now, brother," Cary said, adjusting his Tango6T optic. "Cut the squids some slack. This is probably the first time those Navy folks have ever talked to real-life war fighters on the radio. Meat-eaters like us make sailors nervous."

"They could have at least given us an Army call sign instead of that Trident SEAL bullshit," Jad said.

"Relax," Cary said. "If a Navy call sign is the only thing we have to complain about once the op is over, I'd say we came up smelling like roses."

"Then I hate to be the bearer of bad news, boss. You smell like pig shit."

Strictly speaking, this wasn't true.

While Cary had no doubt he smelled to high heaven, the excrement in which he was covered did not come from swine. In fact, Cary had his suspicions that nothing four-legged had produced the offal. But he kept these thoughts to himself. His normally Steady Eddie spotter was already un-characteristically frazzled. No need to add wood to the fire by letting Jad know that the rice paddy they'd both parachuted into had probably been fertilized with human rather than animal manure. The Green Berets had inserted via a HAHO, or high-altitude, high-opening jump, and it hadn't been a ton of fun. With the outer edge of a tropical storm only sixty miles away, the winds had been borderline no-go. As a holder of the coveted jump-master badge, Cary had several hundred jumps under his belt, including five in combat.

None of them had been as bad as this one.

After a stomach-churning, harrowing flight, the two Green Berets had touched down.

Right into a fetid rice paddy.

Thanks to his next-generation night-vision goggles, Cary had seen the rice paddy coming in vivid detail, but he'd been powerless to avoid it. The storm's outer band had consisted of giant towers of churning air that rose and fell with reckless abandon. Many a one-hundred-thousand-pound commercial airliner had been tossed about after mistakenly flying through so-called clear air turbulence. A two-hundred-pound man hanging from a silk sheet was the equivalent of tossing a toy sailboat into the swirling water upriver from Niagara Falls. After riding a spiraling column of air skyward at better than five hundred feet per minute before falling toward the earth in a second band of turbulence, Cary had steered his chute toward the first piece of suitable terrain and hoped for the best. As per standard operating procedure, or SOP, Jad had followed Cary into the murky water, undoubtedly cursing in at least three languages as he did. The stench was stomach-churning, and Cary had pointedly ignored the bits of flotsam drifting in the water that his goggles rendered in high-definition detail.

Sometimes ignorance really was bliss.

The wet landing had necessitated a rather soggy slog out of the rice paddy and up the adjacent hill the pair of snipers had designated as their hide site. In keeping with long-practiced techniques that had kept the Green Berets safe over the course of more deployments than Cary could count, they covered the last one hundred meters of the stalk by low-crawling across the ground, towing their drag bags. Now the two commandos were filthy, tired, and sore, and smelled of things too terrible to name. But they were also in a hide site undetected.

For a sniper, things often didn't get much better than that.

"You ready to start mapping target reference points?" Jad said.

"Thought you'd never ask," Cary said, panning his optic across the target building.

As overall mission commanders for the raid, the SEALs had the honor of naming all the operational graphics. The head naval commando apparently had a thing for classic rock. The objective had been named Zeppelin, while the stretch of beach where Jack and his SEAL comrades would come ashore was christened Fleetwood Mac. Unlike Jad, Cary wasn't one to get wrapped around the axle when it came to call signs. What he cared about was clear lines of sight to Zeppelin.

"Okay," Jad said, beginning the process the two men had perfected across half a dozen countries.

"You see the break in the woods on the north side of the building? Distance is seven hundred meters, heading zero eight five."

Cary thought he'd found the open patch of woods Jad was referencing, but this was a time to be certain. Activating the laser range finder clipped to his optic, Cary sent a pulse of light energy at the open ground. A moment later the range materialized on the device's LED display.

Seven hundred meters.

"Got it," Cary said.

"Good," Jad said. "I'm designating that as Alpha One."

Cary annotated the information in his sniper's notebook, which already contained a sketch of the target area.

"Roger that," Cary said as he slid back beneath the rifle. "Ready for the next one."

For the next ten minutes the two men delineated their area of responsibility into landmarks that would be easily recognizable under the stress of combat. Then they turned to the more complex aspect of their job—high-angle shooting. Since their hide site was a good fifteen hundred feet in elevation above the target building, the snipers' look-down angle had to be factored into any ballistic solution in addition to the more traditional elements like wind direction and speed, bullet drop, Coriolis effect, and a score of equally arcane-sounding terms unique to their profession.

This took another ten minutes, after which time Trident Main made another appearance.

"Trident 12, this is Trident Main, over."

"Go for 12," Cary said.

"Roger 12, Trident 6 is five mikes from Fleetwood Mac. I say again, Trident 6 ETA is five mikes, over."

"One two copies all," Cary said. "Zeppelin remains green. Will have eyes on Fleetwood Mac shortly, over."

"Roger that, Trident 12. Charlie Mike. Trident Main out."

"Somebody has got to teach that boy radio protocol," Jad said.

"Quit bellyaching already," Cary said. "The fun's about to begin."

"Where have I heard that before," Jad said. "Ready for me to come off the spotting scope?"

With two kilometers and a set of rolling hills separating their hide site from Fleetwood Mac, there was no way the Green Berets could provide overwatch of the beach with their rifles. This was where the disassembled device Jad was carrying in his drag bag came in. The RQ-11 Raven hand-launched drone had a range of ten kilometers and an endurance of better than ninety minutes. A sensor package mounted in the UAV's nose provided real-time imagery in both visual and infrared spectrums. But that wasn't the best part. What truly set the hand-launched UAV apart from its countless competitors was noise. Or, more accurately, lack thereof. Outfitted with a single pusher propeller, the remotely controlled aircraft didn't make the high-pitched buzzing associated with comparable quadcopter drones.

It was the perfect tool for a pair of sneaky snipers.

Cary played his optic across the target building before answering. It didn't look like much. A rectangular single-story structure with an open field to the south and woods to the west and north. A well-traveled gravel path led to the east, terminating in the much more impressive missile assembly building. Lieutenant Wilson, the naval intelligence officer, believed that the building housed the guard force assigned to the small compound.

That made sense to Cary. Since the really interesting work went on in the missile assembly building, that structure was the focus of most of the observable security measures. Cyclone fences topped with razor wire, roving patrols, manned checkpoints, and plenty of cameras would make that building a hard nut to crack.

Zeppelin, on the other hand, had a much smaller security presence. A pair of guards were visible at the building's entrance, and the two jeeps parked in the gravel to the east suggested more were inside out of sight. Not a cakewalk by any stretch of the imagination, but a world apart from its heavily defended cousin to the east.

His survey complete, Cary was in the process

of giving Jad permission to come off his optic and begin assembling the Raven when the building's door opened, emitting a splash of white light. A small form exited, drawing the attention of the two stationary guards.

Then all hell broke loose.

58

MUSUDAN-RI MISSILE TEST FACILITY, NORTH KOREA

JACK WASN'T SURE HE WOULD EVER DIP A TOE IN THE ocean again. Growing up in the Baltimore area, he'd spent plenty of time seaside. He'd learned to swim at an early age and had even taken up surfing over the last couple years. In fact, Jack had been in the process of booking a trip to Australia and New Zealand before the Campus assignment to South Korea had unexpectedly popped up.

Now the oceangoing part of his life might just be over.

"How you feeling?" Brandon said.

"Great," Jack whispered back, concentrating on the view through his HK MP5's EOTech holographic sight. "Just great."

Jack was kitted up like the SEALs with a plate carrier, helmet, radio, grenades, flash-bangs, and an MP5 as his primary weapon, with a Glock 23 in a drop holster. But as the watery infil had just made abundantly clear, looking like a SEAL and being a SEAL were two very different things.

A barely audible chuckle greeted his response.

"I'm gonna let you in on a little secret—if you ever meet some loudmouth in a bar claiming to be a SEAL, ask him how he feels about the ocean. If he tells you he's more comfortable in the water than on land, punch him in the face. He'd be what we call a fake frogman. After a water infil, there isn't a man among us who isn't itching to get his boots back on solid ground. More than one fully qualified naval commando has lost his shit after riding in a SEAL delivery vehicle. You made it to the beach without shitting your pants. That's a win."

"Thanks," Jack said.

While he was certain that terra firma rather than salt water lay beneath him, Jack couldn't speak to the status of his undergarments. The looming tropical storm had churned up the already rough surf, making his time in the SDV less than pleasant. Exiting the minisub into the open ocean hadn't provided much of a relief, and swimming through the surf break had been downright terrifying. Though Jack wanted to believe he'd helped to fight his way through the swirling current, he suspected that Brandon towed him through most of it.

The frogmen, in comparison, had come ashore seemingly unaffected by the raging ocean. After transiting through the beach's dangerous openness, they were now hidden in a small copse of trees that bordered a series of tiered rice paddies.

"This waiting shit's for the birds," Brandon said, as if reading Jack's thoughts.

What the SEAL didn't say was that Kira was late. Three minutes and fifty-four seconds late, to be exact. And while civilian scientists couldn't be expected to adhere to a timeline with the rigidness of Special Operations operatives, her absence weighed on Jack. He'd been on enough operations to know that missions had a feel to them. An inexplicable but tangible sensation that let an operative know when a clandestine endeavor was going well.

Or not so well.

Other than the Russian scientist's tardiness, Jack had nothing concrete to point toward, but he still couldn't shake the ominous feeling. Like the dark storm clouds gathering overhead, the air felt . . . charged. Like something was about to break bad in a big way.

"Trident 6, this is Trident 12, over."

"Go for Trident 6," Brandon said, his voice barely audible.

"Roger, 6. Sitrep as follows. We've got gunfire at Zeppelin. A single individual exited the building, engaged the guards, and is now heading south across the open field on foot."

"Roger that," Brandon said. "Are you able to identify the squirter?"

"Negative. But based on the build, it could be TINK, over."

"Copy," Brandon said. "Can the drone get a better look?"

"That's affirm once we launch. Things got loud right as we were breaking it out. I wanted two guns up, over."

"Understood," Brandon said. "Launch the drone and see what we've got. Hold fast for now."

"Roger, wilco."

Jack's stomach tightened. Chaos at the Zeppelin was not what they needed right now. And to make matters worse, without the drone airborne, no one was keeping an eye on them. Which meant that if Kira decided to make her appearance . . .

The rumbling of an engine interrupted Jack's train of thought just as a fat raindrop splashed against his face.

When it rains, it pours.

59

"GET THE BIRD IN THE AIR," CARY SAID. "NOW."

"On it, boss," Jad said.

Cary could see his spotter squirming in his peripheral vision, but he didn't have the bandwidth to follow Jad's progress. The view through his optic demanded his full concentration.

Cary had done a hasty zero with the SCAR heavy he was carrying on floating targets from the helipad of the USS **Lake Champlain.** Even so, this was not the same long gun he'd carried on combat deployments the world over. A sniper's rifle was like a painter's favorite brush. While they all functioned the same, hard-to-quantify subtleties made each rifle fire a bit differently. This was especially true for a target at five hundred meters.

"Bird's aloft," Jad said, after hurling the Raven into the air. "Video's active. Zooming in on the squirter."

Like most Green Beret snipers, Cary did not maintain a day and a night rifle. Instead he opted to use a clip-on thermal, which attached to the end of his optic, providing him with the ability to detect and engage targets under low-light conditions. But the sensor did not have the resolution to identify a person. For that, Cary needed the high-fidelity gimbal-mounted sensor package carried under the Raven's nose.

"Can't get a clear image of the runner's face," Jad said, "but I'm pretty sure it's a woman."

Cary panned from the running woman to the six men chasing her. Adrenaline was great but would never replicate conditioning. While she'd covered only about fifty meters, the woman was already slowing, while her pursuers were eating up ground with distance-swallowing strides.

This wasn't going to end well.

Cary had a decision to make. Now. The mission operations order briefing had been clear. TINK was designated as precious cargo and should be treated as such. The rules of engagement allowed for the use of deadly force on her behalf. Even so, the current scenario put Cary into a bit of a gray area. The rules of engagement were predicated on the shooter's ability to positively identify both TINK and any threat she faced. Present conditions made that impossible. In a worst-case scenario, the runner wasn't TINK and the men chasing her were

Russians, not Koreans. If this were true, killing the men could have global ramifications.

Had this been a Triple Nickel operation with Captain Alex Brown at the helm, Cary would have pressed the trigger without a second thought. He'd shed blood with his team leader more than once, and knew the young officer would go to the mat on Cary's behalf if things went sideways. But Reaper 6 wasn't on the other end of the radio. Cary was operating with an unknown commander as part of an unknown team.

Better safe than sorry.

"Trident 6, Trident 12," Cary said, whispering into his mic. "I need a decision. Pronto, over."

"One two, this is 6, stand by."

The SEAL got points for promptness, but this was not a stand-by kind of scenario.

The men were now less than twenty meters from the fleeing woman.

Time to act.

"I need you on your gun," Cary said.

"Thought you'd never ask," Jad said. "What's the play, boss?"

"I'll take the lead runner and work my way back. You take rear and move forward. We'll meet in the middle. Shoot on my mark. Ready?"

"Ready," Jad answered.

His spotter's voice already had the zen-like tone the SoCal surfer adopted while settling into his shooting zone. Cary worked to even his own breathing and bring his pulse under control. Five hundred meters was not an insignificant shot, especially against a running target. But Cary ignored his doubts, focusing instead on the white form jostling in his sights.

"Three, two, one, mark," Cary said.

He pressed the trigger and the rifle slapped him in the shoulder. The can mounted at the end of his barrel did much to suppress the gun's report, but the discharge was still very much audible.

As was Jad's.

But thoughts about operational security would have to wait. The form in his crosshairs stumbled, and Cary immediately sent another round into the splotchy green figure. The uninformed often thought of sniping as a one-shot, one-kill type profession. In a perfect world that was true. But at long distances against moving targets with an untried rifle, hit rates fell off sharply. Cary had once read the after-action review from a pair of Delta Force snipers who decimated an attacking group of jihadis from over one thousand meters. The two men had killed an estimated twenty enemy combatants between them, but the duo had required over fifty shots to get the job done.

Cary felt their pain.

On the bright side, Cary was running a gas-driven SCAR rather than a bolt-action rifle. This meant that as his target fell, he could immediately transition to the next man without the time required to work the rifle's bolt with his left hand. On the not-so-bright side, shooting purists believed that a bolt gun's accuracy was superior to a gas gun's. At the moment, Cary didn't really have an opinion.

He was too busy engaging targets.

Cary dropped another man before the event he'd been dreading occurred. Rather than continuing to chase the still-running woman, the remaining pursuers dropped to the ground, out of sight. Cary panned across the field, looking for another form, even as Jad's rifle coughed a final time.

Then the hilltop fell silent.

"You thinking what I'm thinking?" Jad said.

"That our boys have a sniper-detection system?" Cary said.

"The survivors all proned out at exactly the same time."

Stealth was one of the primary weapons employed by a sniper. A good shooter could fire half a dozen shots from a position of concealment without giving himself away. That quantity increased quite a bit when suppressors and camouflage were properly employed. But engineers had made great strides at rendering these advantages obsolete. U.S. operators carried several sniper-detection systems that used a shot's acoustic signature to determine the range and bearing to the shooter.

If the North Koreans or Russian allies had something similar . . .

"I'm thinking we should—"

A series of deep **thump**s interrupted Cary.

Mortars.

"Incoming," Cary said, slapping his spotter on the back.

Then the hillside erupted.

60

MUSUDAN-RI MISSILE TEST FACILITY, NORTH KOREA

"SIR? WE HAVE A PROBLEM."

"I can hear," Pak said.

The sound of exploding artillery had ceased, but the detonations still echoed in Pak's ear. The soldier standing in his office's doorway looked just as rattled. Rim was a member of Pak's personal guard, hand-plucked from a cadre of Special Operations operatives who'd distinguished themselves during missions in the south. The commando didn't rattle easily, and he didn't mince words.

If Rim said there was a problem, Pak paid attention.

"Come in," Pak said, "and shut the door behind you."

As offices went, the quarters Pak had appropriated in the Musudan-ri complex's missile range

control building weren't the worst he'd ever endured. But they were close. Drab, windowless walls
bounded a scuffed, dingy floor. The Musudan-ri
complex was isolated for a reason, and the scientists and engineers who worked in the desolate facility weren't the sort of people who merited the
finer things the ruling class were accustomed to
in Pyongyang. Like the launch tower and rocket
engine test stand complexes, this facility did have a
single room furnished with more fitting accoutre-
ments in the event the boy-king chose to visit.

But Pak had not appropriated the reception
room for his command post.

More than wall hangings, plush carpeting,
or a comfortable couch, Pak needed something
ethereal—connectivity. He had a war to run and
a coup to manage. These tasks would have been
difficult enough in his traditional office back in
Pyongyang. Pak was relying on the remote outpost's hardened communications architecture,
which had been designed to monitor and control the missile tests to ensure he maintained
uninterrupted comms.

Like most things in the hermit kingdom, the ex-
pansive communications nodes had been imported
from outside entities. Much of the infrastructure
had been based on Russian designs, with key im-
provements courtesy of the Chinese, including
the use of their satellites. From here, Pak could
maintain constant contact with his coconspirator,

General Phyo, not to mention the men he'd sent with the general to ensure the squeamish man's compliance.

Just as important, the Supreme Leader and his sister were under twenty-four-hour guard only a few short kilometers away. While the compound still housed a good many soldiers, technicians, and engineers who had nothing to do with his coup, Pak had guarded his exposed flanks by garrisoning his thirty-man protection detail at the complex as well. So far, the men hadn't been needed, but if Rim's presence was any indication, this was about to change.

"Let's have it," Pak said, eyeing the soldier.

Though Rim's crisp uniform was as spotless as ever, his shaved head glistened with perspiration. The commando was normally cool and collected under pressure. Not a good sign.

"Mesun escaped," Rim said.

Pak's hand froze, the tumbler of soju he'd been seeking forgotten.

"Explain," Pak said.

"She somehow got out of her room," Rim said. "I think she may have drugged the guards, but I'm not certain. In any case, she took one of their weapons and made a run for it."

"Your men didn't catch her?" Pak said.

"She had help," Rim said. "Snipers engaged my men. We fixed their location and responded with counterbattery fire, but Mesun escaped."

Pak eased back from his desk, considering what he'd just learned.

"Did you find the snipers?" Pak said.

Rim shook his head. "My men are still looking for both Mesun and the snipers. So far they haven't found either."

"What about her brother?" Pak said.

He refused to refer to the boy-king as the Supreme Leader.

Not anymore.

"Still in bed," Rim said. "I've tripled the size of his guard. The rest of my men are searching the complex. Mesun may be shrewd, but she's no soldier. I've locked down the entire Musudan-ri compound. No vehicles have come in or out in the last twelve hours. With ocean to the east and inhospitable terrain to the west, north, and south, she has nowhere to go."

Which would be true, were it not for the presence of the mystery snipers. Men who were skilled enough to massacre Rim's soldiers and escape from an artillery barrage unharmed. In Pak's mind, this ruled out DPRK soldiers loyal to Mesun or her brother. Troops of this quality originated from one of two places—South Korea or America.

The implications behind either option were concerning, to say the least.

An electronic beep echoed through the room. Pak glanced at the television monitor hanging from the wall to his left. The DPRK formations of tanks and infantry fighting vehicles were arriving at their lines of departure.

The war would soon begin.

"Lead the search yourself," Pak said. "Canvass every potential hiding site down to the last blade of grass. Nothing is off-limits. We have to find her. I'll ask the Russians for help."

"Understood, sir," Rim said. "I'll find her. You have my word."

Pak acknowledged the man's salute with a nod and reached for his phone.

61

CONTRARY TO WHAT HE'D TOLD RIM, PAK WAS NOT calling the Russian contingent for help. A ruler does not ask for help—he demands it. The power that Pak commanded, in truth his very existence, was all predicated on the thinnest of veneers. The notion that he was totally and unconditionally in charge of the Democratic People's Republic of Korea. Even the tiniest crack in this façade would have dire consequences for Pak's quest for power.

Not to mention his life.

So while Pak did pick up the phone as his bodyguard stepped out the door, it was not the number to the Russian garrison that he dialed.

The phone rang as Pak watched the icons representing the KPA lead echelon forces creep toward their invasion routes. He was so tantalizingly close. In less than fifteen minutes, the frontline traces would come into range of the South Korean and

U.S. forces arrayed on the other side of the DMZ. What happened would be anyone's game. Faced with overwhelming evidence that North Korea intended to wage a conventional peninsula-wide war, Pak was confident that the puppets to the south or their Yankee masters would launch a preemptive strike to defang the armored horde.

Even if they didn't, Pak would still win.

As he'd agreed with General Phyo, the reconnaissance units leading the advance would engage in skirmish fires with the South Korea defenders. This would probably provoke an overwhelming response from the South Koreans, decimating the lead KPA elements. But Pak had planned for this by instructing Phyo to rework his order of battle, placing the newer M2020 tanks safely out of reach. Regardless of which way the conflict ended, Pak would have created the conditions he needed—the peninsula on the brink of war, with trigger-happy soldiers on both sides of the DMZ. Then he'd play peacemaker by negotiating a cease-fire and a return to the armistice borders. He might even offer up the bodies of the Supreme Leader and his troublesome sister as consolation prizes.

But only if the slippery woman was still in his grasp.

Pak's plans mattered for nothing if both the brother and sister were not accounted for. Like a shark smelling blood, the Americans would sense weakness in the form of regime instability. If he couldn't convince the Yankees that the country and its nuclear arsenal were firmly under his control, they might still invade. For that matter, China might do the same thing. When it came to nuclear weapons, no one liked instability.

Pak could not allow this to happen, but he also wasn't naïve enough to think that his coup would go off without a hitch. He'd already involved far more people than he'd intended. Each time his circle of conspirators was forced to expand, the odds of the entire venture tumbling down around him increased. This was why Pak had a final bit of insurance. Something that guaranteed that the Americans and the rest of the world would have to listen when he spoke, regardless of what happened on the DMZ.

"Yes?"

"What is the status of the device?" Pak said.

The man on the other end of the phone was more than just a fellow conspirator. In a country such as this one, it was not uncommon to find someone who'd been wronged at the hands of the Supreme Leader. In fact, it would be unusual **not** to have someone you know suffer at the regime's hands. What was unusual was to have had that suffering mitigated before it could lead to death.

The man was such a person.

Several years ago, the man's wife had contracted a cold before one of the Supreme Leader's scheduled visits to the outpost. She'd then had the grave misfortune to sneeze during his remarks. It was a small sneeze as sneezes went—scarcely audible and well covered.

But it had been a sneeze all the same.

Within minutes of the speech's conclusion, two of the boy-king's bodyguards had seized the woman, dragging her from her husband's car. They'd lined her up against a wall and were in the process of raising their rifles when Pak intervened, asking to complete the task himself. This was also not an unusual request. To gain favor with the psychopath and his family, members of the ruling class often jostled for the honor of dispatching the Supreme Leader's perceived enemies. Assuming this the case, the guards had gladly surrendered the hysterical woman into Pak's care before rushing to rejoin the motorcade. They had no more desire to spend another night in the lonely outpost than did most of its miserable occupants.

Pak had waited for the Supreme Leader's motorcade to vanish in a cloud of dust before handing the woman back to her husband. Even then Pak couldn't have said exactly why he'd intervened. He was not running for office, and he had no outsized streak of benevolence. Even so, something had told him that the scientist would make a better friend than enemy.

And he had.

Now Pak was preparing to test just how far a husband's gratitude stretched.

"Preflight checks on the device are complete," the man said. "The missile is fully operational."

"Excellent," Pak said. "How long before the nuclear warhead is mounted?"

A span of dead air was his answer, but Pak counseled himself to remain patient. The man was a scientist. Scientists thought and spoke deliberately. Silence did not necessarily equate to hesitation.

At least that's what Pak told himself.

"We are ahead of schedule," the man said. "It's hard to be precise, but I estimate fifteen minutes. Perhaps less."

"Excellent work," Pak said, before ending the call.

Gratitude stretched a very long way indeed.

62

INTERNATIONAL AIRSPACE, VICINITY OF MUSUDAN-RI MISSILE TEST FACILITY, NORTH KOREA

AT AN ALTITUDE OF SEVENTY THOUSAND FEET AND AN airspeed of four hundred and seventy-five miles per hour, Air Force Captain Eric "Duke" Fagerland was for all intents and purposes an astronaut. Though FAA regulations stated that astronaut wings could not be awarded unless the aviator achieved a height of fifty miles, Eric begged to differ. Unlike the space tourists in national headlines as of late, Eric wasn't strapped to an ergonomic couch staring out the window as a flight computer handled all the work.

No, he was stuffed into a coffin-sized cockpit wearing a pressure suit originally developed in the fifties. Eric's aircraft had been dubbed the Dragon Lady and designed at the famed Lockheed Martin

Skunk Works by the legendary Clarence "Kelly" Johnson. The reconnaissance plane had been the intelligence community's answer to the burgeoning Soviet ICBM arsenal. Originally envisioned with overflights of the Soviet Union in mind, the U-2 was built to go higher and see farther than any other airplane. It succeeded on both accounts.

Unfortunately, the overflights were a different matter.

In 1960, Gary Powers was shot down during a reconnaissance flight, ending the unacknowledged spy missions over Russian territory. Some thought this incident also spelled the end of the Dragon Lady, especially after her sexier and faster sibling, the SR-71 Blackbird, rolled off the assembly line. And while no aircraft built before or since captured the public's mind quite like the Blackbird, seventy years later the Dragon Lady was still flying, while the SR-71 was collecting mothballs.

But that was the past, something Captain Fagerland had little concern for.

He was too busy dwelling on the present.

"Assassin Main, this is Weasel 1, over," Eric said, after thumbing the radio transmit button located on his stick.

"Weasel 1, this is Assassin Main, go ahead, over."

Though the aircraft Eric was piloting had first rolled off the assembly line before his mother and father had shared their first date, the Dragon Lady had undergone some beautifying in the ensuing decades. To a casual observer, the aircraft's exterior might look the same. It wasn't.

Not even close.

Eric's aircraft boasted a larger fuselage, a greater range, a more capable sensor package, and a completely digital cockpit. The large multipurpose display to Eric's left showed a moving map display overlaid with imagery from the jet's ten-band imaging sensor. It was this display that had caused Eric to break radio silence by bouncing an encrypted transmission off an orbiting satellite. Unlike the flight operations personnel located at Osan Air Force Base in South Korea, Assassin Main was elsewhere. They were the customers for the imagery and ISR data Eric collected and could adjust his mission profile in real time. While Eric had his suspicions, he didn't know for certain who his customers were or where they resided. Along with the weather briefings he received prior to each launch, Eric was handed a list of Priority Intelligence Requirements neatly printed on kneeboard-sized paper. These PIRs served as warning flags. If Eric ever discovered one midflight, he was to reach out to Assassin Main and prepare for a change of mission. In the eight months he'd been stationed at Osan Air Force Base, Eric had yet to encounter a PIR. He'd begun to believe that the entire thing was a bogus ploy just meant to ensure he didn't engage the autopilot and take a nap while the cameras rolled.

But the blur of activity centered on PIR number five suggested otherwise.

"Roger that, Assassin Main," Eric said. "Weasel 1 has activity at PIR number five. I say again, PIR number five. Several vehicles and personnel are clustered around the target building. Awaiting instructions, over."

"Weasel 1, Assassin Main copies all. Stand by."

"Weasel 1, roger," Eric said.

Eric touched the upper-right-hand button on the multipurpose display. A second later the image changed to a narrower field of view. The video and digital feeds from the onboard sensors fed into parallel data buses. This allowed Eric to digitally manipulate what he was seeing without interrupting the data stream or affecting what his customers were receiving. He'd just activated a digital zoom, which employed a series of algorithms to enhance the video feed without ever altering the camera's focus. In the new frame, he could clearly see a long, cylindrical object mounted on a transport truck.

Eric might be an Air Force fighter jock at heart, but that didn't mean he wasn't interested in his collection targets. To the contrary, before each mission set, Eric reviewed the exhaustive target data package prepared by the squadron intelligence officer. Though he wasn't briefed on the classified PIRs, Eric knew a mobile missile system when he saw one. That said, the weapons system wasn't familiar.

Rather than the blocky look of an intercontinental ballistic missile, this was narrower. Sleeker. It more resembled a land-based cruise missile than its bigger brother. The section that normally bore the missile's warhead was empty. But judging by the army of people climbing over the rigging, it wouldn't be for long. The details around PIR 5 might be classified way above Eric's pay grade, but he had the sneaking suspicion that he'd just stumbled onto something big.

Big enough to command the attention of people on the other side of the world.

As if hearing Eric's thoughts, the image on the screen flickered, then vanished. In its place was a sea of white static. For a terrifying second, Eric thought he had done something to the video feed. Then the image resolved, albeit a grainier version. Eric realized the malfunction's cause.

Weather.

Though he was miles above the tropical storm, Eric had seen its hungry, white tentacles reaching for the Korean peninsula during climb-out. In fact, he'd briefed a weather abort plan to land at a contingency airfield in Japan if necessary. The U-2's mission package was one of the most advanced sensor suites ever fielded, but its cameras still couldn't see clearly through precipitation-laden clouds.

His operational window was closing.

"Weasel 1, Assassin Main, change of mission.

Continue collection on PIR five for as long as possible, over."

"This is Weasel 1, wilco."

If the flickering video was any indication, **as long as possible** wouldn't be for very much longer.

63

KIRA TRIGGERED THE JEEP'S WINDSHIELD WIPERS AS
another smattering of raindrops exploded against
the dirty glass. She wasn't sure of the sport utility
vehicle's make, only that it was olive drab green,
reliable, and loud. Of these characteristics, it was
the jeep's reliability that made it Kira's vehicle of
choice for her nocturnal drives.

The first time she'd asked the motor pool sergeant for a car at three o'clock in the morning,
he'd given her a rather strange look. Now, after
several days of following the same pattern, her
insomnia-driven routine was well known. Unlike
the trolls who guarded the Supreme Leader's sister, the kindly old man who checked out vehicle
keys seemed like a good enough fellow. Tonight,
he'd even had a glass of warm tea waiting for her.
With the blustery wind coming ever sharper off
the storm-tossed sea, Kira had been grateful for his

thoughtfulness. But the shivers racking her slim frame weren't from the cold. Kira was scared.

Terrified, actually.

Slowing the jeep, Kira downshifted, taking comfort in the straining engine as it powered through ruts in the gravel road. She'd come to associate the sound with leaving the compound behind as the hardball service road transitioned into a gravel strip that led through the sleeping village to the ocean beyond. Though not anything approaching the beaches to which she'd become accustomed, the promontory offered a constant breeze and a view of the ocean—two things that allowed her to forget her current circumstances, at least for a little while.

Kira glanced at the analog clock mounted in the jeep's cracked vinyl dashboard and stepped on the gas. She was late, something Kira avoided at all costs and could little afford tonight. With the drizzle fast becoming a downpour, Kira's tardiness could easily be chalked up to the steadily worsening weather. But like her shivers, the storm wasn't to blame for Kira's schedule deviation.

This had all seemed so simple when Mesun had spelled out what Kira needed to do in the plain, nononsense manner of someone who was accustomed to being obeyed. And though the slight Korean woman had no power over her, Kira's objections crumbled in the face of Mesun's tireless onslaught.

Unlike many of her contemporaries, Kira had not chosen the profession of medicine for money or the quality of life it all but guaranteed in a nation still teetering on the brink of oblivion. She genuinely believed in the Hippocratic oath and had made it her life's mission to help people. This was where Mesun had Kira over the proverbial barrel. If Kira didn't help Mesun, she would be responsible for the woman's murder.

Kira had originally believed that connecting Mesun with her American friend Isabel would fulfill her obligation. Though Kira was anything but a spy, she was not an idiot. Her former roommate's father had been a Special Operations soldier who'd been killed in battle. Kira had reasoned that if anyone would know how to get in touch with the kind of people who could help Mesun, it would be Isabel. After Mesun had sweetened the pot by describing the danger awaiting Isabel in Seoul, Kira had been only too happy to play conduit between the women.

But that had been just talk. Now Kira had progressed to something infinitely more dangerous. If the Korean woman was to be believed, Americans were coming to Mesun's rescue. Men with guns. This was no longer just talk, and Kira was right in the middle of it.

A bright flash of headlights startled her. A vehicle was approaching from behind at a high rate of speed, judging by the jouncing of the headlights along the rut-filled road. Then the white high beams were joined by flashing red and blue lights.

Guards.

Korean guards were following her.

Kira clenched the steering wheel, her knuckles white. This had never happened before. Not once. Something must have gone wrong.

Kira thought through options even as the headlights drew closer. In the end, she faced a simple choice—fight or flight. Kira was a doctor. A healer. She was no more a fighter than a spy.

She chose flight.

Kira pushed the accelerator to the floor even as she switched the windshield wipers to high. She might be late, but she'd seen enough action movies to know that the men she was about to meet wouldn't be. The rendezvous point was just ahead—a grove of trees around the next bend. Men who infiltrated North Korea under the cover of night in the midst of a howling storm wouldn't go home without accomplishing their mission. They would help her just as they'd promised to save Mesun. It seemed like a good plan. Or perhaps it was the only plan a healer could devise while fleeing for her life. Either way, an unexpected calm settled onto Kira as she steered through the storm. She had a fairly large lead on the trailing truck and a solid course of action. Maybe that would be enough.

It wasn't.

A jagged bolt of lightning split the night sky, igniting a tree just off the road to Kira's left. Kira jerked the wheel to the right in response.

Hard.

She realized her mistake an instant after she made it and corrected back to the left.

She was too late.

The jeep's knobby right front tire dug into the lip of the road. The unexpected collision between rubber and mud wrenched the steering wheel from Kira's hands, sending the vehicle careening off the road. Kira screamed as the top-heavy jeep swayed like a punch-drunk boxer, convinced that the vehicle was going to topple.

Then the rocking stopped.

With a sigh of relief, Kira put the vehicle into reverse and revved the engine. The jeep rocked backward as the RPMs redlined, but it didn't move. Heart pounding, Kira shifted the transmission into drive and again gassed the truck.

The engine strained as the jeep surged forward, but the tires refused to budge.

She was stuck.

64

"STAY FROSTY, EVERYONE. WE'VE GOT COMPANY."

None of his SEAL compatriots acknowledged Brandon's command, so Jack didn't, either. While he was a veteran of countless Campus direct action missions, he felt like a fifth wheel right about now. Jack had been more baggage than useful teammate during the infil portion of the mission. Now that they were ashore and waiting to rendezvous with Kira, Jack was assessing his utility to the entire mission.

While TINK had demanded that he accompany the rescue force, Jack thought her demand was more bargaining chip than ultimatum. After all, a drowning swimmer wasn't in the position to be choosy about life preservers. Though he'd now had more than enough time to recover from the unpleasantness of the SDV ride and subsequent

swim, Jack still felt out of his element. The frogmen were more than capable of executing a hostage rescue without him.

But that wasn't all that was bothering him.

The amount of hand-holding Jack had required
during the infil had been a blow to his confidence.
It was one thing to be the fifth wheel, but something else entirely to be a flat tire. Jack's biggest
fear wasn't that his presence was unnecessary. It
was that he would prove to be a drag on the team.
A distraction that might get someone hurt.

Or killed.

So when the sound of the straining car engine
echoed across the open ground, Jack found himself
breathing a sigh of relief. Though she was late, Kira
was still coming. Jack would have a role to play
even as the SEAL commander tried to make heads
or tails over what was happening at Zeppelin.

Then something unexpected happened.

The jeep careened around the bend in the road
just as a bolt of lightning turned a tree into a
matchstick. The sudden flash of light and deafening explosion caused Jack to jump.

The driver fared even worse.

The front tires spun off the road, dragging the
jeep down the muddy slope toward the waiting
rice paddy. The driver braked, bringing the sliding vehicle to a halt just before the water's edge.
Then the truck reversed, trying to claw its way

back to the road. The transmission strained, but the jeep's underpowered engine couldn't shake the vehicle loose.

It was stuck.

And that was when flashing blue lights heralded another vehicle's arrival.

65

KIRA SLAMMED HER HANDS AGAINST THE STEERING
wheel as red and blue pulses sent shadows writhing
across the jeep's interior. First she'd decided to run,
then she'd gotten stuck. If she'd needed any other
convincing that the shadowy life was not for her,
this was it. She was a doctor. What did she know
about clandestine meetings and covert phone calls?

Kira felt her heart rate decrease as she considered
this line of thought. Nothing. She knew nothing
about being a spy, or conspirator, or whatever it
was Mesun imagined her to be. She should conduct herself as such. She was a Russian doctor out
for her evening drive. A drive compounded by a
freak storm and shoddy roads. She was actually
happy to see the approaching guards.

After all, she had just been about to call for help.

Satisfied with the story, Kira gave her reflection a quick nod in the rearview mirror. She had

nothing to feel guilty about. Her newfound sense of optimism lasted for exactly ten seconds. That was how long it took for Kira to recognize the two men climbing from the vehicle behind her.

Porky and Lanky.

And they were smiling.

66

IT TOOK JACK A MOMENT TO MAKE SENSE OF WHAT HE
was seeing. At first he thought the pair of Koreans
were coming to help the driver. That notion ended
a millisecond later when the scrawnier of the two
wrenched open the driver's-side door. His chubby
partner reached past him, leaning into the cabin.
Jack heard a decidedly feminine scream. Then the
soldier reemerged, dragging a woman by her hair.
The **crack** of flesh striking flesh echoed through
the air as the pudgy man backhanded the woman.

She crumpled.

The pudgy one spun her limp form around,
pushing her flat against the side of her jeep.

His partner loosened his belt.

In an instant, Jack was on his feet, moving forward in a shooter's crouch.

"Hey," Jack screamed.

The fat one turned toward the shout. His

DON BENTLEY

chubby face registered shock for a fraction of a second. Then Jack drilled him twice in the forehead with an aimed pair from his MP5. The submachine gun's integrated suppressor muffled the weapon's report, but the bullets still did their jobs. Jack panned right without breaking stride, centering the EOTech's red holographic dot on the Korean's partner. The chubby man's death had given his skinny sidekick an extra half-second to react. He'd done an admirable job reaching for his pistol. Unfortunately, he'd unbuckled his belt. The weapon wasn't where he expected it to be.

Them's the breaks.

Jack pressed the trigger half a dozen times as he continued forward, walking the rounds from the man's stomach up through his chest cavity, until he put the final shot right between the would-be rapist's eyes. Jack had killed many times. Sometimes he'd been scared, but more often than not, he'd been riding the rush of adrenaline. This was the first time he'd killed in the grip of a mind-numbing rage.

Towering over the fallen soldier, Jack shot him once more in the face.

Jack knew the New Testament said that all sins were equal in the eyes of God. That might be so, but Jack was not God. In his mind, there was a special place in hell for rapists, and he'd just stocked the lake of fire with two more souls. Jack thought his childhood priest, Father Sean Cameron, might just agree with his theology. In addition to teaching math, Father Cameron also coached the school's football team. He'd been no stranger to dealing with sin, be it at the line of scrimmage or in the confessional booth.

A hand gripping his shoulder brought Jack's introspection to an end.

"You good?" Brandon asked.

"Am now," Jack said, letting his tactical sling catch the MP5.

"Great shot placement on the first bad guy," Brandon said. "Second one, not so much."

"I hit exactly where I was aiming," Jack said. Turning away from the SEAL, Jack stretched out his hand toward the still-trembling woman with the same manner he'd often used to calm a skittish horse. "Are you Kira?"

The woman nodded, wiping away tears with the back of her hand.

"I'm Isabel's friend, Jack. Are you okay?"

Jack lightly touched Kira's shoulder. She was trembling uncontrollably. Her auburn hair hung disheveled around her shoulders, and the fair skin over her cheekbone was already swelling from Fatty's backhand. Jack's battle rage flared. It was all he could do not to empty the rest of his magazine into the prone bodies. Instead, he fought to keep the murderous thoughts from his face even as he continued speaking to Kira with a calm, steady tone.

"They can't hurt you," Jack said, staring into her hazel eyes. "You're safe."

"Those **zhopa** might not be able to hurt me," Kira said, her voice remarkably calm, "but I'm far from safe. I'm not ungrateful, but your presence here puts me in considerable danger. I started down this path to save a life. Now my own is in danger."

"Listen to me," Jack said, "you've been incredibly brave to come this far. Help us finish this, and I will make sure nothing happens to you. Do you understand?"

Kira looked back at Jack for a moment, weighing his words.

"No, I don't understand," Kira said. "But I believe you."

"Good," Jack said with a reassuring nod. "Where's Mesun?"

"I'm not sure," Kira said. "She was convinced her captors were going to kill her. Tonight. I gave her drugs to tranquilize the guards before I came here. I promised her that I'd bring you to where she was being held. But I'm not even sure she's still there."

"It's okay," Jack said. "You've already done more than enough. My friends and I will take it from here."

"Hold up a minute," Brandon said, fingers pressed to his radio headset. "We've got a problem."

67

"WHAT KIND OF PROBLEM?" JACK SAID, EYEING THE SEAL commander.

"The mission-changing kind," Brandon said. "Come with me."

Jack left Kira in the hands of the team medic and followed Brandon a couple paces away. The SEAL commander had placed three of his frogmen in security positions and set the remainder to freeing Kira's mired jeep. Though the dead Koreans posed a bit of a wrinkle, the overall plan was still intact.

For now.

"Whadya got?" Jack said, leaning closer to hear the SEAL over the sound of the jeep's straining engine.

"A national asset just picked up activity at Site Tango. The weather's playing hell with his ability to collect, but initial analysis suggests the Koreans are preparing to launch a missile. Maybe one armed with a nuke."

Jack stared at the SEAL, his mind trying to process the magnitude of what Brandon had just said. This was the worst-case scenario. The exact situation that had everyone terrified—a cornered regime choosing to go out with an apocalyptic fireball. Almost anywhere that missile landed would become a humanitarian tragedy, but if the warhead detonated above a population center like Seoul, or Tokyo . . . or New York City, the casualties would be incomprehensible.

"Yep, it's bad," Brandon said, correctly interpreting the look of shock on Jack's face. "Bad enough that the National Command Authority is going to risk an all-out conventional war with North Korea to stop it. A strike package of F-18s is being launched as we speak. ETA forty minutes. They will get the job done, but they're certainly not stealth bombers. There will be no hiding the fact that we struck North Korea first."

National Command Authority was military speak for the political decision-makers, but in a case like this, Jack knew there was only one decision-maker—his father. Closing his eyes, he tried to imagine for a moment the pressure his dad must be under. Do nothing and risk a nuke detonating over Washington, D.C. Destroy the nuke and risk North Korean artillery unleashing a conventional Armageddon on Seoul's 9.8 million civilians.

It was the ultimate no-win scenario.

"What are your orders?" Jack said.

"To take my frogmen over to Site Tango for a little look-see," Brandon said. "It's about six kilometers northeast of here. Weather is about to block the national asset's ability to collect additional ISR. If the situation's as bad as the intel folks think, maybe we can stop the launch. Or at least offer a battle damage assessment after the Hornet strike. If not, we wave off the Hornets and hopefully keep artillery shells from falling on Seoul."

Jack nodded. He understood the SEAL's orders completely.

But he didn't have to like them.

"What about TINK?" Jack said.

Brandon shook his head. "Look, I'm sorry. I know this leaves you in a tough spot, especially after what you just promised Kira. But my orders were explicit—everyone under my command flexes to Site Tango."

The emphasis Brandon put on three of those words was subtle, but Jack heard it all the same. **Under my command.** Jack wasn't under the SEAL's command.

Technically, neither were the two Green Berets.

Jack opened his mouth, intending to explore this topic further, but a transmission across the team net beat him to the punch.

"Any station this net, Trident 12 is Firestone. I say again, Trident 12 is Firestone, over."

Jack and Brandon locked eyes.

Firestone was the duress code word. It meant that an element was pinned down, or in danger of being overrun. Or both.

"I got this," Jack said. "Those guys are here because of me. Go save the world with your frogmen. I'll take care of the rest."

Brandon paused for a moment and then slowly nodded.

"Okay, cowboy," Brandon said. "You're up. I hate to hell to be leaving you like this, but I'm afraid I'll be needing every rifle I have. My guys'll bump to the alternate team channel so our radio transmissions don't overlap. Good luck."

With a couple quick commands, Brandon gathered up his men and commandeered the police vehicle. They pulled away in a choking cloud of exhaust, leaving Jack with a muddied jeep, a terrified Russian scientist, and a pair of dead North Korean guards. Jack wished he could say that the current situation was par for the course when it came to Campus operations, but that just wasn't true. He'd been in some dicey situations before, but when things really went south, it was usually just his own life in danger.

Not anymore.

Three people were counting on him.

Four, if he included TINK.

So this was what command felt like.

Taking a breath, Jack keyed his mic.

"Trident 12, this is Scepter. Copy that you are Firestone. Send sitrep, over."

"Scepter, Trident, our primary position was hit with indirect fire. We are currently moving southwest to an alternate position, over."

Jack pulled up the operational map on the Android device mounted to his plate carrier. The two Green Berets registered as blue dots tracking down the reverse slope of the hillside that had been their primary position. The alternate position was the northern tip of a north/south-running saddle. To gain access to the terrain feature, the Army commandos would have to descend into a west/east-running draw, traverse it, then climb back up the saddle. From his rough math, Jack figured the pair had an elevation change of a couple thousand feet. The Green Berets weren't exactly summiting Mount Everest, but at a dead sprint with a full pack, they weren't on a Sunday stroll, either.

"Copy all," Jack said. "Are you currently in contact?"

"Negative," Cary said, his breathing labored. "But that's probably too good to last. We went to work on the men chasing TINK, but they must have been outfitted with some sort of sniper-detection system. If the indirect fire would have been twenty meters further south, we'd be a bloody spot on the hillside, over."

The North Koreans had the ability to detect snipers and indirect-fire assets at their disposal. Neither of these tidbits had been mentioned in the pre-mission intel brief. Jack wondered what else the intelligence analysts might have missed.

"Roger that, Trident. Be advised that the remainder of the Trident forces have flexed to Site Tango. We have a missile readying for launch. Possibly nuclear. Our mission has now become the secondary objective, over."

"Understood, Scepter. Where does that leave us, over?"

That was a damn good question. Jack looked away from his phone to the aftermath surrounding him. The two would-be rapists lay where they'd fallen in the mud. Kira's vehicle was now free and the doctor leaned against it, pointedly not looking at the dead Koreans. The night had swallowed Brandon and his SEALs, and the falling rain pattered against Jack's wet-weather gear, obscuring any remaining sounds.

The smart play would be to have the Green Berets collapse on his position and call it a day. They could either link up with the SEALs and lend a hand or set up a security position at the exfil point and wait for the evac. At this point, war in one form or another seemed all but assured. With the full contingent of frogmen, linking up with TINK had always been a high-risk proposition.

Now it was trending toward a stupid one.

Then again, Ryans weren't known for taking the easy way out.

"Trident, this is Scepter," Jack said. "It leaves us in between a rock and a hard place. TINK is still the key to stopping this whole shooting match. If she's in the wind, I'd like to try and effect linkup, but not if that means hanging you out to dry. If you think you're compromised, fall back to my location. I'll pick you up and we can go from there. But if you're still operational, I'd like you to set up in your alternate hide and talk me onto TINK, over."

"Scepter, Trident, copy all. We launched a Raven before we were compromised. It's still loitering overhead. Stand by while we take a look-see, over."

"Understood," Jack said. "Standing by."

Jack walked toward Kira's jeep as he waited, his stomach churning.

For the first time, Jack thought he understood how John Clark felt after receiving a telephonic shit bomb. No wonder Mr. C. always seemed to be in such a bad mood. Kira pushed away from the jeep, moving to meet him halfway, but Jack shook his head.

"Hold fast," Jack said. "I'll have this sorted out in a minute."

He prayed that was true.

"Scepter, this is Trident, I have eyes on an enemy platoon-sized force. They're conducting a deliberate clearing operation south of our position and are continuing to move south. Assuming they don't change direction, we should be able to provide coverage for you, over."

Now all Jack had to do was find TINK and stop a second Korean war.

Piece of cake.

"Scepter copies all," Jack said. "Continue to alternate site Eagles. Let me know once you're in place and ready to rock. I'm heading north to find TINK. If you can give me a target talk on via your eye in the sky, I'd appreciate it."

"Roger that, Scepter. One more thing. Now that this is an Army mission, my spotter respectfully requests we ditch this bullshit Trident call sign for the much more appropriate Reaper, over."

Jack shook his head.

Two men he barely knew were humping down one mountainside and up another just minutes ahead of a North Korean platoon set on finding and killing them. They'd just agreed to risk their lives again by providing overwatch for Jack. In return, the two commandos wanted just one thing—their ODA team's radio call sign.

Where do we get such men?

"Roger that, call sign Reaper," Jack said. "Welcome to the team."

"Happy to be here, Scepter. Call once you're headed north and ready for target talk on. Reaper out."

Shaking his head, Jack walked through the rain to the waiting jeep and his next problem.

Kira.

68

"HOW ARE YOU FEELING?" JACK SAID, DUCKING HIS head into the Jeep's cabin.

The drizzle was fast becoming an outright downpour, but Jack hadn't taken refuge inside the vehicle to stay dry. It was much too late for that. No, he was purposely placing himself in closer proximity with Kira for a different reason altogether.

Rapport.

As his spycraft mentor, Mary Pat Foley, had explained on more than one occasion, building rapport was the most critical piece in the handler/ asset relationship. The more you connected with a potential asset on a personal level, the greater the strain the budding relationship would be able to endure.

And Jack was about to dump some serious strain on Kira.

"Overwhelmed," Kira said. "Completely overwhelmed."

The doctor's diction reflected her stress. Though her English was still precise, her Russian accent was thickening.

"I understand," Jack said. "I can't imagine what the last twenty-four hours have been like, but you're through the worst of it. I meant every word I said earlier. I'll keep you safe. But how I do it is up to you."

"What do you mean?" Kira said.

Kira's features constricted as she spoke, bringing the red slap mark across her cheekbone into higher resolution. Jack's heart went out to the woman, but the splotchy bruise might just be a blessing in disguise.

"Things can go one of two ways," Jack said. "You can come with me, but that means defecting. Leaving Russia behind. Do you want to do that?"

"No," Kira said, her eyes again filling with tears, "no, no, no. I love my life and my work. I never wanted to be involved in any of this. That woman took advantage of me. I don't know how to get out of this madness."

"I can help," Jack said, "and you've already done the hard work."

"I don't understand," Kira said.

"Everything you just said is the truth," Jack said. "I want you to stick with that and add in a couple other details. Try this—you drove down here to look at the ocean like you do every night. This time a group of armed men were waiting for you. They tried to force themselves on you. Luckily you were rescued by a patrol of North Koreans. Your rescuers were killed, but you slipped away in the confusion. How's that sound?"

"Fine," Kira said, "except that I have to make heroes out of those monsters."

"You do. But they're dead and you're alive. Your bruise will help sell the story. I'm sorry that it has to be this way, Kira. You're a good woman in a terrible situation. I wish we had more time, but we don't. That offer to come with me is still good, but if you want to keep your life in Russia, this is the way."

For a long moment, Kira just stared at Jack.

Then she slowly nodded.

"Okay," Kira said. "I'll say those words, even if they hurt my heart."

Jack gave her shoulder a reassuring squeeze. "You're a brave person, Kira."

"Thank you," Kira said, her voice husky. "What happens now?"

"I'm going to take your jeep," Jack said. "I'm sorry to leave you stranded, but it's the only way the story works. Give me about a ten-minute head start and then begin walking up the road. Flag down the first patrol you see. Tell them everything."

"What about you?" Kira said.

"I'm a big boy," Jack said with a smile. "Besides, there is no me, remember? Just a crew of ruthless men."

"You are a good man," Kira said, giving him a quick kiss on the cheek. Then she slid past Jack and into the pouring rain.

Jack watched until the downpour swallowed her. Then he put the jeep in gear, pressed on the gas, and turned the wheel until the hood was pointed north.

It was time to finish things.

69

JACK DEBATED WHETHER OR NOT TO ENGAGE THE JEEP'S headlights. His night-vision goggles were great for moving across terrain on foot, but driving with them was an entirely different skill. The lack of depth perception that was an annoyance at a slow walk was life-threatening while attempting to pilot a vehicle over rough terrain at twenty miles per hour. Besides, the pouring rain made visibility a nightmare and the wipers rendered the windshield one big green splotch.

After putting about eight hundred meters between himself and Kira, Jack flipped up his goggles and turned on the headlights. The bright beams lanced through the darkness, revealing a rutted road that was already beginning to fill with water. This storm was serious business. For the first time, Jack wondered whether evac by helicopter was still a viable egress plan. He quickly abandoned the thought. He had more than enough trouble today to be borrowing more from tomorrow. Keying his mic, Jack checked in with his favorite pair of commandos.

"Reaper, this is Specter, over."

"Go . . . for . . . Reaper."

Judging by the huffing between the words, the two Green Berets were still humping toward their alternate hide site. But that was fine. Jack wasn't interested in their vantage point. He wanted to know what the orbiting Raven saw.

"Roger, Reaper. Specter is moving north just south of phase line Albatross. Can you give me a talk on to the high-value target?"

"Affirmative, Specter. Stand by, over."

While Jack had never flown one himself, he understood that many of the newest portable UAVs were basically hands-free devices. Between GPS positioning information and sophisticated autopilot software, a human pilot was for the most part an afterthought. To further reduce an operator's workload, many of the devices had a **follow** feature. This nifty bit of code allowed the pilot to tag a moving target in the sensor's field of view and instruct the aircraft to follow behind it, maintaining a constant slant range and altitude.

This was what he assumed the Green Berets had engaged to keep TINK in sight.

"Specter, this is Reaper, we have eyes on the target. There's a wood line located about two hundred meters west of the road you're currently following. The wood line is the eastern barrier for several fields and is generally oriented on a southwest-to-northeast azimuth. Target is skirting the western edge of this wood line, moving generally southwest toward you. I estimate approximately five hundred meters, direct line distance between you and the target, over."

"Roger that, Reaper," Jack said. "Specter copies all. Stand by."

Jack took his foot off the gas, allowing the vehicle to coast as he consulted the satellite map on his phone. The road on which he was traveling headed due north for another hundred or so meters before coming to a T-intersection. The branch to the right went east for about fifty meters before doglegging back to the northeast. If TINK maintained her current direction and rate of travel, this would be the ideal point to intercept her.

Setting the phone on his lap, Jack accelerated, steering around potholes that were quickly become swimming pools. He pushed the vehicle's speed to the edge of what he could control, knowing that his time was limited and growing shorter with each passing second. Between the F-18 strike package streaking toward them, a platoon-sized patrol of North Koreans searching for the Green Berets, the worsening weather, and whatever was happening over at Site Tango, Jack had more ticking clocks than he could count.

Not to mention the North Korean armored brigades moving toward the DMZ.

A sudden gust of wind slammed into the jeep, rocking the vehicle against its struts. Jack resisted the urge to jerk the wheel in response, the memory of what happened to Kira looming large in his mind. Still, he came a bit closer to a treacherous-looking stump than he would have liked. After several more seconds of slogging through puddles, his probing headlights found the T-intersection. Jack spun the wheel to the right, adding more gas as he powered through the turn. Half a dozen seconds later, the road came to the second intersection. Jack followed the branch leading northeast.

Then he hit the transmit button on his radio.

"Reaper, Specter, where is TINK in relation to my current location, over?" Jack said.

"Specter, Reaper, stand by."

Cary's even breathing suggested that the snipers had finally reached their secondary hide site. Jack was grateful. Blundering around in the darkness and rain with nobody watching his backside stuff was not a recipe for success.

Or a particularly long life.

"Specter, this is Reaper, TINK is less than fifty meters from your location. Almost due west, over."

Jack smiled. His plan had worked, and he was now abeam TINK. Now he just needed to grab her. He thought for a moment. With the UAV overhead to guide him, Jack could try to link up with her on foot, but he quickly discarded that idea. TINK was on the run from men who'd tried to kill her. Chances were that she wasn't in a trusting mood. While Jack was confident that he could catch her on foot eventually, the pursuit would take time.

Time that he didn't have.

She needed to come to him.

"Reaper, this is Specter," Jack said. "I'm going to try something. Give me real-time updates on TINK's movements until I say otherwise, over."

"Specter, roger. She's currently moving southwest, headed away from you. Distance is just over fifty meters and increasing, over."

Jack turned the wheel to the left and added gas, angling the hood until the headlights lit up the wood line where he believed TINK was hiding.

Then he activated the high beams.

"Specter, this is Reaper, the target is moving away from your position almost due west. Her rate of travel is increasing, over."

That hadn't worked. TINK must have thought the headlights belonged to the men hunting her. Jack needed to convince her otherwise and fast. Throwing caution to the wind, Jack laid on the horn. He let the blast echo for a good second or two before letting up. Then he repeated the process.

"Specter, Reaper, TINK is turning toward you. I say again, TINK is turning toward you. Now heading in your direction. Distance fifty meters and closing, over."

A moment later, a sopping-wet form popped out of the wood line.

Jack killed the headlights and hopped out of the car.

"Mesun?" Jack said.

"Yes?"

"It's Jack. Would you like a ride?"

"That would be lovely."

70

JACK'S YEARS WITH THE CAMPUS HAD TAKEN HIM TO many exotic places and landed him in the company of just as many unique people. While he'd never stopped to rank these experiences, sharing a jeep's cabin with the rain-soaked sister of the dictator of North Korea was probably near the top.

"Are you hurt?" Jack said.

The woman shook her head. "Just cold. Though I believe that is probably thanks to you?"

Jack turned on the jeep's heater even as he ignored the woman's question. Success in this crazy venture was far from assured. In the event that they were captured or, worse, the woman was playing him, Jack wanted to impart as little information to her as possible. Instead, he responded to her question with one of his own.

"Do you have the cipher?"

"No."

Jack felt the bottom drop out of his stomach.

"Why not?" Jack said.

"The man attempting to overthrow my family is named Pak. He's a powerful member of the Politburo, and his plans are coming to fruition. Tonight. That makes me a liability. I saw an opportunity to escape, and I took it."

"Without the ciphers?"

Mesun nodded.

"Then how do we stop this war?" Jack said.

"We don't," the woman said. "I do. Pak is controlling everything from the range control building located on the northernmost point of the complex. He will hold the final VTC with the generals there. I don't know how he will get around me not being present, but he'll find a way. Perhaps he has a co-conspirator with enough political leverage to sway the generals. That's not important. Getting me to the radio in that building is all that matters. With it, I can talk directly to the military leadership. Once they realize it is Pak, not me or my brother, who's ordered the invasion, the coup will fail and the preparations for war will cease. Simple."

It certainly seemed simple coming from Mesun, but in Jack's experience, nothing was ever as easy as it sounded.

"What about the activity by the rocket engine test stand?" Jack said.

"What activity?"

"Our surveillance assets show what looks like a missile being readied for launch. A missile with a nuclear warhead."

"Do you have a picture?" Mesun said.

Jack hesitated, his tired brain trying to sort through the security ramifications of showing the dictator's sibling imagery from a classified collection asset. Then he mentally shrugged. What the hell—in for a penny, in for a pound. Scrolling through the phone's encrypted storage, he found the image he wanted and enlarged it.

"Here," Jack said.

Mesun took the phone, her wet fingers leaving smudges on the glass. She zoomed in on several aspects of the missile and then the warhead itself. "Of course," Mesun said, handing the device back to Jack.

"You recognize it?" Jack said.

"It's why we are in this mess to begin with," Mesun said. "That is the prototype Russian weapon fitted to an operational launcher. A nuclear-powered cruise missile with no range limitations. A stealth weapon that can skim wavetops and trees, meandering in and out of radar coverage to strike anywhere on the globe. And it's being fitted with a nuclear warhead."

Jack's gut clenched.

"I thought the prototype exploded?"

"It did," Mesun said. "There were two. That

was the price my brother demanded from the Russians—one missile for them. One for us."

"But the Russian missile didn't work," Jack said.

Mesun shrugged. "Depends what you mean by **work.** The missile's nuclear engine worked just fine. A little too well. Thrust was much higher than expected. So was the resulting radiation pollution. The catastrophic failure occurred when the technicians attempted to throttle the engine back. The reactor ruptured."

"The missile's capable of flight?" Jack said, still dumbfounded.

Mesun looked at him like he was a particularly dim-witted child. "Have you not been listening? The weapon flies magnificently if you discount the radioactive jet stream spewing behind it. If Pak launches that missile, he'll have the equivalent of a loaded gun pointed at the head of every nation on earth. The missile could literally fly circles around an obscure portion of ocean or desert for years, waiting for final targeting instructions. Or, better yet, it could be configured with a dead man's switch."

"What do you mean?" Jack said.

"A default setting to fly to a certain city and detonate unless the missile receives instructions to the contrary. With that kind of leverage, no one will dare to interfere with Pak's peninsular campaign."

"The sword of Damocles," Jack said, finally understanding.

"Precisely," Mesun said. "The men mating the warhead to the rocket are undoubtedly Pak loyalists. Pak is the key to everything. He must die."

For the first time since he'd met Mesun, Jack found himself in wholehearted agreement with the dictator's sister. Unfortunately, killing Pak was a little easier said than done.

Like just about everything else to do with this operation.

"I'm not an assassin," Jack said. "Our agreement was to provide you with a means to talk to your generals, not eliminate your political enemies."

"Silly boy," Mesun said, the confidence that infused her voice during earlier conversations returning. "I am more than capable of dealing with my own political enemies. Pak is the key to everything. He is two kilometers away in the range control facility. Help me take control of the radio in that building. I'll do the rest."

Jack stared across the dim interior, considering.

It was a reasonable-enough-sounding plan.

The worst ones always were.

71

PAK HATED RUSSIANS.

Every last one of them.

To a person, Pak found Russians to be arrogant, patronizing, and generally unpleasant people, but none more so than the man currently standing in front of him.

"Would you like to explain why your men are using the far ridgeline for mortar practice?" the man said.

Pak did not want to explain anything to the condescending Cossack, but that was beside the point. Pak hated Russians for a good many reasons, but his country could not survive without them. This was doubly true of his current visitor.

"There was a security incident," Pak said. "My men are dealing with it."

"That's an interesting way of phrasing the

problem," the Russian said, scratching his bushy beard. "Perhaps you would care to elaborate."

The man's facial hair nearly consumed his face. An unchecked reddish-brown thicket covering his lips, chin, and lower neck. Snarled clumps of hair reached past his cheekbones to join with equally shaggy sideburns. His unkept hair made his beady eyes all the more prominent.

Like most North Koreans, Pak found even the idea of a mustache distasteful.

The Russian was downright revolting.

But Pak could not give voice to his thoughts for a number of reasons, chief of those being his survival. The Russian who went by the name of Misha, or Bear, was the head of the contingent of irregular troops garrisoned at what Pak and his men had come to refer to as the Russian Compound. The collection of buildings that normally housed technicians and scientists during a missile test event had been repurposed for the Russian doctors and engineers. Doctors to treat the patients sickened by the unexpected radiation exposure resulting from the previous Skyfall's failure. Engineers Pak had demanded to work on the project as the price for his silence.

After a terse back-and-forth, Moscow had agreed to Pak's terms. The Russians would send the requested personnel, and all would be forgiven. Except that when the doctors and engineers had arrived, Bear and his twenty armed men had come with them. Bear claimed to be employed by the Wagner Group, the Russian equivalent to the American mercenary company formerly known as Blackwater. To Pak, this was a distinction without a difference. In the same spirit in which there was no such thing as a former Russian intelligence operative, Pak knew that the boundary between Russian Spetsnaz and the Wagner Group was so nebulous as to be nonexistent. Bear might not be dressed in an Army uniform, but he was an extension of Moscow all the same.

And right now, Moscow seemed to be less than pleased.

Pak considered lying to the Russian, but didn't. The Wagner operatives had brought with them an impressive number of hardened plastic cases, which Pak assumed were not scientific instruments. Shortly after the group's arrival, Pak's men had reported a startling number of security upgrades to the Russian Compound, including a tethered blimp outfitted with a sophisticated array of gyro-stabilized cameras. If the resolution on those devices was even half what Pak suspected, Bear probably already had a good idea what transpired on the hillside. Lying to him would accomplish nothing and could tilt the relationship's balance even further toward the Russian.

Pak would have to tell the truth.

Or at least some version of it.

"We have intruders in the compound," Pak said, choosing his words carefully. "A roving patrol was fired upon. Fortunately, they were equipped with a Chinese countersniper system that provided a range and bearing to the attackers. The patrol leader requested indirect fire support, which our mortars supplied. After the rounds impacted, the attack promptly ceased."

"Interesting," Bear said, his eyes narrowing. "Who attacked the patrol and why?"

Pak shrugged. "That is still to be determined. Saboteurs from the South are always a risk."

"Undoubtedly," Bear said, "but I find it extremely interesting that saboteurs chose tonight of all nights to conduct their attack. Tell me, what were the guards doing when they were ambushed?"

"Nothing out of the ordinary. Just a standard patrol."

Bear stared at Pak in silence, his beady eyes glittering.

Pak met the Russian's gaze with a stone-faced look of his own. Like all prominent members of the Workers' Party of Korea, Pak had learned how to mask his feelings long ago. To do otherwise was not conducive to a long Party career.

Or life, for that matter.

"Have you captured the perpetrators or discovered their remains?"

"Not yet," Pak said. "But my best man is leading the effort. He's conducting a methodical cordon and search now. We will find them."

"Excellent," Bear said. "Then I'm sure your men won't mind if we assist."

"Assist?" Pak said. "Why?"

This time he didn't need to fake his confusion.

"One of my doctors has gone missing. And not just any doctor. She's been the personal consulting physician to your Supreme Leader and his sister."

"Missing how?" Pak said.

"Just what I said," Bear said. "The doctor has chronic insomnia—a trait apparently shared by her patient. She often goes to check on the sister before driving down to the seaside. The motor pool log shows that the doctor left thirty minutes ago. She hasn't returned. I'm now wondering if her disappearance could be somehow related to the attack on your patrol."

"I don't see how," Pak said.

"Nor do I. Which is why I'm leading eight men to look for her. Please provide me with the call sign and frequency of the man in charge of your search effort. The night is already foul. I'd hate for the inclement weather to result in any more unforeseen firefights."

"Of course, of course," Pak said, "but my patrol leader doesn't speak Russian. I'll send a liaison officer."

"Very thoughtful, but totally unnecessary," Bear said. "We can deconflict our efforts using terrain features."

"Oh, but I insist," Pak said. "As you said, I'd hate for there to be any friendly-fire incidents."

The Russian stared back and Pak could see the man doing the math in his mind. Undoubtedly the Russian contingent was both well trained and well equipped, but they were also only sixteen men. Close to ten times that amount of North Korean troops were garrisoned at the missile test facility. Bear might be able to throw his weight around, but when push came to shove, he still commanded a numerically inferior force at a remote outpost.

"Of course," Bear said, apparently arriving at the same conclusion. "We'll be leaving from our compound shortly."

"My man will ride back with you," Pak said with a smile.

"Excellent," Bear said. "Thank you for the help."

The Russian made to leave, but paused as he reached Pak's door.

"Oh," Bear said, turning back to Pak, "one last thing—is there any way I could speak with the sister? Since she was the last one to see my doctor, I was thinking she might offer insight as to the doctor's state of mind."

"State of mind?" Pak said.

"Yes. The storm was already raging when the

doctor went on her drive. I'm wondering why she would have braved such a tempest."

"Unfortunately, Mesun's personal physician administered her a sedative, and she's currently sleeping. But I'm sure your doctor will turn up."

"I'm sure she will," Bear said.

His flat eyes seemed to harden and then he strode out the door.

Pak waited for the sound of the Russian's footsteps to recede before he let out the string of curses he'd been holding in.

He hated Russians.

Every last one of them.

Snatching the radio handset from his desk, Pak pushed the transmit button.

Rim would be thrilled at the news.

He liked Russians even less than Pak did.

72

"TRIDENT 12, THIS IS TRIDENT 6, OVER."

"Do we tell him we've changed call signs, or nah?" Jad said.

"Let's do the man a favor and answer," Cary said. "SEALs are easily confused."

"Fair point," Jad said.

"Trident 6, this is 12, go ahead, over," Cary said.

Cary wiped the moisture away from his face and pressed his eye back to his rifle's optic as he waited for Trident 6's response. He and Jad had reached their secondary observation post only moments ago, and he was still trying to get situated. As per standard operating procedure, the two had deployed a camouflage netting hide site and wormed their way inside. The netting didn't offer anything in the way of warmth or protection from the persistent rain, but it did help the Green Berets hide from enemy snipers equipped with thermal imagers or light-intensifying devices. Remaining undetected and therefore alive was much more important than being warm or dry.

At least that's what Cary kept telling himself.

"One two, this is 6, we're situated just west of Site Tango. Could you send your eye in the sky this way? It'd be nice to have a little look-see before we get any closer, over."

"What do you think?" Cary said, turning to Jad.

His spotter shrugged, even as he continued panning his optic across his assigned sector. "I think we're running out of time. Jack might have linked up with the sister, but the frogmen have the most pressing mission. Give them the bird."

That Jad didn't even chuckle at the obvious joke spoke volumes about the commando's level of concern. Once again Cary felt the absence of Captain Alex Brown and the rest of Triple Nickel in an almost physical way. Though Cary believed he and Jad had avoided the patrol by evading north instead of south, Cary knew their situation was precarious. Cary was accustomed to being outmanned, since Green Berets operated in twelve-man elements far from friendly lines. But he wasn't usually also outgunned. Army Special Forces normally had access to a portfolio of so-called combat multipliers. These platforms and weapons systems ran the gamut from close air support in the form of AC-130 Spectre gunships to specialized indirect fire systems capable of placing

120-millimeter high-explosive rounds on multiple targets simultaneously.

But not this time.

This time Cary and his faithful spotter were alone and unafraid, hiding from a company's worth of angry North Koreans. What he wouldn't give for an orbiting B-52 loaded with multiple two-thousand-pound GPS-guided JDAM bombs right about now.

"Trident 6, this is 12," Cary said. "Affirm on the bird. She's got about fifteen minutes of loiter time left, but she's all yours. I'll pass you control, over."

"One two, 6, roger all. Standing by for drone handover."

Jad, who had been monitoring the conversation, unfolded the Android device attached to his plate carrier. He pressed his gloved finger against the touchscreen and then nodded to Cary.

"It's done."

"Trident 6, this is 12, handover complete. Confirm you have control."

"One two, 6, confirming control of the drone. Thanks, boys. Trident 6, out."

"So now we're just drone operators?" Jad said. "I'm starting to get bored."

"Reaper, this is Scepter, over."

"Now you've done it," Cary said, before triggering the transmit button. "Scepter, this is Reaper, go ahead, over."

"Roger, Reaper. I've linked up with TINK. She's soaking wet, but no worse for the wear. Thanks for the assist."

"Great news, Scepter," Cary said. "Are we exfiling?"

"Not quite. What's your current status, over?"

"Uh-oh," Jad said.

"Watch your sector while Mom and Dad talk," Cary said, but he had a feeling his spotter was right.

"Scepter, this is Reaper," Cary said. "We are set in our alternate observation post. We have line of sight on Zeppelin, but we do not have eyes on you. The platoon-sized element hunting us still seems to be moving southwest, away from our present location. We are green right now, but they are blocking access to the primary exfil spot, over."

Cary didn't bother pointing out that if the North Korean search team changed directions, he and Jad would be in a world of hurt. Nor did he remind Jack that the worsening storm spelled trouble for their plan to exfil by helicopter. This wasn't to say that these stressors didn't loom large in Cary's mind.

They did.

But at the moment, there was nothing he could do about any of them. When Cary was a baby Green Beret newly arrived to his first ODA, his team sergeant had cautioned him to never borrow trouble. Even if you didn't see it, there was always more than enough to go around.

This operation was proving to be no exception.

"Scepter copies all. Does your current position offer line of sight to Eagles, over?"

"Here we go," Jad said, shifting in the shallow depression that was quickly becoming a mud puddle. "Change-of-mission time."

"Weren't you just saying you were bored?" Cary said. "Quit whining and remind me where Eagles is."

"Getting old is a bitch, isn't it, boss?" Jad said. "In addition to being the best band ever to come out of California, Eagles is the range control building complex. Oh, look at that—Eagles also just happens to be across the valley from our current position at a range of six hundred meters. It's almost like your spotter knew what the hell he was doing when he picked the observation posts."

"Nobody likes a braggart," Cary said. "Besides, if I had a spotter who was worth a damn, he would have found us somewhere dry. I might drown if we stay here too much longer."

"Now who's whining?" Jad said. "Besides, this isn't rain. It's liquid sunshine."

Cary smiled in spite of himself. Most of a special operator's life was some variant of this—lying in the dark shivering, with a muddy hole for shelter. **Embrace the suck** was the mantra most often repeated to new Green Berets by the grizzled veterans, but in Cary's mind that was only part of the solution. Teammates who became brothers were the other half of the equation. There was no one Cary would rather embrace the suck with than Jad Mustafa.

"Scepter, this is Reaper," Cary said. "We have eyes on the red side of Eagles, but there's a ridgeline between us and the green side. We can reposition for better angle, but it will take us to the exfil window if we do, over."

"Roger that, Reaper. Can you put eyes on the green side with the UAV, over?"

"And the hits just keep on coming," Jad said.

"Scepter, that's a negative," Cary said. "We had to pass control of the bird to Trident 6. Can you give us a sitrep? Maybe there's a way we can still help, over."

"Aren't you just the kinder, gentler team sergeant," Jad said.

"Come on, now," Cary said, orienting his rifle toward Eagles. "This guy's some kind of paramilitary spook. He's tough as nails, but he's not an ODA team leader. We've got to remember that."

"Point taken," Jad said. "But I still think you're getting soft in your old age."

Cary had to admit that he was growing older, but he took issue with the idea of his muscular frame growing soft. He was preparing to point out this very important distinction to his still-wet-behind-the-ears spotter when the radio crackled.

"This is Scepter, roger. Sorry about that. Things are moving fast, and I keep forgetting you two aren't in the car with me. Here's the scoop—Eagles houses two things we need: the communications system TINK requires to make contact with the Central Military Commission to call off the invasion of South Korea and a Politburo member named Pak. Pak is the mastermind behind the coup. We take him off the table and the whole thing falls apart."

"With you so far," Cary said. "How do we do that?"

"Two schools of thought on this one, Reaper. Pak's inner circle of loyalists are providing security around the building. He keeps his personal guard segregated from the rest of the missile testing facility personnel. Course of action one is that I pose as one of the Russians and bluff my way into the building with TINK in tow. Once inside, I eliminate Pak and TINK makes the radio call to the generals, over."

"Is he for real?" Jad said. "That sounds like some bullshit the SEALs would think up."

"Uh, roger, Scepter," Cary said. "That seems a bit loose to us. What's the second course of action, over?"

"Second thought is to make Pak vacate the building and come to us. That one's a bit trickier without getting eyes on the site, over."

"By trickier, I'm assuming he means even less well planned than the first harebrained scheme,"

Jad said. "No wonder that dude got himself nailed to a cross."

"Roger, Scepter," Cary said, "wait one." After releasing the transmit button, Cary turned to his spotter.

"Okay, stud," Cary said, "how we gonna do this?"

Jad sighed. "Of his two ideas, I like the second better. We have pretty good lines of sight to the red side of the building. Looks like that's the main entrance. The checkpoint leading to the building forms a natural barrier. If we can funnel dudes into that kill box, it will be like shooting fish in a barrel. But I'm not sure how we get them out of the building."

"Do we ask Trident 6 for the UAV?" Cary said. "I agree with Jack that a look at the entire complex might shake loose some ideas."

"No, the SEALs need the bird more than we do," Jad said. "What I wouldn't give for another pair of eyes."

Jad paused for a moment, thinking. Then a smile slid across his face.

"Hey, now," Jad said, "I might just have an answer to our problem."

Jad abandoned his spotting scope in favor of digging through the rucksack lying beside him.

"What?" Cary said. "You got another UAV stashed in there?"

"Not a UAV per se," Jad said. "More of a loitering munition."

Jad withdrew a pair of tubes from his pack and placed them on the ground. Both cylinders were olive drab in color, but one was a bit thicker and sported a red band that circled the base.

"These are made by AeroVironment," Jad said, as he unfolded the bipod legs from each cylinder, propping them at forty-five-degree angles. "They're called Switchblades. Basically a flying bomb with collapsible wings, a pusher propeller in the back, and a kickass camera in the front. Their loiter time is only about fifteen minutes, but it's better than nothing."

"What's the difference between the two tubes?" Cary said.

"Both munitions are designed for precision strikes with very low collateral damage. Think of them as big shotgun shells rather than small bombs. This one's got the bigger warhead," Jad said, pointing to the thicker tube with the red band. "It's a prototype rigged just for the SEALs. I grabbed them both."

"My man," Cary said, "pop one into the sky."

"Which?" Jad said.

"Bigger is always better," Cary said.

"I knew you'd say that."

Jad opened the Android device on his chest, punched a couple buttons, and then turned to Cary.

"Okay, I've got the ground control system synced

with my ATAK situational-awareness system. We're ready to go."

"Hit it," Cary said.

Jad depressed the firing trigger and the tiny munition shot skyward in a puff of smoke. For a second Cary heard the high-pitched whine of its tiny propeller.

Then the device vanished into the night sky.

"That was easy enough," Cary said.

"I told you," Jad said, keying in waypoints on his Android. "They had to make it SEAL-proof."

"Okay, brother," Cary said, "clock's ticking. Let's do a high recon of the target area and then give our favorite spook a call. Time to put a bow on this operation."

"Already?" Jad said. "I was just getting used to the smell."

The sad part was that Cary was, too.

73

UNDISCLOSED LOCATION, SOUTH KOREA

"READY UP THERE, SIR?"

Lieutenant Mike Reese looked up from the collection of maps spread across his knees to meet his back-seater's gaze. Once again Kassi was looking at him via the mirror hanging from the top of Mike's canopy.

This time she was smiling.

"Maybe you need a better preflight monologue, Miss Shaw," Mike said.

"Come on, sir," Kassi said. "Combat is terrifying. You've got to find humor where you can. Besides, last time I said that we shot up a North Korean SOF boat, ditched our gunship in the East Sea, and lived to talk about it. That's a pretty good day for cavalry pilots."

"Then I don't want to see a bad one," Mike said.

"Plenty of those, too," Kassi said. "I know you're

thinking about the guys we lost today. That's normal. But you've got to put it out of your mind for now. You've got a platoon to lead, sir."

Once again Mike's back-seater was taking care of him.

"Routes are loaded and verified," Mike said. "Weapons check's complete. Sensors are bore-sighted. Good to hook up here. Commo check in two mikes."

"Roger that," Kassi said. "Radios are configured, and the encryption fills all loaded. Ready for engine start."

"How 'bout that," Mike said, verifying that the Hellfire missiles showed the correct laser codes. "We're ready early."

"It's like you know what you're doing or something," Kassi said. "Hey, sir, on that note, flying lead for the entire squadron is a big ask. Remember—your most important responsibility is hitting our time on target. When you start getting task-saturated, feel free to offload radio calls to me—even if it's Blackjack 6 who's calling. If we don't hit the FLOT at our crossing time plus or minus thirty seconds, we're going to be in a world of hurt."

"Tracking," Mike said. "I appreciate the help, Kassi."

His nonchalant answer to the contrary, Mike felt the pressure of what he was about to attempt constrict his chest in a way that even getting shot at hadn't. He was in charge of leading twenty Apaches on an hour-long cross-country flight at the end of which he had to pass over a random piece of terrain at an exact time with only thirty seconds' margin of error.

Too early and he'd fly into friendly artillery or maybe get shot down by North Korean gunners.

Too late and he'd definitely get shot down by North Korean gunners.

It was a tall order, but not undoable. In another variation from traditional deep attack doctrine, the Apache squadron was doglegging to the west for a considerable distance before turning back north to cross the FLOT. The thinking from the Tactical Operations, or TACOPs, folks charged with planning the ingress routes was that since the actual shooting war had yet to break out, subterfuge was the name of the game.

This meant that rather than crossing the FLOT with the shortest route possible in order to reserve more precious fuel for hunting and killing North Korean armored formations, the Apaches would try some sleight of hand. The suppression of enemy air defenses, or SEAD, artillery fire would be concentrated on an area the North Koreans wouldn't expect. In theory, the stretch of land should be populated by fewer air defense systems, which the friendly missile and long-range cannon fire would pummel before Mike and his troopers roared overhead.

In theory.

But either way, the feint to the west would provide Mike with better than forty minutes to adjust his airspeed and ground speed in order to hit his assigned time on target. The operation would still be stressful, but not anywhere near the level of anxiety of a straight ingress in which he had less than fifteen minutes to hit his FLOT crossing time.

"Blackjack 6, this is Sabre 6, over."

Mike's eyes snapped to the radio. Sabre 6 was Lieutenant Colonel Jack's call sign. The boss calling Mike's boss two minutes before the commo check could mean only one thing—change of mission.

"Sabre 6, this is Blackjack 6, go ahead, over."

"Roger, Blackjack 6, we've just received a change of mission. Lead elements of the North Korean advanced guard main body are moving toward Kill Box Alpha time now. We need to flex to ingress route Iceberg and depart in sixty seconds. How copy, over?"

"Shit fire," Mike said. "Switching active route to Iceberg."

"Roger that, sir," Kassi said, her earlier humor gone. "Cranking engine number one."

The deep bass of the General Electric T700 turboshaft engine filled the cabin as the Apache's rotor blades began to turn. With a start, Mike realized that the six other birds in his flight might not have been monitoring the squadron command net and wouldn't know about the change of mission.

Technically, it was Blackjack 6's job to order a troop change of mission, but Mike decided to take the initiative. After all, better another ass-chewing from Captain Tucker after the mission than miss the timeline because his aircraft weren't ready.

"Blackjack elements, Blackjack 16," Mike said, transmitting on the troop internal frequency, "ingress route has changed to Iceberg. REDCON 1 in sixty seconds, over."

A chorus of **roger**s filled the airwaves, but Mike didn't reply. Blackjack 6 and Sabre 6 were once again talking on the squadron net, and he'd missed the beginning of the conversation.

"Cover troop internal, Kassi," Mike said, even as he turned down the radio tuned to the troop frequency so he could better hear the squadron net.

It was a good thing he had.

"Blackjack 6, this is Sabre 6, are you saying that you are unable to execute your bump plan, over?"

"Sabre 6, Blackjack 6, negative, sir. I just need a bit more time to switch birds, over."

"Blackjack 6, by definition a bump plan means that you are able to still execute on the squadron's timeline, over."

Mike swallowed.

Sabre 6 was dragging Captain Tucker across the coals by having this conversation on the squadron net, where anyone and everyone could listen. Like any complex machine, Apache helicopters could be fickle. With this in mind, the troop commander and platoon leaders generally briefed a bump plan prior to each mission. That way, if their helicopter developed a maintenance problem prior to take-off, they could jump in the front seat of another helicopter, "bumping" the original copilot in the process. For the life of him, Mike couldn't figure out why it would take Blackjack 6 so long to gather his gear and hop into another cockpit.

Then he knew.

In addition to being a less-than-stellar commander, rumor had it that Captain Tucker often didn't pay attention during the operations order briefs. He preferred to fly during the mission, leaving the radio calls to his back-seater. Mike was willing to bet that Blackjack 6 didn't want to jump into another bird because his new back-seater wouldn't be able to manage the fight for him. Instead, Captain Tucker wanted to kick both crew members out of the new bird, but this necessitated shutting down the aircraft completely so that the pilots could swap seats.

Which took time.

Time they didn't have.

Sabre 6 was expressing his displeasure with Blackjack 6 in a way that only commanders could—a public flogging delivered on the squadron net.

"Engines one and two are at one hundred percent," Kassi said. "We are REDCON 1."

"Roger that," Mike said, acknowledging Kassi's transmission. "How's the rest of the troop looking?"

"REDCON 1 across the board with the exception of Blackjack 6. We need to pull pitch in fifteen seconds in order to make the new takeoff time. How we playing this, sir?"

That was a good question. What Kassi was really asking was were they going to follow the new timeline or delay takeoff until Blackjack 6 sorted himself out. Rule one of deep attacks was to take off on time in order to stay coordinated with the artillery. But Mike had a feeling that doing so would only further piss off his already agitated commander.

Fine.

If Mike had wanted an easy job, he would have flown Black Hawks.

"Unless Sabre 6 says otherwise, we're pulling pitch in fifteen seconds," Mike said.

"Roger that, sir. Hope you got more ass under your flight suit than you're showing. Blackjack 6 is going to take a bite out of it."

"Miss Shaw," Mike said, as he verified the first GPS waypoint a final time, "I would appreciate if you refrained from checking out my ass. Pretty girls make me nervous."

Kassi's chuckle echoed across the intercom, but the radio crackled with another transmission before she could reply.

"Blackjack 16, this is Sabre 6, over."

Oh, shit.

"Sabre 6, this is Blackjack 16," Mike said, trying

to keep his voice from cracking. Now his boss's boss was calling him.

What in the hell?

"Roger that, Blackjack 16. Are you REDCON 1?"

"Affirmative, sir," Mike said.

"All right, son. Looks like you've got lead and command of Blackjack Troop. You good with that?"

"Yes, sir," Mike said.

"Then carry on. Sabre 6, out."

"Welcome to the big time, sir," Kassi said.

A million thoughts coursed through Mike's brain, each one more intimidating than the last. The ingress route had changed, the mission clock had been adjusted, and, oh, yeah, his boss had just been fired. Now Mike was both leading a formation of twenty Apaches and commanding the six-ship formation that was Blackjack Troop.

So much for having everything under control.

Mike eyed the mission clock, took a breath, and stepped on the floor-mounted radio transmit toggle.

"Sabre flight, Blackjack 16 is Cherry. I say again, Blackjack 16 is Cherry."

His helicopter leapt into the air as Mike gave the takeoff brevity call.

They'd made their takeoff time.

Everything else should be gravy.

74

KIRA HUDDLED BENEATH A KOREAN PINE'S waterlogged limbs, wondering how her life had gone so off course. If curiosity killed the cat, then kindness had to be a close second. The kindness she'd shown to a woman in need had gotten her beaten, nearly raped, and now soaked to the bone and almost hypothermic. All this and she had yet to undergo the potentially most dangerous portion of this affair—explaining her actions to her countrymen.

Unlike the doctors and scientists who Kira considered coworkers, violence was not an abstract concept to the Wagner Group mercenaries. While the rough men had shown her nothing but respect, Kira knew the status afforded her was there only as long as she was laboring on behalf of her country. Texting and then meeting face-to-face with an American intelligence operative most definitely did not fall into that category.

A jagged bolt of lightning snaked down from the sky, turning a tree on the other side of the road into a ball of flame. Kira instinctively crouched lower to the ground, making her silhouette less distinct. She knew that she wasn't supposed to take refuge beneath a tree during a thunderstorm, but that little axiom made a whole lot more sense when she wasn't soaked to the bone and shivering.

Just a little while longer, she promised herself. In another hour or so, the sun would come up, and while the storm didn't show any signs of abating, it would surely be warmer then. Or at least it wouldn't be any colder. Besides, she'd promised the American, Jack, that she would give him and his men a head start before reporting his presence to her minders.

Kira eyed the dark bodies on the other side of the road. She wondered what the Wagner Group mercenaries would think of the dead Koreans. Probably not a whole lot. She'd experienced more violence in the last several hours than she had in the entirety of her life, but the skill and ease at which the American had dispatched her assaulters suggested this was just another day on the job for him. She supposed her Russian bodyguards fell into the same camp.

A pair of headlights washed across the road as a

single vehicle crested the hill before starting down the gravel path. Kira made herself smaller once again. This time it wasn't nature she feared.

It was her fellow man.

Only after the jeep wallowed down the incline did she breathe a sigh of relief. The unmarked hood and doors identified the vehicle as part of the Russian contingent. The people inside were her countrymen, not more lust-filled North Koreans. Kira considered allowing the vehicle to pass, but discarded the idea. She was beginning to shiver uncontrollably. She'd more than fulfilled her agreement with the American.

It was time to get warm.

Pushing herself to her feet, Kira left the safety of the tree for the open road. The rain sliced into her hair, plastering it across her face and sending icy fingers worming down her neck. The headlights played across her body, and she waved her hands over her head, suddenly desperate for the jeep to stop. Kira no longer needed to fake the tears coursing down her cheeks.

She wanted to go home.

Now.

The vehicle creaked to a halt and the doors opened. A moment later, two of her countrymen stood before her. While she didn't know their names, she recognized them both from the compound.

Wagner Group employees.

"Dr. Sidorova," the one nearest her said. "Are you all right?"

"No," Kira said, "I'm not."

And she began to sob.

75

"SCEPTER, THIS IS REAPER, WE'VE GOT SOME GOOD news, over."

The sound of the Green Beret's voice was comforting, and Jack's anxiety dropped a notch. Talking with the two Army commandos felt like having an ace up his sleeve. A plan that seemed ethereal when discussing it with Mesun suddenly developed substance when Jack heard one of the men who could help put it into action speaking into his ear.

"Reaper, this is Scepter," Jack said. "I can use all the good news I can get."

TINK shifted in the seat beside him. After making contact with the Green Berets, Jack had pulled Kira's jeep off the side of the road and into the underbrush. By now the Russian scientist and the two dead North Korean guards had probably been reported missing. The last thing Jack wanted to do was run into a search party made up of Russians or Koreans. At the same time, he didn't want to draw any closer to Eagles without a plan. With that in mind, hiding seemed like the best course of action.

For now.

Jack could almost feel the operational window closing. The F-18 strike package was minutes away and dawn was close behind. Once the darkness faded, so did their exfil opportunity. The Night Stalker air mission commander had made it clear that his Black Hawks would not be going feet-dry onto North Korean soil during the hours of daylight. Originally, the plan for a missed exfil had the team going to ground in a hide position until nightfall. Jack no longer considered this a viable option. Between the mayhem they'd already caused and the havoc they were about to unleash, he didn't believe there was anywhere in the Democratic People's Republic of Korea a dozen Americans would be able to hide.

He was way overdue for good news of any kind.

"Roger that, Scepter. We've got another bird on station. Bad news is that it can only loiter for about fifteen minutes. Good news is that its warhead ought to be good for one hell of a distraction if we use it correctly. We're over Eagles now, check your Android for video, over."

Jack unclipped the device from his chest, holding it so that TINK could also see. Black-and-white imagery filled the screen showing a rectangular-shaped building bordered by open fields to the south, west, and north, and clumps of trees to the east. A single road approached the building from the south, terminating at a checkpoint. In addition to the main building, two other smaller structures filled the frame—one to the west of the building and a second to the north.

"Does this look familiar?" Jack said.

TINK frowned as she studied the Android and then slowly nodded.

"I have never seen it from this angle," TINK said, "but that looks right. The cluster of antennas are a dead giveaway."

She tapped a section of roof on the building's northwest corner with a chipped fingernail.

"What about these two structures?" Jack said, indicating the smaller outbuildings.

TINK chewed her lip as she thought. "I'm not entirely sure, but I think this one houses the generators."

"Generators?" Jack said.

"Yes. Our electrical grid is . . . erratic in this part of the country. Each of the separate compounds on this facility have their own robust backup power supply in the form of gas-powered generators."

Jack felt a tingle of hope at TINK's answer, but he asked a clarifying question to be sure. "Then what's this structure?"

"That is where the gas is stored."

"I was hoping you'd say that," Jack said. Then he keyed his radio. "Reaper, this is Scepter. Stand by for the new plan, over."

JACK SLOWED TO A STOP IN FRONT OF THE CHECKPOINT, his heart racing. Mesun shivered. Jack wondered whether it was cold or nerves prompting her reaction.

"Remember," TINK said, "the guards will be Pak loyalists, but the technicians will not be a part of the coup. They are the key to our success."

Jack remembered. It had been only ten short minutes since they'd developed the plan and briefed it to Cary and Jad. But Jack knew that TINK was talking as much to reassure herself as to make certain her coconspirator understood his role. Though he still wasn't sure what to make of her, he was certain about one thing—the woman didn't lack for courage.

To succeed in their goal, Jack and TINK needed to accomplish three things—gain entry to the building, eliminate Pak, and issue the instructions that would halt the North Korean advance. To accomplish the latter, TINK needed access to the VTC equipment in the telemetry room. TINK thought that Pak's support was tenuous at best and heavily reliant on his own cadre of guards. Once the DPRK cadre of generals and party officials saw that she and her brother were still firmly in command, the uncertainty Pak was using to his advantage would vanish.

And so would Pak.

The ramifications of this operation came at Jack in unexpected waves. While it was easy to sympathize with the well-spoken, shivering woman sitting next to him, Jack also knew that she was part of a murderous regime that was responsible for the deaths of thousands if not millions of its own citizens. On more than one occasion Jack had wondered if the world might not be better off if he simply stepped back and let Darwin decide who ruled the hermit kingdom. Or maybe he should play a more active role in decapitating the entire regime. But every time he entertained that idea, Jack knew it was just wishful thinking. The peninsula was on the brink of war, and Pak was holding a loaded gun to the world's head in the form of the nuclear-equipped Russian superweapon.

In a conversation with his father, Jack had once asked the elder Ryan how he stomached making the kind of pragmatic decisions on the world stage that often traded stability for freedom. Senior had looked at his son for a long moment before giving a reply that had stuck with Jack to this day.

"There are no perfect answers to an imperfect world, son. Sometimes the only choice really is the lesser of two evils. I think the trick is to never give in to evil's stain. Never stop fighting for what is noble and good in the name of expediency."

Jack hadn't liked his father's answer then, and he didn't like it now. But on a dreary cold night, years and thousands of miles from that fireside conversation, Jack finally understood. God willing, his actions in the next few minutes would prevent the deaths of millions, but he was already feeling evil's stain.

The guard scowled, but Jack made no move to dim the jeep's headlights. As TINK had explained, the contingent of Russian soldiers, scientists, and doctors had been issued distinctive vehicles to facilitate quick identification by the compound's organic guard force. Furthermore, the Russians were not intimidated by cranky Korean guards.

"Ten seconds," Jack said, whispering into his mic.

The guard left his shelter for the car, his head bowed in an effort to keep the slicing rain out of his eyes. Unlike their Western counterparts, North Koreans didn't much care about their sentries' comfort. In fact, prevailing wisdom thought that uncomfortable guards were less at risk of falling asleep. The guard manning this checkpoint had no wet-weather gear, which made him all the more anxious to conduct a cursory credentials check and wave the Russian vehicle through.

A scenario Jack intended to use to his advantage.

The guard drew even with Jack's door and motioned for him to lower the window.

"Execute, execute, execute," Jack said, keying his mic even as he rolled down the rear passenger window instead of his own.

The guard instinctively looked toward the rear seat as the glass pulled away from the door's rubber lining with a loud squelch. Jack responded by bringing the pistol gripped in his right hand up to the window. The guard turned, eyes widening. An explosion ripped through the air as the orbiting Switchblade found its target, and Jack pressed the trigger twice.

Glass splintered.

The guard's head snapped back, and he dropped to the ground.

Just that quickly it was over.

But as Jack accelerated through the checkpoint, he knew that it wasn't true.

It wasn't over.

It was just beginning.

76

"YEOBOSEYO," PAK SAID, EXPECTING THE CALLER TO BE
Rim with an update on the search for Mesun.

It wasn't.

"I've found my scientist. She has quite the story."

Pak jerked the phone away from his ear in surprise.

Bear.

The Russian had rung Pak's personal line. A thousand questions flooded Pak's mind. He wanted to know how the Wagner Group operative obtained the number, but didn't ask. Though the Russian was now a mercenary, he'd once been an intelligence operative. He might have done this precisely to throw Pak off balance. Taking a calming breath, Pak placed the handset against his ear and voiced the question he should ask rather than the one he wanted to ask.

"I'm glad you found your missing doctor,"

Pak said, "but what does her absence have to do with me?"

"Not her absence," Bear said, "as much as what she encountered. A team of Caucasian men accosted her. They spoke American-accented English and were going to rape her until two of your guards intervened. She escaped, but your men are dead."

"You're sure?" Pak said, his earlier caution forgotten.

"I saw the bodies myself. After the gunfight, the Americans drove off in the vehicles used by your guards and my scientist. I'm coming to you after I drop the doctor off at our compound."

"Why?" Pak said.

"Where do you think this team of American commandos is headed?"

An explosion rocked the building before Pak could reply. Pak hung up without replying and punched speed dial. The phone rang twice.

"Annyeong haseyo."

"The weapon—is it ready?" Pak said.

The walls shuddered in response to another explosion. Pounding feet and raised voices echoed from the outside hall, but Pak cared only for the man on the other end of the line.

"Yes. The warhead has been mated."

"Launch it," Pak said.

"Yes, comrade."

Pak ended the call and slid the cell into his shirt pocket. Then he picked up his pistol and sprinted from the room. The American presence was unfortunate, but not a game changer. Not if Pak played his cards correctly.

The final VTC with the generals was about to begin. An ongoing attack by the Americans would provide excellent motivation to ensure the commanders commenced the invasion. Even if the military men balked, Pak still had the missile, and he alone possessed the access codes needed to override its guidance system.

Once the weapon was airborne, Pak would be unstoppable.

77

JACK ROARED INTO THE BUILDING'S COURTYARD AND
then swung the wheel hard to the right. As TINK
had predicted, the parking lot was half full with
military vehicles. The jeep's headlights briefly spot-
lighted two additional sentries standing post outside the building's entrance, but Jack continued his
turn, thundering past them.

The vehicle's tires thumped over the curb at the
far end of the parking lot and then they were off-
roading, racing along the strip of gravel that led to
the rear of the building. The rocky path was clearly
made for sentries patrolling the building's perimeter, and Jack had been more than a little worried
that the jeep might prove too wide. But after seeing the amount of soldiers on the far side of the
building, he'd decided this was the only answer.

But he hadn't been wrong about the tight fit.

Hungry tree branches scraped the right side of the jeep even as the building's brick exterior whizzed by just inches away to the left. Or perhaps less than inches, as the snapping sound of the driver's sideview mirror detaching from the vehicle attested. TINK shrieked, but Jack kept the pedal to the metal. Shock and awe were the linchpins of his plan, and both faded at an exponential rate.

Finally, Jack saw the opening he'd been waiting for. Like he was Ichabod Crane emerging from Sleepy Hollow with the Headless Horseman hot on his tail, Jack burst free from the corridor formed by the overhanging tree limbs onto the concrete pad at the building's rear. Dousing the headlights, Jack spun the wheel left, now paralleling the structure's back wall.

The view was spectacular.

To the right, angry orange flames clawed skyward spewing plumes of thick, black smoke from the remains of the fuel storage depot. As Jack rounded the corner, a secondary explosion sent a sea of liquid fire spilling across the concrete. The jeep was a good hundred meters from the billowing inferno, but the concussion still rocked the vehicle.

To the left, a flood of green uniforms poured from the building's rear exit. The secondary explosion knocked several of the soldiers from their feet, but to a man, they stood back up on shaky legs. Several just stared at the flaming pyre as if unsure what to do, but as with armies the world over, a grizzled sergeant waded into their midst shouting orders.

"Quickly," TINK said, slapping Jack's arm, "before they get organized."

Jack didn't need any urging. Slamming the gas pedal, Jack bore down on the still-ajar rear door. As TINK had explained, security for the range control complex was concentrated at the building's front, but the rear entrance was used mainly by soldiers servicing the generators. It was lightly guarded, and Jack intended to put this oversight to good use.

Thundering up to the building, Jack slammed on the brakes, parking the jeep so that it was parallel to the building's rear exit with just enough room for the metal door to swing open without hitting the vehicle. After shifting the transmission into park, he bailed out of the jeep, TINK right behind him. The emergency-exit door crashed open just as Jack was reaching for the handle. He stepped back, allowing the door to reach its widest arc.

A North Korean soldier emerged, stopping when he saw Jack.

Jack shoved his pistol into the man's chest and fired two quick contact shots, using the soldier's body to muffle the pistol's report. Then Jack pushed the dying man out of the way and peered into the hallway, leading with the pistol.

Clear.

Motioning with his off hand, Jack waved TINK past him. Then he took a fragmentation grenade from his vest, pulled the pin, and tossed the device into the jeep's cabin. Jack slammed the building's metal door closed, slid the deadbolt home, and transitioned from his pistol to his MP5. With the submachine gun tucked into his shoulder, Jack flowed down the hallway, TINK at his heels. A **thump** followed by a louder secondary explosion echoed from outside, but Jack was solely focused on the holographic sight. With any luck, he'd just barricaded the rear entrance with a jeep-sized fireball.

If not, he'd just given new meaning to the phrase **burning the ships.**

78

"DID HE MAKE IT?" JAD SAID.

Cary panned his optic across Eagles, trying to understand what he saw. On the front, or red, side of the building, soldiers were rushing around in clumps as their leaders attempted to ascertain the threat and direct their men accordingly. As of yet, no one appeared to have noticed the dead guard sprawled on the concrete, but Cary knew this was too good to last.

The complex's builders had wisely constructed the gas depot a good distance from the building proper. Though the Green Berets no longer had eyes on the building's rear, Cary didn't think the structure was in danger of catching fire right away. While flaming debris and embers could settle on the building's roof, the ever-present rain worked to the North Koreans' advantage. The rain-saturated shingles would stop the inferno from spreading.

Probably.

In any case, Cary had done everything he could to help Jack gain entrance to the building. Though the soldiers milling about by the front entrance provided a target-rich environment, Cary wasn't in a hurry to start shooting. His earlier experience with the sniper-detection system had been eye-opening and he intended to remain undetected for as long as possible. If experience were any judge, Jack would soon be needing their help in some form or fashion. Assuming their fearless leader had actually made it inside the range control building.

"Scepter, this is Reaper," Cary said, "send a sitrep, over."

"Reaper, Scepter, we are inside Eagles."

Jack responded with staccato words. That request for help was probably coming sooner rather than later.

"Reaper copies all," Cary said. "Standing by."

Jack acknowledged with two clicks of the transmit button.

Cary paused, but the radio remained silent. Cary knew that as a solo operator, Jack was probably too busy for a lengthy back-and-forth, but Cary still found the silence unnerving. Or maybe it was just that for the first time since he and Jad had touched down in the fetid rice paddy, there was nothing for the Green Berets to do besides wait. Cary wasn't much for just sitting still, but that was often the life of a sniper.

Boredom Cary could handle. But this was something more. Lying in the mud as the rain plunged
off the bill of his boonie hat in a frigid waterfall,
Cary felt something else—useless. Yes, he and Jad
were ready to cover Jack's exit or create another
diversion with the second Switchblade, but until
the spook emerged, the Green Berets were out of
the fight.

"This laying-here shit is for the birds," Jad said,
reading Cary's mind.

"I feel you," Cary said, "I—"

"Trident 12, this is Trident Main, over."

"So we're back to the SEAL call sign," Jad said.

"Trident Main, this is 12, go ahead, over," Cary
said, ignoring his spotter.

"Roger, 12, we've been attempting to contact
Trident 6 for the last several minutes but have been
unable to raise him. Can you assist, over?"

"Doesn't surprise me that they're having trouble
getting through," Jad said. "The cloud cover and
lightning has to be playing havoc with the signal.
We probably have better line of sight to the satellite
from atop this ridgeline. Want me to handle it?"

"Yep," Cary said. "I'll take comms with Trident
Main. You try to reach the SEALs."

Jad nodded and reached for the radio strapped
to his chest rig while Cary relayed their intentions
to Trident Main.

"Trident 12, this is Trident Main, roger all. If
you're able to make contact with Trident 6, please

advise them that the clouds are now obscuring our ISR coverage of Site Tango. Strike package is still en route, ETA one zero mikes. Anticipate that weather will prevent the fast movers from self-designating the target. They will require an accurate GPS location prior to weapons release, over."

"So much for being bored," Jad said.

Cary nodded, too busy processing the information Trident Main had just relayed to reply. Thanks to heavy cloud cover, the F/A-18E Super Hornets would not be able to use their organic laser designators to direct their JDAM munitions onto target. Instead, the pilots would have to conduct a blind drop. This meant the naval aviators would have to feed GPS coordinates provided by the SEALs into the bomb's guidance computer without ever visually confirming the targets.

Things were becoming complicated fast.

"Trident 12 copies all," Cary said. "Stand by."

"Trident 6, this is Trident 12, over," Jad said.

Cary heard his spotter's voice over his earphones, so he knew Jad was transmitting. Unfortunately, that was the only thing he heard.

"Trident 6, this is Trident 12, over," Jad said.

Still nothing.

Rolling onto his side, Jad began digging through his rucksack.

"The storm shouldn't be messing with this frequency band," Jad said as he worked. "The problem is probably just good old-fashioned range or line-of-sight obstructions. Let's see if a better antenna helps."

Jad pulled a compact object from his pack's outer pocket and expanded it accordion-style, revealing a whip antenna. With concise, practiced motions Jad mated the connector to his radio and extended the thin metal band skyward.

"Trident 6, this is Trident 12, over," Jad said.

The reply was instantaneous.

"Trident 12, this is 6. Thank God. We've been trying both you and Trident Main for the last several minutes, over."

"Trident 6, this is 12," Jad said. "Atmospheric conditions are interfering with comms. Trident Main is trying to get ahold of you. Cloud cover has fully obscured target site. ISR is no longer available, and the strike package cannot self-designate. They'll need drop coordinates from you, over."

"One two, this is 6, please pass the following sitrep to Trident Main. The device has now been mated to the missile. I say again, the warhead has been mated to the missile, and the missile has been elevated to a firing position. We believe launch is imminent. Sending imagery now. Please advise, over."

Cary's Android device registered an incoming data file as Brandon was speaking. Cary touched the icon and an image appeared showing one of North Korea's Chinese-made transporter erector launcher, or TEL, vehicles. The TEL was massive. Its sixteen wheels could support eighty tons' worth of missile and launcher along with a hardened crew cab that jutted off the front of the truck. This missile itself was elevated and ready to fire, and a nose cone was clearly attached to the front of the device.

"Stand by, Trident 6, relaying now," Jad said, glancing at Cary.

Cary nodded and began to transmit.

"Trident Main, this is 12, we established comms with Trident 6. Sitrep as follows—warhead has now been mated to the missile. Missile is elevated and launch appears imminent. I say again, launch appears imminent. Sending imagery. Please advise, over."

"This isn't looking good," Jad said. The spotter was consulting his Android device, scanning through the real-time imagery generated by the still-orbiting Raven. "I count at least fifteen dismounts and two vehicles equipped with crew-served weapons. The SEALs have their organic weapons and not much else. Without close air support or long-range indirect fire to even things up, Brandon's boys are in for one hell of a fight."

Cary nodded but didn't answer. He wouldn't characterize it a fight as much as an ass-whooping. Assaulting a fixed force with a plan developed on the fly and no combat multipliers had the makings of a massacre.

"Trident 12, this is Trident Main, please relay the following to Trident 6—neutralizing that launcher is now their primary task. I say again, neutralizing the launcher is their primary task, over."

Cary felt his stomach clench as he considered the magnitude of Trident Main's words. The SEALs had just been handed the equivalent of a suicide mission. Never in his twelve-year Special Operations career had he ever been asked to do something remotely as certain to end in death.

Then again, he'd also never faced the possibility of nuclear war.

Though he figured he knew the answer, Cary keyed his mic and asked his question anyway.

"Trident 12 copies all," Cary said. "Are there any other assets Trident 6 can employ besides those organic to his team, over?"

"Trident 12, Trident Main, that's a negative. We agree with Trident 6's assessment that launch is imminent. Weather and distance prevent employment of any other combat multipliers. Trident 6 is on his own, over."

"Roger that, Trident Main," Cary said. "Trident 12, out."

Technically Cary should have waited for Trident Main to end the conversation, but radio protocols didn't seem so important right about now.

"Let me have your headset," Cary said, "and get on your gun. Trident 6 deserves to hear this from me."

"You're the boss," Jad said, sliding off his Peltor combination mic and earpieces before handing the rig to Cary.

For the first time in his life, Cary wished this wasn't true.

79

JACK FLOWED DOWN THE HALLWAY, HIS MP5 AT HIGH ready with TINK following behind him. If speed and violence of action were the hallmarks of the type of close-quarters battle practiced by military assaulters, while slow and deliberate more reflected the philosophy of traditional law enforcement, Jack was somewhere in between.

This was by choice.

As TINK had explained during their quick planning session during the drive to the range control building, the people who saw them needed to believe that she was still in charge. She needed to exude the type of confidence that a man and a woman running through the building's halls would not.

But feigned confidence alone would not win the day. This was Pak's stronghold. While the diversion had hopefully drawn many of Pak's guards outside, a man with Pak's aptitude for survival would have planned for contingencies. Anyone in the building could be either friend or foe.

Or both.

With this in mind, Jack's plan was simple—get TINK to the control room as quickly as possible without overtly threatening anyone in the process. While a Caucasian was normally a rarity here, the contingent of Russians helped. Jack figured the average North Korean would have as much success determining the difference between Jack and a Wagner Group mercenary as Jack would trying to differentiate between Pak and TINK loyalists.

Which was to say not at all.

Jack moved toward the double doors at the end of the hallway with a brisk but deliberate pace. His rules of engagement favored a live-and-let-live philosophy. Hopefully the building's occupants felt the same way.

The missile control room occupied the bulk of the building's real estate, which meant that the hallway Jack and TINK were traversing was comparatively short. Staff offices and a small bathroom took up the majority of the space. The main entrance was much more ornate and featured a private room reserved for the Supreme Leader's use. Mesun believed that slinking in the back way would keep her and Jack clear of trouble.

But trouble found them all the same.

The double doors opened, emitting a pair

of Koreans. The men saw Jack and TINK and stopped. TINK shouted something, but her words didn't seem to do the trick. Both guards reached for the pistols holstered at their waists. Jack brought his MP5 onto target and fired twice into the center mass of each man. The suppressor somewhat muffled the shots, but the reports still sounded impossibly loud. The sneak-and-peek aspect of Jack's plan was out the window.

Time to embrace the chaos.

"Stay on me," Jack said, sprinting for the doors.

Jack reached the doors and braced his shoulder against the wood, holding them closed. Letting the Viking tactical sling catch his HK, Jack released his hold on the weapon in favor of stripping a cylindrical device from the webbing affixed to his plate carrier.

"What are you doing?" TINK said.

"Getting their attention," Jack said. "Then it's up to you."

Jack pulled the device's pin, opened the door, and tossed the cylinder underhanded onto the floor.

Then he slammed the door shut to the chorus of startled voices.

A moment later, the flash-bang detonated.

80

JACK HAD HEARD OPERATORS TALKING ABOUT <u>CRASHING</u> The Bang—a term that meant that the assaulters actually entered the target room as the flash-bang exploded. That was fine for men and women wearing hearing and eye protection who'd trained themselves to ignore the 170 decibels and 8 million candela the flash-bang generated, but Jack knew this course of action wouldn't work.

Even so, Jack didn't exactly hesitate.

The moment he heard the concussive blast, Jack wrenched open the door and charged into the room, dragging TINK behind him.

The view on the other side was interesting, to say the least.

Jack found himself at the bottom of a tiered amphitheater reminiscent of a college lecture hall, except the section he occupied was the largest portion of the room. Five gigantic LCD displays hung on the far wall, with the center screen stretching from floor to ceiling. The open bullpen contained a series of workstations stacked one behind the other on the left and right sides of the room, leaving a wide center aisle for observers. The rear of the room featured a balcony with plush seats.

He'd entered from stage right, but the flashbang had detonated almost precisely in the center of the room, just as Jack had planned. Jack dominated the ensuing chaos by striding from the hazy smoke with TINK at his side. Taking her cue, TINK marched past the scorch marks on the floor, planted her feet, and announced her presence with a long string of Korean.

Jack didn't have a clue what she was saying, but the four men in military uniforms staring back from the LCD displays seemed suitably impressed. Apparently, they'd arrived right in the middle of the VTC.

TINK kept talking and the generals kept nodding.

Maybe this was actually going to work after all.

The diminutive woman abruptly finished her monologue.

This was it. The instant in time that would prove or disprove TINK's claim that her presence alone would restore what passed for normalcy in the hermit kingdom. For a long moment, the room was deathly quiet.

Then the silence was broken.

By a gunshot.

81

PAK HAD INSTINCTIVELY DUCKED BENEATH HIS DESK when the flash-bang detonated. He was not a soldier and had never been exposed to such a device. As such, it took several seconds for his brain to comprehend what had just happened. The explosion had not been the result of an American bomb, as he'd first assumed. In fact, other than his ringing ears and his strained eyes, Pak felt fine.

Or at least he'd felt fine until he saw who was standing in the center of the room.

Mesun.

She was already giving instructions. Beside her stood a hulking American wearing body armor and armed with a machine gun. American commandos must have stormed the building. How they'd located Mesun and why they brought her here, Pak didn't know. Nor did it matter.

He'd lost.

Or had he?

Pak cautiously edged his eyes above the desk, for the first time interpreting what he was seeing through his intellect instead of just emotions. Yes, Mesun had already instructed the generals to stand down, and the old bastards were complying. And yes, the menacing giant standing next to her certainly looked American, but where were his companions?

Craning his head around the other side of the desk, Pak cautiously surveyed the room. Other than the single American, the room's occupants were technicians and the like. No bearded warriors guarded the exits, and no commandos barked orders.

Just Mesun and her lone wolf.

As Pak watched, Mesun finished speaking, undoing everything he'd planned. But what could be stopped with a call could just as easily be restarted with another. By now the nuclear cruise missile should be airborne, providing Pak with the world's most powerful negotiating tool. A tool that would bring even the Americans to the table. The more Pak thought about it, the more he believed his plan was still viable. With the missile already in the air, neither the Americans nor the Russians, or any other nation, for that matter, could prevent Pak from assuming power.

Just one person stood in his way.

Lifting his pistol, Pak steadied the barrel against the desk, aiming his hatred and frustration at Mesun.

Then he pulled the trigger.

82

JACK SPUN TOWARD THE SOUND OF GUNFIRE EVEN AS
TINK collapsed. His MP5 transitioned from high
ready to a shooting position without conscious
thought, a testament to hours on the range under
Ding's tutelage. He panned the submachine gun
across the room, searching for a target.

The shot had come from the observation area.
Jack slid the EOTech's crimson holographic circle across rows of plush chairs until he found a
target—a middle-aged Korean man in a black
Mao suit.

A man with a pistol.

Jack centered the red dot on the man's forehead as he took the slack out of the HK's trigger.
Spinning, the shooter ducked behind a bystander
just as Jack's shot broke.

Jack jerked his aimpoint to the left, putting the

round into the doorjamb above the man instead of into his terrified hostage.

The shooter vanished into the scrum of bodies.

Cursing, Jack turned to TINK. While she was still conscious, her clothes were already soaked in blood. Jack started toward her, but the woman held up a shaking hand.

"No," Mesun whispered, "not me. I stopped the war. But Pak can just as easily start it. Find him. Kill him."

Jack stared at the red tide spreading across the floor.

This was the outcome that had haunted him since Jack first conceived of the operation to rescue TINK. Her brother was a cold-blooded murderer responsible for untold deaths, but Jack wasn't here to pick sides in a North Korean power struggle. With a historian for a father, Jack was well versed in America's many failures when it came to choosing a government on behalf of its people. From Vietnam, to Iran, to Afghanistan, the philosophy of picking a leader for the populace always failed, whether that failure took one year or twenty. Jack was in North Korea to prevent a catastrophic war, nothing more. Viewed through that lens, his course was clear—find the man trying to ignite that war and stop him.

Permanently.

With a final look at Mesun, Jack sprinted from

the room, hot on Pak's tail. He received more than a few strange looks from the technicians milling around the bullpen, but they all wisely stayed out of Jack's way. Sometimes it paid to be a six-foot-two, two-hundred-pound American brimming with righteous fury.

The submachine gun didn't hurt, either.

83

"TRIDENT 6, THIS IS TRIDENT 12," CARY SAID.

"Go for 6."

The SEAL's whispered reply immediately put Cary in the other man's shoes. Cary envisioned the naval commando and his team set up in overwatch positions, already guessing the contents of Trident Main's orders. Lieutenant Cates was a professional. With the missile elevated to a launch position, the SEAL knew there was no way he could wait for the F-18s. Just as he knew there was no way he and his small force of men would be able to successfully ambush the larger force and disable the missile without grievous losses. The warhead of a traditional nuclear weapon would not detonate if the missile itself was destroyed.

But Skyfall was different.

The cruise missile relied on nuclear propulsion, meaning that the missile itself contained an active nuclear reactor. Since the device was in launch position, Cary assumed that the reactor was already online and producing power. This meant that the reactor stood a good chance of going critical if the missile was destroyed, creating a miniature Chernobyl on the launch stand. The nuclear event would surely kill or critically injure Brandon's SEALs even if they somehow survived the coming firefight with the fifteen men guarding the launcher. Cary was about to order the SEALs on a suicide mission. It made no difference that he was just the messenger. The words that would send eight men to their deaths would still come from his lips.

"Six, this is 12," Cary said, turning to look at Jad as he spoke. "Trident Main says that you're to . . . hang on a minute now."

"Trident 12, this is 6, say again, over."

The confusion in the SEAL's tone was evident, but Cary didn't care. His attention was fixed on the tube beside Jad.

The tube without the red band.

"You all right, boss?" Jad said.

"That Switchblade," Cary said, pointing at the tube. "It's a limited-effects warhead, right?"

"Yes, sir," Jad said. "It's like a sniper's bullet. No secondary explosions."

"Hot damn," Cary said. "Get it in the air. Now."

"You're the boss, boss," Jad said, configuring the tube for launch.

"Trident 6, this is Trident 12," Cary said, his lips twisting into a smile. "Trident Main wants you to take out that launcher. We're sending you help in the form of a Switchblade with a limited-effects warhead, over."

"Trident 12, this is 6, you're a lifesaver, over. What's the ETA on the Switchblade?"

The elevated tube belched the drone as the SEAL was talking. Jad was already heads-down on the Switchblade's controller, but he held up two fingers in answer to Cary's unasked question.

"Six, this is 12," Cary said. "Switchblade is in the air with an estimated ETA of two mikes."

"Roger that, 12. The missile's launch is controlled from the armored crew cab at the front of the vehicle. We need you to fly the Switchblade right through the windshield, over."

"Tell them to give me a laser spot," Jad said.

Cary nodded before keying the radio's transmit button. "Trident 6, Trident 12 copies all. We've only got one shot at this. Please lase the desired impact area so we're sure we're putting this baby exactly where you want her, over."

"Good copy, 12. Call when ready and we'll sparkle the target, over."

Jad's full attention was still focused on controlling the UAV, but he nodded and raised one finger.

"Roger all, Trident 6," Cary said. "One mike till we're overhead. I'll call sparkle."

For the first time since he'd splashed down in a

rice paddy full of human feces, Cary thought that they might just be turning the corner. He didn't really believe in luck, but surely they'd reached their mission allotment of bad karma.

"Reaper, this is Scepter, I need help, over."

Or perhaps not.

84

WHILE RIGHTEOUS FURY AND HIS MP5 HAD CARRIED
Jack as far as the facility's front door, the rational
side of his brain strongly suggested that he ease
back on the gas before bursting outside. The dis-
tractions Jack had employed to get him into the
building would have lost their shock value by now.
Though he assumed most of the remaining guards
were still at the rear of the building fighting the
Switchblade-induced fire, he didn't want to bet his
life on this supposition. Especially since he had
two Green Berets twiddling their thumbs on a
hilltop overwatch position.

Pausing just short of the front door, Jack activated his radio.

"Reaper, this is Scepter, I need help, over."

"Scepter, this is Reaper, go ahead, over."

"Roger, I'm pursuing a squirter toward the
red side of Eagles. Middle-aged, bald Korean

wearing a black Mao suit. If you see him, take him down, over."

"This is Reaper, roger all. Be advised that I'm using a thermal sight so I can't distinguish clothes or facial features. I've got five potential targets on the building's red side. They're heading toward a jeep. One of them's probably your guy. How do you want to play this, over?"

How, indeed?

Jack paused on the other side of the door, thinking. Behind him, the chorus of shouts and the occasional scream still rang through the air. Another explosion rocked the building. Apparently the fuel depot distraction had grown a little out of hand. Between the chaos at the rear of the building, the dead or dying TINK, and whatever instructions she'd issued in the auditorium, the entire site was in chaos.

But it wouldn't last.

Sooner or later, someone who spoke Russian was going to ask Jack a question he couldn't answer. Five-to-one odds were shitty, even with the Green Berets to balance things out. But they were the best odds he was going to get.

"Reaper, this is Scepter," Jack said, "I need you and your spotter to both engage. Start with the targets closest to the car and work toward the building. Call your shot. As soon as you start dropping bodies, I'll come through the door and engage from my end, over."

The words gave Jack hope as he spoke them.

Maybe this wouldn't be so bad after all.

"Reaper copies all, but be advised, only one gun will be engaging. My partner is busy."

Jack thought about asking what in the hell was more important than his request, but didn't. The commandos were professionals. If Cary said that Jad was unavailable, he was unavailable. If Jack had to do this with just one long gun, so be it. If Jack didn't stop Pak, the carnage would be unlike anything the world had seen in seventy years.

Sometimes no-fail missions really were no-fail.

"Okay, Reaper," Jack said, "I guess it's just us. I'm triggering off you. Call it."

This time, Jack's radio transmission didn't feel quite so comforting.

"Roger that, Scepter. Going in three."

Jacked tucked the HK against his shoulder with one hand and placed the other against the door.

"Two."

Jack turned the door handle, opening the door a crack, picturing how the engagement would go, as he tensed his legs beneath him.

"One."

Jack eased the door open with his hip, both hands gripping the HK.

"Execute, execute, execute."

The door swung open.

Five Koreans had almost reached a jeep.

Pak was in the center of the scrum.

The lead man stumbled as if he'd caught his foot on the concrete. Jack didn't have a clear shot at the Korean in the Mao suit, so he centered the EOTech's holographic circle on the soldier behind him.

A second man slumped against the jeep, half of his head missing.

Jack fired.

His target went down.

Two men left—Mao Suit and a bodyguard.

The bodyguard turned, his AK spitting fire. Jack ignored the high-velocity rounds snapping past his head. He put a burst in the bodyguard's chest and a second into his head as the bodyguard fell.

He panned to the final target but found . . . nothing.

Mao Suit was gone.

"He's on the far side of the car," Cary said. "I don't have the angle."

Dropping to the ground, Jack turned on his side, sighting the HK beneath the jeep.

For a heart-stopping moment he didn't see anything.

Then he saw a pair of feet.

Jack exhaled, waited for the natural pause in his breathing, and squeezed the trigger.

The first round divoted the concrete.

He adjusted.

Fired again.

And again.

The third or fourth round found an ankle. The next a calf. Then a man sprawled onto the pavement. Jack emptied his magazine into the man's prone form.

It was done.

With a shuddering breath, Jack got to his feet and conducted a mag change.

"Reaper, Scepter, I got him. Thanks for the help."

It was over.

"Scepter, Reaper, roger. Be advised that a column of trucks is approaching the gate at a high rate of speed, over."

Son of a bitch.

85

UNDISCLOSED LOCATION, SOUTH KOREAN AIRSPACE

"I NEED YOU TO PICK UP THE PACE BY TWO AND A HALF knots," Mike said, looking from his navigational page to his handheld flight computer.

"Come on, sir," Kassi said. "I am without a doubt the best pilot you will ever fly with, but even me and my chief-warrant-officer magic cannot hold airspeed in half-knot increments."

In an instant, Mike realized his mistake. For the last ten minutes, he'd been completely absorbed in the numbers and seconds, frantically trying to ensure that he crossed the FLOT exactly on time. Between the waypoint clock on his navigational page, the timer clipped to his kneeboard, and his watch, Mike had three timepieces running simultaneously.

He'd also been double-checking everything the Apache's onboard computer spit out against his handheld E6B slide rule while attempting to compensate for winds and other minute variations. All the while Mike had been rattling off a stream of increasingly terse deviations in heading and airspeed to his back-seater. Up until this point, Kassi had patiently obliged, but apparently even she had her limit.

"Okay, Miss Shaw," Mike said, "please increase the airspeed by two-point-zero knots exactly."

"That's more like it, sir," Kassi said, amusement evident in her voice. "Mind if I give you a piece of advice?"

"Please," Mike said.

"I've got a NAV page up as well. The computer says we're going to hit our cross FLOT point at plus-five seconds. Our tolerance is plus or minus thirty seconds. You're well within the margin for error, and we don't get extra credit for crossing exactly on the nose. In less than ten minutes, we'll be across the FLOT and over enemy territory. From now until then, let me worry about our time on target. Spend your energy on something more productive—like getting your platoon and troop ready to fight."

It took a moment for what Kassi was implying to register. When it finally did, Mike could have punched himself. He'd been so focused on the route and exactly hitting his time on target that he'd neglected his other more important job—leading the men and women of Blackjack Troop.

A few of the aviators were like Kassi—troopers who'd served combat tours in Iraq or Afghanistan. But many of the front-seaters were young, inexperienced warrant officers either fresh out of flight school or with no more than a year or two under their belts. Not only were they heading into combat, but they were doing so without the benefit of their commander or the senior platoon leader. If Mike was uncomfortable with the thought of leading an entire squadron across enemy lines safely, CW3 Jay Hogg, the warrant officer Mike had tapped to lead the attack platoon, must be doubly so.

Time to do what officers were paid to do—lead.

Mike reached for his intercom select switch, intending to change frequencies to the platoon internal, but paused. Though his message was specifically for Jay, he had a feeling that the entire troop could benefit from hearing the commander's voice right about now. Gathering his thoughts, Mike stepped on the transmission button.

"Blackjack 9, this is Blackjack 16," Mike said.

"This is 9, go ahead, 16."

"Roger," Mike said. "I just wanted to see how things were going back there, over."

The airwaves were silent for a moment, and Mike

found himself worrying that Jay was thinking too hard about his answer.

He needn't have been.

"Six, this is 9," Jay said. "If I was having any more fun, it wouldn't be legal. I've got two pylons loaded with Hellfires, a tank full of gas, and an army of bad guys in front of me. What more could a gunship pilot want?"

"A cup of real coffee would be great," a new voice broke in. "The muddy water they served back at the TAA isn't fit for infantrymen, let alone aviators."

"As a former infantryman, I agree with that assessment," another voice said. "Though I'm also confident that the amount of cream Blackjack 19 puts in his coffee precludes him from offering an opinion."

"Y'all are a bunch of grumbling old men sitting in climate-controlled cockpits. Try trudging through the rain with a sixty-pound pack on your back."

"As I've told you more than once, you cannot fault us for your poor choices. Flight school starts every two weeks. Maybe you should have submitted your flight packet sooner, 19."

Mike smiled as the radio chatter continued, each voice bringing a face to mind. Todd Askins, Matt Isaacson, Buddy Auten, Ron Thompson, Damon Nicolas. All were troopers Mike was still getting to know, and all were following him into battle.

In that instant Mike felt the enormity of the weight of command. The men and women of Blackjack Troop were depending on him to lead them into battle and then bring them back home.

Him.

A twenty-four-year-old first lieutenant with a grand total of two years in the Army. Mike didn't know what fate held for the aviators of Charlie Troop, 1-6th Cavalry, but he did know this—he would prove worthy of his fellow troopers' trust.

He owed them that much.

And so much more.

"Okay, folks," Mike said, keying his mic to break through the chatter, "now that we've cleared up that pressing issue, let's get ready to rumble. Once we cross the FLOT, the enemy has a vote. That means that things probably aren't going to go exactly the way we've planned. That's fine. Sabre 6 picked us to fly lead for a reason. We're the best damned troop in the entire squadron. We will accomplish our mission. Besides, as Blackjack 9 keeps telling me, this gunship pilot stuff is easy. If all else fails, find yourself a North Korean tank and send a Hellfire through its roof. Cross FLOT is in three minutes and thirty seconds. From now until then, keep this frequency clear. Blackjack 16, out."

Mike released the transmit button and felt some of the tension that had gathered in his shoulders and neck begin to dissipate. For better or worse, they were committed. In less than a minute, the suppression of enemy air defenses, or SEAD, artillery barrage would fall, breaching a hole in the North Korean air defense systems. Then the six attack helicopters that remained of Blackjack Troop would thunder through, followed by the rest of the squadron.

It really didn't get much simpler than that.

"Great speech, sir," Kassi said, the earlier traces of levity gone. "For what it's worth, I'm glad you're my front-seater."

Mike prepared to echo the sentiment, but didn't get a chance. His TSD page flashed as multiple air defense radars powered up. For a second, his threat screen remained clear. Then the dreaded red triangle appeared, solidifying around the blue icon representing his helicopter.

Not only were the North Korean gunners awake, they'd just locked up Mike's Apache.

86

"REAPER, THIS IS SCEPTER," JACK SAID, HEADING FOR the Jeep. "What am I looking at, over?"

"Scepter, this is Reaper, four vehicles, maybe five. It's tough to tell under thermal, but I think they're the kind the Russians roll in. You are not going to be able to exfil through the gate. Recommend alternate egress to the west, followed by a linkup at our position, over."

Sounded reasonable to Jack. Stepping over the dead bodies, he climbed into the jeep and started it. Then he put the transmission into gear and swung the wheel to the left, heading west. He roared past the entrance to the range control building just as headlights from the approaching convoy played across the parking lot.

"I'm heading west, Reaper," Jack said, as the vehicle picked up speed. "Can you talk me onto the alternate egress point?"

"Scepter, this is Reaper, say again, over?"

"The egress point," Jack said, guiding the vehicle off the pavement and onto gravel. "I can't remember where it is. All I see is fence."

"Uh, roger that, Scepter. You're going to have to create the egress point."

"Create it?" Jack said.

"That's affirm. Breach the fence, over."

Of course, Jack mumbled to himself as he buckled his seatbelt with one hand and steered the car with the other. **Of course I have to breach the fucking fence.**

An expert on fences Jack was not. Even so, it looked to him like the cyclone fence had been built with people, not off-road vehicles, in mind. At least he hoped that was the case. Either way, Jack was about to put his thesis to the test. Flooring the accelerator, Jack locked his arms on the steering wheel, tucked his chin to his chest, and breached the fence.

The collision thrashed him against his seatbelt, the restraint biting into his chest and ribs. A length of cyclone rolled up onto the hood and smashed into the windshield, splintering it. Jack swung the wheel to the left and then back right, trying to ditch the debris from his sightline even as he kept the gas pedal pressed to the floorboard.

For the first time, Jack was happy he was in North Korea instead of a modern state that enforced vehicle safety standards. There was something to be said for a good old-fashioned collision that didn't end with an airbag blasting you in the face.

Then his dashboard lit up like a Christmas tree as steam vented from the hood.

Maybe vehicle crash standards weren't such a bad thing after all.

The engine rumbled, coughed, and died.

Jack opened the door while the truck was still rolling, bailed out, and ran for the wood line fifty meters distant. He pumped his legs and swung his arms, trying to ignore the sound of engines closing in from behind him.

"Reaper, this is Scepter," Jack said between gasps. "I need a whole lot more help."

87

**UNDISCLOSED LOCATION,
SOUTH KOREAN AIRSPACE**

FOR A MOMENT, MIKE JUST STARED AT HIS TSD SCREEN,
not believing what he was seeing. A North Korean
air defense radar had locked up his helicopter. And
not just any radar. A fire-control radar linked to a
gun system. Mike thought he had a pretty good
idea which gun system.

A ZSU-23-4.

The ZSU was a self-propelled, radar-guided anti-
aircraft system. Its four 23-millimeter autocannons
could eviscerate a helicopter with armor-piercing
projectiles fired at a combined rate of four thousand rounds per minute. If that monster opened
up on him, Mike knew there wouldn't be enough
of his body left to fill a cardboard box.

With a practice born of countless hours in the
simulator, Mike slaved the Apache's fire-control

radar, or FCR, to the azimuth dictated by the radio frequency interferometer, or RFI, and activated a scan. The maneuver was roughly akin to looking toward something you've heard in an effort to identify what made the sound. In the Apache's case, the RFI **heard** the ZSU's fire-control radar, and now Mike was trying to get the FCR to **see** it.

If the FCR saw something, Mike could kill it.

Mike watched as the green windshield wiper line denoting the radar swept across his screen. A moment later the icon representing the threat moved from outside the gunship's range fan to inside. The RFI had heard the gun system's radar. Now the FCR had seen it and passed the coordinates to one of the four RF missiles hanging on the inboard pylon located on the Apache's starboard side.

All Mike had to do was squeeze the trigger.

But as much as the fingers of his left hand were itching to send a Hellfire streaking on its way, Mike hesitated.

This time the pause was intentional.

If Mike launched a missile, he'd be firing the opening shots ahead of the coming artillery barrage. He'd be announcing his intentions, and the element of surprise they'd worked so hard to maintain would be lost.

Something didn't feel quite right about that.

"Whatcha doing, sir?" Kassi said, the tension evident in her voice.

Mike eyed his TSD page.

A minute and a half until they crossed the FLOT, which meant that the SEAD would begin falling in thirty seconds.

Mike checked the range to the ZSU.

Three kilometers.

Max effective range on those cannons was about two klicks. That meant Mike had about . . .

"Sir? What gives?"

"Ten seconds, Kassi," Mike said, selecting missiles with the weapons-activation switch. "I will launch this missile in ten seconds, come hell or high water."

Mike watched the range to the ZSU decrease even as the mission clock spooled down.

Five seconds.

Mike raised the trigger guard and slid his left index finger over the trigger.

Two.

One.

Mike began to squeeze.

"Blackjack 16, this is Sabre 6, ABORT, ABORT, ABORT. Acknowledge, over."

"What the fuck," Kassi screamed, as she banked the helicopter over in a hard left turn, trying to keep the flight of Apaches in South Korean airspace. "What in the actual fuck?"

"Settle down, Miss Shaw," Mike said, releasing the trigger. "No foul language in the cockpit, please."

Mike's cavalier tone was befitting a gun pilot.

Luckily his back-seater couldn't hear his pounding heart.

"Sabre 6, this is Blackjack 16," Mike said. "Acknowledge abort. We are turning back south and will remain in South Korean airspace. What's happening, sir?"

"Blackjack 16, Saber 6, can't say that I know myself, son. We just received abort instructions from Brigade. I guess we're not going to war tonight."

That sounded just fine with Mike.

88

"ROGER THAT, SCEPTER," CARY SAID, WATCHING THE unfolding debacle through his optic's sterile lens. "When you hit the wood line, you'll see sloping terrain. Follow it uphill until you reach high ground. We're at the very top of that spur. We'll do what we can to slow down your pursuers, over."

"Roger that, Reaper. See you on the high ground."

"Got it," Jad said. "I nailed that motherfucker."

"You disabled the nuke?" Cary said.

"Won't know for sure until we hear from Trident," Jad said, "but I saw the SEAL's sparkle and flew the Switchblade right into the missile truck's windshield."

"Fantastic," Cary said. "Get on your gun. Start working over those trucks. Take left to right. I'll reach out to the squids."

As if he could hear the Green Beret's discussion, Cary's radio crackled with Brandon's voice.

"Trident 12, this is Trident 6, good hits with the Switchblade. I say again, good hits. The launch system is disabled with no secondaries. We've waved off the F-18s. Be advised, we are in contact and falling back to the primary exfil point. Suggest you do the same, over."

Cary could hear automatic-weapons fire in the background of the SEAL's radio transmission, providing a stark contrast to Trident 6's calm voice. The SEAL officer was no Captain Alex Brown, but he might not be such a bad guy to go to war with after all.

"That's a negative, Trident 6," Cary said. "Trident 12 is facilitating a hot linkup with our third element. We will be stationary until then, over."

Cary walked his optic onto the windshield of the lead vehicle careening toward Jack's abandoned jeep and fired his rifle. The round went low, sparking off the hood. Cary adjusted his aimpoint slightly higher and fired again. This time he could see bits of glass fly into the air, rendered as green sparkles under his thermal sight. Cary put two more rounds into the windshield before the truck slalomed to the right. Jad's rifle coughed beside him and a second vehicle ground to a halt, steam rushing from its ruptured radiator.

"Trident 12, this is 6, roger all. Are you in danger of being overrun? If so, we can fight our way to you, over."

Trident 6 was in a running gun battle against a numerically superior foe, and the SEAL officer was worried about the two Green Berets. That settled it.

Cary was officially instituting a one-week moratorium on SEAL jokes.

"Six, this is 12, that's a negative," Cary said as he selected another target. "We're engaging with long guns and expect to be mobile as soon as we effect linkup. Thanks for the offer, but we're holed up pretty good. I'm afraid if you came this way, you'd drag your hostiles with you, over."

"One two, this is Trident 6, roger that. Be advised that our exfil birds are inbound, ETA one zero mikes. The storm's giving them a run for their money, but the Night Stalkers are still playing ball. Don't worry about getting to the secondary egress site. If need be, we will come your way. Also, I'm passing the Raven back to you. She doesn't have much juice left, but you need an eye more than we do."

"Six, this is 12," Cary said. "Thanks for the assist. See you back at the boat."

The SEAL replied with two clicks of his transmit button.

Cary took this as an indication that the running gun battle the SEALs were fighting with the North Korean missile crew was a bit more intense than Trident 6 had let on. Cary could sympathize. All five of the trucks that had been chasing Jack were disabled, but their occupants were now pursuing the fleeing man on foot. The gunmen were bounding forward in three- to five-second rushes, one fireteam providing covering fire while the other moved. Clouds of thermal-resistant smoke drifted across the battlefield, spewing from a cluster of grenades the men had tossed. The combatants were trained and disciplined—two characteristics that spelled trouble.

"Take over the UAV," Cary said, "and talk Jack onto our position. I'll keep an eye on these guys."

"You got it, boss," Jad said, trading his rifle for his Android device.

Cary glassed the battlefield but didn't fire. Between the distance, the erratic and unpredictable movements of his target, and the concealment provided by the drifting clouds of smoke, he assessed his hit probability as extremely low. No sense wasting ammunition.

Before this was over, Cary had a feeling he'd need every bullet he could get.

89

JACK RESISTED THE URGE TO LOOK BEHIND HIM AS HE ran. Instead, he combat-reloaded his MP5 with his last magazine. Jack found this notion strangely comforting. Like sand flowing through an hour-glass, loading his last mag meant that one way or another this goat rope of a mission was coming to an end. With a final burst of speed, Jack made it to the wood line's welcoming embrace. That Jack was still alive was a credit to the Green Beret snipers, not his hundred-yard-dash time. The repeated **crack** of high-velocity rifle rounds breaking the sound barrier was punctuated with the crinkling of breaking glass and the screaming of truck engines redlining.

Jack desperately wanted to steal a quick glance over his shoulder, but didn't. He might not be invited to the Olympic time trials anytime soon, but the quicker he linked up with the Green Berets, the sooner they could start heading for the egress point. By providing him with covering fire, Jad and Cary were surely exposing their position to the pursuing men from the convoy. Jack needed to get to their sniper hide site as quickly as possible.

This was easier said than done.

As promised, Jack had found the sloping terrain and was now making his way upward as quickly as his tired legs could carry him. His breath was coming in huge, shuddering gasps and his side felt like someone was shoving a length of red-hot steel into his spleen. Maybe he should take Lisanne's advice and incorporate more cardio into his weightlifting routine. The thought of the dark-haired beauty brought a smile to Jack's lips. If thinking about your girl while mountain-goating up a hillside one step ahead of a pack of gunmen wasn't love, Jack didn't know what was.

He really was losing his mind.

"Scepter, this is Reaper, we've got eyes on you courtesy of a UAV. Bear to your left, over."

Jack did as instructed, angling to his left, which unfortunately took him into a thicket. Shielding his face with his hands, Jack crashed through the brush. All attempts at stealth were out the window. Jack was concerned with just one thing.

Speed.

"Good correction, Scepter. Keep pushing. Only about one hundred meters more."

One hundred meters more.

Jack could do this.

"Roger . . . Reaper . . ." Jack said between gasps. "How's it look behind me?"

He'd spoken the final sentence in one breath and was now paying the price. Stars danced in front of his eyes as the incline steepened.

"Lead elements are entering the wood line now. If you can move faster, do it."

Jack found his plate carrier's quick release and yanked, sending his chest and back plates tumbling to the ground. Ditching the ballistic armor made his stomach clench, but it was the right decision. If he didn't get to Cary and Jad soon, they were all dead. Jack made a fortress with his arms, trying to keep the reaching brush from damaging his eyes. He felt lighter without the plates and put on a final burst of speed, pouring everything he had left into the sprint.

"Hot damn, Scepter. You can really move. Fifteen more meters and you'll come to the top of the ridgeline. Then take a sharp left."

Jack clicked the transmit button twice. He couldn't have spoken if his life depended on it. His throat burned, and he could scarcely hear over his pounding heartbeat. Just when he thought he couldn't take it anymore, Jack burst through the last of the brush and found himself at the summit. As instructed, he turned left, refusing to slacken the pace.

"We're proned out directly in front of you, Scepter."

Jack's night-vision goggles had come loose during the incident with the fence, but his eyes had done a fairly good job of adapting to the darkness. Even so, he couldn't see anything but trail ahead of him.

Then he spotted two shadowy clumps lying on the ground.

And a figure standing behind them.

90

JACK RAISED THE HK, CENTERED THE RED DOT ON THE figure, and fired in one motion.

The submachine gun spat.

The figure tumbled to the ground.

"Contact rear," Jack yelled, even as he continued his charge toward the two Green Berets.

A second figure materialized out of the gloom and Jack put a burst into him as well.

Then he was in the hide site.

The snipers had set up camp in a slight depression that afforded them line of sight to their target as well as some cover and concealment. The depression was more along the lines of what special operators jokingly referred to as a Ranger Grave than a true foxhole. Either way, it was a hole in the ground, and Jack gladly joined the two Green Berets inside. To their credit, both men responded instantly to Jack's warning. The pair were already methodically engaging targets with a calmness Jack wouldn't have believed were he not witnessing the scene. The commandos deconflicted targets, changed magazines, and generally dealt out death with a proficiency that was nothing short of astonishing.

But it wasn't going to be enough.

The trees were alive with muzzle flashes and the shouts of fighting men. Incoming rounds kicked up dirt to either side of Jack's face and snapped by his head. Cary grunted as a ricochet pinged off his plate carrier. The Green Berets had beat back the initial charge, but the attackers would soon rally. Jack and his two compatriots were pinned down. One well-placed enemy hand grenade would end the whole shooting match.

They were going to die.

"This is my fault, boss," Jad said as he changed magazines. "I had the drone's line of sight zoomed in on Jack. If I'd bounced out a field of view, I would have spotted the fuckers sneaking up on us."

"Bullshit," Cary said, snapping off a pair of rounds at a target to Jack's left. "I should have never agreed to a SEAL call sign to begin with. Everybody knows that's bad luck. Jack—watch our six. I'd rather not get surprised twice in the same gunfight."

With a start, Jack realized he'd completely forgotten about the men who'd chased him up the mountain. Flopping onto his stomach, he oriented the HK back down the hillside toward the facility as he eyed the magazine's round counter.

Six.

He had six rounds left in his primary weapon. Not good.

"Hey, guys," Jack said as he peered into the darkness, "as long as we're making confessions, I've got one. My last name isn't Doe."

"You don't say," Jad said.

"Yep," Jack said. "It's actually Ryan."

"Jack Ryan," Cary said. "Kind of like the President."

Jack said nothing.

"Holy shit," Jad said. "For reals?"

"For reals," Jack said. "You guys wanna grab a beer with my old man after this is over?"

"I can probably work that in," Cary said. "All right, boys, stay frosty. These fuckers are going to get their act together soon. Once they do, they'll come hard. One element will lay down suppressive while the second flanks us. Watch for grenades. Jack, keep your eyes peeled. You may need to spin my direction if Jad and I can't stop the next wave. I've got a CS grenade sitting between us. If it looks like we're going to be overrun, toss it right in front of our hole. Once the gas hits, start moving southeast toward the egress point. With any luck, maybe these jokers will get in a shooting match with Jack's friends coming up the hill."

"Sounds like a plan, boss," Jad said.

"Tracking," Jack said.

Jack said the word, but he wasn't fooled. This hole would be their grave. Jack withdrew the Glock from his thigh holster and laid the pistol on the ground next to him. He had a feeling the final six rounds in his HK weren't going to last long, and his Glock was shooting .40-caliber instead of the 9-millimeter rounds used by the submachine gun. This meant that he couldn't use the Glock's ammo in the HK. Once the MP5 ran dry, Jack would have to make do with his pistol.

As if in confirmation, two shadowy forms emerged from the brush.

"Contact rear," Jack shouted, even as he fired a burst into the first figure. The second rolled out of sight, chased by Jack's rounds.

Then his HK ran dry.

"Transitioning," Jack said, grabbing his pistol.

Cary shouted something back, but Jack couldn't hear over a second voice.

The one coming from his radio headset.

"Trident 12, this is Turbine 35, over."

Jack fired his pistol toward where he'd seen the other soldier take cover, only to be answered back by half a dozen muzzle flashes. Dirt and stones peppered his face as rounds impacted all around him.

"Trident 12, this is Turbine 35, over."

The Green Berets were lying shoulder-to-shoulder, still firing their rifles in short, controlled bursts. Jack's gaze drifted from the men to what lay between them. The CS grenade. Grabbing the munition, Jack pulled the pin and hurled the grenade toward the collection of muzzle flashes. He'd always heard that grenades were supposed to be tossed underhanded so the device didn't collide with underbrush or tree branches and bounce back to the thrower.

But not today.

Only open ground separated Jack from the shooters he was targeting, and the men were a good twenty yards distant. Jack hurled the grenade like he was a catcher throwing out a runner at second. The cannister tumbled through the air, bounced off the ground, and then detonated, spewing CS gas all over the thicket the cluster of shooters were gathered behind.

"CS gas is out," Jack said, slapping the Green Berets on the shoulder. "Let's move."

"Negative," Cary said, still firing his rifle. "Too many in front of us and too much open ground. Won't make it five feet."

Jad grunted his agreement even as he fired a prolonged burst at a group of three men trying to flank them.

"Any Trident call sign, this is Turbine 35. Please come in, over."

"Do you guys hear that?" Jack said.

"Hear what?" Cary said.

"The radio."

"If somebody's calling on the radio, mother-fucking answer it," Cary screamed.

"Turbine 35, this is Trident 12," Jack said.

"Roger, 12. Turbine 35 is a flight of four heli-copters inbound to your position. Two gunships and two slicks, over."

"Roger, Turbine," Jack said. "Trident is sur-rounded and in heavy contact. We are in danger of being overrun. Need immediate suppressive fire."

"Turbine 35 copies all. We have a position fix from your radio, but we'll need you to mark your position, over."

"It's the helos," Jack said. "They want us to mark our position."

"There's an IR beacon in my dump bag," Cary said. "Turn it on. Switch is on the bottom."

Jack grabbed the device from the sack hanging from the back of Cary's body armor, thumbed on the switch, and set the beacon in the middle of the foxhole.

"Turbine, this is Trident," Jack said. "Beacon is on. I say again, beacon is on."

"Roger that, Trident. We've got you. Gunship 1 is inbound. This will be danger close, so get your heads down."

"Down," Jack screamed.

The tiny little hole got even smaller as Jack found himself part of a pile of bodies. The absence of fire from Cary's and Jad's long guns made for an eerie silence, but the quiet didn't last for long. A **brrrt** of miniguns firing three thousand rounds per minute was followed by a **whoosh** and then the thunderclap of exploding rockets. The ground heaved under the impact of the munitions as the earth vomited Jack skyward.

Then the process repeated as the second gunship made its pass.

"Tell him good hits," Cary said as the explosions faded. "Immediate reengage."

"How do you know he hit anything?" Jack said.

"We're still alive."

Jack couldn't fault that logic.

"Good hits, Turbine," Jack said. "Request immediate reengage."

"Good copy, Trident. Gun 1 inbound."

This time the series of explosions was more prolonged as the gunship hit targets on both sides of the tiny foxhole. Dirt and dust filled the air and the smell of cordite and sulfur made Jack want to gag. He risked a glance overtop of the depression's lip as the second gunship's rounds impacted, sending burning embers fountaining upward.

It was quite simply the most awesome thing he'd ever seen.

"Trident, this is Turbine, we've pushed back the combatants, but the LZ is still too hot for a normal extraction. Recommend SPIES, over."

"Turbine, this is Trident, we concur with SPIES," Cary said, after picking up his Peltor from where it had fallen in the dirt.

"What the hell is SPIES?" Jack said.

"You're going to love it," Cary said.

Jack did not love it.

As the two gunships continued to work over both sides of the hill with rocket and minigun fire, another Black Hawk hovered overhead. A moment later, a thick rope fell into the foxhole.

"What the hell do we do with this?" Jack said as Cary grabbed the rope and pulled it across the men. "Climb it?"

"Negative," Jad said. "Just relax. Everything's going to be fine."

With practiced fingers, the sniper attached Jack to the metal fasteners on the rope using a series of carabiner clips and the harness mounted to Jack's body armor. Jack had noticed the D-rings and harness when he'd donned the plate carrier, but he hadn't questioned their presence.

He should have.

About the time Jack realized what was happening, Cary and Jad were checking each other out.

"We're rigged, Turbine," Cary said. "You're clear."

"This is Turbine, roger. Hang on."

The rope went taut.

Jack was yanked into the air with Jad hooked in beside him.

Cary brought up the rear.

"We call this dopes on a rope," Jad said. "Stick out one arm. It will keep us from spinning."

Jack stuck out his arm.

It did not keep them from spinning.

The gunships continued to pour ordnance into the hillside in blinding flashes of light and thunderous explosions. Jack couldn't tell for sure in the dark, but he thought Jad was smiling.

"When do they reel us into the cabin?" Jack said as the helicopter accelerated away from the hill and turned toward the beckoning ocean.

"They don't," Jad said.

This time Jack didn't have to wonder.

The sniper was definitely smiling.

EPILOGUE

JACK BLINKED IN THE SUNLIGHT AS AN EVENING BREEZE washed over his face. At least he thought it was evening. He'd spent time in at least three time zones over the past fourteen days. At this point, Jack wasn't sure if his internal clock would ever read correctly again.

"Excuse me."

Jack stepped to the side, allowing a satchel-carrying businessman to edge between him and a mother surrounded by a cluster of children and more suitcases than she had hands. The business-man was simultaneously berating someone on the phone clutched in one hand while flagging down a taxi with the other. He did an admirable job of pretending not to see the obviously struggling mama.

It was great to be back in Washington, D.C.

"Hi," Jack said, looking over at the woman. "Need a hand?"

With a baby on her hip, another in a stroller, a five-year-old by her feet, and a pile of suitcases on the sidewalk next to her, the woman definitely needed help.

Whether or not she would accept it from Jack was a different matter.

He knew that his current look probably didn't inspire confidence. With no luggage, a shaggy beard, and clothes he'd purchased at the BX on Yokosuka Naval Base, Japan, Jack was definitely out of place among the D.C. professionals and families streaming out of the Ronald Reagan Washington National terminal. Jack's wind-beaten face still bore the aftermath of his time in Korea, though his cuts had mostly healed and the bruises were fading. Perhaps not the visage of someone you stopped to pick up on the side of the road, but Jack thought that the woman's mom radar probably would see through his questionable appearance.

It did.

Or maybe she was just that desperate for help.

Either way, the pretty brunette gave Jack a welcome, if weary, smile. "Thank you," the woman said. "My husband's coming, but he ran into traffic. If you could help us to the curb, that would be great."

"My pleasure," Jack said, grabbing two of the suitcases.

It really was his pleasure.

The little family provided a welcome counterpart to the death and destruction of Korea. True to her word, TINK had stopped the war, though it had cost the North Korean woman her life. From what Jack had gathered, the U.S. had come within a razor's edge of conducting a conventional attack against North Korean lead echelon forces. Word on the street was that an American artillery barrage had been sixty seconds away from decimating the DMZ to clear the way for a flight of Apache attack helicopters.

Other than the naval skirmishes between North Korean SOF fast boats and U.S. and South Korean forces in the East and Yellow Seas, no conventional forces had exchanged fire. After halting short of their lines of departure on TINK's orders, the North Korean mechanized infantry and armor formations had returned to their assembly areas and stood down from their wartime postures.

The North Korean SOF operators in South Korea had posed a bigger problem. Most of the last two weeks had been dedicated to ferreting them out. A turning point in the struggle had come when the two Koreas had reached an armistice of sorts. A revitalized Supreme Leader gave a televised order for all KPASOF still in South Korea to return to prearranged staging areas. If they did so, South Korea promised the men amnesty and repatriation to the North.

The North Korean party line was that the pseudo-invasion was the work of a few rogue leaders who'd acted against the Supreme Leader's wishes. In typical fashion, the Supreme Leader single-handedly stopped the war and dealt with the men responsible. To add veracity to this tale, DPRK media released grainy footage showing three very dead Koreans. No mention was made of TINK or the fact that one of the dead men had been killed by an American wielding an MP5. Nor was there any talk of a Russian doomsday weapon, a contingent of Wagner mercenaries, or a U.S. clandestine effort to avert what would have been the bloodiest conflict in nearly a century.

That said, things were not exactly back to the status quo. While the U.S.–South Korean relationship was on the mend, thanks in no small part to the incredible lengths America had gone to safeguard her ally, no one trusted North Korea. As such, the U.S. 7th Fleet was conducting an extensive series of exercises in the Yellow Sea in conjunction with South Korea, Japan, Australia, and a number of other Western allies.

This was why Jack was just now returning home. Lisanne had been more fortunate. She'd hopped a ride with Ding and the rest of the crew aboard The Campus's Gulfstream after South Korean airspace had reopened two weeks ago.

Jack's SPIES exfil at the hands of 160th aviators had forever sworn him off helicopters of any type. The ordeal had ended at the USS **Lake Champlain,** where Jack had been promptly relegated to the status of passenger along with Cary and Jad. For the next twelve days, the men participated in an untold number of classified debriefings while patiently waiting for a flight off the busy cruiser.

Or perhaps not so patiently.

Either way, after the first round of exercises had concluded, the three men had caught a flight to Yokosuka Naval Base, where they'd exchanged numbers and parted ways. Jack was serious about having the men to dinner at the White House. He was just hoping that the Green Berets were capable of dialing down the profanity around his mother.

Then again, Cathy Ryan was no shrinking violet.

Jack was pretty certain his mom could hold her own against a couple commandos.

After a day spent waiting for a flight out of Tokyo, Jack had finally come to the end of his journey.

"Are you somebody famous?"

The question caught Jack off guard, especially since it came from the woman's five-year-old son. The boy stared at Jack with the single-minded intensity small children could so easily muster. Jack wouldn't be surprised if a future FBI agent lurked behind the boy's blue-eyed gaze.

"Billy, what kind of question is that?" his mother said.

Billy shrugged narrow shoulders even as he refused to break eye contact with Jack. "Daddy said famous people use this airport. I thought he might be one."

"Sorry, bud," Jack said as they reached the passenger pickup area. "Better luck next time."

The mom flashed Jack a grateful smile as he helped arrange her suitcases on the curb, but Billy wasn't so easily swayed.

"Are you sure?" Billy said.

"Positive," Jack said with a wink. He ruffled the kid's curly hair and then pulled out his phone to order an Uber.

Or at least that's what he'd planned to do.

"Hey! Need a ride?"

Jack turned to see Lisanne Robertson leaning against a limousine SUV.

Lisanne Robertson in a black cocktail dress and matching heels.

"What are you doing here?" Jack said, his face breaking into a goofy grin.

"Looking for a date. I've got reservations at Franco's tonight. Interested?"

Was he ever.

Lisanne's hair hung lose about her bare shoulders in a raven curtain. Her dress flattered her athletic build, hinting and hiding in equal proportions, and her olive complexion glowed in the last of the day's light.

But it was more than just Lisanne's appearance

that caused Jack's heart to stutter. He'd missed her. Lisanne waiting for him at the airport made Jack happy in a way that was hard to explain. His grin grew wider.

Lisanne smiled at Jack's reaction, her dark eyes sparkling.

"See, Mom? I told you he was famous."

Billy's unmistakable voice carried across the arrivals area, and Lisanne laughed.

It sounded magical.

Jack covered the distance between them at a near run.

Then she was in his arms.

He pressed his face against her neck. Her warm skin smelled like vanilla, and her hair tickled his face. He breathed her in, not in any hurry to end the hug.

"I missed you," Jack said, as her arm tightened around him. "A lot."

"I missed you, too," Lisanne whispered.

Jack edged back so that he could see her face, his heart thundering.

And then his phone rang.

"We both know who that is," Lisanne said with a smile. "Better answer."

"He'll stop calling."

"He won't. Get it."

With a sigh, Jack dug the burner he'd bought at the Yokosuka Naval Base exchange from his jeans pocket. He'd given the number to just one other person besides Lisanne. It wasn't hard to guess who was on the other line.

"Hey, Mr. C.," Jack said as he answered.

"Jack—you back on U.S. soil?"

"Yes, sir," Jack said. "Just landed."

"Great. Need a ride?"

"No, sir," Jack said, looking at Lisanne as he spoke. "I'm with my girlfriend."

Lisanne smiled again, but her bottomless eyes suggested something more.

He needed to get off the damned phone.

"Good, then I won't keep you," Clark said. "I just wanted you to know how proud I am of the way you handled yourself in Korea. Mary Pat passed along the entire classified debrief, including the account from your Green Beret friends. Things on top of that hill got a little hairy, huh?"

"Yes, sir," Jack said, his voice suddenly hoarse as the sights and sounds of the battle came roaring back.

"You did well, son. Damn well. Did your old man ever tell you how he and I and Ding met the first time? The whole story?"

"I don't think so, Mr. C."

"Not surprised," Clark said. "I guess it's really Ding's to tell. Do me a favor, when you get back to the office, find Ding. Tell him I said he needed to tell you about the Battle of Ninja Hill. The whole story. It will do you both good."

"Yes, sir," Jack said, "will do."

"Great. Oh, and one last thing, tell Lisanne hi for me. Clark out."

For once Jack wasn't irritated that his boss had hung up on him.

He had other things on his mind.

"What was that about?" Lisanne said, as Jack put the phone back in his pocket.

"Just Clark being Clark," Jack said with a smile.

"Did you say something about a girlfriend?" Lisanne said.

"Yep," Jack said. "Though it seems strange to call someone you've never kissed your girlfriend."

"Agreed. Maybe you should do something about that."

So he did.

ABOUT THE AUTHORS

Tom Clancy was the author of more than eighteen #1 **New York Times** bestselling novels. His first effort, **The Hunt for Red October,** sold briskly as a result of rave reviews, then catapulted onto the **New York Times** bestseller list after President Reagan pronounced it "the perfect yarn." Clancy was the undisputed master at blending exceptional realism and authenticity, intricate plotting, and razor-sharp suspense. He passed away in October 2013.

Don Bentley is the author of the Matt Drake thriller series, including **Without Sanction, The Outside Man, Hostile Intent,** and a forthcoming title, as well as **Tom Clancy Target Acquired,** a Jack Ryan, Jr., novel. Bentley spent a decade as an Army Apache helicopter pilot, during which he deployed to Afghanistan as an Air Cavalry Troop Commander. Following his time in the military, Don worked as an FBI special agent and was a Special Weapons and Tactics (SWAT) team member. Learn more at www.donbentleybooks.com.

LIKE WHAT YOU'VE READ?

Try these titles,
also available in large print:

**Tom Clancy
Target Acquired**
ISBN 978-0-593-41432-3

**Tom Clancy
Chain of Command**
ISBN 978-0-593-45982-9

**Tom Clancy
Shadow of the Dragon**
ISBN 978-0-593-34053-0

For more information on large print titles, visit
www.penguinrandomhouse.com/large-print-format-books